Aluminum Showers

Noel F. Keane

iUniverse, Inc.
New York Bloomington

iUniverse books may be ordered through booksellers or by contacting:

iUniverse
1663 Liberty Drive
Bloomington, IN 47403
www.iuniverse.com
1-800-Authors (1-800-288-4677)

ISBN: 978-1-4401-7956-3 (sc)
ISBN: 978-1-4401-7954-9 (dj)
ISBN: 978-1-4401-7955-6 (ebook)

Printed in the United States of America

iUniverse rev. date: 11/03/09

Contents

Foreword

My story is fiction: the characters are composites of personalities I have known in the air traffic control profession or elsewhere. Where I have used real names, I have done so with the individual's permission. Most of the anecdotes in this story actually happened, either to me or to someone I know very well. The names have been changed to protect the innocent. Descriptions of current air traffic technology and methodology are drawn from my own experience as an FAA air traffic controller and manager.

This story is not intended to frighten anyone, or to insinuate that air traffic control is unsafe. I'm so convinced that it is safe that I'll gladly accept any unused airline tickets; I'd prefer Hawaii. But we pay a huge price to keep the system safe; the FAA has to restrict the number of aircraft in the air at any one time. The ones that aren't in the air are sitting on the runway, burning fuel.

Why should you care? You'll know for yourself the next time you check the status board in an airport and find that your flight has been delayed several hours, or look at the price of your ticket; the one you paid an arm and a leg for, only to find yourself jammed in the back of the bus.

Although my story is fiction, there is a realistic, underlying theme behind it: the protagonist's belief, as well as my own, that the air traffic control system could be made even safer, and much more efficient, by utilizing computer technology that has existed in this country for more than fifty years. Your author not only believes in that, but hopes to help promote change through the telling of this story. Unfortunately, congress either doesn't realize, or doesn't care how much more efficient the air traffic control system could be. That awakening will come only after the price of a ticket is so high that no one can afford to fly anymore, or the skies are so crowded that we ram two airliners together. Let's hope neither one of those things happens.

Sit back, relax, and enjoy your flight. Your air traffic controller is a well trained professional, watching over your flight at all times.

...On the other hand. . . keep your seat belt fastened, because the disaster I mentioned could happen at any time.....!

NFK

Prologue

TITLE 18, U.S. CODE, Chapter 2, Sec 32 a (5), (6).

It shall be a violation of law ...for anyone to perform an act of violence against any individual on an aircraft...or to communicate information, knowing that information to be false and under circumstances in which such information may reasonably be believed, thereby endangering the safety of any such aircraft in flight...

Section 34:

Whoever is convicted of any crime prohibited by this chapter, which has resulted in the death of any person, shall be subject also to the death penalty or to imprisonment for life, if the jury shall, in its discretion so direct, or, in the case of a plea of guilty...

ONE

Thirty seven thousand feet above Kansas City, Missouri, Betty Milburn leaned her aching forehead against the small window of a Boeing 777 aircraft. The window was cool, the first comfortable thing she'd experienced since boarding the flight. She looked down toward the darkness outside and her stomach did a flip when she realized that the tiny window was the only thing separating her from the dark world below.

Betty's head pounded from the severe headache that had started the minute she boarded the huge aircraft. A drop of sweat had formed at the end of her nose, but she couldn't use her handkerchief because it had fallen between the feet of the fat man sitting next to her. She had avoided the man's attempts at conversation because his sloppiness had somehow added to her own discomfort: he had coffee stains down the front of his shirt and his middle button was missing, exposing his stomach. A crazy thought went through her head: what if the plane crashed and she ended up tangled with the fat man? Her children might think this was the man they suspected she was romantically involved with. The idea made her Baptist heart shiver.

Betty stared out into the darkness hoping to get a glimpse of something other than her own reflection. If she could just see anything at all it would help her to gain some perspective; get her bearings. The only things visible were the black night and her tense face staring back at her. She rolled her forehead from side to side against the window to help with the headache, angling her body so that her face was as far away as possible from the fat man. She closed her eyes and tried to imagine herself sitting in her

1

own house, or on the ground, anywhere but in the clouds. Flying at night terrified Betty. Daytime wasn't much better, but at least you could look out the window and see signs of life. The ticket on Transcontinental flight Three Fifty Four was a birthday present from her children, an opportunity to visit her sister in Dallas. Other than the train trips to Silver Spring, Maryland that her children weren't aware of, this was the first time Betty had been away from home in years. She knew the children had picked a late flight because it was cheaper, but she didn't have the heart to ask them to change it. They were excited for her; they talked about how much "fun" she would have. She had to take a "Fear of Flying" course from one of the airlines just to muster up enough courage to get on the airplane.

Betty was just about to fall asleep with her head against the window when a loud explosion from beneath the aircraft rocked her world. She screamed as loud as she could when oxygen masks dropped like spiders hanging from webs. Every object in the stricken aircraft became a missile that rattled the bulkheads or garbage that made it impossible to see. Newspapers, shoes, purses, even ipods, sent shocked passengers ducking for cover.

Everything happened in seconds: the sky outside turned to daylight and Betty heard a loud noise like metal ripping apart. A second explosion slammed Betty's head back against the seat. Then she was thrown forward again, her seatbelt threatening to rip her apart. She blacked out for a second, and when she recovered she realized that the aircraft was upside down. When the aircraft righted itself for just a second she looked up and saw rocket-like streams of flames shooting up into the starlit sky. She looked toward the front of the aircraft and saw that there was nothing left; no bulkheads, no wings, not even the cockpit. It suddenly came to her that she would never see her grandchildren again. She screamed again, cursing God for what seemed imminent, but couldn't even hear her own scream. All that was left was a flying tomb that rolled over and over until she no longer knew if she was looking up or down.

The night turned dark again and she saw two, giant balls of fire moving away quickly. Everything was eerily quiet now, and with her hearing gone it was like watching a silent movie. She continued to scream, but she still couldn't hear anything. She tried to grab onto something, anything at all, her hands and fingers clutching at air.

In less time than it takes to count to five, Betty Milburn had been trapped in that "other world," a place where no one knows exactly where he or she is, or how they got there. There was an ocean rushing through her ears and bodies floating all around her. She noticed the faces of fellow passengers as they flew by, the same ones she had stood in line with. Their expressions displayed only bewilderment. Some were missing shoes, shirts, even underwear.

A peaceful feeling came over her for just a few seconds. It was as if she was floating in space with no problems and no worries. That changed in a second when she found herself gasping for breath, discovering at the same time that her arms and legs were covered with a frost–like substance. Strangest of all, she realized that the fat man was still with her, floating right above her head, arms outstretched like a big bird's. She wondered why he wouldn't leave her alone.

She sought refuge in the hope that it was all a dream. Weren't these kinds of things always dreams? She told herself to remain calm; get a grip, think positive thoughts.

The angry cold soon rendered Betty's brain incapable of any thoughts, whatsoever.

Betty Milburn had been converted into nothing more than airborne trash. She would never know who or what had caused her to go rocketing down toward the streets of Kansas City.

TWO

More than seven miles below Betty Milburn's tumbling body, air traffic controller Kyle Matthews was living his own nightmare, staring at the surreal presentation on his green radar screen.

Seconds before, two giant Boeing 777 aircraft had been jumping across the screen on intersecting routes toward Kansas City. Suddenly, the two aircraft disappeared: no fanfare, no forewarning, just vanished like two lights turned off in a building across the street.

"Transcon Three Eleven, how do you hear Kansas City Center, over?"

A pause.

"Transcon Three Fifty Four, Kansas City Center, how do you read me, over?"

Matthews had been giving the performance of his life right before the aircraft were due to pass over Kansas City, acting out a prank that was as old as air traffic control itself. As the two aircraft approached on an apparent collision course, he stood up and shouted: "My God, they're going to hit." Anyone looking at the radar scope might have believed it; the electronic tags that accompanied each aircraft showed the same altitude, 370, thirty seven thousand feet. What an inexperienced onlooker couldn't know is that it was intended to be just a prank. Danny Houston, a computer nerd working in the equipment room in the basement, had changed the westbound aircraft's tag from "350" to "370" to make it look as if the two aircraft were at the same altitude. Houston's computer manipulation was vital in order to carry out the "act:" without it, other air traffic controllers, targets of the prank, would never fall for such an old gag.

"Safe" pranks always occurred when traffic was light, when there was no danger to an aircraft. It was something controllers occasionally did when they were bored. And it wasn't the prank that mattered at all, although the altitude tags were an added element. It was the acting job; you had to be very good in order to get the proper reaction. Veteran controllers would never fall for something like that unless the performance was Carnegie Hall. A visitor or office clerk might be sucked in, but not veteran controllers.

Kyle had prepared his act for days just to prove to his fellow controllers that he still had the quirky sense of humor they thought he had lost. All week long he had been acting mysterious, hinting that he was going to "run two of those big sons of bitches together." Controllers passed it off as just idle banter; sick jokes helped to pass the time when traffic was light.

Now, several seconds had passed; enough time for controllers to notice and for Kyle to enjoy what he had hoped would be their confused expressions. Instead, it was Kyle himself feeling confused; dumbfounded was more like it–and scared. It wasn't unusual to momentarily lose a target when two aircraft at different altitudes overlapped, because one aircraft would block out the other's signal. The difference here was that enough time had gone by for the two aircraft to have passed.

Time seemed to be standing still. Kyle glanced down the hundred foot long row of radar screens in the Olathe, Kansas, Air Route Traffic Control Center. Controllers were going about their business, attached to radar positions through headset cords like hospital patients being fed intravenously. None of them seemed to be paying much attention.

Kyle wasn't sure what to do next. It was standard policy to notify the supervisor when there was a loss of an aircraft target, but Kyle was too embarrassed to function. The blood seemed to have gone from his legs; his nerve endings had become electrical wires and his palms were sweaty.

Kyle turned toward his friend Zack Morrisey, sitting at the next radar position. He wondered if Zack or one of the other controllers had reversed the joke by adjusting the radar controls. But Zack seemed oblivious, sitting back in his chair, relaxed and seemingly innocent, his shirt open at the neck while he scratched himself contentedly.

Kyle checked the controls; nothing out of order there.

He tried calling the westbound aircraft again: *"Transcon Three Eleven, Kansas City Center, How do you hear?"*

No response.

"Transcon Three Fifty Four, Kansas City Center, are you on frequency?"

Nothing from the southwest bound, either.

Zack Morrisey finally noticed the panic in Kyle's voice and looked up. He saw Kyle's perplexed expression and slowly got to his feet, leaning on his one good leg. He stood looking up at his tall friend for a long moment.

Kyle's eyes were still focused on the radar screen.

Zack finally looked down at the scope. He was always on guard for practical jokes, himself. He looked up at Kyle again, then back to the scope.

"Jesus, Kyle, weren't those two aircraft at thirty seven thousand?"

"No," Kyle insisted, swallowing hard, "the westbound was at thirty five thousand. Danny Houston rigged the altitude tag to make if look as if they were both at thirty seven. It just was a joke."

"I thought I heard you clear Transcon Three Eleven to Flight Level Three Seven Zero. I was sitting right here."

"I didn't have my headset cord plugged in all the way. I was faking it."

"Did he acknowledge the clearance?"

Kyle hesitated: . . . "How could he? I just told you I didn't give him a clearance."

"You mean you don't *think* you did."

Kyle reacted angrily: "I know damn well I didn't."

Several other controllers, lured by the strain in Kyle's voice, walked over to look at the scope, stretching their headset chords to the maximum.

"Well...what...happened then?" Zack asked.

Kyle stood frozen, unable to speak. In addition to being frightened, he was embarrassed by his imprudent attempt at humor. It wasn't like him, and everyone knew it. He looked around at the gathering crowd and began to pray, silently, promising God that he would never pull another prank if the two aircraft would just reappear.

A third sweep of the antennae, then a fourth.

"Kyle," Zack said, "I don't like the looks of this."

"It was a joke," Kyle insisted. "You can ask Danny Houston."

A bright spot was developing on the radar scope. It had the look of a thunderstorm just west of Kansas City, but there were no thunderstorms tonight.

Kyle and Zack continued to study each other's expressions.

Kyle swallowed hard and transmitted again, angry because he thought the pilots might be ignoring him.

"Transcontinental Three Eleven, how do you hear Kansas City Center?"

The controllers focused on Kyle while anxiously awaiting an answer from the aircraft.

"Transcontinental Three Fifty Four, Kansas City Center."

Finally, Kyle lowered himself into his seat and pulled off his headset.

"This just can't be. Please God, tell me this cannot be."

He tried not to think of what might be falling out of the skies over Kansas City. He put his hands over his face and tried to block it out of his mind.

Zack's mouth hung open, his eyes big as softballs.

"ALUMINUM SHOWERS, Kyle," he said. "There's nothing left of those two birds but aluminum showers."

THREE

Private investigator Manny Vigil, fledgling law student, crossed Troost Avenue in Kansas City, headed for Sullivan's diner. He was one frustrated man, stomping the ground like a hungry Dinosaur. His laptop had taken another vacation, so he was forced to use the law library to brief his cases. By the time he got there, day school students had removed the very pages he needed.

"I'm too old for this crap," he said out loud. "I shouldn't be going to school with these kids, anyway; the little shits have no respect for anyone." Manny hated lawyers to begin with; his interest in a law degree, although he may not have realized it himself, was really just a desire to prove that he could do a better job than most of the lawyers he knew. He referred to them as "scum sucking, thousand dollar suit thieves." Manny had long since lost his admiration for human nature, anyway. His outlook had started with adults and was gradually working its way down.

He hesitated before crossing Troost, not really sure he wanted to put up with the same old, noisy diner crowd. He knew that at this time of night the patrons would be mostly kids from Rockhurst University, including basketball players just out of practice. Most of the kids would be scrounging money to buy dinner. If that didn't work, some of them would go down the street to the local grocery store, pay for a loaf of bread because it was impossible to hide under their coats, and steal whatever sandwich meat they could hide in their pockets. "Mausie" Sullivan, the diner's owner, knew all about that; she'd been lecturing the students about it for some thirty years, eventually having to fork over a few free meals to keep them from stealing.

Manny decided to eat there anyway; the next closest restaurant was too far away. He started to cross the street, but stopped when a thunderous reverberation echoed across the night sky, followed by a "screeching" sound, like a rusty door in mortal pain. He felt a chill and ducked involuntarily, covering his head. When he looked up he saw two enormous fireballs, like logs spilling from a fireplace, or lava down the side of a volcano. A stream of sparks followed each one, trailing off in every direction, swirling and dancing across the sky. At first he thought he had seen a mid-air collision, but changed his mind when some instinct told him that it had to be something else, something that didn't quite fit. He continued to watch for several seconds, hands still covering his head. After making sure it was safe, he ran as fast as he could toward the diner's front door. But just as he stepped through the doorway, a mass of frozen debris came crashing through the roof of the diner, tore off part of the counter, and rocketed on down through the floor. Manny found himself face down on the hard floor, with sounds of breaking glass all around. He counted to five and then looked up, convinced that Mausie and her patrons were probably dead. But he was amazed to see that everyone who had been near the counter was still alive. Most of them sat with their hands covering their heads, their eyes moving between the hole in the roof and the one in the floor. Manny got up and looked around for a place to hide, just in case Chicken Little was right. But when nothing else fell for almost fifteen seconds, he joined the others and began to look around, cautiously. Everyone seemed frozen in time, waiting for whatever might come next. When the others finally looked up, Manny looked up too, but the only things visible through the hole in the roof were the dark sky and some residual sparks floating down. One by one the patrons began to move to where they could see down through the hole in the floor.

"Be careful," someone shouted. "Those things down there might be extraterrestrials."

"If they are," Manny said, looking down, "they're flying around in airline chairs." The others stepped forward for a closer look. Their gaze followed Manny's until they came to the spot where Betty Milburn and a heavyset companion had become one giant ball of humanity, bound together by their attached seats. It was if they were meant to be together; their shroud nothing more than a covering of meat loaf dinners, silverware, and dinner plates.

Assuming he was wrong and there really had been a mid-air collision, Manny wondered how in the world the air traffic control system had allowed this to happen.

Who was the poor soul that had just ruined all those lives, including his or her own?

FOUR

Air traffic Control Supervisor Paul Hilger hurried toward Kyle's radar position after receiving a call from the Missouri state police. He saw Kyle, Zack, and several other controllers staring at Kyle's radar scope like dazed little children.

"Somebody just called with a report of a fireball over Kansas City. Are all of your aircraft accounted for, Kyle?"

Kyle was too traumatized to answer.

"I think we may have a problem, Paul," Zack answered for him. "We've got two Transcons missing. They were both at three seven zero."

"No they weren't," Kyle insisted. "I told you that one of them was at three five zero."

Zack didn't bother to argue any further.

Kyle forced himself to look back at Hilger: "Danny Houston rigged one of the computer tags so it would *look* like both aircraft were at the same altitude, Paul. It was supposed to be a joke."

Paul Hilger's usual demeanor was that of a college professor's, studious and controlled. Even when a majority of the controllers had gone out on strike and practically left the facility unmanned, he had kept his emotions under wraps. But he was angry now; his eyes were daggers. "A joke? What the hell kind of a joke is that? Call the aircraft; see if they're on frequency."

"I tried that," Kyle said.

"Well, try again!"

"Transcontinental Three Eleven this is Kansas City Center, are you on frequency?"

"Now the other one."

"Transcontinental Three Fifty Four, how do you hear Kansas City Center?"

Three more supervisors came barreling from the watch desk, a look of astonishment and fright on each face.

"The shits hit the fan, Paul," a tall, gangly man blurted out. "The god damned phones are ringing off the wall. People from all over Missouri and Kansas are telling us that bodies are falling in the streets. One of the callers reported a mid-air collision. Others are saying it's flying saucers and all that crap."

"One of the bodies fell through the roof of a church and another one fell at a major intersection," offered another, shorter man. "People are really scared; they're worried it might be some kind of terrorist attack."

"That cinches it," Hilger said, "we've lost the farm. Get Matthews and Morrisey relieved and call the regional duty officer. Then get Raymond and Ron Adair on the horn. This is going to be a long night."

Hilger turned to Kyle, a man he had always admired, "Kyle, you better brace yourself. You know how Washington feels about you, already. If you have a lawyer, I'd suggest you call him right now."

But Kyle's mind was on Laura, the children, and his boss and best friend, Ron Adair, a man who stuck up for him when the government wanted him removed for good.

What would they think when they heard he was pulling a practical joke?

FIVE

Ron Adair had received the call at exactly 9:10PM. The portly, five foot nine bundle of energy raced his 1997 Thunderbird down I-35 from his home in Overland Park, Kansas, switching from radio station to radio station looking for updates. Every station was now covering the story.

Adair was the highest ranking air traffic manager in the seven state region. His friendship with Kyle Matthews' father, Eric, started when they were both controllers and officers in PATCO, the Professional Air Traffic Controllers Organization. Both men had been concerned with the deficiencies in the air traffic system in the late sixties, and were among those responsible for giving PATCO a kick start. After at first trying to stop the 1981 strike, Eric Matthews believed that he had no choice but to support the controllers, and reluctantly went on strike himself. He was fired like the others, but was reinstated because of a technicality. He retired from the FAA twenty years later.

Everyone expected Ron Adair to eventually become the next Air Traffic Director, but like Eric Matthews, he was too outspoken and had to settle for his current position. That characteristic had made both Ron Adair and Eric Matthews a hit with their fellow employees, but not with their bosses. Kyle had been cut from the same cloth: when he thought something was wrong, he said so.

Ron hesitated before using his cell phone to call Richard Carpelski and order him to investigate, because he knew Carpelski would be delighted to hear of any trouble befalling Kyle Matthews. Carpelski had been the manager of the Kansas City Air Route Traffic Control Center during a recent wildcat strike, and had blamed Kyle for instigating, or at least not stopping, the job action that had cost him his own job.

Ron didn't like or trust Carpelski, any more than Carpelski liked or trusted Ron's close relationship with Kyle. But it was Carpelski's job to investigate any air traffic controller's involvement in an aircraft accident, so Adair had no choice but to assign him the task.

Ron decided not to mention Kyle's name.

"I just want you to listen to the tapes and find out what happened. Don't go off the deep end. The FAA will be under close scrutiny, regardless of what happened."

Carpelski was right at home in his new job, evaluating controller performance and recommending corrective action. He liked the feeling of power it gave him and he didn't like any restrictions. He picked up something in Ron's tone of voice: "You mean you want me to determine that the FAA is not responsible for the collision?" he asked facetiously.

"You know better than that. I just mean that you and Matthews have a history. I don't want any funny stuff."

There was a pause. "What. . . what has Matthews got to do with this?"

Ron realized his mistake. "He. . . may be involved."

Carpelski was sure his heart had skipped a beat, but he kept quiet.

Ron noticed the silence. "I'll be at the center in thirty minutes. Let me know when you have something factual."

Carpelski didn't even hear Ron's last remark; he was so excited he slammed down the phone and literally ran to his car.

SIX

After things settled down in the diner, Manny Vigil drove to the spot KCMO radio had identified as the crash site. He picked little pieces of glass out of his face and arms as he drove, shards that he hadn't realized were there. He felt lucky he hadn't been seriously injured, or even killed; another ten feet and he'd have been in the basement with that lady and her traveling companion.

A mile or so from the crash site, Manny stopped his Mustang at the highest point in the area, got out, looked toward the east, and saw the destruction: almost two square miles of downtown Kansas City, Kansas, mostly the stockyards area, had been turned into a human abattoir, smoldering like some evil scene from hell. It was a nightmare, a disaster like the ones you read about but never expect to see with your own eyes. He wondered what impulse had driven him to visit such a depressing site, and decided it must be the nagging thought that he might someday be called upon to describe what he had seen and heard while crossing Troost Avenue.

He walked in the cool darkness until he came to a lighted area that appeared to the center of the rescue activity. He listened to his Sony Walkman, hoping for more details. Information was sketchy, but from what KCMO reported, the remains of both aircraft had fallen just west of downtown Kansas City, Missouri, with most of the wreckage landing in Kansas. He shook his head at the devastation all around him. He had remembered this section of town as just a quiet maze of railroad tracks, water towers, and abandoned warehouses; although, surprisingly, there were some well known eating establishments and an old sports arena here, as well.

As Manny got closer, he saw the carcass of an aircraft and scattered remains of bodies and luggage. It was as if he had walked into a child's playroom in the dark, with toys scattered all about. There were forms and shapes of every kind, but nothing distinguishable. Spotlights tried their best to illuminate the shapes through the hazy smoke. He watched as workers turned over objects they couldn't identify, poking at them with sticks to see if they were bodies or something else. Manny had to cover his mouth and nose to keep out the smell and the smoke. He passed dozens of confused people who were just trying to get to their automobiles so they could go home. They had to navigate around yellow tape to avoid stepping on bodies.

Manny was careful to step over a downed power line that was making snapping sounds and shooting sparks. The sound of coughing could be heard all around. He froze when he looked up and saw the second aircraft carcass, just a hundred or so yards ahead, proof that more than one aircraft had gone down. He marveled at how close together the carcasses were after having fallen from such a high altitude, but knew that many other parts of both aircraft were probably scattered for miles, with some landing as much as ten miles away.

Thinking back to what he had seen in the sky tonight, he couldn't understand his own doubts: it had to have been a mid-air collision, the evidence was right here, scattered all around. And yet the doubts remained: something about the sounds and sights of the collision didn't fit, even if he couldn't understand why.

A closer look revealed that both fuselages were without engines and wings. He looked up to see two national transportation board investigators on top of a nearby warehouse, inspecting an aircraft wing and part of a horizontal stabilizer. He saw that an orderly string of body bags were already awaiting pickup, stacked in rows all around. Investigators were removing other bodies from trees and a creek. One body hung from the top of a telephone pole, seemingly unnoticed. He considered climbing up the pole to bring it down, then thought better of it: he wasn't even supposed to be here, and the body wasn't going anywhere, anyway.

He continued to stroll through the chaos, shaking his head and murmuring to himself. Wallets, purses, even children's toys, were scattered everywhere. He pressed the radio headset to his ear, listening for updates. A KCMO reporter was saying that dozens of city blocks had been cordoned off on both sides of the Kansas-Missouri border in order to keep out the hundreds of cars that were blocking the roads and highways. According to the reporter, the downtown areas on both sides were a mass of confusion and panic. Citizens were reporting broken pieces of aluminum, flaming debris, even bodies falling in their yards. The reporter went on to say that emergency workers on both sides of the state line were in complete shock. She interviewed experienced fire fighters, veterans who thought they had seen it all. Manny listened while they answered the reporters questions; he could almost "feel" them shaking their heads in shock and disbelief, describing how each year they conducted drills to simulate an air disaster, never dreaming it would ever really happen. They confessed that their training had never been designed to cover the widespread devastation they were now witnessing.

Manny heard voices and crouched behind a tree. Two firemen passed by within several feet, but didn't notice him. He remained still and tuned to another radio station in time to hear the mayor of Kansas City, Kansas make a statement:

"Our first thought was that there had been an explosion in the stockyard's area," the mayor said. "But further investigation has revealed that this was probably a mid-air collision."

"No it wasn't," Manny found himself saying out loud. He wasn't sure why he had said it, since he was standing close to the two giant fuselages, but he just knew his instincts were right and that the mayor was wrong. He took one more, long look and began walking back toward where he had parked his Mustang, wracking his brain again to decipher whatever it was that was holding his memory captive.

He took time out to say a prayer for the poor bastard responsible for all the chaos.

Whoever that person was, he or she had to be suffering terribly.

SEVEN

It was almost eleven o'clock when Kyle and Zack were escorted to what controllers called the "rubber hose room," a hole in the wall where they were grilled when they screwed up. The eight by ten room featured four grey walls, four government grey chairs, and a government grey table; a perfect place for a supervisor to deliver a solemn message. The depressing little room looked as if it had been decorated around the time Hammurabi developed the first code of laws. It had been recently painted, but that didn't do anything to improve the austere décor: grey is still grey and metal is still metal.

Kyle flopped his slender, six foot three inch frame into one of the metal chairs, tilted it against the wall, and covered his face with his hands. His skin was pale, he shook badly, and he hadn't said a word since he had left the control room. He was so zonked that Zack had to practically guide him to a chair. He sat for several minutes attempting to fight off the cold chill and queasy stomach that had followed the worst moments of his life. He tried to erase thoughts of bodies falling from the sky, but they kept coming back.

He finally removed his hands from his face, wiped his brow with a handkerchief, shook his head back and forth, and considered the consequences. A mid-air collision was a rare occurrence, something every controller dreaded. Only one or two controllers had ever been involved in one, even if the media did make it seem like an everyday thing. It was a subject controllers rarely even discussed for fear that one might actually happen. The repercussions from such a disaster would affect every other controller as well, including those who weren't even at work that day. New, "cover your ass" rules would be added, rules that would serve no purpose other than to make a controller's job more cumbersome.

He went over in his mind every move he had made before the collision. He couldn't see how he could have possibly made a mistake; he just knew it had to be "pilot error." He told himself that as soon as the FAA talked to Danny Houston and listened to the tape recording, he would be exonerated from everything but the prank. His FAA career was over though, regardless of the outcome of the investigation; his name would be associated with the disaster forever. But those things were insignificant compared to the guilt he would carry around if any action he had taken had killed all those people.

He felt selfish thinking of himself at a time like this, but there was more than just *his* life at stake. He had his wife, Laura, and children Todd and Mary Claire to think of. He was forty-two years old, pretty late to be starting over, and he hated to see his family bear the brunt of such a stupid prank.

There was chaos outside the room: supervisors were running to answer phones, and de facto guards were rushing to keep the media from infiltrating through side doors. Every controller or supervisor who passed by the room waived or gave Kyle the thumbs up; he was just about everyone's favorite. They all enjoyed his good, if sometimes irreverent, sense of humor. He was so absorbed that he didn't notice them.

But while everyone liked or respected Kyle, most of them did think he had been acting strange lately. They worried that his renowned sense of humor had lost its spontaneity, that he might even be depressed. Now, they had to wonder if he might have simply "lost it." Their concerns had been the very reason Kyle had pulled the prank in the first place, to show them that he was all right.

If Kyle *had* been acting a little depressed lately, it was because of his separation from Laura: she had been angry with him ever since he announced that he wanted to run for national president of NATCA, the union that replaced PATCO. He was concerned that the recent wildcat strike in the center was a harbinger of things to come, a sign that the relationship between controllers and the FAA was worsening, and that a national strike like the one that put PATCO out of business could be on the horizon. The current NATCA leadership seemed to enjoy conflict, and Kyle thought the organization needed someone who would use their PATCO experience to guide controllers in the right direction. It was a case of loyalty towards Laura versus loyalty towards his profession, and it was dragging them both down.

When he finally did look toward the door, he saw a passing controller he recognized wave to him. While he appreciated everyone's support, it pained him to realize that the attention he was getting was as much curiosity as anything else.

"Oh my God, Laura. . . ," he said suddenly, jumping up. "Zack, I have to call Laura before she hears about this on TV." His legs were so weak he actually stumbled; he made it as far as the door before running into FBI special agent Red Brockman, who stood blocking the doorway. Kyle had a history with Brockman; he had no desire to talk to him now.

"Get out of the way, Brockman. I have to call my wife."

Brockman, an ex-Marine, loved to intimidate, but that wouldn't work with Kyle. Brockman made a half-hearted attempt to continue his blockade. "We need to talk, *now*, Matthews."

"Later," Kyle said, shoving him aside.

Brockman turned to Zack as Kyle hurried away, making no attempt to hide his feelings. "I'm 'gonna get that smart son–of–a- bitch this time."

"Not on your best day, Brockman," Zack responded, following Kyle out the door.

But he wasn't really that confident.

EIGHT

Laura sounded as if she might explode: "Judas, I've been trying to call you for an hour," she said angrily.

The two had been separated for a month, but that didn't keep them from talking on the phone every day. Their separation was a means of keeping the children from hearing their arguments. Laura had no intention of allowing Kyle to run for president of NATCA, not after the long year they had spent in Washington, D.C., when Kyle had accepted a temporary assignment to the NATCA office. Kyle had been in his element there, but not Laura: where he enjoyed the spotlight, she preferred to be with her children in their own, Overland Park, Kansas neighborhood. She was comfortable at home, riding her bicycle with the children, but uncomfortable when making small talk with politicians. Kyle, on the other hand, was a natural born leader, comfortable talking with anyone. He missed the excitement, a chance to make a difference. He had been fired up about going back to Washington from the minute they got home. Laura felt guilty about holding him back, knowing that he only wanted to change things for the better. Nevertheless, she just couldn't go back to Washington, D.C. again, even if it meant an end to his ambitions. She knew it was wrong, and that he would make a good president, but she was who she was.

"The phone has been tied up," Kyle said casually. "Everyone is pretty excited around here."

"Why are you whispering?"

"I'm on my cell phone, trying to keep out of sight. There are people running back and forth all over the place."

Laura didn't like the sound of Kyle's voice; he sounded uptight, and that just wasn't him: he was the kind of person who liked to laugh at himself. He avoided people who took themselves too seriously. His favorite expression was, "don't sweat the small stuff."

"Why do you have to keep out of sight? What's wrong? They're talking about a crash on TV. The reporters sound pretty worked up."

"We had a mid-air collision," Kyle said casually. "I was working the two aircraft at the time. No one knows exactly what happened because they were two thousand feet apart, right before they disappeared from the scope."

Laura was speechless for a long moment. She had taken the time to learn every detail about her husband's job. She knew more about it than some of Kyle's bosses. "That's...impossible," she sputtered. "What do they think happened?"

"They don't know yet."

"You're leaving something out; I can hear it in your voice."

Long pause: "I may be in a little trouble."

Laura was afraid he was going to tell her that he had had blacked out, or something.

"I was trying to pull a joke at the time. I had a guy in the computer room rig one of the altitude tags to make it look as if the two aircraft were at the same altitude."

". . . You what?"

"I'm afraid you heard me right."

There was a period of silence while Laura attempted to understand what Kyle had just told her. "Kyle, you don't pull practical jokes. That's just not you."

"I know, but everyone had been telling me how depressed I seemed to be lately, so I wanted to show them that I still had my sense of humor. I'll admit it was a dumb idea."

"But if they were two thousand feet apart, how did they. . . collide? You're not making sense."

She didn't give him time to answer. . . "Kyle, wait till you see what's happened downtown, it's devastating."

"But I didn't have anything to do with the collision. I'll prove it as soon as I find Danny Houston."

There was a hesitation on the other end of the line. "Who's Danny Houston?"

"The guy who rigged the data tag."

Laura was becoming more and more concerned. "Where is. . . Danny Houston?"

"He must have gone home. They haven't made contact with him yet, but they will."

"Kyle, I'm not sure what you're jabbering about, but we both know the FAA is going to fire you now. Even if you get backing from this Houston guy they're going to get you for pulling the prank. They hate your guts. You can't survive this."

"They fired my dad and he got back. Maybe they'll overlook my stupidity when they realize it had nothing to do with the crash."

"Overlook it? There are bodies all over the city!"

"I'm talking about the prank. OK, maybe they'll fire me, but at least I didn't have anything to do with the accident!"

Laura interrupted him: "Just a minute."

Kyle heard the phone bounce off of a table and the TV volume rise. He listened and realized that it was some kind of bulletin.

Laura came back on the line.

"I hate to tell you this, but things are even worse than we thought, if that's possible. Deeter Noonan was on one of those two flights. He's presumed to be dead. Now tell me again why they'll overlook your stupidity."

Kyle was speechless. Deeter Noonan had been Administrator of the Federal Aviation Administration. When the local NATCA union went on strike in the center, it made the White House so nervous that it cost

Noonan a chance at a Cabinet post. He resigned, accepted the presidency of Transcontinental Airlines, and blamed everything on Kyle; the two actually engaged in the manly art of fisticuffs during a live TV press conference.

"I wasn't aware of that," Kyle said, still calculating the full impact. He tried to think of something to tell Laura that would comfort her. "This doesn't change anything. I still didn't have anything to do with the crash."

"Don't you understand? It's not going to make any difference; the FAA has you right where they want you."

Kyle mumbled something else, but Laura wasn't listening anymore. "They know you hated Noonan," she went on. "You even criticized him during that press conference. You complained that Noonan was filing exaggerated safety reports on controllers."

"But I didn't know he was on one of those two aircraft."

"Think the feds will believe that? You need to find this Danny guy now."

Laura was not one to panic any more than her husband. The fact that she was panicky now concerned Kyle even more. Might as well tell her the rest: "Problem is, even if we do find Houston he may not be a very good witness."

"Pardon me? Say that again." Kyle's way of minimizing problems drove Laura wild.

"Apparently, I didn't choose my accomplice very well. Zack says Houston is probably the most frightened and unreliable person he's ever met."

"Wonderful. If you were going to pull a dumb stunt, did you have to ask some whack job to help you?"

"I guess I really didn't know him that well."

"OK," she said, "give me all of it. What else did Zack say? Not that he's any exemplar."

"Zack says Houston is not very sociable. He doesn't talk very much. He works mostly midnight shifts to avoid people."

"And this is the man who was supposed to help you pull a prank involving two giant airliners, right?"

"I guess so."

"What do we do now?" Laura asked.

"I should be OK as soon as they review the tape."

"Except for the prank," she reminded him. "You better get Rooster involved right now."

Kyle was surprised to hear Laura suggesting he get help from the NATCA union rep. She was no fan of unions, not after the local strike, and Rooster Brunges was the one pushing Kyle to run for national office. She thought Rooster was like the character in the old time cowboy movies, secretly selling guns and whiskey to the Indians. To Kyle, her suggestion was proof of how worried she really was.

"I agree," Kyle said. "Would you do me a favor? Call Rooster. Tell him to get over here now."

"I'm coming, too," Laura said suddenly.

"I'm not so sure that's a good idea."

"I can't stay here; there's already two or three cars with TV station logos going back and forth up and down our street. I wondered who they were looking for, now I know. I'm starting to feel threatened. Have you talked with Ron?"

"I'm almost afraid to."

NINE

Traffic was backed up all the way from I-35 to the center gate. Ron had left the highway at 9:45PM, but it took him another fifteen minutes to travel the last mile. The huge throng outside the fences, mostly media types and gawkers, shocked him. It had the makings of a riot, and since the crash had occurred less than an hour before, it gave Ron a good idea of how bad the situation was.

All air route traffic control buildings had been built in the boon docks in the 1960's in order to isolate them from what was considered to be the spot where the Russians would drop their atom bombs, the center of major cities. That notion became obsolete when the world built a bigger bomb.

Center buildings were like any other office building, with the exception of a long, windowless control room, and a gaggle of microwave antennae on top. The Kansas City Air Route Traffic Control Center was in Olathe, Kansas, almost twenty miles from Kansas City.

Ron wondered how the media had gotten to Olathe so fast. He showed his FAA badge to the gate guard and instructed the man to keep out everyone except controllers and supervisors.

A TV mini-cam appeared outside the window of Ron's car as he started to drive through the gate entrance. A pretty, blond haired woman dressed younger than her age, stuck her head through the window and wanted to know if Ron was with the FBI. Ron said "no," and inched his car forward.

"Can you tell us what happened," a young man with a pencil and note pad asked from the other window.

"No, I can't, I just got here. Now would you please step back? I need to get through."

"We need to get in and interview the controllers," the woman said, her blond hair blowing in the wind. "Someone called and said that a controller's 'gone nuts'."

"Sorry, we can't let any media people in yet. We're going to conduct an investigation and it's going to take some time. We'll talk to you later."

"Who are you...sir...what's your name?" another reporter insisted. He jammed his mike through the open window.

Ron grabbed the mike and shoved it aside. "Please get that thing out of my face."

The gate guard quickly moved in and pulled the reporters away. Ron drove forward as the gate closed behind him. He noticed that quite a few cars had breached the front gate. The parking lot overflowed, unusual for this time of night.

Curtis Raymond, the man who replaced Carpelski as center manager, came bounding out of his car, hurrying toward the front entrance. Raymond was a New Yorker with all the subtlety of a pit bull He exemplified one of the FAA's biggest problems – pay disparity. A manager's pay was less than that of a journeyman controller's, and since a manager could never recover the money he lost when transferring to a new city, the FAA often ended up with managers more interested in ego satisfaction than anything else. Raymond was a prime example of that.

Raymond was dressed in a three-piece suit and tie, waiving his ubiquitous cigar. Curtis never smoked the cigar, he just waived it around. At meetings, he used it to intimidate his supervisors, pointing it at them like a dagger. No one ever got much of an opportunity to talk when Curtis was present: it was said that he woke up each morning with a stockpile of ten thousand words and rarely went home without using all of them. "Matthews must have gone off the deep end this time," Raymond bellowed as soon as he saw Ron.

"Expecting a big TV interview, Curtis?" Ron asked, eyeing Raymond's suit. Ron was dressed in shorts and a golf shirt, with high-top basketball shoes.

Raymond gave Ron's clothes a disapproving once over. "We're 'gonna get rid of this guy once and for all," he mumbled, ignoring Ron's slam. "It's overdue. I knew something like this was going to happen."

"Why don't we wait and see what happened before we rush to judgment, Curtis?" Ron suggested. "Besides, if you knew it was going to happen, why didn't you prevent it?"

Raymond didn't answer. His round face turned red and he walked faster, stepping in front of Ron so that he could get to the door first.

Paul Hilger was standing in the entrance hall talking to two men in business suits when Ron and Curtis entered. Ron immediately recognized the two as FBI agents. It was the second sign of major trouble. The media had been the first.

Ron ignored the agents and took Paul Hilger aside. He reached up and put his arm around Hilger's shoulder and whispered so that the agents couldn't hear. "I need to talk to Kyle and Zack. Who belongs to all the cars?"

Hilger frowned. "Mostly gawkers who managed to sneak in before we got the gate secured. Others belong to supervisors who were called in to help, or employees who came by to see what was happening."

"Get all unnecessary bodies out of the parking lot right now. Where's Carpelski?"

"Listening to the tape recording."

"What happened Paul?"

"Zack said something about hearing Kyle clear the west bound to climb. That put him right with the southbound."

"Kyle would have to be crazy or drunk to do something like that."

"He was pulling some kind of a practical joke," Hilger said, "but he denies ever climbing the west bound."

"The whole thing just doesn't make sense."

Hilger shrugged his shoulders. "I haven't heard the tape myself, yet."

"How is Kyle taking this?"

"Not well, but he's confident the tape recording will exonerate him."

Brockman and another FBI agent were eyeballing Ron all the while, whispering to Raymond and checking their watches.

"Where's Danny Houston?" Ron asked.

"That's the other thing," Hilger said. "According to the sign-out log, Houston went home long before the two aircraft hit."

TEN

Kelly Edmunds was neither offended nor surprised when the man in the car drove right on by. It was obvious that something important was going on in the air traffic control building, and she hadn't really expected to get any quick answers.

The problem now was how to get into the building. She wondered what the hell kind of building it could be; it certainly wasn't a control tower, and the people at WDAF had no clue. All she knew for sure was that the assignment editor told her to get her butt out to the "Olathe Center," interview a Curtis Raymond, and find out about the aircraft collision.

How could they control airplanes in a place with no windows?

Edmunds had been told for years that she was too old to be a star in the TV reporting business; that her station needed younger reporters to increase their ratings. She learned from others that the real reason was her lack of an "east coast intellectual look."

Most people considered Kelly to be very attractive: she was tall and slender, with long, blond hair and green eyes. Her most attractive feature, however, was a face that always seemed interested, even excited. Her enthusiasm was infectious; people who ordinarily wouldn't talk to anyone else were eager to talk to Kelly Edmunds.

In spite of station politics, or perhaps because of it, Kelly was determined to succeed. Exasperation with her bosses had made her bolder and bolder. She had turned in some good interviews lately; there had even been "feelers" from a national network. But she still needed that one blockbuster story to get her over the hump: one big break and she could tell WDAF to shove it. She sensed a good story here: everyone seemed very excited.

She noticed that every car entering the center parking lot had the same, blue FAA sticker. She wished that she had her print set with her.

She decided to walk further down the street, where cars were stopped in a line of traffic.

"Excuse me," she said to a man in a pickup truck. "I'm supposed to be meeting with a Mr. Curtis Raymond, but I can't get my car close enough to get in. Can you give me a lift?"

The controller in the pickup truck knew Kelly was lying; she didn't have any appointment with Curtis, not at this late hour. The real story had to be that she was desperate to get in any way she could. He didn't care; security was a management problem. Besides, it was pretty boring on the mid-shift, and she was good looking.

"Hop in," he said. "But you better keep your head down. I don't think the gate guard is going to buy that sorry story of yours."

Kelly smiled, got in the pickup, and ducked down as far as she could.

"Don't worry," the controller said, "that gate guard couldn't find his ass with Sonar."

The pickup sailed through the gate without even a second look from the guard. The sticker could have said "USSR," just as long as it was blue.

"What in the world is this place?" Kelly asked as they parked the truck.

The controller laughed. "Not too many people know about these air traffic control centers. Come on in, I'll show you around."

They got out of the pickup and Kelly raced to keep up. "What happened here? Did someone really go bonkers?"

"I honestly don't know anything more than what I heard on the radio. I was told to come in early for the mid shift, that's all I know. I guess we're about to find out."

They managed to get inside without being seen; the individual assigned to guard the door was busy arguing with another reporter. Kelly followed the controller down the hall. "Why do they call this the Kansas City. . . something or other. Isn't this Olathe?"

"It's called the Kansas City Air Route Traffic Control Center because it used to be located at the Kansas City airport. The radio call sign is also 'Kansas City Center'; they just never changed it."

As they entered the control room, Kelly saw that the heart and soul of the building was a long room with flashing lights and several rows of radar scopes. Controllers moved around constantly, but quietly. The long isles of controllers and their green radar scopes reminded Kelly of Star Trek, times a hundred.

Kelly and her companion strolled down the isle closest to the door, acting casual so as not to attract attention. Kelly could see that each radar scope was manned by one to three controllers, some watching the green scopes, others apparently providing assistance. In addition to the blinking lights, there were bells ringing softly, which she learned were incoming messages. She also learned that the ring was intentionally kept at a low level so as to generate awareness without bothering controllers at adjacent radar positions. Other controllers, men and women, strolled or sat behind the radar positions.

"I know what the controllers at the radar scopes are doing," Kelly whispered, "but what about the others, the ones behind them with head-sets on?"

"Those are the supervisors."

Kelly watched the supervisors. They seemed to float from radar scope to radar scope, pointing hear and there and talking into headset mikes that were strung from hook-like posts above every three or four radar positions. They didn't seem to be in a hurry, more like skating on a pond. She learned that they were coordinating, making the transition of aircraft from radar position to radar position as smooth as possible.

"Tell me about this place."

"What do you want to know?"

"All of it," she said excitedly, "and lets go some place where they won't see me. I don't think I'm supposed to be here." She grinned.

They found a quiet place away from the supervisors. It was under some large weather maps projected on the walls. Teams of controllers working computer screens updated the weather information. No one paid much attention to Kelly.

Jack Golenzer, Kelly's guide, was used to working in anonymity. He was only too happy to have this enthusiastic visitor. Golenzer was single and somewhat of a ladies man. He wished he had dressed better; he tucked in his shirt and smoothed his hair subconsciously.

"So tell me."

"There are twenty of these centers in the United States," Golenzer said. "The Kansas City Center airspace is approximately one hundred and fifty thousand square miles and goes from east of St. Louis to western Kansas. Controllers pass the aircraft along from one radar sector to another as the aircraft navigate radio beams, signals from the ground that make up airways. They have complete control from the ground up within their own airspace, except for the airspace they delegate to what are called TRACONs."

"Nevil Shute," she said, half under her breath.

"What?"

"Nevil Shute. I think he was the one who wrote a book called 'No highways in the sky.' I guess those radio beams are the airways he mentioned in his book."

"Whatever," Golenzer said. "Controllers are either assigned high altitude sectors or low altitude sectors. When an aircraft is scheduled to land within a center's airspace, it's handed off to the TRACON that handles that particular airport."

"What is a TRACON?" Kelly asked. She was busy making notes and looking around. She was surprised at the size of the place, and the fact that she had never heard of it, even though it was right here, outside of Kansas City.

"TRACON stands for terminal radar control. It's a facility located at major airports to control arriving and departing aircraft."

"So how do these TRACONs relate to the centers?"

"Each major airport has a 'flow rate,' an acceptable number of aircraft per hour that can be accommodated by controllers in the TRACONs or towers at smaller airports. One of the center's primary functions is to feed airplanes to TRACONs at designated rates. The center tries not to exceed those rates, and at the same time, keep up with the flow so as not to delay traffic. Air traffic has to keep moving, otherwise things will back up all over the country. At high traffic periods, the centers reduce the flow rate to accommodate the lower rate the TRACONs can accept. The national flow rate is managed by an FAA facility in Virginia."

"And the towers?" she asked.

"The TRACONs take the aircraft from the centers and jockey them until they're lined up for the runway, then the tower takes over and clears them to land."

Kelly noticed that the control room was surprisingly quiet, even with the bells and phones ringing. "If all that is going on, why am I not hearing a lot of noise?"

"Because each controller receives communications in a headset. If all the speakers were turned up at once, it would sound like the NCAA final four."

"Why is it so dark?"

"So that we can sneak nosey reporters in without being caught,. . . and to make it easier to see the radar scopes."

Kelly smiled. She noticed that her eyes were becoming accustomed to the dark, and that the lack of light made for a more peaceful environment.

Golenzer was looking Kelly over carefully. He liked her enthusiasm. He wondered if she was available.

"So these controllers are all monitoring airplanes?"

Golenzer suddenly looked angry. "Please, don't say 'monitor;' you could get a monkey to do that. These controllers are practically flying the aircraft. They assign routes, issue clearances for turns and altitude changes, even tell the pilot when to speed up or slow down in order to keep aircraft separated. The planes have to be jockeyed continuously so that they won't run into one another."

"Sorry," Kelly said, afraid she might loose her guide before she got her story. "What about the airports without towers, the smaller ones?"

Golenzer was starting to look annoyed. Kelly's use of the word "monitor" had "broken the code."

"At smaller airports, aircraft are either turned over to a tower, or, if there is no tower, cleared to land by the center controller."

Kelly noticed activity at the supervisor's desk. The same man she had seen drive by in the parking lot was standing in the front of the room, pointing in her direction. She heard someone say it was Ron Adair, the boss.

"We better get out of here," she said to Golenzer, but he was already in motion, going in the opposite direction.

Kelly ducked into the woman's room.

Two women were talking.

"It doesn't make any sense," one of them said. "Kyle Matthews is not crazy."

Kelly was used to eavesdropping; it was part of the job. She acted disinterested and went about her business. She fumbled in her purse for a small recorder and turned it on, almost dropping it.

"Jerry told me that Kyle was pulling some kind of joke. Then, two airplanes collided. The brass from the regional office are all here, and the Carp is listening to the tape recording."

"Jesus," the second woman said. "I never thought I'd see this happen in my lifetime. . . all those people! Kyle would never do something like that."

"I don't know; he has been acting odd lately. I just hope whatever he did had nothing to do with the collision."

"Why is it that bad things always happen to good people?" the first woman asked. "When I was having some personal problems, Kyle was the first one to help me."

"I know, he's always been a good listener, too," the second woman agreed. "I thought the FAA would get him eventually, but not like this."

Edmunds didn't see Golenzer again; five minutes later she was caught and escorted to the front door by two angry supervisors, but not before she had all she needed on her recorder.

"Pulling a joke. . . two airplanes hit. . . , FAA would get him eventually!"

It didn't matter that she had been tossed. She howled with delight as she ran for her camera crew. She found them waiting outside the gate, alerted the station, then made a live broadcast right in front of the center building. The broadcast was picked up by CNN and re-broadcast all over the world. Kelly Edmunds was about to become a star.

ELEVEN

Kyle leaned forward in his chair holding a can of diet Pepsi. Ron had never seen him so upset. His hand shook and sweat poured from his forehead. The two FBI agents were clamoring to get in.

"It was just a joke," he explained. He told Ron how he had called down to the computer room to make sure Danny Houston would cooperate, and how he had checked the computerized aircraft situation display to make sure that the two aircraft in question would pass at approximately the same time.

"The computer technician on duty confirmed that Danny was at work," Kyle said, "but he didn't know exactly where Danny was. 'You know Danny,' the guy said, 'he's probably out looking for parts.' He said that was Danny's favorite cover when he was screwing off. I asked him to make sure he delivered a message to Danny. I said, 'Have Danny call me if he can't deliver. He'll know what I mean'."

"Who was the technician? Will he verify that?"

Kyle shrugged his shoulders. "I didn't ask his name and I didn't give him any details. I guess the only thing he can verify, and that's if you find out who he is, is that I called Danny."

"Go on," Ron said, as Zack homed in on every word. "I need to get this straight because Washington wants a full report. If I understand what you've told me, Transcontinental Three Eleven was Westbound from Washington D. C. to Los Angeles at thirty five thousand feet, and Transcontinental Three Fifty Four was southbound from Minneapolis to Dallas at thirty seven thousand feet."

"That's right. They didn't actually have to pass at the same time to make it look real; they just had to be close. I checked their positions again on the ASD when the aircraft were about thirty miles from Kansas City. When I saw that the data tag on Transcon Three Eleven had changed to three seven zero, I assumed that Danny had done what he said he would do. I'll admit it made me a little nervous to see two aircraft showing the same altitude, but that was the whole purpose of the prank. Then, when they were about ten to fifteen miles apart, I pretended to climb the westbound. I was confident no transmission had gone out, because I hadn't plugged my headset chord in all the way."

"Brilliant," Zack mumbled. Ron turned and gave him a nasty look, then turned back to Kyle and asked, "Did the transmitter light go on?"

Kyle's eyes brightened. "That's right, I forgot about that; the red light on the console didn't go on; that *proves* I didn't have my headset plugged in all the way."

"Did you get a read-back?"

"No, of course not; I told you I never issued a clearance."

"That's something, anyway. Did you make other plans in case Danny wasn't there that day?"

"No. When I saw the two altitude tags read the same; I assumed he was there."

Ron shook his head. "What happened next?"

"Both targets disappeared."

"So what did you do then?"

"Nothing-what could I do? The targets had already merged, so it was too late."

"You didn't try to call either aircraft?"

"Of course, right away, but I didn't get any answers."

Ron looked perplexed: "I can't believe you would do something this stupid, Kyle. Even Morrisey wouldn't pull something like this."

"Everybody was saying I had lost my sense of humor. I just wanted to show them I was OK. Besides, I needed a good laugh myself, considering the way things are at home."

Ron shook his head. He'd seen the identical prank pulled a hundred times, although nothing this elaborate. It was just that he couldn't see his friend being a part of it. He paused and asked the "sixty four thousand dollar" question: "Did you know that Danny Houston left the building an hour or so before the collision?"

Kyle jerked his head up. "I . . . don't believe it. I saw the altitude tag change."

"The sign-out log shows that he wasn't even in the building when those two aircraft collided."

"The log must be wrong," Kyle insisted, "He probably signed out at the wrong time."

Ron rubbed his chin and thought for several seconds. "Well, I know you wouldn't deliberately run two airplanes together, so maybe Transcon Three Eleven copied a clearance intended for another aircraft. We can probably clear this whole thing up when we hear the tape recording."

"He couldn't have copied a clearance intended for another aircraft," Kyle insisted, shaking his head. "Those were the only two aircraft on my frequency."

TWELVE

Ron's game plan had been to stall agents Brockman and Davis until Carpelski finished playing the tape recording, but that flight plan also crashed in flames.

"The White House just called," Paul Hilger said, holding the door open a few inches. "FBI agents Red Brockman and Glen Davis are to have immediate access to Kyle and Zack." The two FBI agents peered over Hilger's shoulder like salivating Dobermans.

"Sorry Kyle," Ron said, sounding very concerned. "Be careful what you say to these guys. That goes for you too, Zack. I don't think Brockman likes you guys very much."

Brockman and Davis came in flashing their FBI credentials. Curtis Raymond followed before Ron could close the door. The two agents sat down across the table from Kyle and Zack, while Ron stepped back and leaned against the wall. Raymond stood next to Ron, his arms folded dramatically.

Kyle had already made a decision not to give the two agents anything except name, rank, and serial number. He would accept whatever punishment he deserved for the prank, but he wouldn't discuss anything else with the two agents, not after their last go-around.

"Mr. Matthews, why don't you just tell us exactly what happened," Brockman said in a squeaky voice. "And we don't want any 'make believe' like the last time." He was the taller of the two agents, with red hair combed up and over in an unsuccessful attempt to cover his bald spot. His reference to "make believe" referred to an incident where Kansas City controllers "invented" an employee and named him "Carl Dingle." Dingle had all the requisites for employment: a social security number belonging to a deceased controller, a locker and a headset. He even received periodic performance evaluations because some of the supervisors were in on it.

Brockman was the unlucky FBI agent assigned to investigate when Carl Dingle failed to cash his paychecks for over a year. Brockman went overboard and pursued Dingle with the zeal usually reserved for one of *America's Most Wanted*. Controllers kept him busy creating false leads. Brockman never did find Dingle, of course, but he did manage to make a fool of himself. He blamed Kyle Matthews because Kyle was the NATCA representative at the time.

"Yeah, no more of that cock and bull," Davis added. Davis was short and stocky, with a deep voice. His collar was too tight, causing him to constantly twist his neck. He looked like his whole body might explode at any minute.

Before Kyle could respond to either of the agents, there was a knock on the door and "Rooster" Brunges stood in the doorway, all five foot four inches and one hundred twenty pounds looking very official. He identified himself as a representative of the "National Air Traffic Controllers Association," and insisted on representing "his client."

When Kyle had first met Brunges, he remarked that the little man's clothes fit him like "sweat socks on a rooster," and the name, "Rooster," stuck. Rooster had a withered face, like a cowboy after too many cattle drives, a mercurial temper, and would fight at the drop of a hat, even though he usually lost. On one occasion, he erupted and attacked Kyle over some imagined offense, and lost that fight, too. No reason was ever given as to why he had gone ballistic, but Kyle and Rooster had been good friends ever since.

The two agents looked at one another, not sure of the rules. Rooster didn't know the rules, either, but the agents didn't know that. They hesitated, concerned that Kyle might refuse to talk if they didn't let Rooster in.

"I guess you can come in," Brockman said, "but just to observe."

Rooster hadn't even gotten settled in his seat before he demanded that any questioning be delayed until the FBI talked to Danny Houston and listened to the tape recording. "The tape recording will prove that my client didn't really make a transmission to Transcontinental Three Eleven," he said pompously, as if he were F. Lee Bailey, himself. "All this could have been straightened out by now if Carpelski wasn't so anxious to hang Kyle that he keeps pissing in his pants and has to change his underwear."

Brockman pointed his finger at Rooster threateningly. "I told you you're here just to observe," he barked. "You're not to speak unless spoken to."

Rooster was on his feet immediately: "I can stand flat footed and pee over your head, Brockman," he shouted. Rooster put great stock in a man's ability to pee. To Rooster, it was like the caliber of your gun or how far you could throw a baseball. He bragged that he, himself, had to stand a foot back from a urinal just to keep from "splashing the walls."

Kyle grabbed Rooster and pushed him down into his chair. Rooster's strength was loyalty, not lucid conversation, and Kyle was much too tired to listen to one of his friend's specious arguments.

"Am I facing criminal charges or is this just an administrative investigation?" Kyle asked.

"Just tell us what happened," Tight Neck said, not understanding the significance of the question.

But Brockman understood it all too well: federal employees were only required to cooperate in an investigation as long as no criminal charges were involved. If so, the employee could exercise his or her Fifth Amendment Rights. Brockman snatched a card from his pocket: "You have the right to remain silent. . . ," He continued to read Kyle his rights, then shoved the card back into his pocket.

"Then I want a lawyer."

"This is just an investigation," Tight Neck insisted.

"Fuck you," Rooster said. It was the only legal jargon he really understood.

Ron almost fell over.

"Now listen, you," Brockman said, "I'm telling you for the last time to shut up."

Rooster was back out of his chair again and ready to fight. "Why don't you go find Carl Dingle," he shouted.

This time it was Ron who pushed Rooster down. "Never mind, Rooster; Kyle's not answering any questions until he's talked to a lawyer."

Kyle said to Brockman, "If you'll guarantee me no criminal charges will be filed and put it in writing, I'll answer any question you want."

Rooster lowered himself back into his seat. "Kyle's right," he boasted.

Brockman glared at Ron: "FAA headquarters said you were to cooperate."

Ron didn't like Brockman, either, but he was too smart and too experienced to make enemies. "We realize you guys have a job to do, but Kyle has to protect his rights."

"Yeah," Rooster said.

"Fucking controllers," Brockman murmured. He crossed one leg and looked out the window. Agent Davis slumped in his chair.

"I guess we might as well adjourn," Ron said.

Curtis Raymond stepped forward. "Not yet," he said officiously. "Matthews, it is my duty to inform you that you have been suspended."

"Says who?" Ron asked.

"The FAA Administrator: his office called a few minutes ago. Matthews is to stay out of the building."

"No problem," Kyle said, standing.

Raymond looked disappointed; he had been expecting more of a reaction.

Kyle walked to the door, Ron and Rooster following.

"You don't have to actually leave the building, Kyle," Ron said. "Just stay out of the control room. Go find a spot where no one will bother you until we listen to the tape."

Paul Hilger met them at the door. "Your wife is here, Kyle. She's in the front hallway."

THIRTEEN

Richard Carpelski listened to the tape recording and tapped his foot nervously.

The playback machine consisted of sixteen channels; each channel recording a separate radar position, twenty four hours a day. It had taken Carpelski almost an hour to locate the correct tape and fast forward to the time the two aircraft had been due to pass.

He monitored a radio station while he worked, listening to gruesome reports from the crash scene. It made him even more eager to hear what had happened. He worked alone with the doors closed because controllers in the center despised him and often made derogatory remarks as they passed by. Carpelski was his own, worst enemy, strutting around in a rigid, military manner. He wore the same brown shoes, white shirt, and name tag, every day. The tag read "FAA-Richard A. Carpelski." Everyone else in the facility was on a first name basis; few wore a name tag; the result was that Carpelski, with his ramrod posture and nose in the air, made himself an easy target. They called him "Carp," a reference to the fish. Most fishermen considered a carp to be worthless; controllers considered Carpelski to be the managerial equivalent. They joked that when you catch a carp, you should throw it back or toss it in the bushes. Worst of all, Carpelski was always looking over the controller's shoulders. He would turn in his own mother to impress the bosses. The controllers deduced that the "A" in his name stood for "asshole."

Kyle took Laura by the hand and quietly moved to a spot in the hall-way near the room where Carpelski sat playing the tape. "We'll wait here until the Carp is finished. As soon as he verifies what I told Ron, we can get the hell out of here. We'll be able to know what he found by the disap-pointment on his face."

"Are you serious?" Laura asked. "They're not going to let you go any-where. Do you have any idea what a big deal this is? The accident is only a couple of hours old and already the president is talking about coming to Kansas City. There were calls for a congressional investigation thirty minutes after those airplanes hit."

Kyle put his finger to his lips, "Not so loud," he whispered, nodding toward passing controllers and staff. Laura had tried to make herself less noticeable by scrunching down, but it was impossible to hide a woman with her looks in a building full of mostly male controllers. Her jeans, Kansas City Chiefs sweatshirt and Kansas City Royals baseball cap could never hide her womanly frame. If Laura Matthews could have seen her-self as others saw her, she might have had more confidence in herself. The smile she offered so easily was missing when she was around strangers.

"Congress won't have anything to investigate yet; it will take at least six months for the NTSB to complete their work," Kyle argued. "Let's not get ahead of ourselves."

As much as Laura tried to remain calm, she was more frightened than she'd ever been in her life. A lack of privacy had been the main reason she wanted to get out of Washington D.C.; now they might end up the most infamous family in America. "No matter what happens now, they're going to hang you for the prank."

Kyle couldn't blame Laura for venting, not after what he had done.

"After you were reinstated I thought I had my life back," she rambled on. "Now it starts all over again. I wish you could hear what they're saying about you on TV."

"Just remember, I didn't do it."

"Unless you did it accidentally," she reminded him.

Kyle shook his head. "Not possible. Wait until Carpelski plays the tape; that's all the proof you'll need."

Laura sighed, whispered, "I hate to bring this up now, but I talked to Danny Houston's wife. He didn't come home and she has no idea where he is."

Kyle studied her expression for a long moment. "You called Houston's wife?"

"Yes. She hasn't seen him and he hasn't called."

Kyle appreciated Laura's initiative; it was the first positive thing between them in a long time. "Well, thanks for trying, anyway," he said, smiling while dying inside. "We'll find him. Did she say anything that might help? Where does he hang out?"

"All she said was that it wasn't unusual for Danny to disappear for short periods."

Kyle shrugged. "That's what Zack said, too."

Laura shook her head in wonderment at her husband's apparent nonchalance. This was a man who would camp in the middle of a blazing forest fire and insist it would rain any minute.

Kyle cleared his throat: "How are the children handling this?" Todd was eleven and Mary Clair was ten.

Laura hesitated: "They're fine. They're not aware of anything much yet. My mother is with them."

He nodded, feeling guilty all over again. "After we hear what's on the tape we're going home. I'll save the FAA the trouble of firing me and resign before we leave the building. I'm never coming back here again, regardless."

Laura put her fingers to her lips. "Listen, I hear something." They knelt and listened, turning their heads so that their ears were up against the wall. The voices were faint, but Kyle thought he heard one of the two aircraft report in.

FOURTEEN

Carpelski leaned forward in his chair and cupped his ears.

"*Kansas City Center, Transcon Three Fifty Four, Flight Level Three Seven Zero.*"

Kyle's voice: "*Transcon Three Fifty Four, Kansas City Center, Roger.*"

Shortly thereafter: "*Kansas City Center, Transcontinental Three Eleven, Flight Level Three Five Zero, over.*"

"*Transcontinental Three Eleven, Kansas City Center, roger.*"

Carpelski was disappointed: the two aircraft were two thousand feet apart, just as Kyle had said. He held his breath.

The silence that followed seemed longer than it actually was: then . . .

"*Transcontinental Three Eleven climb and maintain Flight Level Three Seven Zero, over.*"

Carpelski jumped to his feet, knocking over his chair.

"My God," he said out loud, "he did it. He actually did it! He's a dead man."

Laura threw her hands over her face and slumped to the floor. Kyle pulled her up quickly and looked into her eyes. "No," he shouted, "I didn't say that."

Carpelski came hurtling out of the playback room wearing a huge smile. He didn't even notice Laura and Kyle as he flew by.

Kyle took Laura by the hand and they started running down the hall in the opposite direction.

"Where are we going? We can't leave yet?"

"I heard all I need to hear; something's not right and I'm not staying to find out what it is."

Dave Segal, a controller, passed them in the hall.

"Hey Dave, if you see those two FBI agents, tell them I'm in the cafeteria."

"No problem," Segal replied, wondering why they were going in the opposite direction.

"Cafeteria? I don't feel like eating," Laura insisted.

"We're not, we're leaving," Kyle said.

"Leaving? Are you crazy? We don't even know what happened for sure."

"We need to get the hell out of here, now."

"But that will only make things worse; you'll be a fugitive."

"Raymond said Washington suspended me. That means I can go."

"Where? Aren't we going to challenge the tape first?"

"No, we're going to find Danny Houston. Whatever happens here, I'm sure I'm not going to like it. This might be my only chance to find Houston before they put me away for good."

FIFTEEN

It was dark outside when Kyle rang the doorbell. It took several minutes before a light came on.

"Danny, is that you?" a voice behind the door asked.

Kyle's heart sank when he realized that Houston wasn't home. He'd been hoping for a quick trip back to the center with Houston in tow.

Laura looked around, expecting to be arrested any minute. She figured that either the police or the FBI would be looking for both Kyle and Danny by now, if they weren't already here, hiding behind the bushes. She had pleaded with Kyle to go back and listen to the tape, insisting that they might have misjudged Carpelski's reaction, but Kyle wouldn't listen. He kept saying that if Brockman arrested him it would take away his only opportunity to find Houston. He insisted he would find Houston and drag him back to the center.

"No ma'am, my name is Kyle Matthews, and I'm looking for Danny. My wife Laura is with me."

The door opened a few inches, but remained chained. A tall, tired looking woman peered out over reading glasses.

Kyle bent over to make himself less imposing. "My wife was the one who called earlier."

"It's very late, what do you want? Danny's not home, I've told that to a dozen people already, including the police and your wife."

Laura stepped forward: "Mrs. Houston, I'm Laura Matthews; we talked on the phone. I hate to disturb you, but it's very important that we talk to your husband. Could we come in for just a minute? We really need to find him."

Hesitation. Finally, the door closed and they heard the chain come off. When it opened all the way they faced a nervous looking woman in a worn, blue bathrobe, her head wrapped in a towel.

"Do you work with Danny?" the woman asked Kyle.

Kyle forced a smile: "Yes."

"Come in then, I guess."

Kyle let Laura go in first.

"We need to talk to your husband," Laura said gently. "There's been an aircraft accident. Do you have any idea where we can find Danny?"

"No, I told you he didn't come home or call. I'm worried myself. He went to work at two, and he's usually home by eleven. Danny's quiet, sometimes I don't even hear him come in. When all those people called, I assumed he was in the basement. Sometimes he goes down there and works after his shift, even if he's already worked all day. I went down and looked, but he wasn't there."

Alice Houston was babbling now, letting it all out. "A center supervisor called three times. He didn't seem to believe me when I said Danny wasn't home and that I didn't know where he was. I'll be glad when Danny gets back on his regular midnight shift."

"Is this something that happens often?" Kyle asked. "I mean, does he often fail to come home or call?"

"Well, he sometimes stops at a store and forgets to call first, or he'll stay over and work a couple of extra hours, but he's never been late like this. My husband can be difficult at times because he gets to working on some project and forgets to call. He's very good at what he does."

Alice Houston suddenly looked very nervous: "What is this all about? Why are all these TV reporters calling me? I know there's been a terrible accident, I heard about it on the ten o'clock news, but what has Danny got to do with that? Is he supposed to help with the investigation or something; he sometimes does that kind of work, too."

"I just need him to verify some equipment," Kyle lied.

"I can have him call you when he comes home. Can't it wait?"

"I'm afraid not. I need his help now. Do you know if he's with some-one, maybe someone from work? Could they have stopped for a drink?"

"Danny doesn't drink, and he doesn't have many friends from work."

Laura smiled and tried to sound positive: "I'm sure he's all right Mrs. Houston. . . "

"Alice, my name is Alice." She was warming to Laura's smile.

"Well Alice, I wouldn't worry. Who was the last person you remember Danny being with? Could he be at a neighbor's house?"

"He had a visit from some man a few days ago. They talked."

"Who was it?" Kyle asked, thinking it might have been Carpelski.

"I don't know. He was a big man, heavy set. Danny said he asked for a tour of the center. I remember Danny telling me the man was very interested in the center's radio equipment, but I don't think he was a sales-man or anything like that. Danny thought the request was strange, but he agreed to give the man a tour this morning. I only saw the man for a few minutes; I didn't even get his name."

"What else can you tell me about him? Did he wear glasses? How was he dressed?"

"I don't remember exactly. He was tall, had a really red face and a big stomach." She said it hesitantly, as if not wanting to be critical. "He had red hair too, but not much of it."

Kyle immediately thought of Butch Moore, an ex-controller who held a grudge against his father and every other member of his family, includ-ing Kyle, himself."

"Could Danny be with that man now?" Kyle asked.

"I wouldn't think so, not unless the man stayed with Danny all day. If that was true they would probably still be at the center. Must be some-thing important going on. Like I said, I assumed he was working on the crash investigation. But if that's true, why would a supervisor and those TV people be calling here?"

"Maybe they were having a problem with the computers," Kyle said.

"Maybe. But the TV people wouldn't be asking about that. They asked all kinds of questions, like how long he had worked for the FAA and what he did. Do you think I should call the police? I'm not sure what to do."

"It might be a good idea," Laura said. She couldn't believe the police or the FBI hadn't already talked to her.

"Please, have Danny call me as soon as he gets in," Kyle said. "Better still, have him call the center."

"I'll try. I do hope he comes home soon. I'm beginning to wonder if something's happened to him."

SIXTEEN

It was late, but the beer was still flowing at the Bigger Jigger bar. The discussion for tonight centered around the FBI's attempts to locate Kyle.

Zack Morrisey was the featured speaker, not that anyone else ever got a chance to talk when he had a few beers in him. Morrisey was one of the center's more infamous characters: he had one wooden leg and was proud of it. He had lost the leg in a race between a friend's Buick and the train he hitched a ride on. When the train didn't stop, Morrisey jumped off and his left leg landed between the train and the track. Zack refused to take the loss seriously, and he wouldn't tolerate sympathy. He looked upon the loss as a mere inconvenience, a chance to tell a good story. He referred to his wooden leg as if it were a person, like Charlie McCarthy talking to Mortimer. He developed a W. C. Fields accent and talked to the leg even if no one else was around. He often fell down when walking on anything slippery, and would complain to the wooden leg about it: "Well. . . , I guess you got me down on my fat ass again tonight. . ."

Controllers had taken to rapping on Morrisey's leg for good luck as they walked by on the way to their radar positions.

"Where is Kyle? What's going on?" one controller asked excitedly.

"It was a cluster fuck," Zack said, adjusting the wooden leg. "You should have seen it. The feds were running around in circles. They must have looked in the cafeteria and break room ten times. He flew the coop, he and Laura just up and fucking flew the coop."

"Why run, they're going to arrest him anyway? I heard his voice was on the tape recording."

"What the hell has he got to lose?" Morrisey asked. "He may as well breathe fresh air for a while."

"The FBI was really upset," a third controller added. "I was there. It was great: Brockman was on the phone with Washington, trying to explain how he let Kyle get away. From the look on his face, I guess he's in trouble with his bosses again. Kyle better stay away from him, though; Brockman's so pissed he might shoot him. The asshole's running amuck."

Ron Adair sat back and sipped his beer. "I told the FBI Kyle would be easy to find and that he was probably talking to his lawyer. Nothing is going to happen to him."

"Were they going to arrest Laura, too?" another controller asked.

"They wanted to," Ron said, "until I reminded them that no charges had been filed. Kyle wasn't even supposed to be in the building; Washington suspended him."

Rooster jumped in: "Beautiful, it was just beautiful. Carpelski wanted the FBI to put Kyle and Laura in handcuffs. He screamed and ordered everyone to search for them like he thought he was fucking J Edgar himself. Of course, everyone ignored him."

Morrisey wasn't happy that Rooster was stealing his thunder. He hunkered up in the chair and put his arm in front of Rooster's face. "Shortly after Kyle and Laura left," he said, sounding like Dan Rather, "the news hounds were finally on the scent. The calls were coming in and the news pricks began to ask if someone in the center had gone berserk, like that Kelly Edmunds said on CNN. As usual, the news hounds didn't know shit, and of course they acted hang dog, hoping that someone would feel sorry for them and feed them some dirt."

"Carpelski was the one who called them in the first place," Rooster interrupted, pushing Morrisey's arm away. "He called every TV and radio station in town, blabbing that Kyle had gone nuts. The son of a bitch will have his stupid face all over the TV by tonight."

"No he won't," Ron disagreed. "I told Carpelski I'd wring his neck if I saw his face on the tube."

"You're the only one here who's heard the tape, Ron," Rooster said. "Tell us what was on it."

"Can't talk about that now. We're looking into it."

Controller Dave Cannady, looking embarrassed, asked the question everyone else wanted to ask: "Did he do it Ron? Did Kyle really lose it and deliberately run two god damned airplanes together?"

"If he did, we wouldn't be sitting here talking about how to help him," an angry Rooster answered for Ron.

"I'm sure he didn't do anything deliberate," Ron said. "My guess is that he made an inadvertent transmission. He says he didn't have his mike plugged in, but if he accidentally did, that would explain everything. We still don't know exactly what happened."

"Yeah, a 'party record,' that's happening," Zack said. A party record was an inadvertent transmission made when a controller accidentally had his or her mike keyed. The term "party record" usually meant the "F word" had been used.

"You would know," Ron said with a hint of sarcasm. He smiled as he thought about some of Morrisey's "party records." Zack's most infamous one, the one that nearly got him fired, occurred when a U. S. Senator's aircraft was trying to land at Fort Dodge, Iowa in time to meet up with the president. Due to bad weather, Morrisey, a hard working, but not necessarily a skilled controller, kept the senator's flight in a holding pattern until after the president had already left town. His voice could be heard on the tape recording, saying: "Fuck him; he needs to fly in better weather!" Later on, the recording was even played in the White House.

Zack, who had been accepting free beers in return for his inside view, was now slurring his words. On the way to the Jigger he had stopped at what he called a "warm-up" bar. He and his wooden leg had already gone down twice. "At first I thought Kyle really did issue a clearance," he said. "But when he told me he didn't have his headset plugged in, I understood; we've all tried to shock visitors with that one at one time or another."

The controllers nodded their heads in agreement.

"Is the FBI still at the Center?" Karen Davies asked.

Rooster, who was equally smashed, interrupted, continuing to give Morrisey the evil eye. "The fucking FBI is all over the place. They keep questioning controllers about a conspiracy and complaining that no one will cooperate with them."

Kyle and Laura had slipped into the Bigger Jigger unnoticed, wearing baseball caps down over their eyes. They took a nearby booth and eavesdropped for several minutes, keeping an eye out for cops. The talk was getting louder and more belligerent. Morrissey had elevated agent Red Brockman from snake to pervert, and Rooster kept looking at Morrisey like he wanted to fight.

Kyle overheard controller Jack Weisner say, "We ought to do something to that bastard, Brockman."

"He's a fucking pig," another controller added.

"He's also a federal agent," a sober Ron Adair reminded them. Ron's only reason for being there was to keep them from doing something stupid.

"We should just go on strike," someone said.

"The last time controllers tried that, they fired everybody," Ron reminded them. "I remember the PATCO slogan: 'They can't fire us all!'"

"They didn't fire them all," Rooster said: "Only about eleven thousand!"

Everyone burst out laughing, but it was a sobering reminder.

"They're getting too loud, we better go before we get arrested," Laura said.

Kyle stood: "I've got to straighten things out with them first." He took Laura's arm and they sat in a booth directly across from the controllers.

Jack Weisner saw Kyle and Laura first. "Hey, they're here!" He jumped up and grabbed a seat next to Kyle. The other controllers followed, fighting for a seat next to Laura. Everyone gathered around, with Rooster and several others standing to block the view from the front door.

Kyle smiled self-consciously. "Seems like old times, you guys," he said, accepting one of the two cold beers someone put in front of them. He looked up at the expectant faces staring at him: "I have to tell you guys exactly what happened before the media gets things all screwed up."

"We already heard *some* stuff," Weisner said.

"Well I don't want you to hear 'stuff;' I want you to hear the truth, and I want it to come from me. After that, you can tell me what you think."

He explained exactly what he had done and what he hadn't done, step by step.

The controllers had no trouble understanding the prank, but were still shocked that Kyle had done it; it just wasn't like him. They did think the "altitude tag" idea was ingenious, though.

"Why the hell didn't I think of that one?" Rooster asked.

"Cause you aren't smart enough," Morrisey said, still slurring his words. He was drunk enough now to challenge Ron. "Why the fuck did you let the Carp play the tape, Ron? I thought you were Kyle's friend. The Carp shouldn't have been involved in this at all; he hates Kyle's guts. Besides, that shit-head couldn't find his ass in broad daylight."

Ron's look was almost enough to make Zach sober: "Cause it's Carpelski's job, Morrisey; maybe you better lay off of the beer. You're not the only one concerned."

"I still say it's like leaving Dracula in charge of the fucking blood bank," Morrisey muttered.

"Exactly what was on the tape recording, Ron?" Kyle asked. "We left in kind of a hurry."

"A clearance to Transcon Three Eleven, Kyle. No question about it being your voice, either. I listened to the tape ten times. Now the media knows about it too, thanks to Carpelski."

Kyle's expression was a blank wall. He stared into space.

Laura broke into tears.

Most of the controllers either put their heads down or lowered their eyes: the others studied Kyle's expression and said nothing.

"What about Carpelski, Ron?" Cannady asked. "Could he have switched tapes to get back at Kyle?"

Ron shrugged his shoulders.

"Carpelski is a pussy," Weisner argued. "He wouldn't have the guts to try something like that."

Kyle agreed. "You're right. I'd almost have some respect for the guy if he had that kind of guts."

Laura wiped her eyes with her coat sleeve and looked at Kyle in amazement once again. She would never understand his nonchalant way of looking at things. She supposed it was some kind of male game: "score one for the opponent."

"Maybe Danny Houston and the Carp were in on it together," Rooster suggested.

"No," Morrisey interjected, still sober enough to reason. "Danny Houston is as chicken shit as Carpelski. The shit-head won't even go to a dentist's office; makes the dentist come to his house, knock him out, and clean his teeth there."

Ron turned up an eyebrow, not sure how much of Morrisey's stories he believed.

"How can we help you, Kyle?" Weisner asked.

"I need to find Danny Houston, fast. Find him for me and call me on my cell. Drag his ass to the center if you have to. I'm not going to turn myself in until I find him. Once they get me in jail, it's all over."

Morrisey turned his bleary eyes toward Kyle and pounded on the table, practically incoherent now. "I still say we strike the bastards."

"You won't have to, Morrisey," Karen said. "You're so drunk you won't be at work tomorrow, anyway."

"Good excuse," Morrisey slurred.

The conversation was going down hill. Kyle signaled to Laura that it was time to go. They both stood up.

"You still 'gonna run for NATCA President?" Morrisey blurted.

Everyone cringed. Only Morrisey would be so impolitic.

Kyle glanced nervously in Laura's direction. "I don't know, but the mess I'm in now convinces me that controllers can never have enough representation."

Had there been time for further conversation, Kyle would have seen the angry and embarrassed look on Laura's face. He was saved by the sound of doors breaking and people hollering at the front door.

Someone shouted, "Run. . . Kyle. . . Laura." Controllers started pushing them toward the back door.

Out front, owner "Fats" Miller was attempting to hold off an army of invaders. Fats weighed close to three hundred pounds. He made his livelihood selling beer and whisky to controllers and pilots, and he wasn't about to let the cops grab some of his best customers without a struggle. He could be heard shouting in a deep voice, asking to see a warrant.

Meanwhile, Kyle and Laura were already at the back door. But Brockman was way ahead of them. He came in the back way and grabbed Laura, who was still angry with Kyle. She took out her anger on Brockman by giving him a swift kick in the crotch.

Two agents grabbed Kyle, while Brockman held Laura and tried to catch his breath.

"You're under arrest for murder," one of the agents said to Kyle. "You have the right. . . "

Kyle fought the good fight, but ended up on the floor underneath two federal marshals. Reporters and TV cameramen scrambled through the bar just in time to film the action. There hadn't been this much excitement in the Jigger since Rooster tried to pick up a transvestite. Business would be good for weeks.

As angry FBI agents herded Rooster, Kyle, and Laura out the door, Rooster was heard to say in a loud voice: "Carl Dingle says to go fuck yourself."

The whole scene, including Rooster's censored remarks, would be on national TV by morning.

SEVENTEEN

Peter Brock, Special Counsel to the president, watched Frank Zimmer slowly put down the phone.

Brock had been relaxing in the Gulfstream's soft, leather seats, sipping a scotch and water. He sat up straighter.

"What's wrong? You look ill."

Zimmer, President of the International Brotherhood of Airline Pilots, or IBAP, looked out the window of the Grumman aircraft and remained silent. The two men were on the way to Washington, D.C. for an IBAP convention. Brock was to be the guest speaker.

Finally, Zimmer shook his head and leaned back in his seat, his right hand rubbing his double chin. "I'm all right."

"What was the phone call all about?"

"It was my pilot. There was a mid-air collision. Two Transcon flights collided over Kansas City."

Brock lowered the glass and sat up. "My God, What happened?"

"I don't know. My pilot is trying to get more information, but he thinks that everyone on the two planes is dead, including Deeter Noonan. Kansas City is a mess."

"Deeter Noonan is dead? My God, we were just talking about him."

Zimmer shook his head.

"Something is worrying you," Brock said. "And with all due respect, I know you're not that unhappy that Deeter might be out of the way. This paves the way for you."

"It's not that," Zimmer said. "It's just that I had a conversation with someone last week who actually predicted that Noonan wouldn't be around much longer."

"What are you talking about?"

Zimmer's thoughts bounced between Deeter Noonan's death and the sudden realization that flying in a Gulfstream at forty five thousand feet made him just as vulnerable as Noonan. He found himself glancing out the window, imagining all kinds of things that could go wrong. He conjured up thoughts of wings falling off, or a fighter plane coming through the window. He wondered what his body would look like after it fell from forty five thousand feet. He even visualized the surprised look on some homeowner's face when he came crashing through the roof.

He shivered involuntarily.

"Frank, did you hear me? I asked what you were talking about," Brock insisted.

Zimmer wished he'd kept his mouth shut. Now it was too late. Brock was the one man he needed on his side if he wanted to fulfill his dream of replacing Deeter Noonan. He went over his conversation with Butch Moore, trying to remember Moore's exact words.

"This stranger showed up in my office one day, unannounced. He barged in past my secretary, ignoring her protests. He told her he was sure I would want to see him, even elbowed her aside. I was madder than hell when I looked up and saw this big, red faced man towering over me. My first thought was to reach for the phone and call security."

"Who was he?"

"An ex air traffic controller named Butch Moore. The FAA fired him after the PATCO strike. He wants me to help him get reinstated. He said he could 'get rid of Deeter Noonan' if I did that for him. He ranted about how the FAA had screwed him; he said they owe him a job."

"He said he'd get rid of Noonan?"

"Exactly. And he was so cocksure; he had this knowing grin on his face. He acted as if he knew how badly I wanted Deeter's job, too."

"Jesus, that PATCO strike was thirty years ago. He's too old to be an air traffic controller."

"He's not after that, anymore; like you said, he's too old. He thinks we owe him something much bigger, like a regional director's position. That shows you how crazy the guy really is: he goes on strike against the FAA; now he wants to run one of the FAA's regions."

"What, exactly did he say about Noonan?"

"He asked how I would feel if Noonan were "out of the way.""

"And you said?"

"Not a damn thing. I told him to get the hell out."

"That was wise; did you say anything at all that might incriminate you?"

"No. I'll have to admit, though, I was so eager to have Noonan out of the picture I was drooling." Zimmer looked at Brock sheepishly. "I didn't tell him that, though; that's just between the two of us."

Brock took a drink of his scotch. "Well, the man didn't actually say he was going to *kill* Noonan, and if Noonan really did die in that mid-air collision, I wouldn't give it another thought."

"I guess you're right," Zimmer said. "Can I assume this conversation never happened?"

Brock laughed. "You sound as if you actually believe this man had something to do with the collision."

"You had to be there," Zimmer said. "He sounded like some kind of devil; I wouldn't put anything past him."

"You know him that well after just one conversation?"

"I don't know anything, I just feel something."

"Well, I suppose he could cause embarrassment for you; something like this could certainly be misinterpreted. Are you sure you didn't promise him anything?"

"Of course not; all I did was give him some bull shit about how I enjoyed helping people, just to placate the asshole. And I might have mentioned that I would try to help him, or something like that."

"You shouldn't have even said that."

"What could it hurt? I'm not guilty of anything."

Brock put his glass in a cup holder and looked Zimmer in the eye. "Look, technically, you should have reported Moore to the FBI. As a matter of fact, now that you've told me about him, we both have an obligation to report him."

"You aren't serious?"

"Don't worry, I'm just talking here."

The phone rang. Zimmer picked it up. He listened for several minutes, then slowly put the phone back down.

"What now?" Brock asked.

"Speak of the devil; that was Butch Moore."

"Jesus, how did he get this number? What did he say?"

"He just said, 'I kept my promise, now you keep yours.' I told you, this man is a devil; he scares the shit out of me. Like you said, if anyone hears about my conversation with him, I'll be arrested for not reporting it. That would kill my chances of getting Noonan's job."

Brock sat back and rubbed his chin. "And that means you wouldn't be in a position to convince the other airline CEO's to support the president's air traffic control plan, which is the reason we've been trying to help you oust Noonan. So now I'm concerned, as well. I'm going to have to think about this."

EIGHTEEN

Guards roamed a dark, fortress-like estate in Silver Spring, Maryland.

Inside, Angelo Corlini, an angry man in a silk robe and slippers, sat in the dark and watched the details of the mid-air collision on CNN. He gripped the arms of the chair in frustration as he watched, holding back tears. His daughter, Nancy, a tall, dark haired, thirty year old lawyer, sat by the fireplace. She studied her father's expression carefully, wondering why he was so upset. She had never seen him this way.

A woman reporter named Kelly Edmunds was making a big splash with her story about how the FAA blamed an air traffic controller for deliberately running two airliners together. Edmunds stood in front of a large microwave antennae, explaining the operation of something called an air traffic control center.

When Edmunds finished, Corlini switched channels to pick up the Fox network. The FOX anchorman explained how the controller's prank had backfired and resulted in a mid-air collision. He said the controller had admitted the prank, but denied being responsible for the collision. He went on to describe the chaotic crash scene, with body bags everywhere. He exchanged information with on-scene reporters while the network provided graphic shots of bodies that had fallen on top of buildings. One close up showed a denuded body hanging from a stoplight in the middle of a place called the Country Club Plaza. There was also a picture of a woman named Betty Milburn who had rocketed through the roof of a diner. Corlini watched as some insensitive TV reporter tried to interview Milburn's children while they were boarding a flight to Kansas City.

The scene hit Corlini hard: he turned his head to hide the tears from his daughter.

Nancy noticed; it shocked her.

"Is something wrong, Father?"

Corlini shook his head, turning away so she couldn't see his eyes.

The scene quickly switched to the president's unscheduled press conference, something unheard of at this hour of the night. The president expressed his condolences and stated that whoever was responsible for the mid-air collision would be punished severely. He announced plans to visit Kansas City and called for a congressional investigation to prevent similar tragedies in the future. He praised the FBI for their quick reaction in identifying the person allegedly responsible and said that the man would soon be interrogated in Kansas City.

Corlini had already confirmed through his own sources that Betty Milburn was dead. His only reason for continuing to watch was to see if someone other than the man the president mentioned was responsible. It didn't really matter because he intended to do his own investigation, anyway, so this was just preliminary information. Corlini didn't trust the government: for all he knew the collision was part of a government conspiracy. After all, one of the reporters mentioned that the FAA had wanted to fire this particular controller. If so, and if this was a frame up, then whoever was behind it would have to be punished, as well, no matter how high up in the government it went. It wouldn't be the first time the government had framed someone they wanted to get rid of. The only way to know for sure was to conduct a separate investigation. He intended to punish the controller if he was guilty, but first he would use every means possible to insure he had the right man, and the only man. If there were others, he would punish them as well.

Corlini thought of one other problem: what if the controller, who the FOX network identified as Kyle Matthews, plea bargained, took the easy way out in order to save himself from the death penalty. He couldn't allow that to happen because then he would never know the truth. There could also be others involved, others the controller was covering for. He thought for a long moment before deciding he had to get involved right away.

His attention went back to the TV when he heard a FOX analyst discussing Kyle Matthews. She was having a hard time painting a consistent picture of the man. There were conflicting opinions: rave reviews from his supervisors and fellow controllers, criticism from the FAA's top brass. He was called honest and courageous by controllers and managers, paranoid and dangerous by the FAA. A congressmen who was considering using Mathews' suggestions to help formulate changes in the air traffic control system called him "progressive and innovative," but the president's chief of staff called his suggestions "presumptuous and arrogant."

FOX news went on to show pictures of Matthews, some from TV interviews where he represented the controller union; others showing him wearing a headset and sitting at a radar screen. He certainly didn't look like a killer.

Corlini managed to control himself until the reporter revealed that Matthews had bragged about what he was going to do. Upon hearing that, he became violent and started throwing things, stopping only when he realized he might wake up his wife: no need for her to get suspicious about his secret life, especially since the woman he actually shared it with was now gone.

FOX had just about run out of interviews when they cornered a big toothed, liberal, ex-Colorado congresswoman who called for a congressional investigation into unsafe seats in commercial airliners, as if a better seat could have saved the life of someone who fell from thirty seven thousand feet. Corlini turned off the TV, wiped his eyes once more, and turned to his daughter:

"I need you to go to Kansas City tomorrow."

Nancy got up from a seat next to the fireplace and moved to a chair next to her father. "Why?"

"Never mind 'why,' I want you to hire a lawyer to defend the controller they mentioned on TV. Hire anyone you want for the arraignment, but I want everything else handled by one, specific individual. I'll give you his name."

Nancy thought she must have misunderstood. "What did you say, father?"

Corlini's eyes blazed. "I said you're to go to Kansas City and hire a lawyer to defend the controller involved in the aircraft collision. You're to leave tomorrow."

Nancy loved her father, but she knew he was no philanthropist. "I don't understand; do you know this controller? Is he a relative?"

"Never mind. Just do as I tell you. I'll explain later."

"Father, have you forgotten that I graduated from Georgetown law school with honors? If you need a lawyer, why not let me handle the case?"

Corlini didn't dare tell his daughter that what he needed more than a good lawyer was a lackey who would do his bidding, someone so desperate for a case of this magnitude that he could be bought on the cheap. Nor did he mention that the lawyer he had in mind would be required to insure that Matthews, or anyone else who might be involved, did not plead guilty. Money and a desire for publicity would insure that the lawyer he had in mind would do exactly that. As for Nancy, she was a fine lawyer, he knew that, but she was no lackey. Allowing her to handle the case was out of the question; she would never accept the conditions he had in mind. He flashed one of his "no more questions" looks that she was so familiar with and motioned for her to come closer.

Nancy didn't argue; she got up and moved her chair. She was always careful not to cross her father; she even suspected he could be dangerous, even though he had never harmed her. "Father, are you going to tell me what this is all about?"

Corlini looked into her eyes and forced a smile. He was very proud of his daughter. Nancy had the brains and bearing that made a woman stand out in a crowd and men take notice. She was tall and tan, slender like a fashion model, and had dark, shimmering hair cut in a pageboy style. Yet in spite of her brains and good looks, and the fact she had always been provided the best of everything, she was unpretentious. She was confident, but never boastful, and she was brilliant, always finishing in the top ten in whatever school she attended. She was also what the psychologists called a "synthesist," an individual who questions everything. A synthesist could "what if" you to death. It had almost driven her teachers and college professors crazy, but it was the perfect attribute for a lawyer. And what people couldn't see when looking at her, the thing that topped it all off, was the determination that went with all the rest.

Nancy waited patiently while her father gathered his words:

"You need to follow my instructions to the letter. I don't expect you to agree with me, or even understand why I want it this way, but that doesn't matter. This is very important to me."

Nancy hesitated and reluctantly shook her head.

"You're to hire a lawyer named Tyler Harding."

Nancy practically jumped out of her chair: "Tyler Harding? He was disbarred, for god's sake; it was in the *New York Times*."

Corlini's eyes narrowed, his lips clenched, and he made a fist. Nancy recoiled when she saw the anger her reaction had caused. Corlini didn't allow any woman to question his decisions. He believed that a woman in the work-place was just one more empty kitchen. He kept his business dealings and his friends a secret and never discussed them with her or her mother. He forced a smile, the cusp of an angry outburst, and managed to calm down right before he lost it. "Just do as I say. I have my reasons."

"I'm just saying that Tyler Harding is a loser. Why not hire a good lawyer?"

Corlini ignored her: "You are to explain to Mr. Harding that there is to be no plea bargain, even if the man confesses. There must be a full-blown trial and no insanity plea. If he can't live with that, I'll get someone else. We need to know the truth."

"What makes you think the controller will go along with this? If he doesn't plead guilty he could get the death penalty."

"What choice does he have? He can't afford his own lawyer; a case like this could cost millions."

"He'd have to be deaf and dumb never to have heard of Tyler Harding and his troubles with the bar association."

Corlini just glared at her again.

Nancy realized that it was no use arguing any further. Besides, regardless of whom she had to hire, it would be exciting to be involved in a trial of this magnitude; she could handle Harding.

"What about me, what's my role?"

"A very important role, indeed: I want you to forward information to me daily. I want all the details, names and dates of anyone involved. You'll sit second chair, keep an eye on Harding; make sure he does as you say."

Nancy sighed. "Anything else?"

"Report back to me as soon as you nail down everyone involved."

Corlini looked as if he wanted to say something more.

"What is it, father?"

"Make sure whoever you hire for the arraignment makes a convincing argument for bail."

"No way he'll get out on bail."

"Just have the lawyer make the argument; tell him to make it look good. I'll take care of the rest. Someone will be there to take care of the bail."

NINETEEN

Most arraignments are as dull as a Lawrence Welk concert; this one had all the trappings of a Charlton Heston movie. The only things missing were the chariots.

A line of traffic stretched from the courthouse at 500 State Ave, Kansas City, Kansas, to the Missouri border. It seemed as if everyone in Kansas and Missouri was in a hanging mood. Observers carried signs with slogans expressing the same basic thought: that the death penalty was too good for the "Sky killer," as Kyle Matthews was now known. One of the signs pictured his hands gripping two aircraft as if he intended to crush them; another was a cartoon where his face was depicted as the face of the devil.

Attitudes worsened when the crowd discovered that the media had commandeered most of the seats in the small courtroom, leaving many of the victims' relatives waiting outside, clamoring to get in. Two, separate rooms were eventually cleared to accommodate the overflow, but even those couldn't accommodate every relative, friend, or reporter who wanted in.

"All rise," Judge Patricia Carone's courtroom deputy called out. Carone walked in, sat down, and surveyed the crowd. Carone was tall and beautiful, with long blond hair, and was very young looking for a federal judge. She seemed very nervous.

"You may be seated," the deputy said.

Carone cleared her throat several times: "The matter before us is the United States of America versus Kyle Francis Matthews. Will counsel please enter their appearances?"

"Assistant U.S. Attorney Jack Shecker for the government, your honor." Shecker then introduced his assistants.

"Ronald Burger for the defense, your honor."

Peering down at Kyle, Carone said, "Mr. Matthews, you are charged with, among other things, violating Title Eighteen of the U.S. Code. Do you require a reading of the indictment?"

"We do not, your honor," Burger answered for him.

Kyle had been escorted into the courtroom by two federal marshals. He stood with his hands handcuffed in front of him and glared at the prosecutor. He tried hard not to show fear, but his insides were doing cartwheels. Never before had he been this frightened, embarrassed, or humbled. Here he was, standing before a federal judge, while his very own government prepared to accuse him of violating U.S. laws. He found himself both angry and sad.

"Is the defendant prepared to enter a plea?"

Burger: "To each count of the indictment, the defendant pleads not guilty, your honor."

"Very well, do you wish to be heard on bail, Mr. Burger?"

Ron Burger made his living representing controllers with traffic tickets and such, so he was in way over his head here. He had only agreed to represent Kyle because he feared losing controller clients. He didn't know, nor had he ever met, the woman who had hired him. He was confused and uncomfortable; he couldn't understand why the woman insisted he make a strong statement on bail, since he knew Kyle Matthews was headed straight to jail. He worried that the publics' enmity might extend to him if he made too strong an argument. He reminded himself to have his automobile checked for bombs as soon as he could get away.

"We ask that Mr. Matthews be released on his own recognizance, your honor," Burger answered, thinking that nothing he said would make any difference, anyway.

The crowd erupted, stomping on the floor and booing.

Judge Carone banged her gavel.

"Mr. Shecker?"

Shecker stepped forward and glared at Burger for a long moment before answering: "Your honor, we ask that the defendant be remanded. This has been one of the most deliberate and vicious crimes of all time, and there is no question that this defendant committed the crime."

"Anything further, Mr. Burger?"

Burger stared up at the judge for a long moment, unable to think of anything.

"Say something, Burger," Kyle whispered.

"Look here Mr. Matthews, I presume you know you're going right to jail?" Burger whispered back.

Kyle was tired of Burger's defeatist attitude. "At least she's giving you a chance; make an argument, for god's sake."

"Mr. Burger, I'm waiting," the judge said.

"May I have a moment, your honor?"

"Yes, but hurry."

"What is it you expect me to say?"

"Tell her the FAA won't let me control traffic, so I'm not a danger to anyone. Tell her I have a family and I'm not a flight risk, whatever. Do what the lady who hired you said to do; earn your money. Let's at least go down swinging."

Burger stared at Kyle, attributing his apparent optimism to drugs or a mental disorder.

Finally, he looked up, said, "Your honor, the defendant is an air traffic controller and a family man. He is not a flight risk." He cleared his throat and rambled on for several more minutes, sounding more like he was asking for mercy than for bail.

Kyle braced himself, convinced that Burger's weak argument would soon have him on his way to Leavenworth.

Shecker ridiculed Burger. He argued that Kyle was a madman who should be locked up immediately, confident that the judge would readily agree.

But Judge Carone stunned everyone in the states of Kansas and Missouri by setting bail at five million dollars.

There was a brief pause while everyone managed to catch their breaths. Kyle let out a gasp.

The courtroom erupted in a chorus of loud jeers. Shecker went into orbit, literally running toward the bench and flailing his arms. Judge Carone drew back, but showed no signs of changing her mind. "Sit down," she warned Shecker, banging her gavel, her hands and lips trembling. "Sit down or you'll be held in contempt."

The crowd continued to stand, shouting "no, no, no."

Judge Carone banged her gavel again. "I'll clear the courtroom if this continues."

Kyle studied the judge's expression; he had the feeling she was fighting her own conscience. For reasons he couldn't quite understand, he thought her decision had been made in advance and that she had actually anticipated the crowd's reaction, banging her gavel almost before the outburst began.

"Maybe the judge should tell the crowd I can't afford bail, anyway," Kyle said to Burger. "It might make them a little less hostile."

But a man in a blue, pinstriped suit appeared and quickly stood next to Burger. Judge Carone looked down at the man as if she had been expecting him. He identified himself as Bernard Manzina, an attorney from Silver Spring, Maryland, and said he was there to post bail. Once again, Judge Carone didn't seem surprised, and once again Kyle had an uncomfortable feeling that everything had been prearranged, even staged.

Shecker began to argue again, but the judge ignored him and ordered Kyle released following the posting of bail.

In less than five minutes, Kyle was escorted out of the courtroom by two marshals. He wanted to thank Manzina, but the federal marshals pushed him out through a side door and onto the street before he had a chance. A hostile crowd stood waiting, having figured out where Kyle would exit the building.

"Well, you must be elated," Burger beamed as the two men scrambled down an alleyway through a bellicose crowd. "I'm glad I was able to help you out on the bail thing."

"No disrespect, but you probably didn't have a thing to do with it, Mr. Burger," Kyle answered, still looking back for the lawyer. "The judge intended to let me go all along. I wish I knew why, but I'm sure not going to argue with her. Let's just get the hell away from here."

As Kyle was shoving and pushing his way through the angry crowd, he got a quick glance at a smiling Butch Moore, and remembered what Alice Houston had said about "a fat man with a red face" hanging out with Danny. What was he doing here; was it just to gloat?

The raucous crowd standing in the street soon made him forgot about Moore. He had a bigger problem right now; finding a way to get home alive.

TWENTY

Kyle hadn't expected to be released; could see no way to get past the crowd; and had no way to get home. The situation in the streets ahead was chaotic, even dangerous, and since the federal marshals were gone now, he was on his own; the mob could do just about anything they wanted to. It was time to run, and he wasn't going to wait for Burger. But running was difficult; the mob literally pushed the two men through the mass of microphones being shoved in their faces, shouted obscenities, and shook their fists. Reporters made no effort to be polite, maneuvering for a good sound bite.

"You 'gotta 'lotta nerve pleading not guilty, asshole," someone shouted! "You know you did it; we're 'gonna enjoy watching you fry."

The two men ran faster, with Kyle shoving aside anyone who got in his way and Burger covering his head with both hands.

One reporter managed to keep up, shoving a microphone in Burger's face. "Tell your client to talk if he wants the public to hear his side of the story." Burger mumbled something incoherent and kept running.

"Killer," several people shouted.

Kyle was tempted to stop and shout back, but no one was going to listen anyway.

Burger stumbled, but Kyle caught him before he hit the ground and pulled him back up. Several people behind them began to stumble, as well.

"Look here, Mr. Matthews," Burger shouted, getting his feet under him, "you better have a good criminal lawyer. I'm not experienced enough to handle anything like this."

"That's OK, Mr. Burger, I'll find someone. I suggest you run for your car and get the hell out of here."

"Good luck," Burger shouted, sounding relieved and veering off in another direction.

Kyle picked up speed; he could see and feel the increasing hostility as he ran: T-shirts with slogans such as, "*The death penalty for the sky killer*," or, "*You know you're guilty*," were everywhere. It made him angry and sick to his stomach. How could people convict a man without hearing his side of the story? And how could he extricate himself from a stacked deck if everyone already had their minds made up? As he focused on that, he began to realize how much he needed someone with clout to tell his side of the story. Somehow, he had to find a warrior who would go on the offensive; one that the prosecutors, and even the judge, wouldn't want to confront. But how was he going to afford someone like that?

Morrisey appeared out of nowhere, jogging alongside and dragging his wooden leg. He was dressed in his customary black outfit and talking on a cell phone. Morrisey watched a lot of Jason Bourne movies; he enjoyed playing secret agent, just as long as he wasn't the target. Kyle's spirits rose considerably when he saw his friend along side, but the wooden leg was holding both of them back.

"Do you have a car?"

Morrisey pointed straight ahead: "Rooster's guarding it, fifty yards, a borrowed Cadillac." He managed to take a few more steps before the crowd overtook him and he went down, wooden leg, cell phone and all. Pieces of the phone went flying.

Kyle reached down to help him, sighting the Cadillac at the same time. He pulled Morrisey to his feet and dragged him along.

As soon as they got to the car, Rooster tossed Morrisey's rotund body into the back seat, then quickly ran to the driver's side and jumped in. Kyle held off the crowd until Rooster was in, then jumped into the passenger side seat, grabbed the door handle, and slammed the door shut.

"The cellular phone," Morrisey protested, "I borrowed that, too; I have to get it back."

"It's history," Kyle said. "I stepped on some of the pieces myself."

"What the fuck were you doing on the ground, Morrisey?" Rooster teased.

"Some asshole tripped me," Morrisey grumbled. "My life is now in danger from more than just this mob."

"That's what you get for borrowing from your shady friends," Rooster said. "Just because you drink beer with them doesn't mean you're a made guy. And don't worry about the damn phone; if we don't get out of here, you could loose this Cadillac, too."

"Run over the bastards," Morrisey hollered. "I can't let anything happen to this car."

The Cadillac had been parked in an empty lot before a forest of TV vans had moved in and surrounded it. It was so blocked in now that there was very little room to navigate. The satellite dishes make it look like Jurassic Park without dinosaurs.

The Cadillac made like a bulldozer, going forward one foot at a time. To add to the congestion, the entire block had been cordoned off, surrounded by police cars. The angry crowd had *them* surrounded too, banging on the doors and windows. Two crazies even managed to throw themselves onto the hood, where they stubbornly hung on.

"I'm screwed," Morrisey said. "If those nuts dent this car I'm a dead man."

Rooster drove the car like a battering ram, gently but firmly shoving people aside as he edged his way out of the lot. The two hood hangers-on jumped clear when the Cadillac picked up speed.

"Didn't actually expect to see *you* today," Rooster said to Kyle. "How in the hell did you get away?"

"The judge released me on bail."

"You're kidding."

"It doesn't make sense, I know."

"Maybe the judge thought the crowd would kill you and save everyone the trouble," Rooster said, wondering at the same time if the woman who had called him earlier that day had had anything to do with it.

"Some lawyer I never saw before represented me, guy named Burger. Then another guy showed up and posted bail. The second guy disappeared before I could talk to him. You guys know anything about those two?"

"They couldn't have been from NATCA," Rooster said, "NATCA doesn't have that kind of clout; that would be like getting Timothy McVeigh released."

"Well, someone was behind it. And you should have seen the judge's expression. She was scared shitless."

"Count your blessings," Morrisey said. "What'd these lawyers look like?"

"Burger was a light-weight from Olathe; the other guy was dark completed, mean looking. Looked like someone who worked for John Gotti."

"Sounds more like one of Morrisey's friends," Rooster suggested.

"My friends are not that generous," Morrisey moaned. "Better hope the guy who put up the bail didn't have a mother on one of those planes."

Rooster took a sudden, sharp turn and drove between two buildings, leaving the crowd in his wake. In just a few minutes they were eastbound on Highway 70.

They drove for ten minutes before anyone said anything more.

Kyle finally said, "You're too quiet, Rooster. It's making me nervous."

Rooster was still thinking about a phone call he had received earlier that day: a woman with a sexy voice called and offered to pay for Kyle's legal defense. She insisted on meeting with Kyle personally. Rooster assumed it was probably just some flake getting off on the mid-air thing or wanting to make money writing a book. Still, he knew he couldn't take a chance. What if it was some do-gooder who actually had the money and wanted to help? He knew he had to eventually tell Kyle about it, even if Kyle and Laura did think that most of the things he came up with were bizarre.

The hell with it, he decided. I'll pass the information along and let Kyle make his own decision.

He tried to remember the name of the lawyer the woman said she was going to hire. "Harding," that was it, "Tyler Harding."

"Maybe the woman who called me this morning had something to do with it," Roosted blurted.

"What woman?" Kyle asked, sounding skeptical. After all, it *was* Rooster.

"Someone who says she wants to help. She says she knows someone who will put up the money for a lawyer."

"What's the catch? Is this someone I'm supposed to know?"

"How would I know? She just called out of the blue."

There wasn't time for further conversation, because just as it looked as if they were free of the crowd, two dirty, beat up vehicles converged on the Caddie and blocked the road. One of the vehicles was an old pickup truck, the other an old Buick. Four people materialized from the two vehicles and moved toward the Cadillac.

Rooster opened the driver's side door and stepped out, only to find a shotgun pressed against his forehead. The huge man behind the gun was wearing bib overalls and had hands like frying pans. He shoved Rooster aside and ordered Kyle out of the car.

The other three, a woman and two men, had weapons, too. The woman pointed a thirty eight magnum, while the two men waived Kyle into the trunk of the Buick with their own shotguns.

Morrisey and Rooster tried to fight them off, but were thrown aside like rag dolls. It was all over in a few seconds.

TWENTY ONE

Kelly Edmunds hung around the center all day, hoping for a chance to talk to Ron Adair. She lusted for answers that would complete her story.

Was the FAA really out to get Kyle Matthews like those women in the john said? It sounded like something from a TV movie plot. Other than the mid-air collision, why would a government agency care that much about some air traffic controller in Kansas? But if it *was* true, and the man had retaliated for something the FAA did by running two aircraft together, it would make the story of the century. How was she going to know for sure? Everyone said that Kyle Matthews was a solid citizen, but would a solid citizen really go to that extreme just to get even with the FAA?

Adair's car left the parking lot.

Kelly followed at a safe distance, tuning her car radio for the latest news. Other than the crash itself, Matthews' recent release was the major story, and the over-the-air bickering was still going strong. Comments and speculation ran the gamut; some said the judge should be impeached, others argued that she was within her rights. The host said that Judge Carone had refused to give a reason and had been badly shaken by the public's response. Nevertheless, he said, she remained adamant that her decision had been correct.

Shaken my ass, Kelly thought; son of a bitch *should* be impeached. She turned off the radio, turned on her tape recorder, plugged in her earpiece, and listened to the tape recording she had made in the women's room. That recording would be the foundation for the interview she planned with Adair, assuming he would even talk to her.

Edmunds spent the next twenty minutes following Adair and planning an alternative in the event he wouldn't grant the interview. Adair finally pulled into the driveway of a small, neat house on a tree-lined street in Overland Park, Kansas. A sidewalk ran from the driveway to the front door; another sidewalk climbed a steep hill from the front curb to the front door.

Kelly decided to park at the curb and go up from there. Her plan was to climb the stairs and head Adair off. She parked, got out, and looked up toward the house, but Adair already had the door open. Not a good sign. Maybe he had noticed her following.

Shit.

She stood at the curb and looked up and down the street, expecting competition and preparing to run to the door if necessary. She saw nothing but the quiet neighborhood, with well kept yards and golden colored leaves just beginning to fall. There were only a few people moving about. A shaggy dog started to cross the street, stopped and looked her over, then continued on. The look in his eyes made her feel guilty for some reason.

She slowly climbed the stairs, not wanting to alert whoever might be inside. She stopped short of the front door because for some reason it looked threatening, like the entrance to a forbidden castle. She told herself to be bold: CNN was interested in deep background; this was her chance.

She knocked on the door and ran her hand through her blond hair nervously.

An attractive, smiling woman in her early forties opened the door cautiously. "Yes?"

"Can I speak with Mr. Adair?"

The woman smiled again and called for Ron.

Ron came to the door.

"Can I help . . . oh, it's you." He smiled, "I see you made it into the center without me." His smile indicated to her that he admired initiative; it gave Kelly the confidence she needed. She returned his smile. "May I ask you a couple of questions?"

"I'm tired and I have to go back to the office soon, so let me save you some time: I'm still not sure what happened, and I couldn't tell you if I did."

"Look, that center building was really fascinating. I need to know more about it before I can even begin to do a story. I'm going to do my story anyway, so wouldn't you rather have it be accurate?" She smiled again. "Surely you can spare me a few minutes. I won't ask for any top secret information." She winked. "I promise."

"That's good, because no one gives me any top secret information, anyway."

"See, so what can it hurt?"

Her expression was as eager as a child's. Ron couldn't resist. He sighed, turned and looked at Mary.

"Maybe it will help Kyle," Mary said.

"OK, come on in, but if you do a rip job on Kyle, you better find a good hiding place."

Kelly stepped inside. "Thank you."

"I'll get some coffee," Mary Adair said.

Mary went for coffee while Ron escorted Kelly into the living room. He motioned for her to sit on the couch and took a seat across from her, a guarded expression on his face.

"Do you mind if I take notes?"

Ron sighed: "Go ahead, but there isn't much you don't already know. We had a crash; until there's an investigation, we won't know much more. Even then, the National Transportation Safety Board will take months to release their findings."

"But what about the FBI; they're not going to wait for the NTSB's findings?"

"That's the criminal side of it; the NTSB's job is to find out exactly what happened and keep it from happening again. Either way, it's going to be weeks before we know for sure, so what can I possibly tell you now?"

"I heard some things about Kyle Matthews while I was in the center building. What can you tell me about him? Why did he run away?"

"You mean when Jack Golenzer snuck you in, don't you," Ron corrected.

"I was invited in; he was very nice and showed me around," she answered coyly.

Ron raised one eyebrow and eased back in his chair, choosing his words carefully: "Kyle Matthews happens to be a really good controller. I was a good friend of his father's; we were directors in PATCO at one time. As for running away after the tape recording was played, the thing the media keeps howling about, he had no obligation to stay at the center; he wasn't under arrest. That's about all I can tell you right now."

"Didn't the FAA fire his father for leading the PATCO strike?" Kelly asked anxiously, scribbling in her notebook.

"He didn't lead the PATCO strike. He fought against it, but eventually joined the others because by that time he had no choice; it was either stay and be supportive or be a scab that no one will ever work with again. Eric had actually brokered a good deal with ED Curran, the FAA's Director of Labor Relations, and had come up with a contract where the controllers got everything they asked for."

"So then, why did they strike?"

"Go figure. The controllers were getting pretty heady at that time, thinking they could get even more. The ratification vote was something like six hundred 'against' and a few hundred 'for.' I guess that proves the old adage: 'power corrupts and absolute power corrupts absolutely.' The result was that the government put PATCO out of business in 1981."

"And that's the reason the FAA wants to get rid of Kyle, because of his father? I thought PATCO was a dead issue."

Ron sighed, not sure how much he should tell her. "No, this has nothing to do with his father, although there might be a few people who say 'like father like son.' The thing that's frustrating the FAA is Kyle's controversial views on how to overhaul the air traffic control system. As a local representative of NATCA, he's allowed to express his views with impunity. And because he's an experienced controller, he has the credentials.

Congress listens to individuals who have credentials, and the FAA can't do anything about it."

"Because he's representing the union, not the FAA."

"Exactly."

"I heard through the grapevine that there was a wildcat strike in the center last year. Was Kyle involved in that?"

"He fought against it at first, but when the strike became inevitable, he was forced to do the same thing his father had done, support his members. One NATCA member was fired, and several others, including Kyle, were suspended. They would have fired Kyle, too, but they were afraid to make a martyr out of him. A few people high up in the government wish they would have."

"How high up?"

"No one knows. Kyle's been lobbying for an automated air traffic control system where computers control air traffic; an idea that apparently conflicts with something the White House has in mind."

"Can that be done? Can a computer replace a human being and keep airplanes from colliding?"

"Were you watching TV when that Mars Lander hit the target a million miles away? That was no seat of the pants operation; computers did all of that. Compared to sending a chunk of metal to Mars, separating airplanes would be chump change for a computer. We could probably run the entire air traffic control system with your laptop. The current system is way too slow; human beings can't keep up with high volumes of traffic; but volume isn't a problem for computers, and they don't take coffee breaks."

Ron waited while Kelly took notes. "Tell me more, this is interesting."

"Kyle's idea, as I understand it, would require three initial steps before it was safe to go operational: first, computers would formulate instructions for controllers to issue to pilots, just as the controllers do now; second, computers would bypass controllers and go directly to the pilots, and third. . . ."

"Just a second," Kelly said, "I have to get this down."

She finished writing: "Go ahead."

"Finally, computers would bypass both controllers and pilots and go directly to the aircraft's autopilot. The autopilot would then fly the aircraft. The first step has already been tested by the Massachusetts Institute of Technology. There's other advantages to the plan, as well."

"Such as?"

"Let's say a terrorist commandeers an aircraft with the intention of ramming it into the White House. . . "

Kelly didn't hesitate . . . "I've got, it," she said excitedly, "a controller could take control by simply sending an instruction to the autopilot with his computer."

"Bingo. It may seem far-fetched, but it isn't. There have been a few instances where an emergency in the cockpit has rendered the pilot and co-pilot helpless. . . "

". . . So this way, the aircraft could be kept safe until the pilot or co-pilot regains control?"

"...Or the controller could send an instruction to the autopilot, and the autopilot would tell the on-board computer to fly to an airport with a Category Three runway and land; the way pilots usually land air carriers at major airports, anyway."

"Airliners land by themselves?"

"If the airport is properly equipped, yes, the computer even puts on the brakes."

Kelly shook her head: "Sounds radical, all those aircraft being flown around by a computer."

"If a certain congressman has his way, a computer will also draw up the national airline schedule so that departing aircraft have spacing before they leave the ground. That way, the controllers won't have to jockey aircraft around as much; it would save significant amounts of fuel, as well."

"How could one air traffic controller come up with all that?"

"Because he's one, very smart air traffic controller; too damn smart to deliberately run two aircraft together. Don't forget, father and son have been controlling airplanes for many years; they've seen the system go from non-radar, to radar, and beyond."

Kelly nodded. "Then how come the son isn't smart enough to resist pulling a stupid prank?"

"Touché."

"Matthews' plan sounds too good to be true; what's the catch?"

"Like I said, the White House must have a different plan, and you didn't hear that from me."

"Like what?"

"No one knows. If the president has something different in mind, he isn't saying."

"Are you telling me the president doesn't have a plan of his own and yet he ignores Mathews' plan simply because it's not his administration's idea?"

"It's just rumors. And like I said, don't quote me."

She decided to push a little more. "If Kyle Matthews knows our government would like to make him a target, why does he take such a public position?"

"He believes that the only way to get congress to act is to kick a little butt."

Kelly looked as if she was about to ask something else...

"I've said more than I should," Ron said. "I'm tired and I still have a full day of work ahead of me."

"I'm almost finished, just one more question. Are there significant problems in the air traffic control system, something that should be corrected right now?"

Ron smiled: "I better go see who that is at the back door; I think someone's trying to come in that way."

Kelly smiled and got up from her chair.

Time to find Kyle Matthews.

TWENTY TWO

The Buick's trunk reeked of cow manure.

"Hey, can you hear me back there?"

Kyle could hear perfectly, but he wasn't about to answer: better to listen for a while and see what these people wanted. There were four of them; that was all he really knew for sure: three men, one of them huge, and a skinny woman with a Hawk-like face. The woman seemed to be the craziest.

There was a tiny hole where the side of the truck had been bashed in, allowing Kyle to see the landscape flying by, including glimpses of trees, small lakes, and a country road. The speed of the car made everything a blur, and Kyle's curled up body made it difficult to get his eye close to the peephole.

"I know you can hear me. I cut a hole in the panel so I could talk to you." It was a booming voice, probably the monster with the shotgun. He sounded like a good ole country boy, but his voice quivered, as if he had to control himself to keep from showing his anger. Kyle sensed the man wanted to climb into the trunk and blow his brains out.

Except for an earlier argument, the four were unusually quiet. Then, suddenly, they started laughing; he heard the woman say, "serves the bastard right."

In between his captor's conversations, Kyle could hear the news on the car radio. His release had apparently created a furor. The media was having a field day crucifying Judge Carone and Attorney General Matt

Potorf. Potorf released a statement stating that he was as surprised as everyone else at the Judge's decision, but refused to answer questions.

Kyle made up his mind that he would fight like hell when his captors opened the trunk, shotgun or no shotgun. Two of the men seemed reticent, which he hoped might reduce the odds.

He caught a glimpse of the federal prison in Leavenworth, Kansas, and wondered if he might not have been better off if Judge Carone had sent him there.

After about an hour, the car made several sharp turns over bumpy roads, then slowed down and turned onto what was obviously a gravel driveway. It moved slowly for a while and then stopped suddenly. Kyle heard another car pull up behind, which he assumed was the pickup truck. He expected the trunk to open immediately, but it seemed like forever before he heard footsteps. He braced himself. The waiting was intimidating; he wondered if that was their intent.

More footsteps; they came closer and closer, making crunching sounds on the gravel driveway. The trunk suddenly swung open and Kyle dove out headfirst. He jumped to his feet and started throwing right and left hooks in every direction. But an hour in the dark trunk followed by the sun's glare had made it impossible for him to see clearly. He blinked his eyes continuously, trying to focus, while he continued to take wild swings. Even with the glare, he had no trouble noticing Hawk Face's anger. She grabbed at his face, her fingernails ripping his skin. Other hands clutched at him, as well. He fought aimlessly against the sun and his captors, but it was no use. A final blow to the side of his head sent him flying. He hit the ground hard, his head banging against the gravel. He heard the sounds of a spray can and felt an unbearable pain in both eyes. Pepper spray!

He kicked wildly as they began to drag him. He tried to cover his eyes, but the attackers pulled his arms back to get at his face, kicking and tearing at him. When he was finally able to see, he looked up and saw all four of his captors.

The big, crusty looking man placed his steel-toed boot on Kyle's chest. Hawk Face stood at his side, grinning excitedly. The other two men didn't seem as eager.

"Meet the family," Big Man said. "I suppose you're wondering what this is all about?"

Kyle wouldn't give him the satisfaction of an answer.

Big Man's face hardened: "We had family on one of those aircraft you mangled," he said, still trying to restrain himself. "The least we can do is let you know how they felt. They say you like pranks, well let's see how you like the one we have planned for you. Course we might let you off easy if you ask us real nice."

Kyle remained stone faced.

"OK, shithead," Big Man mocked. He turned to the others: "Ready?" Hawk Face shook her head excitedly.

Big Man removed his foot, and the others dragged Kyle to his feet. They shoved him in the direction of a big barn, a hundred or so feet away. Kyle continued to resist, but several blows to the back of his head made him realize it was useless. He turned to get a better look at Hawk Face, which gave her an excuse to take another swing. Her fist bashed his ear, causing a loud ringing noise. She followed that with a sharp kick to the small of his back; he felt every ounce of steel from the tip of her boot. He did the best he could to keep from going down, constantly twisting his body in a different direction to avoid her blows. Nevertheless, a final blow from behind came with such force that it knocked him to the ground once again, and he was unconscious before he landed. When he came too, he was lying on the floor of the barn. He looked up to see that Big Man was still trying to restrain Hawk Face: "We can't kill him yet, we ain't got to the best part. There's lots of time, lots of time." It didn't help; Hawk Face was in another world, getting angrier by the minute because her blows had failed to make Kyle cry out.

It took several minutes, but Hawk Face finally got control of herself. She looked up at the big man and reluctantly shook her head. He patted her back.

Big Man nodded to the others, "Don't let him die yet. We'll save that for last." They tore off Kyle's clothes, leaving only his underwear, picked him up and shoved him through the doorway of a huge, walk in freezer, kicking him in the back again as he went in.

Hawk Face slammed the heavy door.

TWENTY THREE

Laura Matthews' peaceful world had been turned upside down. She looked out through the front window of her Overland Park home and saw that her quiet street had been turned into a movie set: reporters and their camera crews swarmed all over the neighborhood, looking in trashcans and importuning any neighbor naive enough to come outside.

Television trucks with satellite dishes were arrayed in a long line all the way down the street. They'd been there for several days, coming and going, changing crews, and grabbing sandwiches and coffee from a local 7 Eleven store. When one media truck or jeep left from a choice spot near the front of the house, another would quickly fill the void. Reporters jockeyed for a spot closer to the front door, pushing one another and jamming their vehicles together, demanding every inch of space. Any significant movement in the house, such as a light going on or off, had them leaving their vehicles and moving about. They were like a swarm of locusts, eating up the grass and bending the flowers until they snapped.

The networks had gone all-out, sending their best and brightest to the scene. Famous faces were commonplace. Gawkers from nearby homes began to hang out looking for autographs. The gawkers soon became celebrities themselves, with reporters asking detailed questions about Kyle and members of his family: "Why did they separate?" "Did they often fight?" "Did either of them drink?" "Have you ever seen either of them act peculiar at any time?"

At first it was fun for the neighbors. Then, they too began to barricade themselves inside. Finally, the cops had to be called so that the neighbors could get their cars in and out of their own driveways.

Kyle's next-door neighbors, the Pridgens, got very little peace. They tried, at first, to answer questions politely, but each question turned into a full-fledged press conference. Every time one reporter asked a question, others swarmed in. When the Pridgens finally realized they were being force fed both the questions and the answers, the police removed reporters from their front porch and escorted the entire family out of the neighborhood. Cameramen and women then got up on the Pridgens' roof and used it to photograph the upstairs windows of the Matthews' residence. Laura hung sheets over all the windows to keep out prying eyes. From time to time she even ran out and shooed them away.

When Rooster stepped out of his pickup, he couldn't believe his eyes. *My God, he thought, there's as much traffic here as there was at the courthouse. Maybe I should wait and hope the police find Kyle before I tell Laura the news.* He stood by his pickup and examined the situation for several minutes, trying to decide what to do. Laura wasn't too crazy about Rooster and his shenanigans to begin with: his insistence that Kyle should run for president of the union had made him her enemy.

Rooster stood for a long moment before deciding he had no other choice: Laura deserved to know what was happening. He pulled out his cellular phone and started forward, acting as if he were a member of the media. He walked as fast as possible, excusing himself and moving quickly toward the front door. There were lots of "Hey, who in the hell do you think you are?" When he got to the front porch, Laura happened to be on the other side of the door, eyeballing him through the peephole. She had just finished chasing a famous TV anchorman off of the front porch and was prepared to get even nastier. Rooster banged on the door and Laura jerked it open, ready for a fight. "Not now Rooster," she shouted when she recognized him. But Rooster wasn't taking any chances; he jumped in before Laura could act and quickly slammed the door shut.

Reporters assumed that one of their own had been allowed in for an interview and began rushing forward, tripping over one another. With Rooster's help, Laura was able to keep the door closed. When the reporters finally backed off, she stood there in her sweat pants, hands on hips, glaring at him. She made an imposing figure when she was angry, and she was very angry now. She started to say something she knew she'd regret, thought better of it, turned and went into the bedroom. Rooster followed and watched as she began packing furiously, babbling rapid fire over her shoulder.

"Where is Kyle?" she demanded, her violet eyes flashing. "We have to get the hell out of here. Someone from the media said Kyle got out on bail. How could that be?"

"We're not sure," Rooster said, delaying the inevitable. "The judge surprised us and let him out. Then some guy Kyle didn't even know came forward and put up the bail money."

Laura continued to pack. "Never mind, I'm in too much of a hurry to solve another mystery. I had to take the phone off the hook. I can't even call my mother to arrange to pick up the children, so now I have to go get them myself. How am I going to get out of here? Did you see that mess out on the street?"

Rooster could see that Laura was exhausted. It wasn't really a good time to deliver more bad news, but what choice did he have?

Laura went on babbling, not giving Rooster a chance to broach the subject: "Things are out of control, Rooster. The whole damn world is talking about this thing. They're comparing Kyle to a serial killer for God's sake. One guy on TV called Kyle 'Ted Bundy with a headset'."

She stopped talking and turned when she noticed Rooster's anxious look.

"What?" she asked.

Rooster decided to throw out some good news first, something to soften the blow: "I got a phone call this morning from a lady who wants to help Kyle; she says she's willing to hire a lawyer and put up the money."

Laura looked at him suspiciously.

"Who was she?"

"I don't know, and I didn't have time to find out. She did mention the name of the lawyer though, someone named Tyler Harding."

"Tyler Harding? The same Tyler Harding who made such an ass of himself in court that it made the national news?"

"I'm not sure," Rooster said, his voice tailing off. Rooster didn't really pay much attention to the news.

"Well, let me tell you about him before Kyle does something he regrets," Laura said, still tossing clothes into a bag. She sat down on the bed. "Tyler Harding had this client; he was the county medical examiner; I forget his name. He was charged with selling drugs to children. Harding decided that the prosecutor hadn't proven her case, so when it was the defense's turn, he stood up and said: 'The defense rests.' The jury brought in a guilty verdict in thirty minutes, something of a record in that particular county. Mr. Harding was given a searing lecture by the judge, who then proceeded to list in detail some of the damaging evidence that Harding should have countered. They say it was quite a butt chewing."

"Oh," Rooster said.

"Mr. Harding was disbarred; he was also sued for malpractice. The only reason he got his license back was because he was legally entitled to do what he had done. Harding loves crackpot defenses," she went on. "Once he claimed that his client had been brainwashed; another time he said his client had been hypnotized by a 'mysterious stranger.' It's sad, because his father was a great criminal lawyer."

"I didn't know all that," Rooster said quietly.

Laura worried that Rooster might think she was blaming him for her problems. "It's not your fault Rooster," she said, getting up and forcing a small smile. She turned and continued to pack.

"Maybe she can get him a different lawyer," Rooster said. "I don't think she's actually hired Tyler Harding yet. Anyway, I called Morrisey and he borrowed a car so we could get Kyle home."

"And," Laura challenged, stopping to look back over her shoulder.

Rooster shuffled his feet and looked out the window.

"There's something you're not telling me, isn't there?" Laura asked, staring into Rooster's eyes. "What is it, something about Kyle?"

Rooster tried, but he couldn't quite manage to get it out.

"What, Rooster, you're scaring me?"

"Kyle's been kidnapped," he blurted.

Laura's jaw dropped. "Kidnapped. . . what do you mean, 'kidnapped'?"

Rooster described what had happened. "Probably just some angry citizens taking him for a joy ride."

Laura's face turned pale. She reached back, using her arm for support, and slowly lowered herself onto the bed.

"Don't worry," Rooster said quickly, "Morrisey reported everything to the police. They'll find him."

Laura rolled over and buried her face in a pillow. She had the sudden, sickening thought that she might never see Kyle again.

TWENTY FOUR

The cold air brought Kyle back to life. He shivered as he slumped down in a corner of the freezer. He looked around for something to cover himself with, but there was nothing in the freezer but frozen meat. He was alone, naked except for his boxers, and he was sure he would freeze to death if they kept him there much longer.

As the minutes went by, the cold began to numb the back of his neck. At first it just felt like pinpricks, but pinpricks soon became frozen limbs.

He rolled himself into a ball, using his body heat to warm himself.

His thighs began to ache and he had difficulty turning his head because of the sharp pain in the back of his neck.

He thought about his family. How would Laura and the children survive without a husband and father? Who would support them? They didn't even know where he was; they might not ever know.

The humiliation was worse than the pain. To be someone's half naked prisoner was to be less than human. It came to him that he had actually been a prisoner ever since the mid-air collision.

Time inched by; he could hear his own heart beating. He listened to the beats to take his mind off of his troubles. He tried to keep his brain functioning by thinking positive thoughts: maybe this was just their way of scaring him. Two of the men didn't seem like killers; they seemed detached, as if they didn't completely agree with the big man.

The colder it got, the more Kyle's brain began oozing negative thoughts again: maybe they were going to just let him die here. What if they killed him accidentally by misjudging the time it would take for him to freeze to death?

He tried not to think about Hawk Face. She would be the one pushing the others. Her fingernails were like daggers; given the chance, she would rip him apart with her bare hands. He was still bleeding from the cuts she had already made on his face.

He felt another sharp pain in his nose and forehead; the type of thing he often felt when he drank something cold. It slowly grew until it spread to his sinuses. He tried to swallow, but it made everything else hurt even more. He knew that when the body starts to freeze, the heart beats faster to compensate and will eventually beat itself to death.

He couldn't last much longer.

He started shaking, out of control.

His mind began to drift.

All he could do was wait to die.

The freezer door opened. He almost didn't hear it. His senses had already begun to shut down.

His original intention had been to attack as soon as the door opened. He wanted more than anything to fight back, to get his hands on one of those shotguns. But even if he had a shotgun now, he wouldn't have the strength to pull the trigger.

Footsteps.

"Better come here Harmon. Looks like he might be dead, or close to it," one of the men said.

"Harmon." That must be Big Man, Kyle thought, but what difference does it make now.

More footsteps.

"He ain't dead," Hawk Face said, leaning over until her hot, stinking breath actually felt good on his neck. "Let the mother fucker stay in here for a while."

"Won't do us no good if he can't feel 'nothin," Harmon said. "Take him outside and thaw him out."

Kyle stayed as still as he could, steeling himself. He was shivering badly, yet all he could think of was a chance to go of the offensive. If he could make them think he was dead, they might leave him alone for a few minutes. Now that he was out of the freezer, there was still a slight chance he could regain enough bodily functions to make a fight of it, or at least get a chance to run.

He kept his eyes closed, stalling for time.

Someone kicked him. His body was so numb he could barely feel it.

"He ain't 'gonna make it." The voice belonged to someone other than Harmon, and he sounded worried. Kyle hoped the man might convince the others to back off.

An aircraft engine started up nearby, but it didn't register at first.

Kyle's eyes popped open when the realization finally hit him!

TWENTY FIVE

"He's awake."

No use pretending any longer. Kyle looked around but made no attempt to get up. He wasn't going to cooperate, no matter what they did to him. Two pairs of arms tried to lift him up, but he made himself dead weight; he didn't have the strength to make it up, anyway. He pretended to be lightheaded, hoping for a few minutes to regain his strength, but they finally managed to jerk him to his feet. They held him there, his head drooping. It was as if he was back in the dream he often had where he was running through a pool of water, always one step ahead of his pursuer, but never far enough ahead to get away. He wasn't going to get away this time, either, every time he started to gain some strength, they knocked the strength out of him again.

And this was no dream; he knew that Harmon and the others were just waiting for him to thaw out before they gave him the airplane ride of his life.

He felt a slight tingling sensation; a sign there might be a chance to fight back, after all. They urged him forward, but he stayed limp and made them drag him. If he could stall for just a few more minutes, . . . maybe. . .

Harmon kicked the barn door open and shoved him until he stumbled and fell to the ground, the gravel cutting into his half naked body. He opened one eye and looked up. Harmon and Hawk Face were grinning, happy to see that he would be able to enjoy the experience they had in store.

"Welcome back," Harmon said. "Perfect timing. I was afraid you were going to leave us."

Kyle turned his head slightly and saw that one of the recalcitrant brothers trailed behind. He was pretty sure he knew where the other one was.

"Ronald, you stay here and keep an eye out. Carl will fly the Cessna."

"Who are you people?" Kyle croaked, surprised by how weak his voice had become.

"So, the big shot air traffic controller can talk. We work for that airline you almost put out of business, or at least we did. Word is the company might go bankrupt because of you. The stock was already down, now it's hit rock bottom. You didn't think you were going to get away with it, did you? Carl is a pilot for Transcon, by the way; ain't that a coincidence?"

"So that's what Hawk Face is so excited about," Kyle said, nodding toward her.

Harmon looked angry at first, then threw back his head and laughed. "You mean Marilyn? She's my sister. You should see her go one-on-one with one of those tough guys in a bar. She's one mean lady; likes to fight and never quits."

Hawk Face didn't think the nickname was so funny. Her wide, cold eyes stared down at Kyle.

"I don't suppose it makes any difference now, but I didn't do it," Kyle croaked.

"We figured you'd say that, but it don't matter. Since that chicken shit judge was dumb enough to let you go, we felt obligated to do the job ourselves. This will be a lot quicker, anyway."

"So you, Hawk Face, Ronald and Carl decided to take the law into your own hands?"

Hawk Face had had enough of the nickname: she kicked Kyle in the ribs, reached down and began dragging him. She was as strong as any man; dragging Kyle's two hundred pounds didn't seem to bother her at all. Harmon grabbed one arm and helped her.

"You're sure we want to do this Harmon?" Ronald hollered from behind. "It's broad daylight. Someone might see us."

Harmon glanced back and gave Ronald a vicious look.

"Damn right I do. This is the best part, right Marilyn? This guy called you 'Hawk Face'."

Marilyn was too eager to begin the punishment to respond.

"Don't worry, Ronald," Harmon said. "We'll drop him someplace in another county. Then we'll all sit back, drink beer, and watch the FBI look for him. By the time they find him, he should be nice and ripe."

Hawk Face finally spoke up: "They'll give us a medal," her whisky voice drawled.

They continued to drag Kyle until they came to a dirty little red and white Cessna. Carl was in the pilot's seat, looking out the cockpit window. He didn't look like a killer; he was distinguished looking, with well-combed gray hair and an intelligent face. His expression said he didn't like what they were about to do, which made the whole scene even more surreal. The aircraft looked as if it had been wrecked several times: there were holes in the wing and fuselage and most of the paint had been scraped off. But when Carl revved up the engine, it became apparent that at least the engine had been well taken care of. Hawk Face jumped into the back seat, while Harmon shoved Kyle up and into the passenger seat and climbed in next to him. He slammed the door and motioned for Carl to take off.

Kyle felt like a baloney sandwich, wedged in between Carl and Harmon, whose huge body blocked the passenger side door. He was starting to get some feeling in his limbs, but not enough to put up much of a fight. The situation seemed hopeless. He forced himself to concentrate on an escape plan, anything to keep his mind off of his situation. He thought about Laura and the children; he visualized them standing next to his grave. He needed to do something; make some kind of effort, however futile.

He considered two possible options, neither of them plausible: he could fight and attempt to get out of the aircraft, or wait until they were about to take off, grab the yoke, and force the Cessna into a ground loop.

He made up his mind that if these animals were serious and not just trying to scare him, he wasn't going down without a fight. In the meantime, he continued to hope they *weren't* serious.

He looked out through the cockpit window while Carl revved up the engine again. It looked as if their flight path would take them directly over the barn with the freezer. Visualizing what he was about to experience, he thought of a third option: he remembered a movie where a skydiver had broken his fall by landing on the roof of a house. How about the top of a barn? The idea was pure crazy, but if they were really going to toss him out, what did he have to lose? The problem was, if he was going to attempt a dive he would have to get past Harmon, no small task, and he would have to make his move before they reached fifty to a hundred feet.

He glanced to his right, evaluating his chances. It would require a surprise move and it would have to be fast. There would be only one chance; if that failed he would just grab the stick and take them all down with him; a fourth and more likely option under the circumstances.

He glanced back and thought of another problem: Hawk Face had her arm around his neck, breathing her foul breath down his back. He could actually "feel" her exhilaration. It was then that he knew for sure that these weren't scare tactics; Hawk Face, at least, was dead serious, she wanted him dead and she wanted him to suffer on the way down. He looked out the window to his left and saw Ronald standing next to the barn, watching. He figured that Ronald's job was to pick up the body and hide it.

The engine roared when Carl pushed the throttle forward. The filthy little Cessna kicked up dirt and waddled from side to side as it tried to straighten out and get airborne. In only five to ten seconds, Kyle would have to make his move. He took a deep breath and said a short prayer.

When the Cessna reached what he thought was a somewhat safe altitude, he extended his left arm past Harmon, grabbed the door handle with his left hand, and slammed his right elbow into Harmon's neck. Carl had just given the aircraft a slight turn to starboard, an unexpected move that provided the momentum Kyle needed to get over Harmon's body and out the door. It was the one thing Harmon hadn't counted on; nevertheless, he managed to grab Kyle's arm and hang on. Unfortunately, Hawk Face hung on too; she continued her strangle hold as she came flying over the seat, and all three went out the door.

They were now in free fall. Kyle actually had a second or two to enjoy the surprised look on their faces. For the first time since they had kidnapped him, he was in control - sort of.

Harmon lost his grip first and started falling below, but Hawk Face hung on with everything she had, choking him. "Let go, damn you," Kyle screamed, but she just hung on tighter.

Kyle glanced down in the few seconds available and saw Big Man go through the barn roof. At the last possible instant, he rolled over and made sure Hawk Face got the worst of it. She dragged him through the roof, and they continued on down until they hit a concrete floor, pieces of wood flying everywhere. Kyle's entire weight, all two hundred pounds, landed full force on Hawk Face's body, but she never uttered a sound.

Kyle staggered to his feet and looked around. He saw Harmon's big body stretched out on the concrete, one boot and sock missing and blood streaming from his head. Ronald came toward him, brandishing a pitchfork. He didn't seem quite as eager as his sister and brother, but it didn't look as if he was going to step aside, either.

"I don't want to hurt you; just give me the truck keys," Kyle shouted.

When Ronald looked around and realized that his brother and sister were probably dead, he went from observer to combatant. He glared at Kyle malevolently and raised the pitchfork like a sword. He started forward, eyes wide, teeth clenched.

Kyle grabbed a shovel, sidestepped, and slammed it against the side of Ronald's head. Ronald went down hard, unconscious. Kyle tore his pockets apart looking for keys, but there weren't any there.

He ran to the pickup truck and found the keys in the ignition. He started the truck and roared down the driveway in his boxers, wondering how Ronald and Carl would explain what had happened.

In spite of everything, he thought about Hawk Face and shook his head:

Big Man had said she was a tough lady. She was tough all right, but she was no damn lady.

TWENTY SIX

The pickup truck ran out of gas.

Kyle found himself lost on a pitch dark, country road with no signs of life. His bruised and battered body had also run out of gas. He ended up sleeping in a cornfield.

The next morning, wearing a denim shirt, Levis, and a pair of work boots he found in the truck, he walked for an hour, found a farmhouse, and borrowed a can of gas. He walked another hour back to the pickup truck, put a couple of gallons of gas in the tank, returned the gas can, and drove to a grocery store in Overland Park, Kansas, to call Laura. He noticed two men in a black Mercedes pull in behind him as he was entering the store, but he was too tired to give it much thought.

He hurried through the store with his hat pulled down over his eyes to hide his identity. He was infamous now, his face on national television and in every newspaper. The bruises on his face made him even more noticeable.

He looked around for a phone, holding on to the change he had found in the pickup truck. Big Man and Hawk Face were probably dead, so he didn't think they would mind. Funny how one could be so blasé about the death of two human beings, but that was the world he had been forced to live in.

As he walked down an aisle, the tops of two heads could be seen walking in the same direction down an adjacent aisle. With his head lowered, he turned the corner at the end of the aisle and everything went black. He blinked his eyes several times and managed to take a couple steps forward before he lost his balance and fell face down in the aisle. His last conscious thought was of two, Italian looking faces in business suits, looking down and laughing.

When he regained consciousness, he found himself sitting on the floor with boxes of banana nut cereal, including one lying on his chest. It was nice and warm on the floor though, all things considered, much better than the cold freezer. He tried to remember how he had gotten there, but all that came to mind was the two strangers. There was no one else around now, just his body foolishly stretched out on the floor. He brushed away the box of cereal on his chest and got up slowly, boxes flying everywhere. He stepped on one as he wobbled to his feet; cereal shot forth.

He looked toward the front of the store and saw the two men standing at the entrance, pointing at him, still laughing. He shouted for them to stop, but they ignored him and casually left the store. Neither man had seemed the least bit worried or concerned; nor did they seem to be making an attempt to get away. He ran toward the door, still stumbling, went outside, and caught up with them.

"Get back here, you two."

"Go away," one of the men said, not a threat, more like friendly advice. He glanced at the scars on Kyle's face and laughed some more.

"Which one of you knocked me down?"

"Looks like everyone's knocked you down," the second man said.

Kyle wasn't sure what to do next. He wanted to strike back, jump on one of them and get revenge, but his head had cleared somewhat, and he realized he was in no position to draw more attention to himself. A crowd had already begun to form, drawn from surrounding stores by the shouting. Several of them began to recognize Kyle and started moving in his direction. The two men stopped from time to time to point him out to other passers by. Kyle made a strategic decision to forget the phone call and find the pickup. He crossed the street, running and looking back over his shoulder. The crowd followed. He stopped for a moment, turned around and stood his ground. "Stop right there. I don't want any trouble."

The crowd stopped, but only for a second or two, then they began moving toward him again, faster this time. He saw that they weren't about to be denied.

"You're the guy that caused that airplane collision," a woman said boldly. "My neighbor's niece was on one of those airplanes."

"You're wrong," Kyle said. "Everything will be cleared up in a few days."

"The FAA says your voice is on the tape recording," a man said.

"I don't have time to explain right now, so just leave me alone." He turned and spotted the pickup truck, hurried to get to the driver's side, started to get in. But a disheveled looking man in a leather jacket got there first, grabbing him from behind.

"Wait a minute you, I pay your salary and I've got something to say."

Kyle turned and pushed him away, but the man was determined to impress the crowd. "You're a federal employee. You work for me."

"Not anymore I don't; now get the hell away from me." Kyle grabbed the door handle, but someone hit him from behind and he fell forward against the pickup. It energized the crowd and they began pushing and shoving to get at him. A man carrying a grocery bag got there just as Kyle was recovering; he took a swing and Kyle fought back. The man went down, his grocery bag flying, cans of food rolling in the street. By this time there were eight or nine others swinging wildly. Once again, he shouted for them to stop, but they wouldn't.

Kyle had had enough: he hadn't minded the criticism, even thought he probably deserved it, but things had gone to too far. He exploded, grabbing the man in front of him. The man started to back away, but Kyle hit him and he went down. Another man took a swing but missed. Kyle hit him under the chin, sending him flying. By this time, even the grocery store manager wanted in: he tried to grab Kyle's arm, but Kyle reacted with a one-two punch to the side of his head, sending him backwards.

Sirens wailed. Kyle abandoned the pickup truck and began running down the street.

Many in the crowd ran after him. But just as some of them were about to catch up, the two men from the grocery store stepped in and stopped them in their tracks.

Kyle looked back, surprised and puzzled. His attackers had become his protectors.

A police car pulled up alongside. Two cops got out.

Thank God, he thought.

"It's him," the first cop said. "What the hell happened to his face?"

"Are you all right?" the second cop asked.

"I guess so," Kyle said.

"Good," he said, and shoved him to the ground.

The first cop looked down at Kyle, swung his foot and kicked him. "Too bad those people didn't kill you, asshole," he said. "Could have saved the taxpayers some money."

They got back in their police car and drove away.

TWENTY SEVEN

Nancy Corey looked up at the tall skyscraper that housed Tyler Harding's office. The building sat in the center of an exclusive area in downtown Kansas City, Missouri, and was the tallest and most modern building on the block. She wondered how a man with such a poor reputation could afford an office in such an opulent setting. Then she remembered a law school chum telling her that Harding was the son of Dexter Harding, a former giant in the field of criminal law, and that Dexter's former law partners kept Harding around to keep from losing his father's clients. They even allowed Tyler full use of secretarial and paralegal help, not that they thought he would have any use for it.

A man who couldn't take his eyes off of Nancy's rear held the front door open for her. She, nodded, smiled, and went in. He continued to watch her backside, shaking his head.

Everything inside smelled of old money. The long, marble entrance hall was so highly polished that Nancy could see her own, long legs upside down. She felt right at home in her designer suit and alligator briefcase, her high heels clicking as she walked the fifty or so feet to an elevator.

She hadn't bothered to call for an appointment because she was sure she wouldn't need one: Tyler Harding would take the case, even with the conditions set down by her father. And even if he wouldn't, that was all right too, she would be glad to handle the case herself. She wasn't into begging, and she didn't intend to start today. On the other hand, she had to make an honest attempt or her father would learn the truth, although she would never disobey him anyway: she would do her duty without her father or anyone else riding herd. She was a like a Marine–always follow-ing orders. She figured she was better than a "few good men," anyway.

"Tyler Harding?" Nancy asked, holding the door open and looking into his office.

Harding had been sitting with his feet up on the desk. They dropped quickly when he saw the tall, statuesque creature standing in the door-way.

"Yes," he said defensively, standing as if in the presence of royalty.

Nancy strolled to his desk and held out her hand. "Nancy Corey."

Tyler's lascivious eyes examined Nancy all over, his mind conjuring up all kinds of scenarios he knew she would never let him carry out. He actually found it hard to breath: the woman was luscious, with style and beauty she didn't seem to be aware of. But there was another side to her, too, something that said she wasn't to be taken lightly.

"What...can I do for you?" he finally sputtered.

"It's what *I'm* going to do for you. May I sit?"

Harding nodded, still speechless.

Nancy took a few steps back and found a leather chair. She sat and crossed one elegant leg, looking him in the eye. "I'll get right to it. You need clients. I have one for you that will put you back in good graces, might even make you famous."

Harding continued to stand, not sure what to say.

Nancy eyed him curiously. She wondered why a short, stumpy lawyer would dress like such a dandy: his horned rimmed glasses were garnished with an oversized chain, and he wore a double breasted, striped suit that was so large it covered his stubby body like a tablecloth. He looked more like an owl than a lawyer, anyway, always cocking his oval eyes sideways, the oversized chain swinging back and forth. To top it off, he blinked continuously.

"What makes you think I'm *not* in good graces? I don't know what you're talking about."

Nancy had done her homework; she was sure he knew exactly what she was talking about: his career was a disaster. Surprisingly, she had learned some positive things as well: lawyers who had worked with Harding said he could often be brilliant. She learned that he had been moot court champion in law school, always "thinking on his feet," outwitting his opponents. His classmates stopped being surprised after a while. When he hit bottom they decided it must have been overconfidence; that he must have stopped preparing for his cases, convinced that all he had to do was show up in court.

"Please, sit down, will you," Nancy said, as if it were *her* office.

Harding quickly lowered himself into his chair, looking chagrined.

Nancy smoothed out a wrinkle on the sleeve of her suit while Harding continued his psychical examination. She was used to childish men eyeballing her; this one was nothing more than a child sitting behind a desk, in an office that belonged to someone else.

"Look, I don't want to sound judgmental," she said, "but I read about your troubles with the bar association. You need business badly, and I've got a great case for you. Are you interested, or shall we continue this pretense, because I'm really in a hurry and I don't have time to spar with you about this?"

Tyler's desperation got the best of his ego. "OK, I'm interested," he said. "But is it all right if I ask who the client is?" His half-hearted sarcasm was an attempt to gain some control.

Nancy ignored it. "You've heard about the mid-air collision, I assume?"

Harding frowned and shook his head slightly. "Who hasn't?"

"I want you to handle the case."

Tyler had all he could do to keep from floating upward. He loved publicity, and airplane crashes always meant publicity. He had even given some thought as to how the case should be handled. His heart leaped. "Is the client related?"

"No, I haven't even met the man yet."

"But you represent him?"

"I'm not going to represent him—you are, and I'm the one who can make it happen."

"How?"

"Trust me. Are you interested or not?"

Tyler was very definitely interested. "You can get any lawyer in town to plead the man out, unless he actually wants the death penalty. What's left for *me* to do?"

"He's not going to plead guilty; he's going to trial and you're going to defend him. This could make you famous, and you'll handle it without some cumbersome legal team. It will be just you, with the whole world watching."

"You must know something I don't. From everything I read, the man predicted he was going to do it, and then did it. I'd be better off prosecuting. Is there something I don't know?

"By the way," he said before she could answer, "how do you know he won't plead guilty if you don't represent him?"

"Because my job and yours is to see that he doesn't. The deal is this, and I can't say much more: I'm an intermediary for a man who is willing to pay all of Mr. Matthew's legal fees as long as he doesn't plead 'guilty,' 'insanity,' or post some-other garbage. That's the deal. You don't need to know any more than that right now."

"An insanity plea might be all that's left," Harding insisted.

"That is not my decision. My client wants to make sure the man is as guilty as he seems to be, and he won't know that for sure unless and until all the facts are presented at a trial. If the man pleads guilty or some insanity defense, it will be a whitewash and my client will never know the real truth. He's concerned that the controller could end up in some mental institution, or a recreational playground they call a prison. If that were to happen, he might get away with murder."

"Why would someone spend all that money when the truth is right there on the tape recording? Doesn't he read the paper? A trial could cost a million bucks."

"That's my client's problem. Deal or no deal?"

Harding shrugged his shoulders and suppressed a smile. "When do I start?"

"Then you agree to my terms?"

Tyler cocked his head, smiled his best weasel smile, and threw up his hands without really saying anything.

"I'll take that as a 'yes.' As soon as Matthews agrees to let us represent him, I'll call you."

"And if he insists on pleading guilty?" Tyler asked anxiously.

"Then he pays for his own defense and you and I are out of it. I'll pay you for your time."

Tyler couldn't wait to brag to his father's ex-partners. Then he remembered something else Nancy had said: "You said 'agree to let *us* represent him.' I thought you told me I was going to handle this case myself?"

"Except that I'll be sitting second chair."

"You," Tyler protested. "How many criminal cases have you tried?" Although by this time he didn't really care.

Nancy was tired of his blinking eyes. "All you need to know is that I'm a good lawyer. I can do a lot of the leg work."

Tyler glanced at her legs involuntarily. He had no doubt.

Nancy recognized her own metaphor and blushed. She got up and moved smartly toward the office door. Harding followed like a lap dog.

"So that's it? I'm hired?"

"For now," she said, walking out the door and slithering down the hall.

Harding stood and watched her glide down the hallway, wondering why anyone would pay a million bucks to help a man who was so obviously guilty, but not really caring. Maybe whoever was paying had an ulterior motive; or she did.

But that didn't make any damn difference, either; he had his own ulterior motive.

TWENTY EIGHT

Manny Vigil's cell phone rang as he was entering the Missouri University law library.

"Badger, I need your help," Ron Adair said.

"I 'gotta class in ten minutes. What is it?"

"I need you to look into something for me. Kyle Matthews, the controller the FBI says ran those two aircraft together, is a friend of mine."

Adair had nicknamed Vigil the "Badger" because it was said that a badger never backs down, even when mortally wounded. Like the badger, Manny was intense, even ferocious, when he was after something. But it had also been said that a badger could turn over in his own skin, which in Manny's case would take about a month: he weighed in at over two hundred and sixty pounds. Manny's size tended to disguise his intellectual gifts; gifts that became apparent only after you got to know him. He had a logical and organized mind, which he kept sharp by working as a private investigator and doing crossword puzzles. He enjoyed solving things one step at a time, a trait that made him good at both. It was not a good idea to debate Manny Vigil unless you had your facts straight and lots of time on your hands. He had been "around the block," too: conducting aircraft investigations for the FAA before opening his own office as a licensed private investigator. He still had contacts in the FAA, the NTSB, the FBI, and had recently worked for the new Transportation Security Administration.

Manny dropped into a chair; brushed aside a stack of papers left behind by some slob, and put his backpack down on the table. He moved his cell phone to his left hand and rubbed his semi-bald head with his right. The thin halo of hair that stretched from his left ear to his right ear was the only hair he had left. "You've got five minutes," he said.

"Kyle Matthews would never intentionally run two airplanes together," Ron said, sounding genuinely bewildered. "Revenge is out of the question. The people who work with him every day don't believe it either."

"OK, so you're smarting because he's a friend, but let's face facts: I was told that Matthews bragged about what he was going to do."

"It was just a joke, a prank."

"Some joke. What about his friend, the one working next to him, he heard Matthews issue the clearance. End of story."

Ron wasn't surprised that Manny had the facts down cold.

"The Transcon pilot must have mistakenly followed a clearance intended for another aircraft. It's possible he was on the wrong frequency, listening to a clearance intended for someone else."

"The FBI checked the tapes for the other radar positions; that never happened."

Contacts, another of Manny's assets: he knew things only the FBI and the FAA were supposed to know.

Ron had no comeback. "I'm afraid that's right," he finally said, "except that it would take a month for them to check every recording for that day: there's thirty or more radar positions."

"So what the hell do you want me to do, destroy the tape? That's about the only thing that will save your friend's ass now?"

"I don't know," Ron sighed. "It's just that I've never known Kyle Matthews to lie."

"Maybe he blacked out, something temporary. Is it possible he did it and doesn't remember?"

"I just talked to his doctor; Kyle's in excellent physical and mental condition."

"Well then, how does *he* explain what happened?"

"He thinks our quality assurance guy played back the wrong tape, maybe even switched tapes."

Manny's interest swelled. "You mean intentionally? Does Matthews have that kind of an enemy there?"

"I assigned a man named Rich Carpelski to review the tape before the FBI or the NTSB got there. Carpelski's a prick with ears and he despises Matthews. But to be honest, I don't think he has the guts to do something like that. I checked the tape recording myself; it looked OK."

"But he could have accidentally picked up the wrong tape, right? I remember checking a few tape recordings at that center when I worked an airline crash case before; controllers are a little sloppy when it comes to logging the times and channels."

Ron Hesitated: "Maybe, but it's unlikely. I checked the logs myself; unfortunately, they look fine."

Manny had as much regard for Ron's intelligence as Ron had for his: Ron was a skeptic, not easily fooled. Still, Manny believed he was being sucked in, like watching a hook floating by with a fat worm attached.

"If I remember right, Matthews' dad took the fall for the collapse of PATCO. I heard he was responsible for causing all those controllers to lose their jobs. I also heard Deeter Noonan once pointed the finger right at him. Good reason for Mathews to be hostile toward the FAA."

"I've been friends with Kyle and his dad for years: neither one of them had anything against Noonan, even if they didn't like him. Look into it, will you Manny, give me your opinion. The FBI took the tape recording right after I looked at it. You have contacts; maybe they'll let you look at it."

"I'll talk to someone in the FBI, see what I can do. But don't sell those guys short, they're good people. If that tape's been jacked with, they'll know it."

"Yeah, but this isn't just a routine investigation. The government thinks they already know what happened, so all they're doing now is going through the motions. I talked with FBI Director Carl Perkins and he sounded as if he thought it was a slam-dunk. Besides, I still have a mid–air collision to deal with. The FAA will expect me to take preventative measures. I need to know how and why this happened, every damn detail."

Manny trusted the FBI and the NTSB, but Ron was right; human nature was at work here. Even dedicated NTSB and FBI investigators would have no reason to argue with the tape recording.

Finally: "OK, Ron, I'll look into it as best I can."

"Be careful Manny, there's a ton of pressure coming from Washington. The investigation just started and the government is already asking why Kyle doesn't plead guilty."

TWENTY NINE

Manny Vigil stood toe to toe with Kansas City Center manager Curtis Raymond, furious because Raymond refused to let him enter the building. Manny had very little patience with bureaucrats to begin with.

"I'm a private investigator representing Kyle Matthews and I'm here to speak with Rooster Brunges. I have a right to be here, so get the hell out of my way."

Manny's size was imposing, more like a roadblock than a human being. His large, demanding eyes bored in until Raymond was suddenly unsure of himself. Raymond was used to being the bully, the biggest man in town, but it wasn't working here. He took a step back and straightened his body to its full height. But even at a stout six two, he was no match for the Badger.

"Mr. Adair never. . . never said anything to me about you. I can't let anyone in right now."

Not to be denied, the Badger's eyes bulged and he stuck his chin in Raymond's face, spreading his legs like a Sumo wrestler. "Look, dumbass, I'm going in, so you do whatever you think best. But first, get that damned cigar out of my face before I shove it down your throat." He pushed Raymond aside and marched toward the front door.

"You'll have to be escorted," Raymond insisted, following behind.

"I know two people who won't like that," Manny said, stopping to turn and broach Raymond again.

Raymond stopped, blinked his eyes. "I . . . don't know what you mean . . . who?"

"Me and the fat prick who tries to saddle me with that escort, that's who." He turned, opened the door, walked in.

"You can't threaten me," Raymond whined, following at a safe distance.

Manny had been to the center many times as a private investigator; he knew his way around. He drew stares as his huge body moved between two rows of radar scopes with a fulminating Raymond trailing behind. "There's certain areas where you can't go," Raymond continued to insist.

Manny ignored him and walked up behind a controller standing next to a scope. The man turned, flinched, and backed away.

"Where can I find Rooster Brunges?"

The controller hesitated for a second and then pointed towards the men's room. "He's in there, but I don't recommend you go in just yet."

Manny heard loud noises as he walked in that direction; it sounded like a drunken brawl inside. He hesitated, walked in, and stood for a long moment, unable to believe his eyes: a short, skinny man stood with his head immersed in a sink full of water. A bunch of other men, and several women, surrounded the washbasin, shouting and cheering loudly.

"Come on Rooster, you can do it. . . come on. . . no. . . don't stop. . . goddammit, I've got ten bucks on you. . . keep your head down."

"What the hell. . . ," Manny said out loud. He nudged one of the rapt controllers and pointed to Brunges for an explanation.

"Little peckerwood bragged he could hold his head under for three minutes," the controller explained, laughing. "There's some pretty big bets riding on this."

Manny remembered the old saying that air traffic control was "hours and hours of boredom, punctuated by moments of sheer terror." He figured this must be what happens during the boring parts.

Rooster's head started to rise, falling far short of three minutes. But when he tried to extricate himself, a tall man standing behind him reached into the sink and pushed his head under. "Damn you Rooster, you ain't coming up yet; I bet fifty bucks on you."

Rooster fought so hard that his feet were practically off of the floor. Water flew everywhere. Controllers laughed and cheered even louder.

Everything changed in seconds when a man who turned out to be the watch supervisor came barging through the doorway. He pushed Manny and the man holding Rooster's head aside, grabbed Rooster by the collar and jerked his head up. "Jesus, you guys, don't we have enough people looking over our shoulders already? I want everyone out of here. Get back to work."

The room was suddenly very quiet. Then, everyone scrambled to get away.

The supervisor turned to Manny and looked him up and down. "Who in the hell are you?"

"Manny Vigil. I'm a private investigator. But I'm not here to look over anyone's shoulder. Ron Adair gave me permission to talk to Brunges."

"Bob Grey, watch supervisor," the man said without shaking hands. Turning his attention to Rooster, "You're an idiot, Rooster."

"Did I make it?" Rooster asked, gasping for air. Water dripped from every part of his body.

Grey gave Rooster a paper towel, shook his head, "no." "Now get this place cleaned up. And next time you make one of your stupid boasts, let me know. I'd like to make a few bucks myself."

Grey turned and bolted from the room, shouting and telling controllers waiting around outside to get back to work. He ordered one of them to "get the hell in there and help Rooster clean the place up."

The controller walked in, then stuck his head back out the door to make sure Grey was gone. He patted Rooster on the back, laughed, and grabbed a mop. Manny waited until Rooster dried off and then introduced himself. "Ron Adair suggested I talk to you," he said. "I have some questions about Kyle Matthews."

Rooster cleaned his ears with a towel and looked Vigil over carefully. He didn't like talking to strangers, and he thought he had heard sarcasm in Vigil's voice."

"You from the press?"

"No. I'm a private investigator working for Ron Adair."

Rooster hesitated. The mention of Ron Adair's name had softened his resistance. He stood, glaring at Vigil for a long moment. "Let's go to the cafeteria."

They took a corner table, away from the crowd. Rooster put a pack of cigarettes on the table and continued to clean out his ears with a handkerchief.

"I'm probably just wasting my time," Manny said, acting disgusted. "Ron tells me that Matthews' voice is on the tape recording. Why would he want to protect a creep who would do something like this?"

Rooster was on his feet in a second, his volatile temper taking over. "Why in the fuck are you here then?" He grabbed his cigarettes and started to leave.

"Whoa there. . . ," Manny said, surprised at how little it took to set Brunges off. He'd been hoping for a reaction, but this was over the top. "Ron Adair said you'd want to help Matthews."

"You don't need me, your mind is already made up," Rooster said, all puffed up.

Vigil found it hard to keep from laughing. This little prick actually thought he was tough. All the same, Rooster's loyalty impressed him.

"Only a crazy man intentionally runs two airplanes together," Rooster went on, his eyes flashing and his finger jabbing at Manny's face. "Kyle Matthews is not crazy."

Manny had to agree: he *had* come to the center with his mind made up. "Come on, sit down. I was just testing you."

Rooster hesitated for a long moment. It looked as if he might leave anyway. He glared at Manny for a few more seconds before sitting back down, fighting hard to contain his anger. He slumped in his seat and shook a cigarette from the pack.

"Look at this from my point of view," Manny said cautiously. "I don't know this friend of yours; all I know is that his voice is on the recording. I need something to work with if I'm going to help him."

Rooster took a drag from the cigarette, said, "Some pilot fucked up, that's all there is to it. It ain't the first time, either."

Manny paused, giving Rooster more time to cool off.

After a long moment: "What about Carpelski? Any chance he jacked with the tape recording?"

"Carpelski's a dip shit; he's too stupid and too cowardly to do something like that. He might have fucked up, though; he's real good at that."

"Someone else, possibly? Did Matthews have enemies in the center? How about this guy Danny Houston? I understand he wasn't even in the building when the collision happened?"

"Danny Houston is as dumb as Carpelski. The man could fuck up a steel ball. I can't believe Kyle would even talk to that little shit. You can forget about him, too."

"So you think Kyle's story about Houston helping him was just bull shit?"

Rooster's eyes narrowed to slits. "I didn't say that; if Kyle said the little prick agreed to help, then he agreed to help. But if that asshole did agree to help, he lied, probably afraid to say 'no.' The little shit's like a water bug, always scurrying around. I can't see him and Kyle in the same room together."

"What about Matthews' attitude before this happened? Did he seem all right?"

"Ain't nobody in this place 'all right,' but he's no different from the rest of us. He's been kinda quiet the past few months, that's all. He's separated from his wife and the FAA bird dogs him every minute, waiting for him to make a mistake."

"Because of his views, you mean?"

"Yes. He's been talking to some congressmen, guy named Crimmins. The guy likes Kyle's ideas, probably plans to steal them and take credit. Going over the FAA's head is a capital crime for a controller."

"Ideas?"

"Yeah, ideas to computerize our job. It's a political thing. The FAA is jealous; they think he's stepping on their toes."

Manny had heard the same thing from Ron. There was no way to know if it was true or just a good friend talking, but it didn't make sense to Vigil. Why would the FAA be so angry about an employee's suggestions that they would be out to get him? After all, Matthews was an experienced controller; he should know what was needed.

Manny said, "Why wouldn't the FAA listen if an employee wanted to make suggestions?"

"Like I said, when an employee talks to a congressman, managers get very nervous, paranoid is more like it. The guy gets singled out as a trouble maker."

Manny: "Surely the government isn't stupid enough to blame a controller for a mid-air collision just because he's making suggestions. They can't get away with that kind of stuff in today's world; not with all those fucking talk shows."

"Maybe not, but if those assholes in Washington can help supply the gasoline, they won't lose any sleep over it. And it doesn't have to be the FAA: suppose some NTSB bureaucrat assumes Kyle is guilty because his boss says he is, and decides to ignore evidence? He might think it's better to do that than to embarrass his boss."

Manny sat quietly for a few seconds, scratching his head. A government plot was nonsense, of course, but it *was* possible the feds were rushing to judgment a little. The little man made some sense, even if he did think he could hold his head under water for three minutes. Until now, Manny had just assumed this would be a short, routine investigation for a friend. Now he was asking himself if this could possibly be something more. He was getting anxious to meet Kyle Matthews.

Rooster interrupted his thoughts.

"My turn to ask a question. What about this Tyler Harding guy, can we trust him not to fuck this thing up any worse than it already is?"

Manny jumped a foot. "Who said anything about Tyler Harding? What's he got to do with this?"

"He's 'gonna be Kyle's lawyer."

THIRTY

Manny left the parking lot in a flash, dialing Ron's home phone and mumbling to himself. *Tyler Harding? Not in his lifetime! That was a deal breaker.*

Ron's wife answered the phone and said Ron had gone to meet with a lawyer at a hamburger place called Winstead's, on the Country Club Plaza.

Manny caught up with Ron inside the restaurant, sitting in a booth with Tyler Harding, having a hamburger and coffee. "I would never have agreed to help you if I'd known Harding had anything to do with this," he said, walking up from behind.

Ron jerked his head around and threw up his hands: "Wait a minute, you don't understand." He knew that Manny and Harding were oil and water, but his plan had been to prepare Manny beforehand; now it was too late. "I know you guys have had your problems, but let's not jump the gun here. Once you realize the circumstances, you'll understand. Sit down, let's talk about this."

Manny shook his head and glared at Harding; "I'll stand."

Harding scooted over in the booth; worried that Manny might smack him.

"Congratulations, Harding," Manny said sarcastically. "This sounds like something right up your alley: lots of publicity followed by a plea bargain and a big payoff."

"Mr. Harding hasn't even agreed to represent Mathews yet," Ron said feebly.

Manny wasn't deterred: "That's bull shit, Ron. You may as well know up front that I won't work with this sleazebag. My mother always said, 'tell me your company and I'll tell you what you are.' I wouldn't want my mother thinking I kept company with this creep. You've latched on to the worst lawyer you could possible find. I'll admit this bird has some talent: I watched him handle a case in federal court and he wasn't bad. Trouble is, he never 'walks it like he talks it.' I hate to see a guy with talent go down the shitter, but what I hate even more is to see him take some unsuspecting client with him. This shyster would walk barefoot over rattle snakes to get his hands on a case like this."

Harding just grinned. He was used to criticism; some said he thrived on it. "Someone offered to pay Mr. Matthew's expenses if I would take the case, Manny, so apparently *he* thinks I'm good. He'll pay your expenses, too, if I decide to hire you. Matthews could never afford this kind of representation himself."

"You little runt. Do you actually think I'd take money from a loser like you? I won't do it, not even for Ron. Even if I had the time to spare, I wouldn't want my reputation sullied."

"Am I really that bad, Manny?" Harding asked petulantly. "Mr. Adair thinks this might just be an unfortunate accident. We can win this, I know we can."

"Unfortunate for everyone but you, you mean. Who's the nit-wit willing to pay for your questionable services, anyway?"

Harding hesitated. "I'd rather not say just yet."

Manny frowned, said, "Ron, I hope you're going to warn Matthews, because if he lets this idiot represent him and the public finds out, it'll be guilt by association."

"I can give you some relief from law school, if that will help, Manny," Harding said, oblivious to Manny's insults. "I have friends at Missouri University."

Manny cringed: "I don't need your fucking help; and what makes you think anyone at the university would talk to you anyway?"

Harding showed all his teeth, as if it was just a good joke. He would flatter the devil if necessary. "You're the best at analyzing tape recordings, Manny. I know you must be dying to get involved."

"Talk to your client, for Christ's sake. Who knows more about air traffic control recordings than he does? Or won't he talk to you?"

Once again, Harding ignored the insult. "I haven't met Mr. Matthews yet, I only talked with an intermediary. But I'm sure he'll be happy to let me represent him. And when I do, I'll need all the help I can get. This is as much a case for a private investigator as it is for a lawyer."

"That's good, because he certainly isn't getting a lawyer. And you still haven't told me who's backing this."

"The intermediary is a woman. She came to my office and said her client doesn't want to be identified. This woman is real sharp, very classy; you don't want to miss meeting her. She looks like something out of Vogue. I'm sure that whoever she's representing has plenty of money."

"I didn't ask who the messenger was; I 'wanna know who's paying the bill? Is this somebody who wants you to argue that the defendant is from Venus and is only following planetary orders, the kind of defense you've used in the past because you were too lazy to do the job right?"

"I've learned my lesson, Manny. I'm going to play this one strictly by the book."

"Good, cause if you don't I'll turn you in to the bar association myself. I'll be watching to make sure you keep your promise."

"Why not talk to the woman yourself before you decide? I have a meeting planned for tomorrow, one o'clock."

Manny finally sat down. It was against his better judgment to get involved with Harding, but he knew Harding was right when he said this might be Matthews' only chance for representation."

"OK, I'll be there, but like I said, I'm 'gonna do my own sleuthing until I'm satisfied I know all the facts. In the meantime, I'll help Ron as long as you follow the rules; I just won't associate with you. And when things go to hell, as I'm sure they will, you better be after the best deal for your client, even if you have to get down on your hands and knees and beg. If you piss off the government with your grandstanding, I'll be all over you."

Harding grinned and shook his head. He didn't dare tell Manny what Nancy's orders were.

He had no intention of following them anyway.

THIRTY ONE

By 9:45 AM the following morning, the media had gotten word that Tyler Harding would represent Kyle Matthews, and that their first meeting was scheduled for 1:00PM, in Harding's office.

By 12:45 PM, the building overflowed with reporters from all over the world. They were stretched out from the curb in front of Harding's office building, all the way inside and down the hall to his office, carrying microphones, mini-cams, and jockeying to get to the front of the line.

Kyle, with Rooster in tow, forced his way into the building, swatting at reporters holding outstretched mikes. Things weren't a whole lot better inside: Dexter Harding's former law partners hadn't gotten the word in time to hire the necessary security people.

Kyle, head down, jammed his outstretched hands forward like the beam of an icebreaker. Reporters were forced to give ground as he bulldozed his way forward, one step at a time towards Harding's office. Employees from surrounding offices stood in their doorways or spilled out into the hall, gawking and scrambling for a better view.

Undaunted by his pleas, reporters jabbed their mikes in Kyle's face, asking questions in rapid-fire bursts. "What happened to your face?" "Why do you think the judge let you out on bail?"

"Now I know how serial killers feel," Kyle shouted, leaning over to broadcast in Rooster's ear.

"I told you they wouldn't believe that bull shit story about how you fell off of a roof."

"Well, I did, sort of."

"Hell, I don't believe it myself and I'm your friend, so what makes you think these bloodthirsty bastards will buy it. Your face looks like a meatball dinner, by the way; they know you didn't end up looking like that from falling off of a roof, not unless you landed face first. You haven't been home long enough to fall off of a roof, anyway."

If he lived long enough, Kyle thought his story about how he taught Big Man and Hawk Face how to fly might be something to tell his grandchildren, but he wasn't going to talk about that now, not even to his best friend. He was confident that the two remaining brothers wouldn't tell anyone about it either, not unless they wanted to go to jail.

"Laura didn't believe my story, either," Kyle shouted above the din.

"What is the truth, anyway? Did those hillbillies do that to you? How'd you get away? There was a story in the newspaper about two dead bodies found in Leavenworth."

"I was beaten, thrown into a freezer like a piece of meat, and tossed out of an airplane. Then, I ran away."

"OK, so don't tell me then, see if I give a shit." Rooster shouted, pushing reporters aside. Rooster hated secrets. "But you better make up something more believable than the crap you're putting out now, cause if these sharks find out you had something to do with those two farmers, you're in deep shit."

"Like I'm not already? And just when everything was going so well. Speaking of things Laura didn't believe, did you hear what she said when we left?"

"You mean, 'have fun with your lawyer friend'?" Rooster asked.

"Yeah, and I don't think she was talking about Harding."

"Corey's picture was in the paper; that's what she was talking about."

"Jealous over some woman I haven't even met," Kyle grumbled.

"Woman's Intuition," Rooster said.

"Are you sure *you've* never met Corey, Rooster?"

"Why do I get the feeling you don't trust me?"

Kyle looked over and raised an eyebrow.

"She called me, that's all," Rooster protested.

"You have to admit that some of the things you come up with are pretty screwy."

Rooster didn't have a chance to respond. They were at Harding's office door and reporters had it blocked. "I'll wait outside," Rooster grumbled, turning back into the flood of reporters and shoving them aside. "I'm not taking the blame if this doesn't work out."

Tyler Harding peered out through the half open door, bracing it with his foot. Kyle ducked in through the crack, saying, "You better get some help if you expect any of us to get out of this building alive."

Harding stepped aside while his secretary repelled the last of the boarders. He turned, smiled, and examined Kyle's face though thick glasses. Kyle examined him, as well, surprised by what he saw: he'd been hoping for someone who looked like the typical TV lawyer, tall, studious looking, wire rimmed glasses; but Harding looked more like some cartoon character, with slicked back hair and an oversized, pinstriped suit and Phi Beta Kappa key. He judged Harding's smile to be plastic; the same smile he'd seen on Burger's face at the arraignment. He immediately distrusted the man. "We've got more security on the way," Harding said.

The two men shook hands, but Kyle's eyes had already locked in on the woman leaning against the far wall, her tan arms crossed in front of her body. She was a knockout; with a slim, perfectly constructed face, high cheekbones, and dark, shoulder length hair. She appeared to be Italian or Native American. Her clothes, a dark blue suit and heels, looked expensive. Kyle's mother would have described her as "knowing money." He immediately thought about a character from the comic strip, *"Terry and the Pirates,"* something his father liked to read when Kyle was a child. One of the characters was a beautiful, dangerous looking woman who wore a silk dress and a flower in her hair. The "Dragon Lady," that was it! She seemed out of place in a room with the unctuous Tyler Harding and the large, bald man sitting in a corner chair, who he assumed was Manny Vigil. If the lady was architectural perfection, brick and glass, then Harding was aluminum siding and the bald man a bouncer from a two-bit dance hall.

Nancy Corey stared back, but said nothing. It was as if she was entering information into her computer and waiting for it to download. Her expression wasn't unpleasant, but the folded arms revealed distrust, maybe even a trace of anger.

Kyle gave a nod in her direction; she gave him a slight shake of the head in return. He knew he should turn away, but found it difficult.

Manny Vigil got up from the couch. Ron had told Kyle all about the man with a patch of hair that circled his bald head like an aircraft circling the globe. Ron had called him the Badger. Was he working for Harding, or the woman?

Harding waited a few seconds for the reporters to stop banging on the door, then smiled and stepped forward to make the introductions.

"Mr. Matthews, this is Nancy Corey, she'll be sitting second chair."

The two stared at each other again. Neither one moved or made an attempt to get closer. "And this is Manny Vigil. I understand you two have a mutual friend?"

Kyle shrugged affirmatively, continuing to steal glances at Corey. A waft of expensive perfume floated his way. In the comic strip, the Dragon Lady wore seductive perfume, too. Kyle didn't know perfume from manure, but he knew expensive. He finally managed to concentrate long enough to nod his head at Vigil, who stood with his arms folded like Corey's. Both of them appeared to have deliberately positioned themselves as far away from him as possible. He was a bug under a microscope; today's get together would be more like a doctor-patient conference than a lawyer-client meeting, with the doctors wondering if the patient's illness was self inflicted. He didn't really mind, he was willing to accept their presumption of guilt; after all, it was his stupid prank that had brought him here.

Harding pointed to a chair and Kyle sat down, continuing to mull over the differences between the three. An air traffic controller would describe them as "not being on the same frequency." They did seem to have one thing in common though: none of them trusted their client.

Nancy Corey's expectations were taking a beating; colored by what she had seen on TV or read in the newspapers. She had assumed that the man they would represent was a Lee Harvey Oswald type, some smart aleck flake who wouldn't admit he'd screwed up and was looking for someone to save his ass. The man standing in front of her was nothing like that: he seemed calm, very much in control, neither apologetic nor defensive. She saw him as "politely defiant," though slightly embarrassed. He was also taller, more athletic, and much better looking than his pictures, even if his face *had* been beaten to a pulp. All in all, the man she saw standing in front of her seemed conservative and non-threatening. It occurred to her that the media might have deliberately painted a negative picture of the man because he wouldn't give them an interview. It was unnerving; she had been looking forward to hating him. At the same time, she wondered if she was cutting him too much slack. After all, there *was* that tape recording.

Manny had been studying Kyle too, and with pretty much the same reaction. He had assumed that Ron's praise was nothing more than one friend defending another. He had been prepared to dislike and distrust Matthews, just another spoiled government employee performing a dangerous prank and making excuses. Like Nancy, Manny was struck by Matthews' calm, confident manner. He, too, noticed that Kyle seemed embarrassed rather that apologetic. It was puzzling. Ron had said something about Matthews being in a fight. From the looks of things, Manny thought it must have been more like a war.

Kyle was beginning to feel like a grade school kid who had forgotten his homework. "I don't mean to sound unappreciative, but maybe someone could explain who's paying my legal fees, and why. Not that I don't appreciate the help, but I feel all of this would be unnecessary if we could just find Danny Houston. I sure don't want to waste anyone's time or money."

His three defenders exchanged stunned looks: "Waste anyone's time or money?" The man was facing multiple murder charges and he was worried about that? "That's one thing we can't tell you Mr. Matthews," Harding answered cautiously. "The person paying the bill has sworn Ms. Corey to secrecy. Even I don't know who it is. It's apparently just someone who wants to help, someone who believes that everyone deserves good representation."

"Then why didn't this 'someone' come and talk to me?"

"I don't know that, either. Your benefactor insists on remaining anonymous. I can only tell you that we're here to help, and that we will do our best to defend you."

Kyle had been warned about Harding. He knew about Harding's propensity toward crazy defenses, but he reasoned that he could always back out after he had listened for a while. "So what can I tell you? I guess we might as well talk about it since I'm here."

THIRTY TWO

It was the first time Judge Maureen Stone had ever received a phone call while flying at thirty five thousand feet. What popped into her head was that someone in the family had died; she never even considered that the phone call might lead to her dream job, a permanent seat on the federal bench.

"Yes, I'd be glad to," she said after a short conversation. "Yes, I can handle that. Thank you, your honor!"

Stone snapped her cell phone shut and sat back in her business class seat, smiling to herself. Here she was, a temporary appointment to the federal bench, and suddenly the chief judge calls and asks if she wants to reign over the mid-air collision trial, the biggest case of the year, maybe even the century.

She grabbed a leftover Lincoln newspaper and immediately saw that the case was still headline news. But reading further, she was shocked to see a familiar face right under the headline. She read the article and learned that her best friend from Lincoln high school, Marilyn Debold, had been killed in the mid-air collision. She hadn't seen Marilyn in many years, but they had been very good friends at one time. Maureen hadn't had that many friends when she was young. She had been tall and gangly, not popular with the other students. Marilyn was the only one who had refrained from calling her "Olive Oil," a nickname she detested. It made her angry to think that some whacko had taken Marilyn's life.

Now she had a real dilemma on her hands, a classic conflict of interest. Stone realized that she should call the chief judge back immediately and recuse herself. If the press found out about Marilyn Debold, she would be finished for good; judges were supposed to know better, especially federal judges. Of course, she could always say she didn't know Marilyn had been killed in the crash, but that would be risky; she was sure some busy body in the media would eventually learn the truth and expose her.

Then, there was her husband, Al.

Al was an ichthyologist, a scientist who had half the ocean in glass tanks in their living room. Al could be simple minded at times, even though he was a Stanford PHD with a very high IQ. Like most scientists, and especially those from a rich family, he was not impressed with material goods or anything else that couldn't be understood without a slide rule or computer. He was also a moralist: from time to time he had chided Maureen on her demeanor in the courtroom. He thought she wasn't studious enough and took her duties too lightly. He considered her to be a "seat of the pants" operator, not worthy of the federal bench. It was conceivable that Al might even report her to the authorities if he found out about Marilyn Debold. At the very least he would demand that she recuse herself. He was that righteous, and he had good connections.

Maureen remembered that she had already talked to Al about the case right before she boarded her flight from Kansas City to Lincoln, Nebraska:

"Can you believe it, Al," she remembered asking him, "according to a reporter on TV, this controller is actually going to plead 'not guilty.' He deliberately wipes out two aircraft and all those people and he's going to plead not guilty."

She recalled Al's self-righteous answer: "Maybe he *isn't* guilty."

Maureen would never get over how people like Al were naive enough to believe in the presumption of innocence. How could anyone be that ignorant? It was rare for an innocent individual to be charged with a crime. And even if the prosecutor failed to prove his or her case, which was usually what happened, the verdict was almost always "guilty." If the occasional innocent person was convicted, well. . . serves him right; if he wasn't guilty, he wouldn't have been charged.

As the aircraft left Nebraska's airspace and hurtled into Missouri's, Maureen thought more and more about the risk. She was almost ready to call the chief judge and ask to be excused. But after a few more scotches she managed to work up some courage. She wasn't sure if it was the scotch, or the fact that she became very angry whenever she looked out the window and visualized Marilyn falling to her death. Whatever it was, she was beginning to get excited: this case could get her that permanent seat on the federal bench if it went well. Others had been catapulted to that lofty position on less.

Indecision caused her to change her mind several times. She kept reaching for her cell phone and putting it back again. Finally, after another scotch, she made her final decision: she was going to go for it. This was just too great an opportunity to miss out on, especially for someone without strong credentials.

The chief judge had mentioned that Tyler Harding was going to represent the controller. Harding was a jackass, full of hair-brained ideas and braggadocio. It was a sure sign the controller was desperate. I'd love to deal with Harding, she thought to herself. I'd string him along; let him carry on with one of his crazy-assed defenses, then cut his balls off. He'd never know what hit him. I'd end his law career and send that murderous controller to the gas chamber at the same time.

Stone remembered that the Chief Judge had also mentioned that Deputy U.S. Attorney General Spencer Mallek, Attorney General Matt Potorf's number one man, would be the prosecutor. If they were sending in the big gun, it meant the White House considered the case crucial. She chuckled to herself: Tyler Harding and Spencer Mallek; one brainless idiot and one pompous asshole! This could be fun, if only she could get away with it.

She was still worried about Al, but by this time she didn't care anymore. One big break and Al would have to take back every negative thing he had ever said about her career. In the meantime, she had to make sure the fool paid attention to his fish and didn't find out about Marilyn.

She took another drink and said it out loud.

"I'll show you, Al."

*   *   *

She took a cab from the airport and arrived home at dinnertime. Al was cooking something French from a cookbook. He was using a timer and washing each pot and pan as he went along. His fastidiousness always pissed Maureen off because she never measured anything. He was a better cook than her, too, although she preferred hamburgers or hot dogs rather than some shit from France. She didn't like the damn French anyway.

Maureen watched Al for a sign that he'd heard about Marilyn De-bold. If he had, he hadn't mentioned it. She had already thrown away the Lincoln newspaper, and since Al didn't watch anything on TV except the Discovery Channel, anyway, she thought she was probably safe. Al was whistling to himself, enjoying his cooking and taking an occasional trip to the living room to talk to his fish. "Dinner will be ready in just a few minutes, honey," he said.

Maureen wondered again how a grown man could get any satisfaction out of staring at fish for years. She figured the only way to learn anything about fish was if the "fucking things could talk back." She had learned that in Al Stone's world, however, there was always hope; he would spend the rest of his life hoping for some revelation. He even had the nerve to call the fish "my subjects."

Maureen grinned as she thought about what she was about to do: she enjoyed bringing Al back to earth with the common folk.

She looked at the gourmet meal, simmering on the stove.

"I hope you didn't fix anything for me, dear," she said. "I ate on the plane."

THIRTY THREE

When everyone was seated:

"Let's start at the beginning," Harding said, blinking his eyes continuously.

Kyle looked around at the furnishings: expensive leather chairs and couches were scattered all about. Paintings by famous western artists, including one by Remington, stood out against the beige wallpaper, and gold lamps provided just the right amount of light. Kyle recalled the old adage: the more expensive the lawyer's furniture, the bigger the bill. It occurred to him that he'd never have gotten past the front door if it weren't for some stranger. Could it be someone he knew? Probably not.

Harding said, "The story the FAA tells is that you actually bragged about running two airplanes together. The cafeteria cook told the FBI he heard you announce your intentions during lunch. He said it shocked him because you sounded serious. According to him, there were about twenty witnesses. Is he telling the truth? Did you say that? You told Ron Adair it was just a joke."

The question embarrassed Kyle, even though he fully expected it. He paused, wishing he didn't know what Harding was talking about.

"I said lots of things to set up the prank. I wanted to make sure the controllers looked at the altitude tags because that's the only way they were going to take the bait. It was all part of the set up. Those guys are always pulling something on me, so I wanted to get back at them. I certainly wouldn't have said something like that if I really meant it."

Manny examined Kyle carefully, waiting for some sign of guilt, even hoping for it. It would make things so much easier. Kyle seemed embarrassed, but he certainly didn't seem nervous.

Manny: "Well then, why don't you explain how the two airliners collided?"

"One aircraft ended up at the wrong altitude for some reason," Kyle said. "I have no idea why; I wish I did."

"You left one thing out," Manny said. "He was at the wrong altitude because you *changed* his altitude. It's your voice on the tape recording."

"Either the tape was switched or the pilot was listening to someone else's clearance on a different frequency," Kyle insisted. "He didn't get a clearance from me."

Harding was taking notes. "Explain what you mean by 'switched'."

"Someone either switched tapes or played back the wrong tape. It could have been one from another day, for all I know. My voice is on a lot of old tapes; we keep them for fifteen days, even longer if there's litigation pending. We pretty much control the same scheduled flights every day, so it wouldn't be hard to find a flight from another day with the same flight number and my voice on it. Some of the log entries are so hard to read you can never be sure exactly which tape you have. There are times when we have to spend hours looking for the right tape."

"Are you suggesting that someone switched tapes deliberately?" Harding asked hopefully.

"I don't know, I guess it's a possibility; the guy who examined the tape is certainly no friend of mine. But I'm more inclined to think it was just an honest mistake."

"Now you're telling us the FBI doesn't know what it's doing?" Manny scoffed. "I happen to know they checked that particular tape recording very carefully: it was the correct tape recording and there was no splice. You'll have to come up with something better than that."

Kyle was beginning to get annoyed: "If you're not a controller, it's difficult to sift through a stack of tapes and find the right one immediately. Tapes from Monday will sound pretty much like the ones from Sunday.

And if they weren't logged correctly, it may take hours. There are times when the only way we can differentiate is by knowing a controller's voice. Besides, I thought you private investigators were supposed to check the facts before you made up your mind. Have you listened to the tape yourself, or had anyone with experience listen to it?"

"We intend to," Harding said quickly. "But first we need to get some information from you."

"What else can I tell you? Check the tape recording yourself, or better still, see if they'll let *me* take a look at it. And what about Danny Houston; he can verify what I'm telling you." He looked over and wondered why the Dragon Lady wasn't saying anything. She just leaned against the wall, her arms still folded.

"How about this scenario?" Manny suggested: "You intended to pull a prank, just as you said, but you accidentally pushed the headset chord in all the way and communicated. If that's the way it happened, just tell us; we need to know now, before this thing gets completely out of hand."

"That's not the way it happened; I was very careful. It's not something I'd forget. There's a light on the console that goes on whenever we transmit. I would have seen it."

Manny walked over and stood behind Kyle, looking over his shoulder.

"Let's see if I have this right," he said. "Someone, you don't know who, takes an old tape recording and exchanges it for the real thing, and yet the FBI, the FAA, and the NTSB, with all their expertise, can't figure it out. Is that your story?"

"All I'm saying is that one tape looks like every other tape. If someone logged an old tape incorrectly, it would be hard for anyone to tell the difference."

"And if we were to believe someone switched tapes, who should we suspect?"

"Richard Carpelski, the guy who first examined the tape. He was in the playback room for over an hour, all by himself. He hates my guts and he had access to the logs and all the tapes."

Kyle's eyes went from one blank face to another, stopping when he got to Corey. She had a habit of tossing her head back periodically to adjust a stubborn lock of hair; the habit became more frantic as Kyle's denials persisted.

"I've heard that controllers work under terribly stressful conditions," Harding said, one eye on Nancy. "How did you feel right before the accident? We understand you were having family problems."

Nancy reacted for the first time, moving her hands to her hips and tossing Harding a threatening look.

"There were only two aircraft on the frequency," Kyle answered, "how stressful could that be? I've had as many as thirty or forty."

Harding started to say something else, but decided against it after reading Nancy's hostile look. He studied his notes instead.

No one said a word for a long time. The only noise was the sound of automobile traffic out on the street.

"Any questions, Nancy?" Manny asked.

Nancy had been expecting a quick confession; she wasn't prepared for this. To make matters worse, Harding was edging toward the stress thing, which meant he was planning some kind of cop-out defense. She was also conflicted; the idea that any decent lawyer would recommend anything other than a guilty plea to a client so obviously guilty would be nothing less than malpractice. So why was she thinking Harding might be right? Nevertheless, she had a job to do for her father. It was time to put her foot down. She slowly pushed herself away from the wall and moved closer, leaning back against a desk and positioning herself so she could look directly into Kyle's eyes. She stared at him with a dubious expression. "Do you really expect us to believe your 'somebody else did it' hogwash?" She cut off his answer with a wave of her hand. "What about Deeter Noonan? You knew he was on one of those flights, didn't you?"

"I'd heard he was going to Dallas, but I didn't know when."

"In view of your history with him, do you think a jury will believe that?"

"Look...lady, whatever your name is, I know how all this looks, and I know I pulled a stupid prank, but I'm not crazy enough to commit murder. Like I said, Danny Houston can back up my story. If you really want to help, go find him." He got up and walked toward a window, turning his back on the others.

"Then where the hell *is* this Danny Houston?" Nancy insisted.

Kyle looked out the window. "I don't know. And I can't go looking for him myself because those berserk media people follow me everywhere I go. He turned and pointed at Manny: "He's a private investigator; ask him where Danny Houston is."

"Maybe I need to clarify something," Nancy said. "We don't give a damn if you're guilty or not. We just want the truth so we can start putting together some kind of defense."

Kyle turned and jabbed his finger in her direction: "What the hell kind of lawyer are you, anyway?"

"The kind who doesn't want a bull's-eye painted on her client's chest. Assuming we can't head it off, there's going to be a trial, followed by a guilty verdict. The final step in the process is lethal injection. Do you get my drift? We don't have a lot of time here."

Kyle turned and started for the door. "I don't need this crap. I can get more satisfaction talking to a wall. I'm out of here."

He paused in the doorway and looked back:

"Thanks for your time, 'wall.' Let me know when you want a two way conversation."

THIRTY FOUR

Nancy Corey stirred her iced tea, chin in hand, disgusted with herself. She'd been filled with resolve when she boarded the flight from Kansas City to Washington, D.C., but resolve had turned to jelly when she got her first glimpse of the Potomac River and remembered that she was about to meet with her father.

The Matthews meeting had been a disaster. She'd been a puppet, her father the puppet master, forcing her to say and do things she had disagreed with from the get-go. A real professional would have begun the process by listening to the tape recording and talking to Danny Houston before making up her mind. She still believed Matthews was guilty; that bullshit story about switched tape recordings sounded more like something out of a movie script. But that wasn't the point: she had failed to live up to her own standards, and that she couldn't deal with.

The iced tea wasn't helping her generate courage, so she ordered a glass of wine.

Antonio Corlini came through the doorway of the Sans Souci restaurant wearing his usual dark blue suit, silver tie, and dark sunglasses. His two, burly, ever-present bodyguards trailed close behind. Nancy forced a smile and rose to greet him. He smiled in return and gave her a kiss on the cheek.

Waiters rushed to the table; Corlini waved them off.

"Well, how is it going?" he asked, tucking a napkin under his collar.

"Not well, I'm afraid."

"Oh," he said, unconcerned, "do you need help?"

"No, it's just that Kyle Matthews is not what I expected." She didn't dare mention that he reminded her of someone she was once in love with, someone her father stopped her from seeing.

"And why is that?"

"He insists he's innocent. He thinks this whole thing is either a mix-up or a conspiracy. He's so calm and rational; it's hard to believe someone like that could do something so horrendous."

"But that's good; just what we're looking for. Who does he think is behind the conspiracy? Can he give us names, because that's exactly what we want? I need to investigate everyone involved."

"He says he doesn't know. He suspects that the government might have played back the wrong tape. Another possibility is that someone named Carpelski could have switched tape recordings, the ones that record air traffic control communications."

"Excellent. I'll check on this Carpelski fellow, find out all about him. Maybe I'll even bring in additional private investigators. As for Matthews' demeanor, don't let yourself be fooled: people who seem calm and rational can be guilty of atrocious acts. Many killers seem sane and rational after the fact. You never know."

Corlini looked around for a waiter.

"But what if the mid-air collision resulted from a blackout, or stress?" Nancy asked. "Our best chance to save him would be an insanity plea, which is what Harding is pushing for. He may not be much of a lawyer, but he's right about that."

Corlini threw his napkin down on the table. "I explained this to you before; a guilty plea, or some other illusory defense, will bury everything; we would never know if anyone else was involved. What if he's protecting someone? If we don't know exactly what happened, we can't be sure of anything. He could plead guilty even if he's innocent, just to avoid lethal injection. No, I will not allow any of those options, not until I know the truth, all of it, every last detail. A trial will require the government to reveal whatever evidence they have and everyone involved, that's the only way I can be sure. Don't forget, he works for the United States government; they might even be in on it."

"Oh, father."

Corlini stared menacingly. "You don't think it's possible? Don't forget, the ex-FAA administrator who was killed in that crash had many enemies, including some who envied the position he held. Maybe someone wanted him dead."

"And you think someone in the U.S. government would ram two airplanes together, just to get his job?"

"Maybe Matthews was getting even with Noonan for past grievances," Corlini went on. "I read where he and his father both fought with Noonan. Whatever generated it, I want this trial to reveal any possible conspiracy."

Nancy noticed that her father was grinding his teeth as he spoke.

A waiter brought salads.

"Why is this so important to you, father?"

"I feel for all those innocent people," he said, picking up a salad fork and poking at his salad.

Nancy concentrated on his expression, noticing the way his eyes dropped. She knew he was lying, but that was about the only thing she knew, except that he wasn't going to change his mind.

"Cheer up," he said, not looking up at her. "You told me the man says he's innocent, so you'll have lots of chances to defend him. Don't concern yourself."

"I want the defense to be professional," Nancy protested. "I guess I'm not really sure if you're offering to help this man or see him punished."

Corlini put down his fork, touched the napkin to his lips, glared at Nancy. "I want the truth, that's all. I've told you that more than once. Everything will make sense in due time. I want justice to prevail; let the chips fall where they may. In the meantime, insist he give you all the details. Squeeze him until you're sure, one way or the other. If that doesn't work, we'll have to try something else."

"And if he changes his mind and decides to plead guilty?"

"Then he's on his own; I hope you've made that clear to him."

"At least let me hire a better lawyer; I feel like I'm sending a baby down the river in a crib."

Corlini glared at her again: "A daughter's job is to honor her father and do as he says. You need to trust my judgment. It's a man's job to make the decisions. Don't think about anything else.

"Besides, he continued, when he saw the hurt look on her face, "I asked you to hire Harding because we need a lawyer who will follow orders. You're a smart girl, think about it; the government will try for an easy way out, offer a deal: Harding's not going to want a deal; he wants to drag things out, make a big splash, get his name in the paper. In a way, that's what I want, too, but for different reasons. I'm after all the details."

"But. . . "

"That's the end of it."

They picked at their salads in silence.

Nancy decided to take a chance, ask a question that had been haunting her:

"Do you have any idea why Judge Carone allowed Kyle Matthews to get out on bail?"

"Not your problem, let's have some lunch," he said.

THIRTY FIVE

"I can't take much more of this," Kyle said, as he watched Rooster stare out the window. "This flea bag motel is so disgusting I'm almost ready to turn myself in. We've called every lawyer in town and no one will touch my case. What's the use?"

"I love this place, myself," Rooster said. "Morrisey and I hid out here during the strike. The Oasis motel is my second home."

"It figures. What's so interesting outside?"

"I think we're being watched. I called Morrisey and told him to get us the hell out of here. He's on the way."

"Good. I don't care where we go as long as we leave this place. I couldn't stand another week here."

A fifty-foot motor home rumbled into the parking lot ten minutes later. Kyle and Rooster, baseball caps pulled down over their heads, made a run for it, tearing across the parking lot and into the motor home. Rooster slammed the door shut. "Go," he shouted. Morrisey, still dressed in black, gunned the engine and they roared away.

Kyle took a seat, said to Rooster, "I think that guy in front of the motel recognized me. We can't come back here."

Rooster looked out the window and shrugged: "We're not. I've already checked us out."

"Where'd you get the rig?" Kyle asked, turning to Morrisey.

"We borrowed it from a motor home salesman," Rooster answered for him, taking a seat. "We told him we were thinking of buying several of them for our company."

"What company?" Kyle asked, peering through the window for one last glance at the nosey man in front of the motel.

"A company where we buy and sell motor homes."

"Didn't know you guys were in that kind of business," Kyle said, smiling. "Doesn't sound like much of a money maker."

"Why not? We'll buy cheap, make a big profit."

Kyle rubbed his two days worth of beard and looked toward the back. "I'm surprised that salesman didn't look up your company in the phone book," he said, squinting to see who was in the back.

Rooster: "Hey, who cares? You said you needed mobility; I got you mobility. We could always take this rig back if you'd rather stay at the Oasis. I figured it was better to keep moving."

Kyle smiled and waived the thought away, having forgotten for a second how sensitive Roster was. He was now able to make out three bodies in the back, one stretched out a couch, the other two sitting in chairs. All three stared back at him.

Rooster noticed Kyle staring and tried to distract him: "This is our office for a while. We can keep moving and still do our business."

"Maybe not," Kyle said, still trying to identify the three bodies, "I think that guy in front of the motel took down our license number."

"No problem," Roosted said casually. "He won't be able to trace it."

Kyle took one more look in the back and eyed Rooster suspiciously. "Is that who I think it is?"

Now it was Morrisey's turn to change the subject: "This thing's got it all, even a phone and a fax."

His eyes now adjusted, Kyle recognized his former defense team. "Shit."

Rooster said, "Sorry, but we knew you wouldn't come if we told you."

From the back: "Blame it on me if you want to," Manny Vigil said loudly.

Kyle turned and hollered at Morrisey. "Stop and let me off."

"Why not hear what they have to say, first," Rooster insisted. "Like you said before, we've tried every lawyer in the state."

"I'd rather go with the public defender."

"A public defender couldn't handle this case, even if you were lucky enough to find a decent one. This is a capital case, calls for someone with that kind of experience. At least Harding has handled a case like this before. It would cost you a million bucks to get someone with his experience. The lawyers say they have a plan, something you might agree with. I'd like to hear it myself. You still have the final decision."

He waited while Kyle sat and stewed for a long moment. Kyle realized that Rooster was correct; he was trapped, he had no other alternative. Even his personal banker, a lifelong friend of the family, had turned down his request for a loan.

"Let's talk," Rooster said, standing.

Kyle shook his head and reluctantly got to his feet. He followed Rooster, staggering to keep his balance as the motor home made several sharp turns. Manny gave him some room on the couch and he threw himself down.

"OK, let's hear this plan," he said.

Harding, dressed in a rumpled suit and looking desperate, cleared his throat. "I realize our first get together didn't go well. We talked it over and you were right: we did have our minds made up. But I think we've come up with a compromise, a strategy that will satisfy you." He turned to the others for support, but neither of them said anything or offered any apologies. Nancy's body language was less rigid than before, but her facial expression indicated she hadn't changed her mind about his guilt.

"We're going to challenge the tape recording," Harding said. "We'll prove that the tape they relied on is not the right one."

Manny leaned forward, not sure if he had heard right. That was not what they had agreed to.

"Here's what we have in mind, Kyle," Tyler said, ignoring Manny's shocked expression. "We ask Mallek to let us examine the original tape recording in the presence of the media. Since you insist the FBI has the wrong tape, let's make them play it in front of the public. If we can prove it's the wrong tape, or demonstrate that the tape has been tampered with, you'll be off the hook."

Manny jumped to his feet, almost falling over because the motor home was rocking back and forth. "No, no," he said, waiving his ham hands like a traffic cop on a busy street. "Here you go again Tyler, off on one of your crackpot trips. This is not what we agreed to. We agreed to check out the tape ourselves, not grandstand. There is no reason in the world to show our cards until we have a chance to look at the tape ourselves. This is wrong, typical Tyler Harding bullshit. You don't go into battle until you study the terrain. All you're after is publicity for Tyler Harding."

Kyle realized for the first time that there was more substance to Vigil than just a huge body and a funny looking ring of hair. His initial reaction was that Manny was right.

Manny turned to Nancy for support: "Tell him, Nancy."

Nancy hesitated, thinking of her father. "I'm not so sure it's such a bad idea, Manny. I'll admit it's a risk, but if we don't demand to see the tape now, we won't get to see it until right before a trial. By then, it may be too late. Why put everyone through all of that if we can prove they have the wrong tape? Besides, his sponsor would want us to do this."

Kyle knew that Manny was the only one who had it right; he also realized that his own tendency was to jump the gun before he had all the facts. Nevertheless, Laura and the kids were already going through hell. They couldn't endure much more. He wanted this one chance to get out from under, to cease being someone's prisoner.

"Manny's right," Kyle said, "it's a big risk. Ordinarily I would agree we shouldn't show our cards so soon. But I'm positive I can prove that I didn't issue that clearance, and I'm willing to go for it. Let's don't ask, let's demand. We should also demand to see all the recordings and logs from that day."

Harding looked pleased. "You're right, we won't ask, we'll demand."

"You're all going to be sorry as hell," Manny said. "I know how deliberate the FBI is when they examine a tape recording, they're very thorough. This is playing right into the government's hands."

"Maybe you think I *did* issue that clearance," Kyle challenged.

"Doesn't matter what *I* think, can't you see that? It's just bad tactics."

"Maybe," Kyle said, "but I'll take that chance. My family can't go through a trial."

"No matter what you think you can prove now, the government will make you prove it in court, anyway," Manny said. "So why take the chance?"

"All the more reason to get the media involved," Harding argued. "The networks will turn on the government like a pack of wolves. They will demand that the government put up or shut up. When we show potential jurors how the government tried to frame a controller, the feds will have to drop the case. Opening this up to the media will also give Kyle a chance to tell his side of the story."

"You mean tell Tyler Harding's side of the story, don't you?" Manny said. "And what do we do when the tape turns out to be authentic?"

Tyler shrugged his shoulders.

Manny turned his head and spoke directly to Kyle: "Don't let him do this, Matthews. This man who calls himself a lawyer has just given you the worst possible advice. He's appealing to your emotions, your desire to extricate yourself with one, fell swoop. He wants your emotions to override your common sense. Has he mentioned any other options at all, like any decent lawyer would do? You can't make a proper decision until you at least know all your options. When this goes wrong, and you can be damn sure it will, he'll remind you that you agreed to it."

Nancy was so impressed with Manny's argument she wanted to cheer, but she couldn't; Harding's idiotic plan was exactly what her father wanted, an opportunity to learn exactly what Matthews or others had done. Once again, she was ashamed of herself.

"I hope you're wrong," Kyle said, "but I can't put my family through a trial if there's any way out. Besides, I'm the only one who knows the real truth."

Manny flopped down into his seat, looked out the window; shook his head.

Kyle couldn't wait to call Laura. Finally, there was light at the end of the tunnel.

THIRTY SIX

The government's response to Harding's request was a flat "no." Spencer Mallek actually laughed at the idea. He argued that Kyle's attorney would get to see the evidence at the proper time.

But the media loved the idea: an average Joe denied the right to confront his government; that was grist for the mill. As soon as they heard of Harding's request, they began to push and shove, demanding that the government put up or shut up, and blowing aside any arguments to the contrary.

Harding released statements questioning Mallek's integrity. He said Mallek was being unfair and wasting the public's money, insisting his own experts could save the cost of a trial by proving the tape recording was a phony.

The two sides went back and forth for weeks. Mallek insisted that federal regulations prohibited the examination of an original air traffic control tape in the first place. He promised that copies of the tape would be provided in the time frame established by law. The media ridiculed Mallek's strict adherence to the rules. Editorials complained that, while Mallek might be technically correct, this situation was different: the entire case was the tape, and only the tape.

The skirmish went on and on. But behind the scenes, the Department of Justice was buckling under the pressure. Mallek stalled until the FBI lab confirmed its findings once again, then called a press conference and magnanimously stated that while such a meeting was unprecedented, he had decided to grant Harding's request "in the interest of fairness." He announced that a meeting between the parties would be held in the Federal Courthouse in Kansas City, Kansas. One representative from each of the various media types would be allowed in, and COURT TV would be the network feed. "The government," Mallek said to a large media throng, "wants to get the complete truth, that's the least it can do for a valued employee, gone astray." When questioned by one persistent reporter, Mallek refused to say what would happen if the tape proved inconclusive. He simply smiled and said knowingly, "It won't be."

Kyle was convinced that the worst was now over. His confidence level had reached an all time high.

The light at the end of the tunnel burned a little brighter.

THIRTY SEVEN

Satellite dishes practically obliterated the sky in front of the courthouse. Hundreds of reporters sprawled on the courthouse lawn, scouring the area for whatever interviews they could muster.

Mallek arrived in a black government car, accompanied by two FBI Agents. He smiled and waived to the crowd, but wasted no time plowing his way through the throng of people and into the federal courthouse.

Kyle, Harding, and Vigil had managed to sneak in a back entrance, unnoticed. Nancy Corey had gotten there much earlier, "guarding the chicken coop." The FBI wouldn't let her touch anything, but she hovered over their shoulders anyway, making sure the playing field would be level.

The FBI, with the help of the FAA, had set the stage ahead of time: flight progress strips that Kyle had used, each one about two inches high and six inches long, were taped to the walls of the courtroom in sequential order. They represented Transcon Three Fifty Four and Transcon Three One One, and showed their altitudes, times, speed, and route. Court TV focused their cameras on those two little pieces of evidence as if they might collide and explode themselves, filing the courtroom with dead bodies.

Harding had been expecting a hearing with a federal judge. But to his shock and surprise it was Spencer Mallek who walked in and took a seat at the head of a long conference table.

"Where's the judge?" Harding asked.

"What judge?" Mallek said.

"We were supposed to have a judge preside over this hearing."

"This is not a hearing," Mallek insisted. "I'm required to preside because I'm responsible for the original tape recording." He then turned his head away from Harding and took papers from his briefcase.

The participants took seats on either side of the table: Harding's team, Manny Vigil, Nancy Corey, and Larry Robinson, a computer expert, on one side; Mallek's team, two FBI agents and an unidentified representative from the Justice Department, on the other.

Mallek didn't even wait for everyone to be seated: "Mr. Harding, this is FBI Agent Blake." He pointed to the stern looking man sitting closest to him. "He is responsible for protecting the tape. Your people can inspect it, but only Agent Blake will be allowed to handle it. He will conduct whatever tests you require, just as long as the tape isn't damaged in any way.

"Proceed, Agent Blake."

Blake stood and held the metal roll containing the tape recording. He told everyone how the FBI determined that it was the correct recording, and explained how each control position was recorded. He showed how controllers logged the times and dates for each twenty-four hour period at midnight each day, and showed them the log for September first. He then walked over and put the tape on a playback machine, selected the appropriate channel, and threw the switch. "We have determined though voice prints that the voices you will hear are those of the pilots and Mr. Kyle Matthews," he said.

Kyle gripped the arms of his chair. He was finally going to hear what Carpelski had heard. It was like waiting for a jury verdict.

The recording went on for several seconds without anything being said. Then, everyone heard the two aircraft report in on Kyle's frequency. Agent Blake pointed to the times on the corresponding flight progress strips and on the recorder's digital readout.

Larry Robinson stood and walked over to get a closer look. Then: "Transcontinental Three Eleven climb and maintain Flight Level Three Seven Zero," over.

Kyle jumped up out of his seat. "That cannot be the tape from September first," he shouted. "I did not make that transmission. . . "

". . . We're not going to honor that argument here, Mr. Matthews," Mallek said derisively, his lips puckered. "You and your attorneys have made all sorts of irresponsible claims about the authenticity of this tape, questioning the integrity of the U.S. Government itself. If you can point out some discrepancy on the tape, or the logs, we'll be glad to listen. We will also play any other tapes that you request. Agent Blake will assist you if you'd like to inspect the tape, the log, or the flight progress strips. He will unroll that portion of the tape for your inspection so you can be assured it has not been spliced or otherwise tampered with." He smiled for the TV cameras.

"You're not listening," Kyle said. . . ".where's the read-back from the pilot if I issued that clearance. . . ?"

"...This is not a courtroom," Mallek interrupted. "We are not going to argue the case here. You and your attorneys will have that chance when we go to trial."

Mallek pushed his chair back and got to his feet. "I will allow you ten minutes to inspect the tape further and ask questions of Agent Blake." He walked over to the side of the room and stood with his arms folded.

Kyle took several steps, pushed Larry Robinson aside, and examined the tape and log carefully. Manny and Nancy stayed at the table, their heads down. Manny covered his face with his hands.

"It looks like the correct tape to me," Robinson whispered to Kyle. "No splices or anything, either."

Kyle wasn't sure what to do next. He examined everything again, going back and forth between the tape and the logs. Finally, he just stood and stared, unable to move.

Mallek looked at his watch, waited exactly ten minutes, came back to the table and began stuffing papers into his briefcase. "I see no reason to prolong this any further," he said to Kyle. "If neither you nor your expert have any further questions, we're adjourned."

"I'd like to caucus with Mr. Robinson," Harding shouted.

"You've had had ample time for that," Mallek said over his shoulder. He picked up his briefcase and marched triumphantly toward the door.

"Do something," Harding said to Robinson.

Robinson threw up his hands.

Reporters crowded the doorway as Mallek and his crew exited, cameras and mikes thrust in their faces. They followed as he walked briskly down the hallway. Others waited in the doorway for Kyle and his team.

"I thought that went well," Nancy said.

"Are you happy now?" Manny asked Harding.

"He never intended to listen to us," Kyle said.

"What did you expect?" Manny argued. "You had to know he had the goods once he agreed to meet."

Kyle got up and followed his team toward the door. They had to push their way through the crowd of reporters.

"What am I going to tell Laura?" Kyle asked. Manny grabbed him by the arm and pulled him forward. "Hurry, lets get the hell out of here, unless you want every potential juror in the state to see this." They began running.

Harding looked back and shouted, "Danny Houston will confirm Kyle's story."

The light at the end of the tunnel had gone out, and had taken Kyle's only chance with it.

THIRTY EIGHT

Kyle had been missing for a week.

He had told Laura that he was tired of the motor home, and had reluctantly agreed to go to another shabby motel owned by one of Morrisey's friends. Once they were situated, he had said, Rooster would go get the lawyers. After that, they would begin preparing what little case they had left. Laura assumed the reason he hadn't called was because he feared the FBI might trace the call; nevertheless, it bothered her that she couldn't talk to him. She feared that the tape playing episode might have shoved him over the edge. She begged Manny to go and find him.

Manny hadn't gotten a call either, so he just drove from one end of Kansas City to the other, checking motels that Morrisey's wife said he had been known to frequent. He thought it was a waste of time, but for Laura's sake, he kept looking anyway: that's what Badgers did. Harding and Corey were also helping, calling some of the same motels.

Judge Carone had resigned. The FBI assumed that whoever took her place would soon rescind Kyle's bail, so agents were now looking for him all over town. They not only searched his neighborhood and places he frequented, but were even checking airline and ship schedules. They were also looking for Danny Houston, thinking his disappearance might be part of a larger conspiracy.

Mallek wasn't having a good week, either: he had enjoyed the media coverage following his face off with Harding, but now the media was all over him again, asking why he hadn't at least had Kyle followed after the tape playing fiasco. Mallek blamed the FBI; the FBI blamed Mallek.

Manny felt partly responsible for the whole debacle, even though he had warned against it. He had promised Ron to look out for Kyle, and he had failed. That wasn't acceptable for a man like Manny: Badgers weren't supposed to fail. He listened to talk shows while he drove, and continued to call Rooster on his cell phone every five minutes. Most of the listeners ridiculed Harding's strategy, but Kyle's naivety was also being criticized: callers wanted to know why he knowingly allowed himself to be embarrassed in public. Some passed it off as ego, but Manny saw it differently: only an innocent man would have agreed to such a public thrashing. To Manny, instincts were everything, and his instincts said that Kyle had to be innocent, in spite of the tape recording. There was still a possibility that he had accidentally issued the clearance, of course, but if it was just an accident, then there was no crime. He had tried to convince Nancy of that, but her reaction had been the opposite: she found the FBI's demonstration convincing, and seeing no logical reason to believe Kyle, became more intransigent than ever. Manny couldn't really blame her; the evidence did seem overwhelming. Nevertheless, he had to find a way to change her mind before she took away the checkbook.

Manny's cell phone rang, but before he could answer he heard Laura Matthews screaming incoherently: "Manny... I need your help...I need Kyle...please...Manny..."

Manny had the Mustang in a U-turn before she finished talking. "Laura, what's wrong...what's happened?"

But the line had gone dead.

He slammed down on the gas pedal and glanced at his watch. It was 8:31 a.m. He dialed Rooster's cell phone again, turning a corner on two wheels at the same time, and almost knocking over a mailbox.

This time he was in luck: "Morrisey's RV sales."

"Rooster, it's Manny, damn it. Where are you guys? Laura's been looking for Kyle for days."

"Couldn't take the chance the FBI was tracing our calls; I answered because I recognized your cell number."

"Never mind; where's Kyle?"

"With me; we found some shitty motel and we've rented a copy machine and stuff. I sent Morrisey to tell Harding and Corey to meet us here because I don't trust the phones. Didn't they call you. . . ?"

"Shut the hell up and take Kyle home as fast as you can. I'm on my way there now."

"I was just about to go to Radio Shack to buy a fax machine. What's the hurry?"

"Laura called, she's freaked out. Either I lost the signal or she hung up before I could get anything out of her. Never mind the fax machine; get the hell over there."

"We're on our way."

Manny arrived just five minutes after he hung up. He jumped out of his Mustang and stared at the house in horror. Smoke billowed up from the back yard and rose ten feet higher than the house itself. He ran in that direction, noticing as he rounded the corner that the black cloud was actually coming from the garage in back of the house.

He grabbed a garden hose near the back, turned on the faucet, ran toward the garage and aimed it. The trickle of water that came forth was like spiting on a forest fire. He saw Laura standing in the back doorway, looking helpless.

Manny heard a noise coming from the garage that sounded like someone trying to claw their way out. He threw down the hose, tried the garage door, which was locked, then ran toward a side window. He stared in, squinting to keep the heat and smoke from searing his eyeballs. He balled up his fist and smashed a hole in the window, backing away immediately when a burst of heat and smoke shot from the hole and seared the skin on his face.

Sirens wailed in the distance, making a hell of a racket and adding to the confusion.

"Manny," he heard someone shout. He looked to his right and saw Kyle running toward him from the front of the house, carrying an axe and pointing toward the garage door. Manny shook his head knowingly and followed. He watched as Kyle first tried to open the door and then slammed the axe against it. He hit the door again and again, but all he was able to do was to tear off some of the wood. He finally gave up on the axe and the two men began ramming the door with their shoulders. Rooster and Morrisey appeared at their side and joined in. The four men finally managed to forge an opening big enough for Kyle to squeeze through, ripping his pants and shirt in the process. Manny followed, and the two moved blindly through the smoke filled garage, feeling around on the floor.

Kyle was the first to see the crumpled body, but the smoke quickly overwhelmed him and he had to turn his head away, his eyes burning from the unbearable heat and smoke. Manny's hairline had been singed until it looked as if it might catch on fire. He, too, gave up and began feeling his way back to the doorway, where he finally stumbled and fell. Kyle attempted to drag the unidentified body, but it was so charred and mangled that he couldn't find anything to grab hold of. He fished around until he found a man's belt, grabbed it with his left hand, then turned and got hold of Manny's shirt collar with his right hand. He dragged both of them toward the garage door entrance until he saw daylight. A fireman standing next to Laura assisted until the three were clear of the fire.

Kyle left Manny and the body with the firemen, ran to Laura, picked her up and hugged her.

"Are you hurt?" he asked.

"I'm OK. I couldn't believe it when I smelled the smoke. I thought it must have been coming from the house behind us. By the time I realized it wasn't, it was too late."

Kyle put her down and looked around at the large crowd that had gathered. "I better check on Manny and then get the hell out of here. There's a rumor that my bail has been rescinded."

They found Manny sitting next to a tree. Medics were checking him out. He seemed dazed.

A crowd of gawkers attempted to get closer to the garage. Firemen pushed them back, dragging one recalcitrant photographer off and escorting him to the street in front of the house.

Manny finally regained some of his senses and noticed Kyle and Laura looking down at him. "Are you guys all right?" He asked, sounding as if he couldn't get enough air in his lungs.

Kyle: "We're fine, but *you* don't look good at all."

"Just a little dizzy. How'd I get here?"

"That man dragged you out of the garage," a paramedic answered for them, pointing toward Kyle. "Sit still while I check your vitals."

"Get the hell out of here, Kyle," Manny said. He started to get up, but the medic pushed him back down.

"Not until I find out who that is," Kyle said, pointing to the garage.

"I'm going with you," Manny said, pushing the medic aside and getting to his feet.

They moved to the garage, kneeled and examined the badly burned body. Nothing was left except a charred lump of clothes and bones. The skin was falling off, and what was left of the face was covered with blisters as big as softballs. The shoes were smoldering and there was a pair of eyeglasses that had melted into a pile of plastic. Even the cops and firemen had to turn their heads.

Kyle saw something that appeared to be metal. He took two fingers and removed some small pieces of clothing that covered what had once been an arm, but was now just a bone. He carefully turned the arm over and found an identification bracelet. He nodded to Manny and Manny moved in for a closer look. Manny rubbed some dirt off of the bracelet while Kyle watched expectantly.

"What's your worst nightmare?" Manny asked, holding the bracelet up.

Kyle didn't hesitate: "Danny Houston's dead body."

THIRTY NINE

With his bail having been rescinded by Judge Raymond Bradford, Carone's replacement, Kyle couldn't take any more chances; he had to consider himself a fugitive.

He couldn't go looking for Carpelski in public because FBI agents were everywhere and just about everyone knew who he was. He couldn't go back to the hotel either, because he was sure that it was being watched by now. He stretched out on the roof of the armory where Carpelski regularly attended reserve meetings, positioning himself right above the back door and next to the parking lot. From there, he could see whoever came out. Time was running out: with Danny Houston dead, the pressure on the FBI to find him would force them to add additional manpower. The fact that they hadn't already found him was a miracle. He hadn't talked to Nancy Corey, Tyler Harding, or Manny Vigil in days. He hoped they hadn't given up on him, but he knew that the Mallek fiasco was as good an excuse as they would ever need to dump him. Not that he blamed them, he knew he must look guilty as hell under the circumstances. Worst of all, he'd used poor judgment. Air traffic controllers were used to quick action and quick results, but that was no reason to flail at windmills. Once again, that weakness had cost him.

He was exhausted, and after waiting for over two hours, fell asleep on his back while staring up at the sky.

He heard movement and immediately rolled over. He could still feel the results of the beatings Hawk Face and the others had given him. His eyeballs felt like sand traps and there was a dull ringing in his ears. It took all of his will power and effort to get to his knees. He took a second or two to remember where he was, shaking away the cobwebs. He peeked out over the edge of the roof. There was only one way to save himself now, and that was to catch Carpelski at one of these Thursday night meetings and beat the truth out of him. He heard a door open down below. Uniformed men and women began pouring out of the building. He waited and watched, wondering what he would do if Carpelski should try to run for it.

He inched forward and looked down.

The top of a head appeared, looked left and right, and started walking toward the nearby parking lot. Kyle recognized Carpelski's walk immediately. Controllers all knew that walk, like someone tiptoeing through a minefield of guilt. Life is difficult when you have a lot of enemies. He almost felt sorry for him.

Carpelski suddenly broke into a trot, as if he knew he was being stalked.

Kyle scrambled down the drainpipe, circled around, and approached Carpelski from the front of his Volvo. Carpelski didn't see him until he was almost inside the Volvo. Kyle blocked the door with his body.

Carpelski staggered back. "I didn't do it," he blurted.

"Didn't do what?" Kyle shouted, grabbing Carpelski's shoulders and pinning him up against the car.

"You know *what*," Carpelski said. "I didn't switch the tapes. The FBI wouldn't even let me near them after you raised such a stink."

"Then how did my voice get on that recording?" Kyle asked bitterly. "Even an ass like you knows I'm not capable of murdering innocent people. Either you or Danny Houston is behind this, maybe both of you. But Danny Houston's dead now, so it's just you."

"Houston's dead?" Carpelski blustered, dribbling spit all over himself.

"That's right, pretend you didn't know. Now tell me what the hell the two of you cooked up."

"I didn't even know the man. None of you guys at the center ever talk to me. Why don't you ask Houston's friend, the big guy he's been hanging around with?"

"What guy; what's his name?"

"I don't know; just some big guy who looked like he was a heavy drinker. You can't blame this on me. I just played the tape and reported what I found."

Kyle had a sinking feeling Carpelski was telling the truth. It was difficult to be sure because the man had never before been observed in that state. Still, deep down, he had known all along that the FBI would never have given Carpelski a chance to switch tape recordings. They would have thoroughly analyzed the tape themselves and then kept it under lock and key. Carpelski couldn't possibly know anything more than what he'd already told Ron. It had been wishful thinking, something far from reality that you reach for when you have no other explanation, and Kyle had to admit to himself that he had been reaching all along.

Kyle hesitated, not sure what to do next. Carpelski had pretty much described the same man that Alice Houston had described. Once again, it sounded as if it might be Butch Moore, a sworn enemy of the Matthews family. He remembered that he had also seen Moore standing by the courthouse door after he had been released on bail. But what could Moore possibly have to do with any of this? After all, it wasn't his voice on the tape recording.

Moore or no Moore, he had to challenge Carpelski, just to make sure. He doubled up his fist and drew back his arm. "You're a damned liar, Carp," he hollered. "You and your friend Raymond have been trying to get rid of me for a long time. Now you're going to tell me the truth. Who is this big guy you're talking about? What's he got to do with this? Who killed Danny Houston? Tell me or I swear I'll kick your useless ass right here."

"I told you the truth, I swear," Carpelski squealed. "I don't know anything more."

A bear-like arm grabbed Kyle from behind, causing him to lose his grip on Carpelski. Before he had time to react, Carpelski jumped into his Volvo, locked the door, and started the engine. Kyle clawed at the door, but the Volvo roared off, ricocheting off of another vehicle and bolting from the parking lot. He watched his last hope fly away.

Kyle twisted his head and saw that the arm belonged to Manny Vigil, who still had a hold of his neck. "Freaking Volvo, I should have known. Why is it all assholes drive Volvos?"

"Beating the crap out of Carpelski wasn't going to help, anyway."

Kyle relaxed; Manny let go.

"You're just in time to keep me from making a fool of myself again."

"Just to clarify things, I'm guessing you managed to make a fool of yourself before I even got here."

Kyle gave an agreeable nod and leaned against a concrete wall. He crossed one leg and casually picked tiny pebbles from his hands, shaking his head.

"The one armed man gets away again," he said. "I hate to admit it, but the son-of-a-bitch is probably telling the truth. He had nothing to do with this. I'd have known if he was lying, he's such a pathetic bastard. Well, I guess that's it, I'm flat out of ideas now. If you're looking for explanations, I don't have any."

Manny sat next to him on the wall.

"I thought Ron said you were a fighter. Are you giving up?"

"I can't fight something I don't understand myself."

"You said that after listening to the tape recording, you were more positive than ever that you didn't issue the clearance. Have you changed your mind?"

"No, goddammit, but whose 'gonna listen to anything I have to say now?"

"If you recall, I advised against that meeting."

"You're right, it was my fault. Patience is not one of my virtues."

"It's not one of mine, either, so let's forget all about the Mallek screw-up and talk about what we can do now."

Kyle nodded his head.

"If it's all right with you," Manny said, "I've decided to devote full time to this."

"What could possibly be in this for you? You know I don't have the money to pay you. And what about law school?"

"I love puzzles. Listening to that tape recording and watching your reaction hooked me. Law school can wait. I'm tired of it anyway, a bunch of old assholes teaching a bunch of young assholes. Besides, I saw something the night those two aircraft hit, something I can't quite put my finger on. I'm not doing this just for you; I'm also doing it for me."

"You saw the collision?"

"Let's not go into that right now. If you're telling the truth, and assuming you didn't just screw up, someone must have it in for you, big time. And if someone does have it in for you, it has to be someone really clever and resourceful. If you're interested in finding out who that is, then you need to stop acting like a fucking commando and start looking. I'm going to need to know who your enemies are, and we don't have time to fool around."

"I hope you know what you're up against," Kyle said, shaking his head. "If you're suggesting that someone other than Carpelski framed me, I can't help you."

"Yes you can; it's the same asshole that set fire to your garage and killed Danny Houston. Use your head; think of everyone you ever had a beef with. But first, let's go to the crash site. They ran me out of there yesterday, so I didn't get a chance to really see anything. My friend Fred Bell will be there today; he might let me look around. I'm not sure exactly what I'm looking for, but I need to know why I'm so confused about what I saw that night. I'll just have to do this like I do crossword puzzles, one piece at a time."

FORTY

Frank Zimmer found it hard to contain himself: the status he'd always coveted, fought for, even lied and cheated for, was now his. All that was left now was to fly to Phoenix, stand in front of a cheering crowd, and be anointed president of Transcontinental Airlines. Many a man had had to be eliminated, cut down, even run over, before Zimmer could even make it to the short list. But thanks to his promise to convince other airline CEOs to back a White House project, he was about to reach the summit. He was saving his first presidential flight on Transcon for after tonight's ceremony. In the meantime, he was going to enjoy the luxury of his company Learjet and slip into Phoenix unnoticed.

Instead of boarding the Learjet right away, Zimmer decided to have a drink in the Denver Jet Center lounge to calm his nerves; flying had become much more frightening since the ghastly collision over Kansas City.

Nerves sufficiently calmed after consuming two drinks, he snapped his fingers and pointed to his co-pilot, who had been patiently waiting nearby. The co-pilot picked up his luggage and followed him out. They climbed aboard the Learjet and Zimmer settled down in a soft, leather seat, near the rear of the aircraft. He reached for a magazine and looked around for the flight attendant, intending to have one more scotch to help him sleep. But when the engines came to life, he changed his mind, put his head back, and closed his eyes.

Something brushed against his leg. He looked up, assuming it was the flight attendant, but found Butch Moore standing there instead, staring down at him. It sent cold shivers down his spine. "What in the hell are you doing here?" he said, looking around to see if anyone had seen Moore come aboard. "You can't be here, I'm just leaving town." He jumped up and practically ran toward the front of the aircraft, shoving the surprised flight attendant aside and motioning for Moore to follow. He ran from the aircraft, crossed the tarmac, and entered a side door into the COMBS AVIATION building. Moore followed and they entered a small office. Zimmer motioned for Moore to close the door.

Moore, a big grin on his red face, closed the door and stood, hands on hips.

Zimmer thought about threatening Moore, see if a bluff would work, but decided it would be smarter to determine Moore's asking price first.

Moore said, "Why are you hiding from me?"

Zimmer steeled himself, doing his best not to show fear. "Jesus, Moore, that flight attendant saw you. Can't you understand that we can't be seen together? If you want my help you'll have to be more careful."

"You won't answer my phone calls." Moore hissed, his blank eyes darting back and forth. "You promised to help me. You're the fucking president of an airline, what are you waiting for?"

"Look Butch, I'm going to help you, all I'm asking is that you be patient. I can't do this overnight. The government has barred you from further employment because of those false transmissions. There's no way I can go through the normal channels; this has to be done politically. There aren't that many open positions in FAA management, anyway, so I'm going to have to go over the FAA's head. The government will fight this all the way; can't you see that? I need more time."

"I think you're backing out," Moore said ominously. "Have you already forgotten what I did for you?"

Jesus, Zimmer thought to himself, this idiot is out of control. "Backing out of what? And why do you keep saying you did something for me? You didn't do anything for me, and I didn't promise you anything. You're crazy."

"I got rid of the guy standing in your way, and I'm about to get rid of the guy standing in the White House's way."

"That doesn't make sense."

"Well then, let me make it a little clearer for you: I got rid of Noonan, and I made sure no one would ever listen to Kyle Matthews' ideas again. You're involved, so don't even think of backing out. And you'd better hurry, because Matthews' PI is smart and he's been sniffing around. There are things you have to do right now."

"Butch, calm down. We need to be careful. What are these things you say I need to do?"

"The private investigator; the guy helping Matthews, he's been to the crash site and he'll probably be going back. He's already suspicious."

Zimmer threw open his hands: "What about it? Suspicious of what? Start over."

"Matthews' PI, Manny Vigil, is a friend of Fred Bell, the man in charge of the crash investigation. You need to get Bell the hell out of there before Vigil learns the truth. Call someone now; have them put me in charge of the investigation. Give them some story about how Bell is needed somewhere else. Tell them we already know what happened with the mid-air, anyway, so Bell isn't needed. Once Vigil gets a close look . . . you know, once he sees what's there, we're both in trouble."

"I never heard of Vigil or Fred Bell. For god's sake, get the fuck out of here. Don't get me involved in your shit."

Moore came closer, his red face puffed up like boiling water. Zimmer could smell his hot breath. "Don't you understand, you fuck, I bombed those two airplanes."

"Oh, my God," Zimmer said. "Oh, my God!"

"Don't worry; the FBI isn't paying attention anyway; they think they already know what happened. But if Vigil spends much time at the crash site, he won't have any trouble convincing them otherwise. You need me in charge of this investigation. I'll keep Vigil away until it no longer makes any difference what he sees. I'll end the fucking investigation for good. Call Peter Brock; tell him to get Fred Bell out of there. Have him put me in charge. Tell him it's just temporary, or whatever, I don't fucking care. That should be easy for a man with your connections."

"That's settles it," Zimmer said, pointing toward the door. "Get the hell out of here and don't ever contact me again."

Moore trembled like a man rolling through a shock wave. Zimmer was surprised the man could even function. There was no way to know if he was serious, just plain crazy, or what. One thing was for sure, though, Zimmer thought, if Moore really did put bombs on those aircraft, if there was no mid-air collision at all, then this nut case could end several careers.

Zimmer changed tactics, forced a smile, said, "Look, Butch, I have an important meeting in Phoenix, but I promise I'll call you just as soon as I get back. We can sit down and talk about this."

"Fuck you. You need to make that call right now. And if Fred Bell is already suspicious, which I'm sure he is, you better convince him to keep his mouth shut. From now on, no one can see any of that evidence except me and whoever I designate."

Zimmer thought about it for several seconds: "OK, I'll do just as you say; I'll call Peter Brock, see if he'll assign you to that NTSB committee."

Moore's glazed eyes stared through Zimmer as if he weren't there. "Assign, my ass, I have to be in total charge. It won't work any other way. It's not going to be easy to cover up all that I have to cover up. I'm going to have to bring along several of my friends to help me. I'll assign them to my committee myself, just as soon as you complete that call."

"That's not possible."

"Fine, then I'll just call Peter Brock, myself."

"Ok, Ok, I'll see if I can have Brock put you in charge."

Finally, Moore seemed to focus again. He shook his head up and down slowly, smiled. "By the way," he said, reaching into his shirt pocket and pulling out a small recorder. "I've tape recorded our conversation. I also have a recording of your conversation with Peter Brock on that fucking Gulfstream, including the part where you agreed to cover up our first conversation. That's just in case you're lying."

Zimmer tried not to show concern, but he was now more frightened than ever. He remembered what he and Brock had discussed, and it might be just enough to put him in jail or get him fired. He wished he had never talked to Moore in the first place.

"I'll call you as soon as I talk to Peter Brock," Zimmer mumbled, feeling numb.

Moore started to say something else, but stopped. He stood for a few more seconds, waived the recorder in Zimmer's face, and left the room.

Zimmer sat staring at the phone for a long time, trying to think of a way out. But after a long three or four minutes, he realized that there just wasn't a way out. He was trapped. He couldn't take chances, not after he'd just landed his dream job. What if this nut was telling the truth? The easiest way out of this was to have someone throw him out of the Learjet, but even that might not solve things; what if he had made arrangements to leave his tape recording with someone, have them deliver it to the FBI in the event of his death?

Finally, he picked up the phone and called Brock. If the White House didn't want a conspiracy on their hands they would have to do as he asked: put a nut case in charge of one of the highest profile airline crashes in history.

FORTY ONE

Fred Bell raged on for almost a minute, walking fast and looking back to where Kyle followed ten or so yards behind. "What in the world were you thinking of, bringing him here?"

Bell was the NTSB's number one accident investigator. He had grown up with airplanes and engines, learning to fly on his father's farm at the age of thirteen. He was arguably the most knowledgeable expert in the field. He was also a tough man in a fight, but he was no politician. When he had to face up to his bosses, he was quivering jelly.

Manny said, "You know as well as I do that it will take months for the NTSB to issue a report. Without your help, it'll be impossible for us to get any information. Six months from now will be too late; I need to know exactly what happened and I need to know now."

Kyle strained to hear what the two men were saying, his face partially hidden by an oversized baseball cap and dark sunglasses. He looked around at the devastation as he stumbled forward through the mud and debris. The ground had been scorched from fires that had burned for days. Carnage was all around; it made him sick to his stomach. The impact of what had really happened in the skies over Kansas City had finally become reality. Black body bags were neatly lined up in rows, as if neatness could camouflage horror. One by one, the bags were being carried away by men wearing orange suits. He swallowed hard as he surveyed the wreckage and thought of the families of the innocent dead. For the first time, he understood the public's rage, and it terrified him. Television news could never capture the smells of a crash site. Would he ever be able to face the public and convince them he was innocent?

Trucks hauled away numbered pieces of the two aircraft. Ordinarily, those pieces would be carefully reconstructed in Kansas City's Mid-Continent airport hangar to determine the "probable cause" of the crash. But Manny had heard that the NTSB might shortcut that process because they were sure they already knew the probable cause. The official position, however, was that they were "vigorously investigating every detail." Manny had warned him to stay in the car. He was beginning to understand why.

"He has a right to be here, Fred. It's his ass on the line."

Bell's craggy, weathered face twisted into a sneer: "From what I hear, he deserves it. I can't be seen with him; I'm investigating the very collision he caused. Anything he hears me say could influence his or my testimony at a trial. The NTSB Chairman will shit bricks if she finds out he's here. I'm already hearing rumbles from the front office that I might be taken off of this assignment. Why isn't he in jail, anyway? I heard his bail was rescinded."

"It was, but I'm keeping him out of sight until we can find something to help him. What about the black boxes? Have you found them yet?"

Bell ignored the question and pointed back toward Kyle. "Just keep him away from me. The pressure is bad enough already."

"How about Matthews, you don't think he's under pressure?"

Bell grunted his disgust; he knew better than to argue with Manny Vigil. He stopped suddenly, squatted, picked up a small piece of metal and rolled it around in his oil-stained fingers. He quickly shoved it into a small plastic bag.

"What is that, Fred?"

"Nothing."

"Let me see it."

Bell tried to put the bag in his pocket, but Manny managed to snatch it.

"Damn it, Manny, you're not even supposed to be here."

Manny paid no attention. He studied the small piece of metal, said, "If this piece of metal came from the crash, then there was a bomb aboard one of those aircraft. Look at these markings; this pitting could only have been caused by a bomb. I thought I had seen something like this when I was here before, that's why your buddies chased me away."

Bell kept his eyes down, clawing around in the dirt. "Of course it's pitted; what do you get when two aircraft hit, you get an explosion."

"I'm talking about an explosion from a bomb, not from two aircraft colliding, and you damn well know it."

Bell's face made for a poor liar. He grabbed the piece of metal and started walking again, keeping his eyes as far away from Manny's as possible.

Manny kept pace. "Talk to me, Fred. If this was a mid-air collision, how come that piece of metal looks like that?"

Bell started to answer, but before he could, Manny had seen something else and dropped down to his knees. He actually gasped: "Look at this piece of luggage; it has the same kind of markings we saw after the Lockerbie crash. That's how we determined there was a bomb on board that Pan Am flight, remember?"

Bell stopped and examined the luggage. "You've been watching too many CSI shows, Manny. The two aircraft exploded when they hit; that's what caused those markings."

Manny shook his head. "No way; only a bomb could cause luggage to be rutted like this. That's why you're so anxious to get rid of me, isn't it, because you knew it all along? You NTSB guys have been brain washed into calling this a mid-air collision in spite of the evidence. The bosses don't want complications."

"The FBI is in charge of the criminal investigation, Manny. Do you really think I'm so important that the FBI will let me determine whether or not there was a bomb on board one of those aircraft?"

"They wouldn't dare challenge you; you're the expert. Once they listened to that tape they had all the evidence they needed, anyway. Whatever you say is going to be the final word."

"Two aircraft collided, that's all I know," Bell insisted and began walking again. "When two aircraft collide, they explode. And when they explode, shit flies all over. I have no reason to think it was a bomb."

"Bull shit. You're selling out."

"Look," Bell said, practically pleading now, "I know it looks suspicious, but since we know there was a mid-air collision, it stands to reason we would see stuff like this. I listened to the controller tape just like you did; that's the end of the story. Doesn't matter what you or I say, anyway, that's the way it is. I'm retiring in six months; if I went to my boss and said there was a bomb involved, with no more evidence than some beat up luggage and some pieces of metal, all hell would break loose. Now, get the fuck out of here and take that crazy controller with you."

"That's it? You're going to just roll over on this?"

"There's going to be a complete investigation."

"You mean a complete investigation with a predetermined finding made by Washington."

"You better leave now, Manny, big brother is watching. My boss is on the way here, and he's already pissed at me because someone reported seeing you hanging around once before."

"What about the cockpit recorder? Have you listened to that?"

Bell slowly shook his head. "My lab guy did."

"When can I get the results?"

"You need to ask the FBI; we just talked about that. I don't even have access to those."

Manny frowned. "Don't tell me you're turning into the bureaucrat you and I always despised, Fred. You, of all people, know how long it takes the government to fork over evidence. It could take months, even years. I'm trying to head this off, maybe even save a man's life."

Bell looked back and glared at him. "Good luck with that."

"One day you complain about bureaucrats and the next day you are one. I can't believe what I'm hearing."

Bell took a few more steps before stopping and turning around.

"OK," he said, walking back. "I'll have my lab technician make you copies of the CVR tape just as soon as I can."

"I need to listen to that tape now, Fred."

"Are you crazy? You can't."

"Why?"

"First of all, you'd need a playback machine, and the closest playback machine is in my temporary lab in Kansas City. I sure as hell can't let you in there."

"What's on the tape? There's something you're not telling me; what is it?"

Bell continued walking. "All I know is that our lab tech is having a hard time interpreting the data."

"Why?"

Bell shrugged. "I'm not really sure, it's complicated. And like I said, you can't use our machine; it would be the end of my career. Your lawyer will have to wait for discovery. And if I'm replaced, don't expect the next guy to help, either. The heat is on big time." He jabbed his finger in Manny's face. "And you were right; this is a done deal, so stop harassing me. The pressure is on to get this over with."

"You know I can't do that Fred."

Bell sighed, shrugged his shoulders. "I know, Manny."

FORTY TWO

Manny climbed a hill to where Kyle had retreated and was now standing next to the Mustang, staring out toward the crash site.

"Why'd you run off?"

"I thought I'd better get out of there so you could work things out with Bell," Kyle answered without looking back.

"What're you looking at? Come on, let's get out of here; I've learned some very interesting stuff. Now I need to listen to that CVR tape."

"Wait just a minute; two guys just drove up in a government car. One of them is arguing with Bell."

Manny took a closer look. "That's Bell's boss, John Callahan. I used to work for him. Fred said he was unhappy about me hanging around the crash site. I know how chicken shit Callahan is; it wouldn't take much for him to take Fred off the case."

Kyle pointed: "It's the other guy that concerns me. That's Butch Moore, the guy I told you about. What the hell's he doing at a crash site?"

Manny followed Kyle's eyes: "What else can you tell me about him?"

"He made false radio transmissions during the PATCO strike, just to harass the FAA. He could have easily caused an accident. He's called everyone he could think of during the past twenty-five years, asking for help to get his job back. He even called the Vatican, if you can believe that. He's nuts and he's dangerous. His brother owns a big car dealership, so he could be making a good living, but he's obsessed because the FAA fired him. It pisses him off that other controllers finally went back to work."

"If he made false radio transmissions, I'm not surprised the FAA turned down him down. His brother probably turned him down, too."

"Any binoculars in the Mustang?" Kyle asked.

Manny reached into the Mustang, pulled out a pair of binoculars.

Kyle adjusted the binoculars and studied the scene for a long moment. "What was it you found that was so interesting?"

"There was a bomb on one of those aircraft."

Kyle's eyes went wide and he almost dropped the binoculars. He jerked his head around: "A bomb? You're sure?"

"Damn sure; the signs are all there. I saw a piece of metal that had been pitted by a bomb blast and some luggage with little shards of metal that also came from a bomb. And there's something else: Fred said his lab guy was having trouble interpreting the CVR data. Don't know what that means, but if there was a bomb, then maybe the CVR is connected. Fred won't let me in his lab, so I'll have to call another friend in the FBI. I'll get in somehow. . . ."

". . . Jesus, Mary and Joseph, a bomb. I can't believe it!" For the second time, Kyle began to feel hope. "Let's go back down there and brace those guys."

"Not now, I need to listen to that CVR tape first. Callahan won't listen to us anyway. Tell me more about Moore."

Kyle went back to the binoculars. "Oh shit, Moore's wearing an NTSB badge."

Manny grabbed the binoculars and looked for himself.

"He's also looking up at us and pointing. Didn't you tell me Houston's wife said something about this guy?"

"All she said was that it was a big guy with a red face, but the description sure fits. Carpelski said something similar."

"Stay here, I'll talk to Callahan and see what this is all about."

As soon as Manny started walking in Callahan's direction, both he and Bell hurriedly ran for their cars. Moore also started walking away, shouting orders to everyone around him.

Manny came back a few minutes later. "Callahan's gone, but I talked to one of the NTSB guys and he says somebody in Washington put Moore in charge of the entire investigation. The guy said he never even heard of Moore, wanted me to tell him what I knew."

"Well, you sure as hell won't get in that lab now. If you think Bell is difficult to deal with, wait till you try dealing with Moore."

FORTY THREE

They left the crash site and headed back to their motel.

Manny hadn't said a word since they got into the Mustang.

Kyle: "What are you thinking about?"

Manny took his time answering: "I'm trying to match what I heard the night of September first with what I saw at the crash site; that suitcase and that little piece of metal. Bell tried to hide them from me, but I'm convinced there was a bomb on one of those aircraft; no doubt about it."

"What exactly *did* you hear that night?"

"Two loud booms. When I looked up, my first impression was that it was a mid-air collision, but something kept telling me I was wrong. After what I saw at the crash site today, I'm thinking that one of those loud booms could have been a bomb going off."

"Or the second one could have been a bomb going off," Kyle suggested.

"Then what was the first one?"

Kyle threw up his hands: "A mid-air collision?"

Manny sighed: "I guess the only thing I know for sure is that there was a bomb involved, somehow."

A Ford Taurus came veering around the corner and passed Manny's Mustang on the right side. The driver leaned on his horn and presented his middle finger to Kyle as he zipped by, then swerved in front of the Mustang, missing by an inch or two. In his attempt to insult Kyle, the driver had apparently taken his eye off of the road, causing him to miss seeing the stoplight ahead. He roared right through it.

A Cadillac, crossing the same intersection from the left, sideswiped the Taurus, bouncing off of and striking a third vehicle coming from the right. The Taurus then hit a telephone pole.

Manny pulled up behind the wrecks and they both got out.

Bloody faces showed from the windows of all three vehicles. The sound of sirens could already be heard down the street.

"Judas," Kyle said, looking into the Ford Taurus, "this poor guy was so busy giving me the bird he lost control. I suppose I'll get blamed for this, too." He opened the door and reached in to assist. But before he could, the man began screaming at him. "You, I don't need help from someone like you. Get the hell away from me."

Kyle explained that he was only trying to help, but the man continued to shout, pointing at Kyle as if he were Jeffery Dahlmer.

Kyle threw up his hands and retreated. Other passersby were already running toward the Taurus, anyway.

"Come on Manny, let's go before somebody spots me."

Manny had already been retreating toward the Mustang.

They got in and drove in silence for about ten minutes.

"*Now* what are you thinking about?" Kyle asked.

"That crash reminded me of one other thing; I remember now that one of those booms I heard that night was louder than the other, kind of like the noise the Cadillac made was louder when it sideswiped the Taurus, than the noise the Ford made when it hit a telephone pole."

"How does that help?"

"If the first sound was louder than the second sound, which I think it was, it might mean that the first one was a bomb. It would also help to remember if there was any delay between the two."

"Why?"

"I don't know, but I'm going to keep thinking about it. Maybe two things happened at once, or maybe one thing, like a bomb going off, led to another, like if part of one aircraft came off and hit the other one."

"If there *was* a bomb, where could it have come from?"

"Maybe someone carried it aboard."

"That would be hard to do in this day and age."

"Dream on," Manny said.

"You think it's easy?"

"No, but it can be done. Not every flight attendant, pilot, ticket taker, or baggage carrier, pays attention one hundred percent of the time. We're lucky if anyone pays attention ten percent of the time."

"Well then, as much as I hate to say it, the first sound you heard could been two aircraft colliding, and the second sound a bomb that someone carried aboard."

"Or maybe there was no mid-air collision at all, just two bombs going off, one on each aircraft."

"I like that theory; I just wish the NTSB would buy it."

"I'm just saying anything's possible. I need to get into that lab."

"You're nuts, you know that, don't you?"

"Yeah."

After another three or four more minutes of silence, Manny said, "Is this a bad time to throw some more shit into the game."

"What now, I don't think I can handle much more."

"The Dragon Lady."

"What about her?"

"I need to tell you something, but don't go blotto on me."

"What is it?"

"I called Maryland University."

"And?"

"They never heard of Nancy Corey. The closest they could come, based on when she said she had graduated, was a Nancy Corlini. Same thing goes for Georgetown law school."

"Why would she lie about her name?"

"Beats me; every time I try to get something more, I hit a dead end. I tried some of my best sources, the FBI and the Department of Justice. It's like they're scared to talk about her or her family. I couldn't get a damn thing out of anyone."

"Could be just a coincidence."

"I don't believe in coincidences, but I do believe in cover-ups."

FORTY FOUR

Karen Davies had insisted on meeting at midnight.

After three trips running back and forth through the University of Missouri parking lot, Kyle still hadn't located her.

Karen was very reliable, with excellent instincts, so Kyle decided he would wait as long as it took. Remembering her phone call, he thought she had sounded nervous, unusual for someone with her balls-to-the-wall confidence; one of the coolest controllers he had ever worked with.

Standing and waiting in the darkness reminded him of his father's stories about the PATCO controller strike, meeting in the dark to avoid federal marshals and their subpoenas. His father had mentioned many times how exciting those times had been, even with the threat of jail hanging over their heads.

Kyle heard a low whistle and turned to see Karen standing in the shadows, motioning for him to come. But as soon as he started walking, she moved in another direction. The faster he walked, the faster she ran. Pretty soon they were both running. She would stop for a few seconds, look around, and begin running again. She had on a long coat and floppy hat, which made it appear as if a ghost was floating across the parking lot.

When Kyle finally caught up with her: "I have to be careful, I could get in a hell of a lot of trouble if the FAA knew I was meeting with you. I needed to find a spot where we couldn't be seen."

She slipped Kyle a large envelope, eyeballing everything around her at the same time.

"A friend gave that to me. You can't tell anyone where you got it."

Kyle took a few steps toward a lamp post and opened the envelope. He studied the contents while Karen continued to scan the area.

"What is this?"

"A computer extraction: it shows the flight paths of the two Transcon aircraft you allegedly bonked."

"Thanks, but is there something in particular I should be interested in? I'm not good at evaluating these things."

"Take a closer look, numskull. According to that printout, the two aircraft never occupied the same airspace until after they were on the way down."

Kyle moved even closer to the light pole and studied the document carefully, his heartbeat doing a fast staccato. He told himself not to get too excited, but it didn't help. He thought about what Manny had been saying from the beginning, that he didn't believe what he had heard was a mid-air collision. He thought it must have been wishful thinking on Manny's part at the time, but now this."

"There's something else you should know: Curtis Raymond faxed a copy of that extraction to Washington. He also sent them a letter, warning them that the extraction could be a big problem if your lawyer managed to get a copy. "

"You saw the letter?"

"No, but Rooster did. You know how he's always ransacking Curtis's desk."

"So, Washington knows about this?"

"Yeah, unless they have their heads up their asses, or haven't looked at their mail yet."

Kyle let out a long sigh and smiled: "Should I be expecting an apology."

Karen laughed: "In your dreams, hotshot. That's just a copy, by the way. The original is under heavy guard. I managed to get my hands on it just long enough to make the copy."

"You're telling me I'll probably never see the original."

She shrugged.

"You were taking a big chance, Karen."

"That's what friends are for, numbskull."

"How accurate is this thing?"

"Don't expect me to know that; I just steal computer extractions; I don't work for the frigging FBI."

"I can't wait to show this to Nancy Corey. Maybe now she'll believe I was telling the truth. I might even be able to convince the FBI."

"In your dreams again, big daddy. Other than you and me, Curtis Raymond and the dimwits, no one else knows about this. I doubt if the FAA will even mention it to the FBI. I heard Curtis talking on the phone, making up some lie about how the computer must have been out of whack. He's too far out on a limb to admit he's wrong now. He's probably been warned to keep his fat mouth shut. I'm just guessing about all this, but I'd bet my retirement the original extraction will be history as soon as FAA Washington gives Curtis the word from the bird."

"I can't believe they would do that. I'll go the Freedom of Information route, catch them in a lie. They can't keep this hidden forever. I don't even know why they would want to."

Karen looked around and mumbled, "You still don't get it, do you, Captain America: where the information has been destroyed, there is no freedom of information."

"Well, anyway, this is great, Karen, thank you. I would never have known about this."

"No problem. By the way, the FBI is trying to force controllers to rat on you. They won't get anywhere, though; I actually feel sorry for anyone attempting to question a controller."

Kyle smiled: "My dad told me about the aftermath of the PATCO strike when FAA security cops questioned the controllers. They ended up chasing false leads, running around in circles."

Karen kept looking over her shoulder. "You mean like you and Rooster did with Brockman?"

"Jesus Karen, why do you keep looking around? Do you really think you're being followed?"

"I don't know, but I saw two guys hanging around right before you got here; two mean looking guys in suits. They looked like characters from that Soprano show."

Kyle looked around himself. "Those are probably FBI agents." Then he remembered the two men from the grocery store. "Whoever they are, we should probably get the hell out of here. Thanks for getting this for me, Karen. I owe you."

"Getting what for you? I didn't give you anything, numbskull. Good luck." With that, Davies bolted and ran. Kyle followed her towards the parking lot, having forgotten how fast she could run. When they had played softball together, Karen covered all three outfield positions at the same time, intercepting fly balls headed in Kyle's direction.

She quickly disappeared into the darkness.

FORTY FIVE

"I'll come right to the point," Warren Ramsey said.

The President's Chief of Staff hunkered up behind his White House desk, glaring at Attorney General Matt Potorf, Special Counsel to the president, Peter Brock, and William Hufnel, FAA Administrator. It was one of those "I don't have time for any bull shit looks."

Ramsey, short and stocky, had dark, slicked back hair, and wore an expensive, gray suit with gold cufflinks. His tie was the traditional blue and red pin stripes.

"Can I assume we have a rock solid case in Kansas City and can anticipate no problems?" He covered all three men with his obsequious smile, but his real target was Potorf, who sat in between Brock and Hufnel. And while he worked hard to look unconcerned, there was an undercurrent of angst in his expression.

Hufnel wondered why *he* had been invited: these powerful men were the ones determined to prosecute Matthews, so why did they need him? He studied a picture on the wall behind Ramsey, hoping someone else would answer the question. He'd been thrilled to be summoned to the White House for a meeting with the big boys, something he could brag about to his family, but as he was signing in at the front gate, he suddenly remembered an old adage about White House meetings: "Careers are made and broken here." He worried that his might be one of the latter.

"We don't anticipate any problems," Matt Potorf finally answered, his long legs stretched out in front of him. Potorf had gone from barely passing the bar exam to the most powerful lawyer in the country. He had been happy to leave his former life, where he had spent most of his legal career plea bargaining. He had attended dozens of these, "cover you ass meetings," and knew just how to act. He wasn't about to be intimidated or offer anything more than what was asked of him. He seemed surprised by Ramsey's concerned expression; was there a problem with the NTSB investigation he hadn't been told about?"

"Then why is that man still on the loose? His bail has been rescinded, why hasn't he been caught?"

Potorf shrugged. "He's just been lucky, running around in a motor home or hanging out in flea bag hotels. We'll catch him. Where can he go? It's just a matter of time; we're not really worried about it; all he's doing is making the public more and more angry."

Hufnel noticed that all three men were stealing glances in his direction. Peter Brock, in particular, would make eye contact, then look away quickly. Hufnel had intended to bring up Curtis' computer extraction, but did they want him to mention it or not? Did they even know about it, and if they did, were they ignoring it? For all he knew, the pressure he'd been getting meant they weren't interested in evidence, they just wanted Matthews out of the way. He thought about broaching the subject, but the way they studied him caused him to decide against it. On the other hand, maybe that was *why* they kept looking at him, expecting him to mention it. Did he dare tell them he ordered the extraction destroyed; would they consider that a good thing or a bad thing? After hearing Potorf's positive response to Ramsey's question, there were two, distinct possibilities: Potorf knew and had decided to let Hufnel be the scapegoat if the shit hit the fan, or Potarf hadn't gotten the word. All three of these powerful men had numerous contacts; any one of them could have found out about the extraction.

Brock was studying him again; his beagle eyes hiding a Rottweiller personality. He, too, dressed expensively; a dark brown, tailor-made suit garnished with a gold watch chain that hung conspicuously from his pocket. Everything about these men was a front, and Hufnel knew it:

bland expressions masking the hearts of skilled politicians who could care less if some "Kafka" got the gas chamber.

"I can't understand why the man doesn't just plead guilty," Ramsey grumbled to Potorf. The case seems rock solid."

Potorf: "We think it's because he got bad advice from his attorney at the arraignment; some hick lawyer from a small town in Kansas. He has a different attorney now. He'll come around."

"Yeah, Tyler Harding," Ramsey scoffed. "It wouldn't surprise me if Harding rides this thing until he sucks out every drop of publicity. His Father was Dexter Harding, I think you knew him, Peter?"

Brock shook his head: "Thank God it's not the father defending. He was the best. Seems like I *have* heard that the son is not cut from the same cloth."

"No," Potorf agreed.

Brock smiled. "Let us count our blessings."

Ramsey frowned again, his beady eyes giving Hufnel the once over. "Yes, well let's get back to the issue. It is true, is it not, that it was Matthews' voice on the tape recording and that there are no other issues?"

Hufnel swallowed hard and allowed Potorf to answer.

"Yes," Potorf said confidently, after glaring at Hufnel again for a long moment.

"We've checked that out, no possibility of error?" Ramsey insisted, his squinty eyes rotating between the three men like cattle prods.

"None," Potorf said. Once again, his eyes focused on Hufnel.

"The president doesn't want any mistakes," Ramsey said. "It's critical that we get this mess over with as soon as possible. It's not that we don't want justice done, but this controller has been a thorn in our sides for years. He has the ear of an important congressmen who is hell bent on pushing his crazy ideas. We already have a billion dollars invested in our own plan; it would be a disaster to turn back now. We need to silence the voices of anyone in opposition; convince congress that our plan is the best possible way to improve the air traffic control system. We don't need some crazy controller saying otherwise."

Once again, Hufnel was sure he was getting a mixed message. His conscience almost came to the surface, but he just swallowed again.

To their surprise, the door opened suddenly and the President of the United States, Franklin Wright, came strolling into the room. He had a deep tan and the body of a swimmer, slim and powerful looking. His thick gray hair was perfectly combed in a short, youthful style.

The three men rose to attention. Hufnel's eyes focused on the president's thousand-dollar suit. He couldn't wait to tell his wife and children: the president had come in to meet with William Hufnel!

The president shook hands with the attorney general and smiled profusely. He nodded to Brock and Ramsey, then turned to Hufnel with presidential flair. "Mr. Hufnel," he said, grasping his hand in a strong grip. "Good to see you."

"Thank you, Mr. President," Hufnel blurted. The president knew his name!

Potorf quickly grabbed a chair for the president. The four men waited until he was seated before they sat down themselves.

"I visited with some of the families whose loved ones were killed in the crash," the president said. "Terrible, just terrible! This whole thing is causing shock waves. Fortunately, we don't have the speculation that usually follows these tragedies; for once we know what happened."

The president turned to Ramsey: "Exactly where are we with this case?"

"These gentlemen don't seem to think we have a problem, Mr. President." Ramsey said.

The president turned and focused on Hufnel.

Once again, Hufnel just couldn't get up the nerve to mention the extraction: "That's right," he mumbled.

"Good," the president said, smiling as though this was the biggest thing on his plate. "Sometimes when people tell me there's no problem, it reminds me of what others told Ronald Reagan about Iran Contra."

There were several smiles, but Hufnel just sat there, stone faced, ashamed and frightened.

The president's expression turned serious again. "I hope you gentlemen realize that we have a lot at stake here. We want justice done and we don't want to pre-judge this man. I think, however, it's fair to say we definitely have the guilty party. Now we need to seek swift justice, heal the wounds. I wouldn't expect the NTSB or any of the other agencies to spend too much time reaching alternate conclusions. The public wants closure."

The president looked at each man once again. Hufnel swallowed.

"Can I expect what I have to say next to remain in this room?"

The four men shook their heads.

"Our neighbors to the South and to the East have an interest in this; they are the ones who have the most at stake. They will build our new air traffic control system. It's an important part of my foreign policy, to sooth strained relations by allowing foreign countries to join with us in a few of our endeavors." He turned and asked Hufnel, "How is the media in Kansas City reacting to this?"

No one was going to bail Hufnel out this time. He cleared his throat. "The eh. . . the same as everywhere else, I guess. They seem very angry that Matthews is still on the loose, but that's only making it worse for him." Hufnel wished his voice was stronger, more decisive. He also wished he had more guts.

"Good," President Wright said. "You're all doing a fine job. Tell the FAA people in Kansas City I said that."

"Yes, Mr. President," Hufnel said. It was now too late for him to speak up. All that was left, if it came to that, was to hang fast and come up with a good cover-up story.

"Well, I have a dozen more things to do," the president said, rising and holding out his hand with another big smile. "Glad to see you all." He shook hands all around and was gone.

"Well, I suppose that's it," Ramsey said. "You gentlemen seem to have everything in hand." He stood, came around to the front of his desk, smiled and reached out his hand to each one of them.

Hufnel took Ramsey's hand and tried to return the smile, but found it impossible. The entire situation could easily turn to shit, with him holding the bag. He suddenly realized that there was only one sure way out: get Matthews to plead guilty by blackmailing whoever it would take. He was glad he didn't have to come to the White House everyday.

FORTY SIX

As soon as Hufnel had gone, the other three went outside and settled in a garden area were they were sure there were no microphones.

"I hope this thing really is under wraps," Warren Ramsey whispered. "If Matthews weasels out of this, Crimmins will make him look like a martyr and we'll be left holding the bag. That son-of-a-bitch can't wait to jam this controller up our asses."

"Mathews is dead either way," Potorf disagreed. "A jury will never believe him now, regardless; they'll hang him for the prank as much as for the collision."

Ramsey shrugged: "Good point, but I'm not convinced. I've seen things like this turn to shit before."

"It's hard to believe one air traffic controller could cause us so much trouble," Brock said.

Potorf gave an agreeable shrug. "This thing has to get settled soon. Crimmins is close to introducing legislation that will steal Matthews' ideas right down the line. If we screw this up, congress will support him and the president will accuse us of turning a slam dunk into a rim job. We need this over with."

"Can that really be done, replace controllers with computers?" Brock asked. "Sounds like bull shit to me."

Potorf: "Not without a shit pot full of money, but yeah, I think it can be. I've given his ideas a lot of thought, and, frankly, it's about the only idea that makes sense. Even the FAA's long term project managers would admit that. I know because I did some checking." He smiled: "Keep that between us."

"Then why doesn't the president take Matthews ideas and use them himself, beat Crimmins to the punch?" Brock asked.

"Because he's already committed to the Russians and the Mexicans, which is something Crimmins doesn't know or he would have pulled the trigger by now."

Brock: "I still can't understand why the president thinks that allowing the Russians and Mexicans to build our air traffic control system is so important. The project seems pretty insignificant to me."

Ramsey: "You need to look at the big picture: every county is looking to form the relationships they will eventually need to protect themselves from Iran, North Korea, or one of those other nuthouse countries looking to build a hydrogen bomb. This is an attempt to make some small inroads with the Russians and the Mexicans. The project itself is insignificant, just as you said, but it's damn important to those two countries. It's important to us too, because if we can get closer to the Russians politically, considering their size and power, there won't be a country in the world that will dare mess with us."

Brock shruged. "It still seems kinda Mickey Mouse."

"I told you it's just a first step, something to set the wheels in motion. We can't screw this up. We can handle the Mexicans if this thing turns to shit, but if the president breaks his promise it will piss off the Russians big time, might even start another cold war. The Russian economy is in big trouble, and now that they don't have a need to make more nuclear bombs, they have to start doing business with other countries. Doing this one little job for us could lead to much more important contracts for them. As for Mexico, what better way to fight illegal immigration than to provide them with jobs, give them a reason to stay home? It's not the money; a billion dollars is still a relatively small amount, it's the prestige. But once Crimmins learns what the president is up to, he'll introduces his legislation and the president will be shit out of luck. Crimmins will tell American workers that the president is about to turn his back on them, and the next thing you know the Ruskies are warming up their missile silos and a billion more wetbacks are pouring over the border. And don't forget that idiot in Venezuela, Hugo shit-for-brains. The president is scared to death of him. We might need the Russians help if Hugo turns off the spigot."

Brock: "Well, I think it's too late for Crimmins already. He won't dare introduce anything with Matthews name attached to it."

"Get real; he'll never even mention Matthews. By the time he writes up his legislation it will sound like he could design the system himself."

The three men sat in silence for a long moment:

"Does the president know we're taking credit for this deal, with the Russians and Mexicans, I mean?" Brock asked, looking around.

Ramsey smiled. "He knows. He doesn't mind if we make a few rubles and pesos. I wouldn't be surprised if the president isn't expecting a few rubles and pesos himself."

Potorf and Brock exchanged surprised looks. "How can he get away with that?"

"Because he's the president," Ramsey said. "It's easy to keep things like that a secret when you're the president. Besides, by the time we get paid for this we'll all be out of here, including the president; no one will even remember who the hell we were."

Potorf whistled out loud. "That's good. It makes the president our shield in case something goes wrong."

Ramsey's eyes turned hard. "Nothing is going to go wrong. We're in the clear, unless one of you develops a 'Chuck Colson' complex."

"A billion dollars," Brock said. "How is the president going to get that past congress without Crimmins finding out?"

"Something called the Airport and Airways Development Act. It was supposed to be used to improve airports and such when it was signed about twenty years ago, but the money was never spent. Something about boosting the balance of trade numbers, or some damn thing. All it will take is for the president to spend it."

"So there's nothing at all to worry about?" Brock asked.

Ramsey scratched his head and rubbed his chin. "There might be one thing."

"Like what?" Brock asked.

"I'm worried about the expression I saw on Hufnel's face. I've seen that guilty expression a thousand times. He's hiding something. I wouldn't be surprised if the government's case isn't a little weaker than he lets on."

"In what way?" Brock asked.

"I don't know; I just know he's a weak link."

Brock jumped in quickly: "I have someone close to the NTSB investigation. I'll see if there's a problem."

"Do that. Get back to me right away, because if he *is* hiding something, we have to do something about it. We can't afford problems. Promise Hufnel something if you need to, but keep him in the dark."

Brock shrugged.

Potorf smiled. "I wouldn't worry if I were you; with Spencer Mallek prosecuting, that controller will soon be out of our hair forever."

FORTY SEVEN

Deputy U.S. Attorney Spencer Mallek had been in a "kill" mode ever since he learned that Kyle Matthews couldn't be found. He entered his Washington office raging at everyone, slammed down his briefcase, and threw himself into his leather chair. He considered it an affront to the entire judicial system and a black mark on the Department of Justice that a killer like Matthews was still running around on the loose. The death of Danny Houston had only heightened his anger. He vowed to make Matthews pay dearly for his free time. One of the other prosecutors told everyone that Mallek had been heard to say he would "find Matthews, rip off his head, and shit down his neck."

But Mallek would never have said such a thing. A Mormon Bishop, Mallek never dealt in vulgarities. On the surface he was a devout and dedicated family man, a believer in justice for all. The other two thirds of the iceberg, the part he tried unsuccessfully to conceal, were pure contempt for anyone he considered less intelligent or less competent than himself, which included just about everybody.

Mallek was tall, six foot seven, and gangly. He moved about like a stork, head bobbing and birdshot eyes boring in from behind wire rimmed spectacles until others turned their heads away. He was indifferent to anyone's feelings and he never stopped categorizing everyone he met to see if they met his standards. They seldom did.

There was something other than Kyle Matthews that was eating on Mallek today, as well: he had been told that Tyler Harding had been hired to represent Matthews. How dare someone like a Tyler Harding have the nerve to challenge a Spencer Mallek? Fellow prosecutors whispered among themselves that Mallek was lucky it was Tyler Harding defending, and not his famous father, Dexter. Mallek had heard the whispers, too, but he ignored them. He knew who Dexter Harding was, but he certainly wasn't in awe of him. Mallek considered himself God's prosecutor, not to be compared to, or conquered by, mortals. After all, this controller was nothing more than a mass murderer. He salivated when it occurred to him that Harding might try one of his "theoretical defenses." That would give him an opportunity to preach to the court about the evils of esoteric schemes, something he had always wanted to do. Juries were sick and tired of criminals anyway: the newspapers were full of editorials decrying the recent outbreak of defenses based on insanity or "post something-or-other."

The phone rang. "Mallek."

He listened for a long moment before screaming at the caller, ranting and raving at the assistant because she had been unable to solve the same problem Mallek had been unable to solve himself.

He slammed down the phone, calmed himself somewhat, sat back in his chair, and thought some more about Kyle Matthews. Upon further reflection, he took comfort in imagining what it was like for a man with a target on his back to be running like a hunted animal. Let the man boil in the stew of public disgrace for a while, he thought. There was no hurry to prosecute: the man was as good as permanently removed from society anyway. The notion that Matthews had to continuously run and hide was so inviting it actually began to cheer him up.

Mallek had always wanted to do one big job for God. Ridding the world of this animal would do exactly that, not to mention what a pleasure it would be. He would be Kyle Matthews' bête noire.

He looked through a file on his desk for several moments, then pressed the intercom button and called for Jerry Rhinehart, an attorney and his chief clerk.

Rhinehart came in holding a thick file. "What is it?"

"I'm surprised at all the documentation we have on this defendant."

"And?"

"He seems to be quite a big deal in the eyes of some congressmen."

"Well, he's certainly made quite an impression on Congressman Crimmins," Rhinehart agreed. "He often quotes Matthews concerning his views on updating the air traffic control system. He talked about Matthews during a CBS interview, just a few weeks ago."

Mallek, as if talking to a child: "You don't get it, do you?"

"Get what?"

"That's why he did what he did, for recognition."

Rhinehart couldn't believe his ears: "Cause an accident that killed all those people just for recognition?"

"Exactly."

"That's crazy," he said before he could stop himself. "He already had all the recognition he could ever want. I'd call articles in the New York Times recognition. I wish someone would quote me in the New York Times."

Mallek's temper flared. No one dared to say his ideas were crazy. "He was angry because the FAA suspended him, don't forget that. And don't forget he almost struck the FAA Administrator during a TV interview. The two ended up in a wrestling match."

Rhinehart strangled a smile. "I remember that. I think Noonan was the one who lost his cool, though."

Mallek was near boiling point. "Like father, like son. He should have been fired just like his father."

"His father was reinstated. He actually retired from the FAA."

"Well, that won't happen here. Department of Transportation officials will testify that Matthews was getting even with Deeter Noonan for ignoring him. We'll make sure the son stays fired."

Rhinehart looked confused: "But he wasn't being ignored, we just talked about that. He was in the media limelight long before the crash."

"If he's so wonderful, why did they suspend him?"

"I don't know," Rhinehart said, struggling to control his own anger. "I guess the bureaucracy was on a roll and couldn't stop,"

Mallek stared at him for a long moment. He had no sense of humor and he wasn't familiar with colloquialisms. "On a roll? I don't understand what you mean."

Rhinehart enjoyed annoying Mallek whenever he could, even if it *was* dangerous. "All I can tell you is that Kyle Matthews has a great reputation."

Mallek had had enough; he stood and shook his finger at Rhinehart: "Well, don't let your naiveté get the best of you. And remember who you work for. Are there any surprises here, anything I should be worried about?"

Rhinehart blanched and looked at his notes: "No, just what I've already told you: Matthews' reputation doesn't fit with a man accused of deliberately causing a mid-air collision. A jury will take that into consideration. If you're looking for something negative in his background, it's not there."

Mallek practically screamed at him: "Then he's just a sloppy performer, that's all. We'll get him one way or another. Don't worry about it. Once again, you better decide which side you're on."

Rhinehart knew he had gone too far; nevertheless he went on: "I'm just trying to say that you shouldn't underestimate Kyle Matthews. In any testimony he gives, he will be considered an expert in air traffic control. He is a director with the current controller union, NATCA, and his opinions have always been well respected by the media."

It galled Mallek to think that Rhinehart would consider a mere air traffic controller as competition. "Yes, well consider this: Mr. Matthews will be charged with one of the most heinous crimes of the century, and we will use his so-called expertise against him. We will tell the jury that he used his expertise as a weapon. I don't think there's much to be concerned about here. And for the record," he continued, "when I get through with Mr. Matthews, even Mother Theresa wouldn't believe him. Besides, Mr. Harding probably won't allow Mr. Matthews to testify, he will claim that Mr. Matthews heard voices, or was under great stress and is not in his right mind."

Once again, Rhinehart was walking a thin line, but he was determined to tell him everything: "There is one more thing that may or may not be important. Someone is paying big bucks to defend Matthews."

Mallek raised an eyebrow. "Don't tell me, let me guess: neither you nor any of my other assistants knows who that is, do you?"

"No," Rhinehart admitted sheepishly.

Mallek rose dismissively. "We won't worry about it then."

Rhinehart wasn't quite finished. "We're waiting for the NTSB to tell us what the cockpit recorder says. We don't expect it to be any different than the FAA tape recording."

Mallek acted as if he hadn't heard him and stormed out of his office.

FORTY EIGHT

"Sounds like my lawyers are unhappy," Kyle said, turning up an eyebrow and stopping at the door of Manny's cabin. They could hear loud arguing inside.

Manny said, "Maybe we should wait until those two birds finish slugging it out."

Kyle circled the shack, looking around in every direction.

"Don't worry," Manny insisted, "no one ever comes here except for the guys I hunt with. There's poison ivy everywhere, helps keep everyone away. Let's listen and see if we can hear what they're up to."

Manny put his ears to the wall and whispered, "There's something funny going on between those two, and I'd sure like to know what it is. They're definitely not telling us everything."

"The hell with it, let's just go in," Kyle finally said.

The inside was comfortable, but not luxurious, just a typical stopping off point for hunters before they were off to the woods. The furniture consisted of three stuffed chairs, two stuffed couches, a small refrigerator, and shelves with boxes full of everything from bug spray to empty whiskey bottles.

"Nice," Kyle mumbled sarcastically.

"Would you rather we talked in a jail cell?" Manny said. "I'm sure the FBI has one all ready and waiting for you."

Kyle gave him one of those "I was only kidding" looks and concentrated on Harding, who looked whipped.

"Well," Nancy said, "pull up a chair. Now that we've heard the tape recording, maybe we can finally get down to business. Tyler's brain-dead plan was a mistake; I think we can all agree on that. I'll admit it was partly my fault, too. I apologize for that. Anyway, we're back to square one now, but at least we know there's nothing wrong with the tape. It's up to you now, Kyle. What's it going to be? Where do we go from here?"

Kyle waited for Manny to answer, but Manny just leaned against the wall, arms folded. He obviously wanted to hear what Nancy had to say.

Kyle: "My position hasn't changed: I didn't do it, tape recording or no tape recording. Listen to what Manny and I learned before you decide where we go from here. We've learned some things that will change your mind."

"We'll get to what you guys learned later, but first you need to understand something: we're your lawyers, whatever you tell us is privileged. No one else will find out unless you agree to tell them. After you explain exactly what happened and give us the details, we'll figure out how to prepare your defense. We can say that while you were pulling the prank you accidentally keyed your mike, if that's what you want. Never mind what the cafeteria cook or anyone else says, because we'll argue it was all part of setting up the prank; you never really intended to do it. The cook will have to admit he had no knowledge of your real intentions; he's no mind reader."

Kyle got up from his chair: "What in the hell are you babbling about?"

"You heard the tape recording: you issued the clearance that caused the crash. No one switched tapes."

Manny moved away from the wall and shook his head. "You're not listening, Nancy. Wait until we tell you what we learned before you formulate your plan."

"I don't want to hear anything more until he admits what he did. We all heard the tape; now it's time for the truth."

"You have an excellent reputation," Harding whined, coming to life and getting up off of a couch. "Once Nancy and I know the truth, we'll put on a great defense. Just tell us exactly what happened. Don't worry about my screw-up with Mallek. You were confused, but now you remember exactly what happened. It will sell."

Nancy bit her lip and brushed back the same stubborn lock of hair. "We need to know where you stand, Kyle," she said. "Do you agree with us or not?"

"Is this the part where I confess and you save me?" Kyle scoffed.

Nancy's eyes tightened: "You heard what Larry Robinson said, and I don't think you still believe Carpelski was involved, so what else is there?"

"You want me to just make up something, that's what you're going to use to defend me?" Kyle asked.

Nancy sighed and, for the first time, seemed embarrassed. "No, I just want you to tell us the truth. Your sponsor insists on it."

Kyle turned and started for the door.

"Wait a minute, Nancy," Harding said, moving to head Kyle off. "Let's listen to Manny first."

"I'm not negotiating," Nancy said, shooting Harding a warning look.

"You know my position, Kyle," Tyler said. "I still believe that you were overworked, stressed out."

Kyle stopped, put his hands on his hips. "You're both wrong, and *I'm* not negotiating, either."

"Wait, hear us out," Harding insisted. He hesitated for a long moment, as if realizing this might be his last chance. His hands came to a point in front of his face: "We both know the words stress and air traffic controller go hand in hand; mention the words air traffic controller and a jury will immediately picture a man or woman bent over a radar scope blanketed with aircraft targets. They will sympathize with the difficulties of your profession. Use that to your advantage." Tyler became animated, waiving his arms as if addressing a jury. "I can see their faces; they will be enthralled when you tell them how chaotic your job is. They will see the government as the enemy for not providing you with better equipment."

"Yeah," Nancy said, "right up to the time the prosecutor turns on the playback machine and the jury hears that damn tape."

Tyler became even more animated, as if he suddenly had a brainstorm. He turned toward Nancy expectantly, his eyes opening wide: "How's this for a compromise, Nancy. I don't know why I didn't think of this before. He cocked his head and smiled broadly. "We can do just as you suggest, admit he accidentally keyed his microphone, but still use the stress angle. Yes, that's it. . . we admit he did it, but it was accidental; he was pulling a prank and accidentally keyed his mike because of the stress he was under. He was tired, overworked."

Tyler studied Nancy expectantly. Her eyes said "Hell no," but he jumped back in anyway. "I understand you have to do what you have to do, Nancy, but I strongly suggest you tell Kyle's sponsor this is the only way."

"Wait a minute," Manny said, hands on hips. To Harding: "What do you mean, 'Nancy has to do what she has to do'?" To Nancy: "What does he mean when he says you have to do what you have to do?" He glared at Nancy. She glared back but refused to take the bait. "I can't believe we're still debating this."

"Never mind, I think I can answer that question myself," Manny said. "You came here with someone else's plan, didn't you, Nancy? You're insisting on a confession because you're under orders. No wonder the two of you have been acting so strange. I suggest you tell us what those orders are."

"Yeah," Kyle said, "I'd like to know myself."

Nancy wasn't about to back down. She stood and said, "My orders, if that's what you want to call them, are just to make sure we know the whole truth before we proceed. What's wrong with that?"

"And if he confesses; what then?" Manny insisted.

Nancy hesitated before answering: "He pleads 'not guilty.' Then we go to trial and make Mallek prove otherwise, without all that stress crap that Tyler is so fond of."

Manny laughed out loud. "I must say this is unique. Let me see if I have the correct scenario: you want your client to tell you he's guilty, but then you insist, no you order him, to plead not guilty, without the option of a plea bargain or a diminished capacity defense that might save his life. Have I got that right?"

Nancy put her hands on her hips and looked at Manny defiantly. "Kyle's sponsor doesn't want a cop–out, like that insanity crap. Besides, we both know that never works anyway. Look at him, does he look insane to you. I'd say he looks pretty stable."

"And of course Harding had to agree to this or he didn't get the case," Manny said disgustedly. "You two worked this out before we came here."

"I thought we had," Nancy admitted, "except that now Harding just wants to take the easy way out and collect his money. I can't allow that."

Manny started to say something else, but Kyle cut him off, waiving his hand in the air. "Save your breath, all of you. I'm not stressed out. The only stress I'm feeling is from my lawyers." He started toward the door again.

"You're going to go this alone, then?" Nancy asked, surprised. She followed after him.

"I have no other choice," Kyle said over his shoulder. He stopped and pointed at her. "But before I go, chew on this for a while: there's a little thing you lawyers should think about occasionally. It's called evidence. Manny is trying to tell the two of you something, but you're not even objective enough to listen."

FORTY NINE

Harding followed Kyle out the door, leaving Nancy standing with one hand on her hip, the other holding a cold cup of coffee.

Manny sat and waited for her to calm down.

"What's Kyle talking about?" Nancy asked after a pause.

"It's possible this wasn't a mid-air collision after all."

Nancy's jaw dropped: "What the hell do you mean?"

"A bomb, that's what I mean," Manny said, sounding like he couldn't believe it himself.

Nancy lowered herself into a chair. "Explain."

"I'm not sure I can, at least not to anyone's satisfaction. I just know there was a bomb on board at least one of those two aircraft. I saw evidence of that at the crash site. How that computes, considering what we heard on the tape recording, I don't know. I've been trying to match what I saw at the crash site with what I saw and heard the night of September first, but I can't make it fit. All I'm sure of is that I heard two loud booms, and one of them must have been a bomb."

Nancy sipped her coffee. Her expression said she wasn't buying it. "You deduced all that from a visit to the crash site and what you think you heard that night?"

"There's more: a controller friend of Kyle's gave him a copy of a computer extraction, a printout. According to that extraction, the two aircraft were never at the same altitude until after they went down."

Nancy swiveled her eyes and her cup of coffee in Manny's direction. "Are you telling me the FAA's own computer extraction proves there was no mid-air collision?"

"That's what it looks like."

Manny pulled the extraction from his coat pocket. "All we have is this copy; the original was sent to FAA Washington, along with a letter giving Curtis' interpretation. And since we don't have a copy of his letter, we're not even sure what it said. Maybe he fashioned his interpretation to match what the FAA already believes."

Nancy shook her head back and forth slowly, as if she couldn't quite believe it.

Hearing no argument, Manny went on: "One more thing: my friend said that the NTSB is having trouble interpreting the CVR tape."

"What does that mean?"

"I'm not sure. I need to listen to the tape myself, but the NTSB has the only playback machine."

"My god, this all sounds so unbelievable."

"What can I tell you? It is what it is. I went to the crash site and saw the bomb evidence myself. I know what luggage looks like after a mid-air collision, and I know what it looks like after a bomb explodes on an aircraft. I was at Lockerbie, and I wasn't there on vacation."

"Or you saw the results of two aircraft loaded with fuel smashing into one another and exploding. Maybe there were secondary explosions from something else, something in the luggage compartment, or whatever."

"I doubt the airlines are allowing explosives in the luggage compartment, but it is possible that someone carried a bomb on board one of the aircraft. There are all kinds of possibilities; we need to check these things out before we make any decisions."

"Unfortunately, we can't use the 'Manny Vigil thinks there was a bomb defense,'" Nancy pleaded. "Any testimony from you will be suspect, anyway. This is a death penalty case. The government is going to go all out, and we have nothing but your opinion. We need to think long and hard about this. Even if what you say is true, it isn't proof, and we can't possibly come up with the proof in time. The government is entrenched in this thing; they're going to come up with a real good reason why it couldn't have been a bomb. Once the jury hears the tape recording they'll laugh at your bomb theory, anyway."

Manny sighed. He spoke very slowly now, as if this would be his last attempt to convince her: "Let's look at the big picture for a minute. Ask yourself this question: If Kyle was guilty, why would he agree to have that tape recording played in front of the whole world?"

He paused while Nancy held her chin in her hand and shrugged.

"And why would he chase Carpelski all over town trying to get a confession if he already knew what had happened?"

Nancy had already asked herself the same questions.

"And how about the fire at Kyle's house: is Kyle stupid, so stupid that he'd kill Danny Houston and dump the body in his own garage, not to mention burning the garage down and putting his wife at risk? For that matter, wouldn't Kyle be out of the country by now? I sure as hell would be!"

"Do you think Mallek knows any of this, or cares?" she asked.

"I don't know. But if you're thinking about asking him to meet for another listening session, forget it. I don't think Mallek is going to chance that a second time."

Nancy looked thoughtful for a long moment: "This all sounds promising, but the NTSB has the CVR tape and we don't even have a copy of Curtis' letter."

"And the FAA will probably interpret the extraction however they want to, anyway; I know that," Manny agreed reluctantly.

"That's a lot to overcome," Nancy grumbled.

"Look at it this way Nancy, your client says he wants the truth. Well, now we have a chance to get at it. You need to think about this." He studied her expectantly.

Finally, she threw up her hands. "How do we get a copy of Curtis' letter?"

Manny, hiding a smile, said, "Are you sure you want me to tell you?"

FIFTY

Thanks to Ron, Manny had no trouble getting permission to drive the motor home into the center parking lot; but he had to hide the rest of the defense team to get past the gate guard.

It was dark in Curtis's office. Nancy reached for Manny's arm. "I could get disbarred," she whispered angrily. "I shouldn't be here."

"Shhhh," he whispered back, tossing papers from Curtis Raymond's desk drawer. Andy Fisher, controller and veteran in the amateur spy business, worked alongside, ransacking Raymond's other drawers and pilfering files. It wasn't the first time Fisher had gone through Raymond's desk drawers. He practically owned most of Raymond's files, convinced that the government had it in for him and the other controllers because of the NATCA strike.

"For Pete's sake," Kyle whispered, "we can't take all day. Raymond could walk in here any minute."

"Don't worry," Andy said, not bothering to lower his voice, "he's in the cafeteria, blowing smoke. I do this all the time. Karen's at the radar scope right next to the supervisor's desk and Rooster is standing next to the cafeteria door, so we're good to go. They'll warn us if the bulbous prick starts coming this way." He continued to wallow in Curtis's papers, checking each one and tossing it aside.

Nancy succumbed to the excitement and began pulling files from a file cabinet. "Shouldn't we be putting this stuff back in the drawers if we can't use them," she suggested. "I'd just as soon the FAA didn't know we were in here."

"No time," Kyle said, tugging on Fisher's shirt. "Let's go. This was a bad idea."

Andy pulled away. He'd found something interesting and moved closer to a lamp on Raymond's desk. He cursed when he read what was there.

"Is that the letter?" Manny barked over his shoulder.

Andy didn't answer. He continued to read, his mouth hanging open.

Rooster suddenly ran into the room, his finger in front of his lips, and waived everyone out. Andy didn't move; he continued to stare at the piece of paper. Manny grabbed him by the arm and dragged him to the door.

They managed to escape down a side hall unnoticed, run out the back door, and make it to the motor home in less that a minute.

Once they were safely ensconced in the motor home: "I think one of the supervisors suspected something," Rooster explained. "Karen said he was headed toward Raymond's office. That was close."

Andy, a Huck Finn look alike, was still in a trance.

"What the hell's wrong with you, Andy?" Rooster asked. "Did you find the letter or not?"

"No," Andy answered dejectedly.

"Then why are you so goggle-eyed?" Kyle asked.

Andy, to Kyle: "Before I tell you, promise you won't kill the messenger?"

"Just spit it out," Manny said impatiently.

Andy looked at them all cautiously.

"Well, what is it?" Kyle insisted.

"Your psychological evaluation."

Kyle shook his head. "I don't remember any psychological evaluation, other than the one we took before we were hired. What did it say?"

"It said you are highly intelligent, well motivated, even a natural peer leader, that kind of shit."

"They couldn't have been talking about me."

"I'm not finished. I didn't get a chance to read it all, but it said something about how your goals are 'inconsistent with FAA goals,' or something like that. There's also something there about how you're capable of stirring up trouble. It sounded like Senator McCarthy and the Communists, or something."

"In short," Rooster finished for him, "they would do anything to get rid of you."

"Right," Andy agreed. "They even recommended he be transferred to another facility, somewhere like New York, where he would be just another loudmouth. I think Nome, Alaska, or Cleveland might also have been in the cards. All of this was written before the. . . well you know. . . the crash."

"I think you're exaggerating," Kyle said.

"No, I'm not. The assholes planned to transfer you. They think that because of the strike you may be suffering from 'post' something or other. There were some 'four semester words' in there that I didn't quite understand. What's a fugle...or a fugue?"

"Beats me," Kyle said.

Nancy volunteered. "I think it has something to do with a condition where you have blackouts and don't know quite where you are at times. Sounds more like a medical evaluation."

"It's also Kyle's way out," Harding said excitedly. "It's in their own words, a blackout, that's exactly what we need."

"Forget it," Kyle said. "The only blackout I ever had was one night at the Jigger when I drank too much, it was my birthday."

"And we don't have the damn evaluation, anyway," Andy said. "I dropped it when somebody grabbed my arm. We'd have to go back inside."

"Never mind," Nancy said. "There's got to be a record of it somewhere. We'll ask for it in discovery if we think it will help. Our problem right now is that we still don't have a copy of Curtis's letter. The fact that the FAA intended to transfer Kyle isn't going to help that much, anyway; we need that letter."

"We still have my copy of the computer extraction," Kyle reminded her.

"That's not worth the paper it's written on. The FAA will say the computer was fouled up, or that we falsified the findings. Without the letter from Curtis to Washington, we have nothing."

"Well, anyway, I have to go," Andy said, getting up. "Can I talk to you for a minute, Kyle?"

"Sure."

Once outside: "Who's the fox?"

"Fox?" Kyle teased.

"Don't give me that crap. Who is she?"

"Oh...you mean the Dragon Lady?"

Andy looked confused. "Dragon Lady?"

"That's what I call her. She says she wants to help me, but I'm not sure I can trust her."

Andy grinned. "Who cares? I say let her help all she wants."

"What was it you wanted to talk about, Andy, we need to go."

"The bastards said I was a thief."

"By bastards, I assume you mean our esteemed FAA flight surgeons?"

"Yeah, those pill pushers did a psych evaluation on me, too. They said I had the instincts of a thief."

"A thief?"

"Yeah. The sons 'a-bitches said I was stealing from FAA files."

Kyle suppressed a smile: "Well, isn't that what we were just doing?"

Andy started to say something, then stopped. "Well . . . yeah, but that's different."

Kyle couldn't resist: "Exactly how is it different?"

Andy just stared at Kyle for a long moment. "I'm not sure; I guess I just always thought that taking FAA files is like screwing the warden's daughter, a bennie."

Kyle hadn't intended to laugh, but he couldn't help it. He shook until his side hurt, causing Manny to open the motor home door and look out.

"Can I sue the FAA?" Andy asked.

Kyle laughed again: "I can see the headline now: 'Controller sues FAA for calling him a thief. Controller got his information by breaking into FAA manager's desk!"

FIFTY ONE

It was 10 P.M., but the lights in the NTSB's headquarters in Kansas City were still burning.

Manny had wanted to go in alone, sneak in without being noticed. He even had in mind breaking in, if necessary, but he was overruled: the entire defense team, which now included Laura, insisted that they wanted in on the action. It was going to make getting in much more difficult, but they said it had to be that way. If anyone was going to be arrested, they were all going to be arrested.

Kyle flashed his FAA ID at a tired security guard looking through the glass door. The guard opened the door part way to let them know they couldn't come in. But before he had time to react, the entire team entered and quickly began walking down the hall.

"Hey, you can't all be in here. Who are you? Is someone expecting you? Let me see that ID again."

Kyle gave the guard a nondescript waive of the hand and they kept going. "Mr. Moore said it was OK. We're on his committee."

"Quick, before he calls the cops," Manny said. The others picked up the pace, practically running to catch up. They found the lab, and Manny, finger to lips, whispered, "Whoever is in there is going to explode when he sees us. "I'll deal with him. Just remember, we're not leaving until we get some answers."

They entered and saw a slender man with glasses sitting at a work bench, staring at a scope showing lines of various lengths. He looked up when he saw five bodies come through the doorway. "What the hell are you people doing here?" He pointed to the door. "Get out."

Manny closed the door and blocked it with his body. "Not yet. We have some questions." The man studied the door as if he couldn't believe the security guard had allowed five people to just walk in. He had been warned that *Manny* might try to breach the gate, but he was completely unprepared for an assault from five people.

Manny opened the door a few inches and looked down the hall. He saw the security guard coming, phone or radio up to his ear. He quickly closed the door and locked it. "Tell the security guy to go away and I promise we'll only be here a few minutes."

"I can't talk to you. They'll have my ass on a rack. Thanks to you and your friend, Fred Bell has been removed and some maniac is in charge. Fred's probably been shuffled off to Washington or some other god forsaken place."

"We'll be quiet," Manny said, holding his finger to his lips. "Nobody other than that guard is likely to be here at this time of night, anyway. We're only asking for information we're entitled to."

"Bull shit, you told that same story to Bell. Get out of my way." He tried to move Manny aside, but Manny had spread his body so that there was no room to pass.

"We haven't asked our questions yet."

The guard banged on the door. "Mr. Andes, are you all right?"

"I know who that is," Andes said, pointing to Kyle. "Leave now or I'll have the FBI come and get him."

"Not until I hear the CVR tape," Manny said. "Fred told me there was something there you couldn't decipher, and since you have the only playback machine, I need to use it. It will just take a few minutes."

The guard continued to bang on the door.

"No way I can allow that; I'll get fired."

"We can help you decipher the tape," Manny insisted.

Andes appeared to be considering it. He hesitated for a long moment. . .

. . . "Let us help you. Kyle and I both have experience interpreting these things."

There was more banging on the door.

"I've been ordered not to talk to anyone associated with Kyle Matthews. You're going to be arrested just as soon as that guard calls the FBI. Is that what you want?"

Manny spread his legs and put his hands on his hips. "If you call the FBI, you might never be able to interpret that tape. If we can do it right here and now, why not let us? Are you afraid to admit you need help?"

Andes knew he wasn't going to be able to interpret the CVR tape by himself. He'd been over it a dozen times. He couldn't figure out why there were differences between the CVR tape and the center tape, and his boss was getting tired of his excuses. If someone could explain it to him, it might get him out of a jam. He thought about it for several seconds, then shouted to the guard, "I'm all right. You can go back to your station."

There was a long pause before they heard footsteps start back down the hall.

Andes sighed, "Don't ever use my name; I don't want to be involved. And after I play the tape, I want all five of you to get up quietly, go out the back door, and never tell anyone you were here. I'll talk to the guard after you're gone."

They nodded their agreement, and Andes motioned for them to sit on one of the stools arrayed alongside the work bench. He pointed to one of several playback machines. "I've been scrutinizing this damn thing for days. Draw your own conclusions, because I don't have any. He looked around for any disagreement. Seeing none, he reached over and flipped the switch on one of two, complex looking machines.

As the lights on the machine began to flicker, Manny was reminded of some of the embarrassing CVR conversations he had listened to in the past. They often revealed the pilot's or co-pilot's innermost thoughts, expressed in a way he or she would never have expressed them had they known anyone would ever hear it. It was often just small talk, but occasionally contained explicit sex and vile language. And because the tapes automatically erased themselves every thirty minutes, there was little concern their remarks would ever be heard outside the cockpit, unless their flight ended up in disaster, in which case unseemly conversation would be the least of their worries. Manny actually considered listening to CVR tapes an invasion of privacy.

"What is that machine, what we are listening to?" Nancy asked.

Laura was glad Nancy had asked because she had been wondering the same thing. It also gave her a chance to get a better read on Nancy. The two had had only known one another for a short time, but Laura had been impressed. Nancy seemed intelligent and confident, not just a lawyer hoping to cash in on a big case. She couldn't completely dismiss the notion that Nancy's interest might be Kyle himself, but that didn't really worry her. Other women might laugh at that naiveté, but she knew Kyle too well for that. He was more likely to actually run two airplanes together than to cheat on his marriage. What did worry her was the Dragon Lady's insistence that he not plead guilty. Not that she wanted him to plead guilty and spend his life in a prison, but she knew it might be the only way to avoid the death penalty. Kyle could be very trusting at times, inclined to act before thinking. She wanted him to think long and hard before taking Corey's advice. And before making *any* decision, she wanted him to learn why this woman wasn't up front about her reason for wanting to get involved and her refusal to say who was paying for Kyle's defense.

"This machine plays back the cockpit voice recorder, or CVR tape," Andes explained. "The media calls it the 'black box.' There are actually two black boxes. The other one is called the DFDR. And they're not black, they're orange, so they can be seen easily." Andes seemed pleased that someone had asked. He pointed to the playback console.

"Channel one is the pilot, channel two is the co-pilot, and channel three is the CAM, or Cockpit Area Microphone, an open microphone in the cockpit. Channel four is the radio traffic coming into the aircraft's receiver. We should hear everything that was said at the time of the accident."

"Is this like the center recorder?" Laura asked.

Now it was Nancy's turn to study Laura. She, too, had been impressed. It gave her a new respect for Kyle, although she wasn't surprised to see that he was married to someone strong and credible. She wondered how two such seemingly stable personalities could have separated.

"Not exactly," Andes said. "Basically, the CVR is a thirty minute Mylar loop. . . "

. . . Kyle finished up for Andes. "Center recorders record for a twenty four hour period, not just thirty minutes. The principle is the same though; to record what was said, with a time channel overlap to record the exact time of each transmission."

What about the DFDR?" Tyler asked. "Have you listened to that?" He didn't really give a damn, but he wasn't going to allow Nancy and Laura to be the only ones showing interest.

Andes fiddled nervously: "We have already extrapolated what was on the DFDR and made copies for our sub-committee," he said, squirming in his seat. "Unfortunately, that information is locked up in the safe and I don't have access to it. Someone in higher authority apparently doesn't want it released yet."

Kyle shot Manny a questioning look; Manny returned it. Andes was obviously holding back. They eyed him suspiciously, but he wouldn't return their looks.

The playback machine sprung into action with sounds of static and disjointed conversations, some from the cockpit and others from air traffic control frequencies.

They heard the pilots talking back and forth, chit chat about a dry cleaning store that one of them owned. It obviously came from the CAM, the open cockpit mike.

After a long moment, they heard Kyle issue the fatal clearance. The pilot read back the clearance and repeated the details.

Kyle almost jumped off of his stool: "That read-back wasn't on the center tape," he said excitedly.

"It must have been blocked out," Andes insisted.

"No. If the pilot had acknowledged a clearance it would have been on the center tape. Play it again."

Andes hit rewind and they listened to the tape again.

"I guess that proves he got a clearance, anyway," Andes smirked. "If that's all you have, you all need to go now."

"Not yet," Kyle insisted. "Let's hear the CVR tape and the center tape played simultaneously."

Manny gave Kyle a questioning look. "Why, Kyle?"

Kyle held up his hand.

Andes saw the exited look on his Kyle's face, sighed, "Give me a few minutes."

They sat silently while Andes set up a center playback machine. Laura kept her eyes aimed at the floor; it had been embarrassing, listening to Kyle give the fatal clearance again.

While they waited: "What was on the DFDR, Mr. Andes?" Manny insisted. "Anything unusual about the altitudes?"

Andes' sideways look was all the answer Manny needed.

"We already know the two aircraft were never at the same altitude," Kyle prodded.

Andes, surprised, "Where did you get that idea?"

"We have our sources."

"Well, you didn't get it from me. And you won't get it from anyone else in the government, either. We've been told to keep our mouths shut. You didn't hear me say *that*, either."

"This happens to be my life we're talking about here, Mr. Andes," Kyle said: "If you know something that could help us, we need to know it, too."

Andes hesitated. "All I can say is that there are differences there, too. If you call me as a witness, I'll lie."

After a minute or so, "The machine is ready. These two decks will play the Center and CVR tapes simultaneously. Each deck has a time channel in the background."

He turned on the machines. There was the usual static and chitchat. Then, the clearance:

"Transcon Three Eleven...Transcon Three Eleven. . . climb and maintain Flight Level Three Seven Zero. . . climb and maintain Flight Level Three Seven Zero." Only one read-back from the pilot was heard, the one from the CVR.

Kyle jumped up, shook his fist, said: "I knew it; there was a read-back on the CVR tape, but none on the center tape. That means there were two separate clearances recorded. I don't know how or why, but it proves I wasn't lying."

"The FAA will have to listen now," Manny agreed.

Kyle to Andes: "Are you sure you started both tapes at exactly the same time? There's a one or two second delay between the two."

"I'm positive," Andes said. "The time channels are in perfect sync."

"You're the recording expert," Manny said. "How is that possible?"

Andes threw up his hands and shook his head.

Kyle stood. "Let's go; there's only one way those two transmissions could be different, and that's if there were two separate transmissions. I have no idea how or why it was done, and I certainly can't explain it yet, but I will be able to; I have to be able to."

FIFTY TWO

"Who in the hell is Butch Moore?" Warren Ramsey ranted, busting into Peter Brock's office and slamming the door.

"Why, who said anything about him?" Brock asked, rising with a shocked expression.

"I asked you who he is," Ramsey insisted angrily. "And I want the truth, no bull shit. Frank Zimmer called me; he's worried about this guy for some reason."

Brock had been expecting a dressing down if Ramsey found out about Moore's qualifications, but he couldn't allow himself to be intimidated; in Washington, intimidation was the final bell.

"You don't need to shout, Warren. I put Moore in charge of the mid-air collision. I told you all about it at the time."

"Well I need to know a lot more now; who is he and what's his background?"

"He's just a fired, ex air traffic controller," Brock finally admitted, after evaluating his lying or not lying options. He's been pestering everyone for years, asking for his job back and holding a grudge because we won't allow it."

"You put one of the people Reagan fired in charge of a major NTSB investigation? What were his qualifications?"

"He's an electronics expert; the NTSB needed him to evaluate the black boxes," Brock lied. "I figured that investigation was pretty much pro forma, anyway."

"You put him in charge of a major investigation because he wants his job back? Shit, that was what, twenty five years ago when the FAA started re-hiring those people? I thought that was a dead issue. No one gives a shit about that anymore; give him back his damn job and be done with it. We don't need complications right now."

"He's not interested in that any more; he's too old. He wants a management job in the FAA. He says the government owes him, big time. The man is nuts: he's demanding to be reinstated and made manager of one of the FAA's regional offices. No way the FAA will allow that; they don't want him back in any capacity. I needed to shut him up."

"Shut him up? Why?"

"Because he's been threatening to reveal some things that could complicate the Kyle Matthews case. It wasn't a big problem; I just thought we should keep him quiet until the trial is over."

"Complicate how?"

"He claims that he had something do with the mid-air collision."

"For Pete's sake, we already indicted the guy who caused the mid-air collision. What could this Moore say that could possibly affect that?"

"He had bragged that he was going to get rid of Noonan, even before the crash. Now he wants to take credit. That could have complicated the investigation."

"I remember you asking me if you could put Moore in charge, but you never mentioned any of this other crap. Zimmer said that Moore is threatening to hold a press conference and tell the truth about the mid-air collision, and that he doesn't care if he goes to jail himself, whatever that means. Is this man holding any cards at all? What's this got to do with Frank Zimmer?"

Brock had a hard time breathing. He slowly lowered himself back into his chair and tried to calculate how much trouble Moore could actually cause.

"Moore is using a conversation I had with Zimmer as a hammer. It has Zimmer running scared."

"What conversation?"

Brock hesitated for a long moment: "When Moore first called Zimmer he hinted that he had caused the mid-air collision. Zimmer didn't report it."

"Well, he obviously should have, but what's that got to do with us?"

"Zimmer told me about his conversation, and I didn't report it either. Unfortunately, Moore has a tape recording of my conversation with Zimmer and is threatening to report both of us."

Ramsey picked up one of Brock's chairs and shoved it against the wall. He stood, hands on his hips, his face red: "You went ahead and made some nut job head of an important committee knowing he was a threat, and you didn't even mention it to me? You had Moore by the gonads from the very start; you should have reported Zimmer's conversation to the FBI and had Moore jailed. Now it's too fucking late; he may have *us* by the gonads. If we told them now, the FBI would inform Mallek and Mallek would be obliged to inform Matthews' lawyers."

Brock waived Ramsey's admonishment away: "No, no. As long as Matthews is convicted, Moore's braggadocio doesn't matter; it will be just one more whacky confession; the FBI gets them all the time."

Ramsey continued to stand with hands on hips, seething, cooling down. After a long moment he looked up and bored into Brock's eyes. Brock couldn't handle it; he lowered his own eyes.

"There's something else you're not telling me," Ramsey said slowly. "I know when you're holding back. Out with it."

"There isn't anything else," Brock lied, eyes shifting rapidly now.

"Out with it, I said."

Brock sighed, hesitated, said, "Moore claims that some NTSB investigator named Fred Bell allowed Matthews and a private investigator named Manny Vigil to visit the crash site. Vigil claims to have seen bomb fragments imbedded in some luggage."

"Bomb fragments?" Ramsey asked incredulously.

"It's nothing to worry about; the bomb fragments, if there actually were any, probably resulted from an explosion following the collision."

Ramsey struggled to comprehend. He stalked the room, looking at Brock as if he might jump up and kill him right then and there. He got control of himself, slumped in a chair against the wall, thinking.

"I hate to bring this up," Brock said, "but we actually need Moore's help now. If there *was* a bomb, we're 'gonna need Moore to keep a lid on things until after Matthews is convicted. By then, it will be too late for anyone to do anything about it. That's another reason I put him in charge; he's in a position to influence the outcome."

Ramsey screwed up his face like a man wrestling with the devil: "Is it possible a bomb had something to do with bringing down those two aircraft and we blamed an air traffic controller? If there was, and we haven't reported Moore's conversation with Zimmer, we could all be accused of a cover-up. Remember Watergate?"

Brock wrung his hands and hung his head like a condemned man. Because he *was* a former prosecutor, he would be held to an even higher standard than the worst felon, and he knew it.

"We need to discuss something else while we're at it," Brock said, hurrying to change the subject.

Ramsey looked up quickly: What now?"

"There's a rumor going around about a computer extraction from the mid-air collision. According to the rumor, the extraction proves there was no collision at all, and that the FAA knows it. Yet, when we had that meeting with Hufnel, he never mentioned it. I called him today and asked him why, but he said everything on the computer extraction checked out. I'm not sure I believe him. Maybe there was something there he didn't want us to know, or maybe he thought we wanted it covered up. I remember how nervous he looked when the president questioned him."

"Anything else, for God's sake; this is turning into a pile of unhealthy shit. You better check out that computer extraction yourself. As for the bomb thing, I guess that will just have to play itself out."

"Hufnel says the extraction was flawed and he destroyed it before it could be misinterpreted, so I don't know what else I can do. I shut up after that because I was afraid someone might also be recording *our* conversation."

Ramsey sighed: "Well, we're probably screwed one way or the other now, but I guess there's no turning back." He got up slowly. "We just have to plow ahead and make sure Matthews pleads guilty, because if he doesn't, we could all go to jail." He pointed his finger at Brock: "I've heard about this guy, Fred Bell. He's one smart investigator. If he starts believing that bomb crap he might bellow to the press. I suggest you send him some place far away; get him the fuck out of the country and tell him to shut his mouth."

"He's already in Russia. The Russians have been asking for some technical help, so I sent him. What do you want me to do about Hufnel?"

"Nothing; you've screwed up enough.

I'll handle Hufnel myself."

FIFTY THREE

The Metro escaped from the ground and rose up to cross the Potomac River, giving Ron his fist glimpse of the Washington monuments in over six months. Those monuments had always given him goose bumps; for a true patriot like Ron, they were important symbols of America, something to cherish forever.

During this short trip to Le 'Fant Plaza and FAA headquarters, Ron had time to wonder why the FAA Administrator had asked him to come on such short notice. No doubt Kyle Matthews had something to do with it, but what could he tell the FAA Administrator that the FBI or the NTSB couldn't? On those rare occasions where the top brass needed to talk to a regional subordinate, they usually just picked up the phone.

Whatever it was Hufnel wanted, it was fine with Ron; he had a few questions, himself. If the rumor was correct, and the computer extraction showed that the two aircraft were never at the same altitude, then Curtis was lying. And if Kyle really had been subject to an impromptu, illegal psychological evaluation, Hufnel should know about that, too. Curtis had steadfastly denied the existence of either; not that lying was unusual for Curtis.

A secretary guided Ron to the Administrator's conference room, where Gerry McGuire, newly appointed National Air Traffic Director, sat waiting at a horseshoe conference table that took up most of the room's space. Ron thought that if the table could speak, it would probably say: "don't get comfortable, you won't be here long."

McGuire stood up to shake hands, smiling and wearing a "what in the hell are we here for" look. The two had worked together for years.

Ron started to ask a question, but stopped when McGuire put a finger to his lips and pointed to the walls. Ron shook his head up and down, remembering that the walls probably had ears.

Before they had time to exchange another message, William Hufnel huffed and puffed his way into the room, followed by his usual entourage of sycophants carrying laptops. Ron figured Microsoft would be out of business without FAA sycophants and their laptops. He didn't use a laptop himself, and he didn't trust anyone who did; he kept his important notes stuffed in his back pocket.

Hufnel, looking harried, introduced himself to Ron as if he had never met him before, one of his subtle, "put adown" tactics. He reminded Ron of Senator Claghorn, without the sense of humor. Next he quickly shook hands with McGuire and took a seat at the head of the table. Sycophants took their cue and grabbed seats on the side opposite from Ron and McGuire.

Hufnel asked for a recap of the mid-air, which McGuire could easily have provided without the expense of flying a man all the way from Kansas City. Clue number one.

Ron flicked at a piece of lint from his pants and carefully considered his answer; he wasn't going to provide any more information than necessary until he found out why the master had called. Finally, he looked up and gave the Administrator a less than informative, two-minute report, leaving out the one thing Hufnel had wanted to hear the most.

Hufnel just stared at Ron. He then asked casually, too casually, if it was true that Ron and Kyle Matthews were good friends. Clue number two.

Ron said yes and made no bones about it. He made it a point to describe what a good controller Kyle was and how he had always been very dependable. He had to fight to keep from smiling when he noticed the pained expression on Hufnel's face. He glanced over and saw McGuire stifle a smile, himself.

"Well, you know you can't be too careful about this man," Hufnel said. "The whole world is watching us." Clue number three.

"What do you mean?" Ron asked in his best 'just off the turnip truck' manner.

"I mean," Hufnel said, sounding exasperated, "that we could all loose our jobs over this. There were signs that all of us should have noticed about this man, Matthews. Our failure to do so could reflect very badly on all of us."

"Signs?"

"Signs," the Administrator repeated, growing visibly agitated.

McGuire had his eyes closed, like a man about to receive a scud missile. Ron was walking the plank and taking McGuire with him. He decided to try and smooth the waters: "What the Administrator is trying to say, Ron, is that FAA doctors have known for some time that Kyle Matthews has been under stress. We probably should have done something to head this off a long time ago."

"Bull shit," Ron said. "If you're talking about the results from some illegal psychological study conducted by FAA quacks, I haven't even seen it yet. Maybe we should send the quacks to consult with the legal office instead of letting them use one way mirrors to bolster a trumped up charge."

Even the sycophants cringed this time, their fingers banging away at their laptops.

"What psychological study?" Hufnel asked innocently.

"The one the FAA doctors conducted."

Hufnel turned to McGuire, "Is this true?"

"Not that I know of," McGuire said. "If there was, it was done before *my* time. That kind of thing could cause a major problem if the media got their hands on it."

"Yeah, a major problem for Washington," Ron grumbled.

"If that were true," Hufnel said, "I would agree with you that our doctors should never have conducted such a study without the man's permission. I can assure you, however, that no such study exists or Mr. McGuire would have certainly known about it."

"Unless no one told me, either," McGuire interjected. "When I mentioned that Matthews was under stress, I was just talking about the routine stress that goes with the job."

Hufnel threw McGuire a quick dagger. "If Matthews was under stress, your supervisors should have been aware of it on a day to day basis. FAA doctors don't supervise our controllers; all they know is what you people tell them. You're the ones who will look bad in the eyes of the media. You should have been more careful."

"Oh, I get it," Ron said. "The FAA didn't do an illegal study, but if they did, it was Gerry McGuire's fault, or mine?"

McGuire closed his eyes; Hufnel blinked.

"Well," Ron said. "With all due respect, this is a bunch of typical FAA 'pass the buck' horse shit and you might as well keep passing it along because I won't allow any of it to stick to me."

Hufnel seethed, his teeth clenched. Ordinarily, he would never allow a subordinate to talk down to him. Allowing Ron to do so was a sure sign that he needed something badly. He took a deep breath and went on talking as if the three were just having a friendly conversation:

"Well, I can understand how you feel . . . considering Matthews is a good friend... our doctors..."

"No, you don't understand. Good friend or not, Kyle Matthews is also a good, conscientious controller and a staunch citizen. I don't know exactly what happened on September first and I've never said I did, but I do know that Kyle's mental condition was not a factor. I'm willing to concede that he pulled a dumb stunt; it's even possible he did something to cause the accident, but it wasn't deliberate, I'd stake my life on it. And please, don't refer to your lackeys as doctors. Those incompetents will rubberstamp anything you put in front of them. The only reason they work for the FAA is because they're not successful enough to afford malpractice insurance."

Hufnel forced a smile. He took a long time clearing his throat.

"Well, all I'm saying is that we may all be staking our careers on this situation."

Ron wasn't finished. "What about the computer printout? I heard the two Transcon aircraft weren't even at the same altitude when they supposedly hit? I also heard there was a report sent to Washington confirming that."

"Where. . . did you hear that?" Hufnel stammered.

"Then it's true?"

"Of course not," Hufnel scoffed. "I. . . don't. . . not sure what you mean."

"I suggest you check with the center," Ron said. "You might start with Curtis Raymond."

Hufnel recovered his composure. "I don't have to check. There is no such report or I would know about it. Where do you come up with these things? I heard that the computer extraction was flawed, but that was just a problem with the equipment; the center staff disregarded it."

"So the extraction was flawed? Who says it was flawed? I've seen a copy of it and it looks as if the aircraft never got together. As the regional air traffic manager, I'd like to see the original and judge for myself. If I'm as responsible for what happened as you implied, let me at least see what I'm responsible for."

"I saw that copy, it was sent to the FBI. One of Matthews' sneaky friends tried to make it look like the original. The FBI disregarded it."

Ron decided to gamble: "What about the DFDR, what were the altitudes of the two aircraft? I heard the DFDR also showed they weren't at the same altitude."

Hufnel looked dazed. The meeting was not going in the direction he'd planned. He gathered himself and edged forward in his chair. "We all need to be very careful and precise about what we say to the media concerning this subject. I've just come from a meeting with the president and he's keeping a close eye on what's being said to the media in Kansas City. We don't want anything said that could be used against us. I don't know where you get your ideas. The NTSB is in charge of the black boxes; I have no idea what they revealed."

Ron was now sure that the computer extraction would have exonerated Kyle. Hufnel would never take the kind of abuse Ron was dishing out if it didn't.

"Well, I can see that this whole incident has been stressful for all of us," Hufnel said, rising from his chair. The sycophants rose in unison.

"Oh, one more thing," Hufnel said as if it had just occurred to him.

Here it comes, Ron thought, the real reason for this little get-together.

Hufnel cleared his throat again. "Have you suggested to your friend that it might be wise to plead guilty? That would resolve all of this, and it might be his only chance to avoid the death penalty."

Ron just glared at him. "In case you don't know it, the man you're referring to has a name, it's Kyle Matthews."

Hufnel's face reddened. He held out his hand, but Ron ignored it and left the room, leaving Hufnel with a handful of air.

"I thought you handled that well," McGuire whispered as they entered an elevator. "Why didn't you just call him an asshole and get it over with."

"You mean I didn't? Let's go back," Ron said.

They both burst out laughing.

But Ron wouldn't be laughing for long.

FIFTY FOUR

Wearing work pants and a shirt with the letters "Mid America Air Conditioning," Kyle waited until the receptionist left before he ran past her desk and down the hall. He found the door to Spencer Mallek's office open, put down his empty toolbox, and walked in.

Mallek jumped up and immediately began looking around for an escape route. "Get out of here, Matthews," he screeched, unraveling his elongated body from a chair and making a move toward the door.

Kyle's eyes widened when he saw FBI Director Carl Perkins standing behind Mallek's desk. Perkins, a short, bulldog of a man in the Hoover tradition, wore a light brown suit and brown tie. His hair had been shaved around the ears like the Marine he once was. He had never seen Kyle in person, so it took several seconds before he realized who he was. Kyle's timing had been perfect: Perkins had apparently been going over a case with Mallek; maybe even Kyle's case. The Director's eyes flicked to the door, wondering how Kyle had managed to breach security.

"I just came here to give you some information," Kyle said. "I didn't know Mr. Perkins would be here, but I'm glad he is."

"You're a fugitive and now you're under arrest," Mallek said. He started to run to the hallway for help until he realized that Kyle had the doorway blocked. "Don't bother looking for a marshal," Kyle said. "I made sure everyone's at lunch."

Mallek's eyes begged Perkins for help; he knew he couldn't handle a man of Matthews' size by himself, but Perkins just stood there, too dumbfounded to react. "Where in the hell are the marshals?" he shouted.

"Relax," Kyle said. "I just have a couple of things to say and then I'm out of here."

"You had your chance when we played the tape recording," Mallek scoffed.

Kyle ignored Mallek and spoke directly to Perkins: "Did you investigate the bomb damage at the crash site, or did Fred Bell even have a chance to tell you about it before the NTSB put some crazy man in charge of the investigation? There was a bomb on one of those two aircraft."

Mallek and Perkins exchanged surprised expressions.

"If you're talking about the luggage," Perkins said, looking down his nose, "Mr. Bell told me all about it. He said the markings on the luggage resulted from the collision and subsequent explosion. When two aircraft collide, there's going to be an explosion; everyone knows that."

Mallek shook his finger at Kyle. "This sounds like another of your fishing expeditions. I suppose now you expect us to go to the crash site with the media and sift through the debris; more theatrics. There was no bomb. If there had been, Mr. Bell or one of the other investigators would have informed us."

"Unless they assumed that they already know what happened and decided to ignore evidence," Kyle countered. "Or maybe someone thought you wouldn't want to know."

"What's that supposed to mean?" Perkins barked.

"The man in charge of the investigation, Butch Moore, is the same jerk you once accused of making false transmissions to aircraft. He's an enemy of my family, and he'll hide evidence to get at me. You don't care about evidence any more; the damn tape recording is all you care about. Butch Moore wants to see me convicted and you guys are making it easy for him."

"Nonsense," Mallek said forcefully. "No one man can influence our interpretation of the evidence."

"You can't interpret what you haven't seen."

"I don't know who this man Moore is," Perkins said, "but I can tell you it doesn't work that way. No man control's what we see or do. If there's actual evidence of a bomb, the NTSB will inform us and we'll take over. Our agents have been at the crash site from day one."

"You don't know Butch Moore. And what about the FAA's computer extraction? I've seen a copy of it. It shows there was no mid-air collision at all."

Mallek's eyes swiveled to Perkins. The FBI had never mentioned anything about a bomb or a computer extraction. He studied Perkins' expression for signs. And who was Butch Moore?

"All I'm asking is that you check those things out," Kyle went on.

"Of course we will," Perkins said. "Now, why don't you just let us take you in and get this over with? You're only making things harder on yourself."

"Don't worry about me, I'll turn myself in when I'm sure you're doing your job. Just don't let Moore interfere."

With that, Kyle quickly walked out of the room.

Both men ran after Kyle, shouting for help. They found a marshal and ran with him as he looked for Kyle in the parking lot. The marshal continued to search for several minutes, but came back shrugging his shoulders. "He's gone."

Mallek screamed at the marshal, demanding to know why he had left his post. He then returned to his office, where he sat and pounded on his desk. "Matthews is going to pay for his insubordination. I guarantee it."

"He sure isn't what I expected," Perkins said.

Mallek looked confused: "How do you mean?"

Perkins shrugged: "I guess I was expecting a madman or something. Matthews seems pretty rational."

"Well if he's rational, what's all that stuff about a bomb and a computer. . . whatever?" Mallek asked. "And who is Moore?"

"I don't know," Perkins said. "You heard what I told him, I'll check into this immediately. He gathered up his papers. "That crap about a bomb is ridiculous, of course, but it's time I check out the status of the case, anyway. I have a plane to catch, so document what Matthews said and send me a copy. I 'wanna make sure I cover all the bases. I'll check and see what the FAA has to say about a computer extraction, too, put that to bed once and for all."

Mallek slowly shook his head. "He's guilty; I'm sure of it."

"He damn well better be; we're too far along to be backing up now. I'll be in my office for a few days, in case you hear anything."

FIFTY FIVE

Mallek slumped in his chair and removed his glasses, his knees reaching the top of his desk. He rubbed his eyes, thinking.

Matthews' sudden intrusion had shaken him for reasons he couldn't quite understand. He had been prepared to enjoy prosecuting the case, ridding the world of another bad seed. But it was always much more enjoyable if you detested your opponent, and now he wasn't so sure how he felt. This was the second time he had come face to face with Kyle Matthews, and for the second time he had come away conflicted. He had studied Kyle's expression carefully when he barged into the office, expecting to see something sinister, maybe even evil. Instead, what he saw was a man who seemed relaxed, completely under control. It threw him off, almost ruined his day.

The more he thought about it, the more curious he became. Could there possibly be something to what Matthews had said, or was it just the ramblings of a desperate man? Wouldn't he have been notified if there had been any evidence of a bomb at the crash site, or some significant computer data? Wouldn't he be the first one on the list? He had always argued that murderers were cowards, but would a coward hunted by the FBI walk into a federal building disguised like that? Small doubts about the government's case had already begun to creep in when Matthews had insisted on having the tape recording played in front of the whole world. That kind of thing was suicidal unless you were innocent or just plain stupid. The man who walked into his office today was neither suicidal nor stupid; more like strong and confident.

Mallek was not naïve: it wouldn't be the first time someone at a higher level had stacked the deck on him, but that usually involved something trivial, such as exaggerating the strength of a case or the credibility of a witness. He had been on a few other cases that didn't quite seem on the up-and-up, but he had never deliberately prosecuted an innocent man. Besides, he had his career to protect. No sense in allowing himself to be made a fool of. He sighed audibly. Why couldn't this case be as uncompli-cated as he had thought it would be?

He sat stewing for a long minute, dialed the Washington, D.C., NTSB office, and asked for Fred Bell. The secretary put Bell's supervisor on the phone. The supervisor explained that Fred Bell was out of the office on assignment.

"What does that mean, 'on assignment'?"

"He's in Russia assisting their government on an unsolved case," the supervisor said, as if reading from a script. Mallek picked up on his tone immediately.

"Is there any new evidence concerning the mid-air collision that I should know about?"

The supervisor answered without hesitation: "I'm not aware of any, sir. You might want to check with the FBI."

Mallek hung up the phone.

The supervisor's answers seemed to have been rehearsed. And why did the secretary put the supervisor on the phone just to tell him where Bell was? Why not just say that Fred Bell was not at his desk, or one of the other excuses secretaries always gave? Was it possible the supervisor was ordered to pass the word himself so that there would be no slip-ups? In any event, it sounded like a prepared answer.

Mallek was sure that Perkins wasn't hiding anything; Perkins was a straight shooter.

He called the attorney general's office in Washington.

Matt Potorf wasn't in. His administrative assistant explained his absence as if she were reading from his yearly agenda.

Mallek was a veteran of the political runaround; he recognized it when he smelled it.

He just didn't know the reason.

FIFTY SIX

Ron was in the middle of the Rocky Mountain Region's daily ATSCON, or Air Traffic Systems Conference, a telephone briefing that took place early each morning between FAA Washington and its regional offices.

Conducting the teleconference was a representative of the Systems Command Center in Herendon, Virginia, which included the Central Flow Control office, called "CF squared." That office was responsible for keeping air traffic flowing throughout the country at an even, manageable rate, based upon what the regional offices identified as their anticipated delays or special problems at the major airports. Special attention would be paid to major cities with bad weather or equipment problems, such as an inoperable instrument landing system. Extra resources would be pulled in to make the necessary repairs immediately.

The collective system of airports and their related electronic equipment was known as the National Airspace System, or NAS. It constituted the principal series of transportation arteries in the United States, and it had to be kept going at full capacity.

Ron's branch managers were always present in order to provide first hand reports on special problems. Such a problem might include anything from low staffing to visits from members of congress or the media. If someone important was due to visit, everyone in an air traffic facility would be ordered to be extra careful: the facility would be made spic and span, with full staffing and all employees ordered to keep their mouths shut. Ron called it "putting all the prisoners back in their cells and cleaning up."

Things were fairly normal today. There were the usual, routine reports just to show that everyone was at work and functioning, but nothing earth shaking.

Ron was interrupted by a phone call from "AT1," the Air Traffic Director, Gerald McGuire. Phone calls from AT1 during an ATSCON were somewhat unusual, since the Director could pass along necessary messages through the ATSCON itself. When a separate phone call was necessary, it usually meant the Director didn't want an audience.

Ron left the room and picked up the phone on a secretary's desk. "I had a phone call from Hufnel earlier this morning," McGuire said.

Ron screwed up his face. "That must have been a thrill. What did the wind bag have to say?"

McGuire remained silent for a long moment. "He said I had to replace you."

Ron put the call on hold and went into an unoccupied office. He closed the door, noticing the secretary's disappointed expression.

"'Replace me'?" Ron asked after sitting down. "He can't just order you to do that. What's the charge?"

"Insubordination, or at least that's what he says. Actually, he doesn't need a charge."

Ron thought nothing could shock him anymore, but he was shocked now, mostly because of what Mary would think. "I can't believe it," he said. "That's what I get for asking questions."

"Apparently, some of those questions hit home. All the little laptop computer boys are busy filling out statements concerning your behavior."

"Well, they won't get a virgin," Ron said, with more bravado than he felt.

"For the record," McGuire said, "Hufnel claims he investigated thoroughly, and officially denies your contention that the FAA did a psychological report on Matthews. He says if it did exist it was done without FAA approval and he can't find anyone who's heard of it. He also claims that a computer malfunction caused the printout to be faulty, and that there was no letter to Washington on that subject."

"I really screwed that one up," Ron said dejectedly. "I gave him an opportunity to bury everything."

"Well, anyway, I'm looking for a qualified replacement, but it looks as if it will take me quite a while to find one."

"So I'm safe for the time being?"

"I haven't told you the bottom line."

"I can't wait."

"Hufnel hinted that if you will use your head and do what is best for your friend, convince him to plead guilty, all is forgiven. He was very emphatic about that."

"Why is that prick so frightened, Gerry? Where's all the pressure coming from?"

"It's not just him, it's everyone in Washington. The rats are scurrying."

FIFTY SEVEN

Kyle and Laura sat at the kitchen table in her mother's house. The only light came from one, small, lamp. Kyle had waited until dark before sneaking in through the basement door. He wore jeans, a clean T-shirt, loafers, and was clean-shaven for the first time in a week because Laura had insisted it would give the children more confidence.

Laura's parents had gone to bed, and after explaining Kyle's situation to their frightened children, Laura and Kyle had finally gotten Mary Clair and Todd to bed, as well. The children didn't really understand what their father did for a living in the first place, much less how much trouble he was in. When they had visited him in the air traffic control center, they just assumed it was like one big Nintendo set. Kyle always put off explaining the serious nature of the business, believing that it was too soon and way too complicated; but now that their classmates were teasing them and they were afraid to go to school, it was time for a more detailed explanation, which he provided right before they went to bed. They were smart kids and grasped the situation well, or maybe they were just happy to see their father.

The conversation afterward centered on Kyle's next move. From time to time one of them would sneak a peek out the window, looking between the slats in the blinds so as not to attract attention. With the lights out, whispering only made things seem more ominous. There was a single TV truck lurking in front of the house next store, but other than that, nothing on the street was moving. There was no way to be sure the truck wasn't an FBI stakeout, so they were very careful not to rattle the blinds. Any movement at all could end Kyle's freedom for good.

When Laura informed Kyle that Ron had been relieved of his job, he became very angry: "I can't believe Hufnel had the guts to do that."

Laura: "They're running scared; but can they actually remove him without a hearing?"

"Yes, as long as he keeps his pay grade. They'll shuffle him off to some piddley assed job doing paperwork. Hufnel will probably ban him from entering FAA facilities, too, anything to put the pressure on."

'What's that all about?"

"Hufnel thinks Ron can talk me into pleading guilty."

"Something's not right, Kyle. I can understand the publics' anger, but why would the government go to this much trouble just to fire one air traffic controller?"

"It started when some of the things I've said in the past upset them. Now they're using whatever happened to those two aircraft as an excuse to get rid of me."

"But why use Ron, as well?"

"Maybe they're no longer sure it was a mid-air collision and they need an easy way out. Maybe Fred Bell said something to someone and the word got around. Mallek looked completely conflicted when I barged in on him."

"Do you think he knows about the computer extraction and the other stuff, or are they keeping him in the dark?"

"Not sure."

"What will happen to Ron in the long run?"

"They'll make it hard on him for a while, put the pressure on him so he'll put the pressure on me; at least I hope that's all they'll do. Ron loves that job. Now I have Ron and Mary on my conscience, too."

"I'm beginning to understand why controllers think they need a union to protect themselves," Laura said. "A bureaucracy that large needs an independent entity to keep it from running amuck."

"I call it a countervailing army."

They sat in silence for several more, long moments.

"Don't get mad when I ask this," Laura blurted.

"I know what you're going to ask, and the answer is still no; I haven't changed my mind about pleading guilty. I'll admit, I've asked myself over and over if that's what I should do, but I'm not going to do it."

Laura hesitated, "It might save your life."

Kyle sighed, said, "I'd rather be dead than in prison."

There was another long pause before Laura said with tears in her eyes, "Maybe you should at least turn yourself in. The longer you continue to hide out, the angrier the public is becoming. There won't be a juror in the state that isn't prejudiced. Besides, I can tell how tired you are. You're going to ruin your health."

Kyle hesitated before saying, "I guess you're right. I was hoping Manny and I could get the FBI to move before I went in, but it looks like that's not going to happen. I'll just have to let Manny carry the ball until the trial."

Laura's head was down, her arms wrapped around her legs and her chin resting on her knees. "If this goes to trial, maybe you'll be able to use everything you and Manny learned there."

"I don't know, once the government gets me in court, it'll be hard for them to turn back. They'll steamroll me all the way."

"Is there anything I can do?" Laura asked. "I feel so helpless."

"Nothing I can think of. I'm still hoping the FBI will at least talk to Manny about what he saw at the crash site. He has all that accident investigation experience; why wouldn't they listen to him?"

Laura sighed, said, "They should consider what he heard the night of the collision, too, that's valuable information."

"I've become convinced there's no way they'll ever listen to my private eye."

Laura, after thinking about it: "You're right. It would be different if some stranger had seen and heard what Manny did. The FBI would have to listen then."

"Probably wouldn't make a damn bit of difference: as Caesar said when he crossed the Rubicon: 'The die is cast'."

Laura got up and poured them a cup of coffee.

"At least my lawyers seem to be getting along better," Kyle said over his shoulder. "Maybe Nancy will come up with something. I've given up on Harding."

"Nancy Corey is full of shit," Laura said suddenly.

Her language shocked him; it wasn't like her. "I thought you were impressed with Nancy?"

"You've always been a big believer in instincts, haven't you? Well, my instincts tell me she's hiding something. I'll admit she's impressive, but the whole thing stinks: the idea that some stranger would pay for your defense and have no ulterior motive is nonsense. As for Tyler Harding, he's not even worth discussing."

Laura's own instincts were right on, but he wasn't about to tell her what Manny had learned about Nancy's orders, not on top of everything else. "I don't have much choice; I can't afford a different lawyer. If those two can help at all, well . . . "

"I say you should ask for a public defender. At least you'd know who you're dealing with."

"It's too late for that. Tyler and Nancy are already preparing discovery motions. Besides, Manny will keep them in line. And I still have hope that Nancy will come around."

"Manny is the only one who has your best interests at heart," Laura insisted.

Kyle didn't disagree: "He's turned out to be a Badger all right, just like Ron promised. He thanked me for pulling him out of that fire, and never once mentioned that he was the first one to enter the garage. By the way, he was angry when I told him I went to see Mallek. He said it proves I haven't learned a f. . . well, never mind how he put it. The gist is that I'm still acting like a commando. He's right, I shouldn't have done that; it was stupid."

"Don't expect me to argue with that," Laura said. "You never did have any patience."

Laura sat down and they drank their coffee. She suddenly sounded very serious.

"I want to help you get through this thing."

"You have been helping me."

"No, I mean I want to be fully involved. I want to be active. I get tired of listening to the TV. I need to do something."

"Just hang with me," Kyle said. He smiled and patted her on the knee.

They sat quietly in the dark until Laura started to laugh.

"What's so funny?"

"Rooster says his phone is tapped," she said.

"That's baloney. Controllers always think their phone is tapped. It started with the first controller sickout in nineteen sixty-nine. Rooster reads too many detective magazines, anyway."

"He sure sticks by you though," Laura said. "So do Andy and Morrisey. You learn to appreciate your friends when you're in trouble."

Kyle thought about all the people trying to help: Morrisey, Andy, Karen Davies; pretty awesome support for a guy they had every reason to believe was guilty.

"I'm pretty lucky to have them on my side, all right," Kyle said, his hand cupping his chin. "I'd sure like to justify their confidence."

"You're thinking about something important. What is it?" Laura asked.

"Something you said about a stranger observing what Manny observed."

"I doubt if anyone but Manny would have noticed anything unusual, anyway. Manny is a natural born skeptic."

Kyle shrugged.

"What you need is a Polaroid," Laura said. "Fat chance of that."

"Yeah, not many people take pictures of the sky at night," Kyle agreed. But the conversation had started something buzzing in his brain.

"El Photo Grande, the big picture." Kyle mumbled, standing up suddenly. "That's it, that's what's been going around in my head. . . the big picture, something Mallek has to believe!"

"What. . . what are you talking about?"

Kyle was already headed for the back door. "Sometimes people do take pictures at night," he whispered. "You said you wanted to help; well maybe you just did."

FIFTY EIGHT

Finding a needle in a haystack would have been easy compared to the miracle Kyle was looking for. It was a one in a million shot, and it had to happen before the FBI found him.

The man guarding the door of the WDAF TV studio in downtown Kansas City recognized Kyle immediately: he was even wearing a "Sky Killer" t-shirt, a sure sign he would turn Kyle in if given the chance. He backed away as if his life were in danger.

"I need to see Bob Lewuellin," Kyle commanded. "We went to school together. Does he still work here?"

"It's midnight, he's . . . not here now," the man stammered. "There's only a skeleton crew inside."

"Get him on the phone. I'll wait."

The man started to argue, changed his mind and scurried inside, attempting to lock the door behind him. Kyle jumped inside before the man could react. "I'll be right here. And don't call anyone else."

The man shook his head and ran down the hall. He returned with another man several minutes later.

"My God," the second man said when he recognized Kyle. "We've had reporters and cameramen looking for you all week. He smiled and held out his hand. "I'm Lou Partee. None of our reporters are here now, but if you're looking to tell your story, I'll interview you myself."

"I'm not here for that. I need to talk to Bob Lewuellin. I have something important for him."

"I'll call him right away; it's late, it might take a while for him to get here."

Kyle shrugged his understanding. "Just make sure you don't call anyone else. If you do, you and Lewuellin can both forget about an interview."

"No problem," Partee said. He motioned for Kyle to follow, and the three men went into an office stuffed with cubicles and TV monitors. Partee sat in one of the cubicles and picked up a phone.

Kyle found a seat; Partee kept one eye on him while he talked. There were only a few station personnel on duty tonight, and as soon as they realized who Kyle was they began looking for a strategic position where they could get a better look at him. They wandered around aimlessly, talking in whispers and sneaking glances in his direction. One or two peered through office doorways.

Lewuellin made it to the station in fifteen minutes, wearing shorts, flip flops, and a Rockhurst University T-shirt. Kyle didn't recognize him at first; whatever hair remained was gray and sparse, and he had put on considerable weight. He pumped Kyle's hand and made halfhearted remarks about how he knew Kyle was innocent all along. Kyle didn't believe a word of it; the comments sounded self-serving, bordered on contempt.

"I need your help," Kyle said.

Lewuellin seemed disappointed. "I thought you were here for an interview."

"No. Not now."

Lewuellin's enthusiasm dropped like a rock thrown from a bridge. "What . . . kind of help?"

Kyle explained what Manny thought he'd seen on the night of the collision.

"So?"

"We have reason to believe there was no collision after all. If there's any chance that someone on your staff might have been shooting video that night, there could possibly be a shot of what my private investigator saw. He was standing in the middle of Troost at the time."

Lewuellin's interest level dropped to something in between "what business is that of mine" to "what's in it for me." Kyle sensed that Lewuellin's next move would be to call the FBI.

"If you have evidence there was no collision, let's go on camera, let the public know."

"Wouldn't do any good; the government won't listen. I need something tangible. You guys cover events at night, like a school board meeting, or one of those get-togethers where the police meet with the public. I know it's a long shot, but if you can find anything helpful at all, Charlie Gibson or Katie Couric will be calling you, and *you'll* be the one being interviewed."

Lewuellin blinked; "Video that shows the collision? That's crazy."

"I'm talking about an international story here, with your station featured prominently. I'm talking Peabody award, or whatever you guys get."

"You actually believe we might have something that would be of interest to the networks?"

"Exactly."

Lewuellin licked his lips. "That would be the coincidence of all coincidences. Besides, didn't the FAA already conclude it was a mid-air collision? I'm sure the networks would love the story, but why not just let me do the interview; tell the public what your PI saw?"

"No. Like I said, no one is going to believe what my private eye claims to have seen. Besides, what's it 'gonna cost you, couple of hours having someone check the video tapes for that night?"

Kyle saw Lewuellin's eyes widen, then widen even more as he apparently thought of something. He turned and said to Partee, "You guys can go. I'll handle things from here."

The two backed away, looking disappointed. They moved to one of the offices.

"I don't like talking about this in front of station employees."

Kyle noticed a sudden change in Lewuellin's attitude: all of a sudden he seemed interested.

"If I found such a video," he asked, puckering his lips and rubbing his chin, "what do you suppose that would be worth? Say you and I decide to combine video like that with an exclusive interview. Wouldn't a network like CBS or NBC pay big money for something like that?"

Kyle's eyes hardened: "I'm trying to save my ass and you're talking about making money from this? Don't you have an obligation to your employer and the public?"

Lewuellin grinned and looked around: "Sure, but I also have an obligation to myself and my family."

"I don't have time for that. I need something right now, something I can give to the FBI. They're going to arrest me any minute now."

Lewuellin stood with his arms folded. "No deal. Either we sell the whole package, assuming I can even find what you need, or it's no go."

"Never mind," Kyle said. "I'll find another station." He turned and left through the nearest door.

Lewuellin followed him outside: "You're wasting your time," he shouted. "If anyone had such a video it would have already been shown on the evening news." He shouted even louder as Kyle moved away: "You shouldn't even be here unless you're willing to tell us your side of the story. People are very upset with you, including the people who work at this station. This whole affair has been a shock and a disgrace. Our viewers would be very unhappy if they thought I was trying to assist you."

Kyle thought about turning back and punching Lewuellin's lights out. He knew Lewuellin would have everyone in the station looking for the video just as soon as he left. The FBI would be notified, too, if they hadn't already been. He stopped, turned, moved toward Lewuellin and put his finger between Lewuellin's eyes: "Look, asshole, you owe me. Remember the times you used my notes before a big test? You were a damn disaster, always behind the eight ball. How about the time you borrowed my car and drove it into a muddy field because you were dead drunk. It cost me two hundred dollars just to have it towed. You never paid me a cent, even after all your promises."

Lewuellin turned, realizing that station employees were standing in the doorway. "Don't you people have something to do? Go back to work." He turned back to Kyle, flashing one of his obsequious smiles. He shuffled up and put his hand on Kyle's shoulder. "Look, Kyle, to find what you're looking for would just be dumb luck. But if I did find something like that, an interview with you would close the sale, give it legitimacy. It would be worth a million dollars to a show like *"FIRST EDITION."* What's wrong with making money for your legal defense? If you won't cooperate, maybe I'll find what you're looking for and make some kind of a deal myself."

Kyle stared into Lewuellin's eyes. All he saw there was greed. It was as if the two had never even met. "You're saying you don't give a shit if I go to jail? This is what friendship means to you?"

Lewuellin shrugged indifferently.

"You son of a bitch," Kyle said. He shoved Lewuellin hard, turned and walked away.

Lewuellin recovered and followed him. "Let me interview you," he begged. "I'll tell your story, then we'll look for some video, I promise."

"You always were a sorry bastard," Kyle said over his shoulder. "I'd rather be in my situation than live the life of a gutless ass like you."

Undaunted, Lewuellin repeated his offer. "There's big money here. It could pay for your defense. If I can't find something here, I may be able to get it from another station.

"We need to keep this between us," he shouted to Kyle's backside.

FIFTY NINE

It wasn't easy finding a cab in downtown Kansas City at midnight.

It was so quiet on the street that Kyle could hear Lewuellin shouting orders to his employees inside the station. If there *was* video from the night of the collision, Lewuellin would find it. On one hand, it could still help if something he found was shown on television, but the downside was that a pitiful bastard like Lewuellin might make a bundle.

Kyle looked up and down the deserted street and decided he'd better find one with more traffic. There was no time to waste; Lewuellin would have his people scrambling for the video and calling the FBI at the same time.

He reached Manny on his cell phone and explained the situation: he needed Manny to call every TV station in Kansas City, Missouri or Kansas City, Kansas until he found something. He had an additional incentive now: to screw a rat out of his cheese.

A cab drove leisurely around the corner; Kyle stepped into the street waiving his arms. The cab slowed and came to a stop, but before Kyle could open the back door, a woman came running up from behind and put her hand on his shoulder. When he turned around, she handed him an envelope. "I found this while you were arguing with Lewuellin. It's marked September one and it looks promising. You were out of there so fast I didn't have a chance to see much of it, so I don't know if it's what you need or not. I'm going to trust you to give me the story first if you find anything useful. Good luck. And by the way," she winked, "we're not all assholes like Lewuellin."

She ran off before Kyle could ask questions.

Kyle got in the cab, gave the driver the hotel address, and tore open the package. There was a DVD inside, along with a sheet of paper bearing the WDAF logo. He looked out through the back window and saw the woman running back toward the WDAF building. Then he looked down and read the note:

"I don't know if you're innocent or not; all I know is that there's something fishy going on: the government has clammed up and I can't get to first base. I'm as anxious to learn the truth as you are.

"Good luck, Kelly Edmunds."

SIXTY

It was 5A.M:

The defense team had already assembled when Kyle got to the Red onion motel, another one of the rag-tag safe houses the defense team rotated to while hiding from the FBI.

Everyone was tired except Kyle; he was just excited. They grumbled as he inserted the DVD. He wasn't overly optimistic, himself, but if Kelly Edmunds had risked her job to give him the DVD . . . well then, there could be something there. Nevertheless, even *he* thought the whole idea was crazy.

He leaned against a wall and looked around at all the annoyed expressions. Everyone except Tyler was dressed in shorts and a T-shirt, sitting barefooted on a couch or lying on the floor. Tyler sat back in a chair with his eyes half closed, wearing a suit, a loose tie, and apparently suffering from too many Vodka Gimlets.

"What's so important you couldn't wait till morning?" Nancy complained. She looked to be the only one somewhat alert: her hair had been combed and her shorts and T-shirt were neat and clean.

"You tell me after you watch the DVD. Kelly Edmunds said there might be something worthwhile on it. Probably nothing we can use, but since she took a chance giving it to me, judging from the fact she was dressed like the spy who just came in from the cold, I owe it to her to at least look at it."

Manny sat looking like a beached whale. He needed a shave, and what little hair he had left over from the fire stuck out from the sides of both ears. It was his turn to do the whining: "You haven't even seen it yourself, yet you dragged us here at this time of the morning?"

Kyle ignored his sarcasm. "Avoid throwing out your brilliant criticisms until after you've seen the DVD two or three times. We'll take a few minutes after we're finished playing it, then we'll discuss it; I don't want anyone to go off half-cocked. If you see anything useful at all, analyze it the way a potential juror would. After all, that's who we'll have to sell it to."

Everyone sat up a little when the TV screen lit up. All they saw at first was a dark night. What followed was a shot of a church shaped like a fish.

"That's St. Francis church on Troost, across the street from Rockhurst University," Kyle said. "Laura and I were married there." The time and date superimposed in the upper left hand corner read, "Sept. 1, 8:30PM."

"I'll take your word for it," Manny said.

Kyle moved the DVD forward until the time read 08:57.

"Looks like some kind of celebration," Nancy said.

"I think it's a mass letting out," Manny disagreed.

Heads went up and down.

The crowd had formed two lines on either side of the sidewalk, facing the church and waiting.

"It's a wedding," Laura said, as a bride and groom suddenly appeared. The people along the sidewalk began to applaud and throw rice.

The cameraman focused on the bride and groom, but swept the camera back and forth from time to time to show the crowd.

"Who are they; anyone recognize either one of them?" Harding asked?

"Never mind," Kyle said. "We don't care about that."

After a few seconds the bride and groom began running toward the camera. The camera swiveled and followed them to the parking lot in back of the church. The picture went up and down as the cameraman ran to keep up.

Suddenly, there were several bright flashes of light in the background, followed by oohs and ahhs from Kyle's defense team.

Kyle played the DVD again, trying not to get too excited. This was what Kelly Edmunds must have noticed, he thought. He forced himself to remain calm, not to jump to conclusions. The others did as requested and remained silent, although by this time they were on the edge of their seats. Nancy was sitting straight up, her palms on her cheeks, thoughtful.

They waited patiently while Kyle played the DVD a third time. They continued to watch in silence. He replayed the DVD two more times, then turned to them: "Well?"

They seemed unsure of exactly what they had seen.

He sighed and played the DVD again.

"Heat lightning," Harding said.

"There was no heat lightning that night," Manny said. "I checked."

"One last time," Nancy insisted, now on her feet.

There was a smile on Manny's face as Kyle hit the play button again.

"I saw flashes of light," Laura said.

"And if there was sound you'd have heard at least two, loud booms," Manny suggested, standing up.

Kyle smiled and played the DVD for the eighth time, finding it hard to keep from shouting out loud.

"Two flashes," Harding said. "There were two flashes."

"Or maybe three," Nancy disagreed. "But what caused them?"

"I know what caused at least one of them," Manny insisted, "it was a bomb exploding."

"Too bad we can't hear anything," Laura said.

"We don't need to," Manny insisted. "One flash of light might explain a mid-air collision, but two or three means that something else happened. The NTSB will have some explaining to do. It's a crack in their case."

"But will it be good enough?" Nancy asked. "Isn't that wishful thinking?"

Kyle stood and ejected the DVD from the playback machine. "Maybe, but at least we have *something*."

"Don't get your hopes up," Nancy insisted. "That DVD isn't exactly conclusive."

"It wasn't that clear to me either," Harding agreed. "Others might say it was just heat lightning."

"Damn it, I just told you there wasn't any heat lightning that night," Manny said. "We can prove that easily."

"Laura was right, she told me I needed a picture, and this is it," Kyle said." He smiled at Laura, but she wasn't looking. She was glaring at Nancy with a foul expression.

Nancy noticed Laura staring, too, but just assumed Laura didn't agree with her. "Well, I guess it's something, anyway," Nancy grumbled, not realizing that sparks were about to fly.

"It's more than 'just something'," Laura said with fire in her eyes. "We finally have something people can actually see. It's a damn miracle, that's what it is."

Harding mumbled something negative, and Laura gave him the same foul look she'd given Nancy. Harding didn't notice, but Kyle did: he'd been the victim of that look before: Laura at flash point.

Nancy didn't notice either exchange and went on: "I don't think the DVD will be enough to keep the government from going forward. If only we had a witness other than Manny, someone with no axe to grind."

"That's not going to happen," Harding said innocently.

Laura Matthews had heard enough: she bolted from the couch, waiving her arms: "Damn it," she said. "Can't the two of you say something positive for a change?"

It was suddenly very quiet, as if all worldly noises had been shut off.

Nancy seemed startled. "I just meant. . . "

"You just meant to be negative, as always," Laura bellowed, loud enough to be heard down the block. "What is it you're after anyway? And why don't you just tell us who you're working for? You don't belong here; you belong in some corporate office, or drinking champagne in a Rolls Royce."

Then it was Tyler's turn to get burned: "And you," Laura said, pointing at Tyler. "Big hat, no cattle, that's you. Just 'cause your daddy was an important lawyer doesn't mean you'll ever be one. You remind me of a toad. Daddy's not going to help you now, so get that silly grin off of your face."

Manny thought he might as well get everything out on the table: "Laura's right, and since we're clearing the air here, why don't you tell us who you really are, Nancy *Corlini?*"

Nancy stammered, "What. . . what do you mean?"

"You know what I mean. Exactly who are you, and why are you lying about your name?"

Nancy seemed resigned. She got up, put on her jacket, headed for the door. "I'm doing what Kyle's sponsor wants me to do, and he has his reasons," she said over her shoulder.

"OK then, just tell us why he insists that Kyle confess and still plead not guilty?"

She stopped at the door and looked back. "Because it's his money and he wants it that way. Shall I tell him you don't want his help?

"I thought so." She stepped out, but quickly came back in and slammed the door. "FBI," she said, "they're all over the place."

SIXTY ONE

The Matthews' team was now meeting in out of the way cabins; hotels were no longer safe. The Mathews' cabin sat on a hill facing west, surrounded by gobs of trees.

"I wonder if I'll have to spend the rest of my life hiding out in the woods," Kyle said.

"Count your blessings, anything is better than jail," Nancy said. "As much heat as the FBI is taking from the media, we don't dare go into the city."

Kyle and Laura had purchased the place on the cheap, hoping to build on it. There was a small fishing lake about a hundred yards behind the cabin, and a ramshackle shack that once held an aluminum boat, a small outboard motor, and life jackets.

"That was close. I hope the FBI can't see this place from the air," Manny said, lying on a couch with its stuffing hanging out. "Where in the hell are we?"

"It's called Tanglewood Lake; we're in Lynn County, Kansas," Kyle answered.

"Looks more like Siberia, except it has trees."

Nancy's eyes floated to the ceiling, unable to believe Manny lived such a sheltered life. "You don't think they have trees in Siberia?"

"What do either one of you know about Siberia, anyway?" Kyle asked, sitting back in an old wooden chair, his hands behind his head."

"I'm assuming it doesn't have trees," Manny said, "too fucking cold for trees to grow there."

Kyle was too tired for specious arguments. "I hope I did the right thing, leaving Laura like that. There just wasn't time to think."

Nancy said, "She'll be OK: the FBI can't do anything with Harding there."

"Yeah, I guess even Harding can handle that situation."

After a long moment: "Speaking of trees, who owns this woodpile?" Manny asked.

"Laura and I bought it about ten years ago for thirty-four hundred bucks. The salesman said it would increase in value because it was the last lot on the lake. All the others had been sold."

"He sure saw *you* coming: we're sitting in the middle of a damn forest. It would take a year to clear this place out. Do you still expect to make money on this place?"

"Hell no; they built another lake right around the corner, three times as big as ours."

Manny laughed out loud. "Sucker, you fell for it didn't you? I thought you said there was a boat in the shack outside. I didn't see one?"

"Somebody stole the boat, the outboard motor, and every other damn thing."

Manny laughed even harder.

"When do you think it'll be safe to leave this place?" Nancy asked. "I feel cloistered."

Manny's cell phone rang.

Kyle, startled, jumped up. "Who could that be?"

"Probably someone looking to sell you more land," Nancy said, frowning.

Manny grabbed his phone. "Should I answer it? It could be the FBI."

All three were on their feet now, unsure if Manny should answer or not.

Manny shrugged and answered, anyway. He listened for several seconds before putting his hand over the mouthpiece. "It's Butch Moore."

Kyle was stunned. "Are you kidding? How did he get your number? What does he want?"

"He said he has something important to discuss. He wants to talk to you." Manny held out the phone.

Kyle threw open his hands and looked at Nancy. "Should I talk to him? It could be a trap."

"My suggestion is that we get the hell out of here, now," she said.

Manny shook his head: "If the FBI knew we were here, they'd be knocking down the door already."

Nancy disagreed: "Moore found the phone number, why not the FBI? And if it's that easy to find a number, why not an address?"

Manny shrugged: "It's up to Kyle."

Kyle hesitated, grabbed the phone, too curious to ignore the danger.

"What the hell do you want, Butch?"

"I need to meet with you and Manny and talk about that DVD."

Kyle's heart beat a little faster. "What DVD?" he asked stupidly.

"The one you got from WDAF. It could be evidence of a crime, and since I'm in charge of the NTSB investigation, I need to discuss it with you before I turn it over to the FBI."

Kyle was speechless. Finally: "You have my DVD?"

"Yes, I picked it up at Harding's office."

Kyle, angry: "Harding left that DVD so his secretary could have copies made. I intended to give it to the FBI, myself."

"Well, I have it now, so that won't be necessary."

Kyle didn't say anything for a long moment: "So why call me? We both know you're not out to help me."

Butch, sounding hurt: "That's not true. I may have my duty as lead investigator, but I also want to be fair. I want the truth. I know this has been difficult for you, so I thought I'd help. You're wrong about me. If the DVD really does help your case, I'd like to know why. I'm giving you and Vigil a chance here."

Kyle held his breath. "Where are you?"

"I'm on Eighty Fifth Street, but the DVD is in a hangar at the Johnson Country Airport with all the other evidence. My team is working there for the duration."

"Just give the DVD back, Moore. You have resources, ask WDAF for another copy, or go to another TV station."

"Well. . . ," Moore said innocently, "I tried that. I called WDAF and every other TV station in town. You somehow managed to find the only useful shot. By the way, a Mr. Lewuellin wants his DVD back; he says he's going to sue you."

Kyle thought of something and put his hand over the mouthpiece. He turned to Manny. "Did Harding's secretary make copies? Call her. I'll stall."

"No. I'm beginning to think Nancy is right: Moore might have the FBI with him. Let's just get the hell out of here."

"They probably know I'm here, anyway. It won't take but a second."

Manny reluctantly borrowed Nancy's cell phone while Kyle got back on with Moore.

"Just give the DVD back, Moore. I'll take my chances with the FBI."

"I can't; I'm required to protect the chain of evidence. If you don't meet with me, you won't see a copy until the government gives you one, which could be right before your trial."

Kyle kicked the chair. He knew instinctively that Harding's secretary wouldn't have a copy. Moore was very thorough; he would have made sure of it.

Manny grabbed his arm: "Harding's secretary says she didn't have time to make copies. Moore flashed an ID, took the original, and left before she could call us."

Kyle clenched his teeth and stood with the phone in his hand for several seconds, trying to control himself: "So when and where do we meet?" he asked, feeling sick.

"How about one o'clock?"

"I can't make that. It'll have to be three or three thirty."

Moore hesitated: "OK, meet me at the Ramada Inn on Eighty Fifth Street at three, and we'll go from there. And bring Vigil with you. I'll call my committee members and tell them we go back to work at three thirty. We can all take a look at the DVD together."

Kyle ground his teeth to keep from exploding: "OK, what room?"

"Meet me in the bar. You can follow me to the hangar."

Kyle slowly hung up the phone. "He wants us to meet him. What the hell is he up to?"

Nancy: "He's going to have the FBI waiting for you."

"No, I don't think so. Moore needs to know exactly how I think the DVD will help me. Besides, now that I think of it, he won't call the FBI until he has what he wants; he enjoys seeing me chase my tail. One thing's for sure, though, he isn't doing me any favors. We need to be ready for anything; Moore's sickness runs deeper than just sending me on a wild goose chase. He has something Machiavellian up his sleeve; I can hear it in his voice."

Manny: "I guess we have no choice; we have to get that damn DVD back. I'll call Morrisey and have him go to the Ramada Inn right now, scope out the place, look for FBI agents."

Kyle started toward the door, gathering his things. Manny followed. "How'd he know about the DVD in the first place? He couldn't have bugged our motel rooms; we didn't stay in any of them that long."

"Harding's office; we talked about it there."

Manny's head went up as he thought about it, "He's probably had that office bugged from the beginning. I should have thought of that."

"He's been following us, too, knows every move we make. That's one of his specialties."

"Wonder why he wants *me* there?"

"I don't know, but there's a good reason, you can be sure of that."

"Are we misjudging this guy? Is it possible he really wants to help?"

"Butch Moore helping me, sure; like Michael Jackson would help out at a Cub Scout camp."

SIXTY TWO

Butch Moore had been feeling more and more threatened lately; questions from the FBI, the NTSB, and the media had been coming at him like bullets all week. The heat was on; he needed to close the investigation as soon as possible.

Everything depended on timing; events had been worked out down to the minute: at three O'clock, assuming Mathews and Vigil arrived on time, he would go to his room upstairs and retrieve the device he had hidden beneath a mattress. In the meantime, he had no choice but to wait. He sat on a barstool, tapping his finger on the bar and staring out at the parking lot.

He hated lounges; he considered them nothing more than smoke filled rooms overrun with drunken idiots. What's more, he hated sitting at a bar with rich yuppies. He had already changed seats twice just so he wouldn't have to talk to some yuppie lawyer. Unfortunately, this was the only spot where he had a clear view of the parking lot. Once Matthews and Vigil arrived there would be just enough time to activate the device, come back downstairs, and leave for the airport.

He wondered if either of them had believed his story. Of course not: he didn't underestimate them, especially after the way they managed to come up with the DVD. It had taken hours of searching, a lot of luck, and a gullible secretary to get his hands on it.

Getting Matthews and Vigil to the hangar on time was what mattered now. If his timing was right, he would get them there at about the same time as his committee members were arriving. The FBI would question why there were barrels of gasoline and used oil around the hangar, but he had that covered, too: his excuse was that those items were supposed to have been removed before the evidence from the mid-air was hauled from the crash site to the hangar. It wasn't his fault if the company he paid to haul the stuff away had the wrong date; he even had a receipt with the correct date.

The groundwork had been completed: the committee members would be there in about an hour; and as long as Matthews and Vigil got to the hotel on time everything would be perfect.

While he waited, ignoring drunks attempting to make conversation, he rehearsed the speech he would make to his committee members and the fire department: "God I'm sorry about this. I can't imagine what happened. I wish I could have been here on time." The best part would be when he asked Vigil and Matthews to verify that he had been with them when the explosion occurred. On second thought, he would generate an official report, including depositions from everyone present.

He was so looking forward to this.

SIXTY THREE

He studied his watch for the tenth time.

He looked out and saw Vigil's Mustang pull in. Perfect: success depended upon the two sets of witnesses arriving just as the fire blossomed, yet too late for anyone to do anything about it.

Time for act one.

He took the lobby elevator to his room and retrieved the box. Even though he couldn't actually see the Johnson County airport itself, he had a line of sight to the hangar. He aimed the box in that direction, turned it on, and pulled down on the toggle switch. "Good by Matthews, you fuck," he said proudly.

He quickly dismantled the box, dropped the parts in the toilet, and ran from the room, back down to the bar.

"I thought Moore was going to meet us here," Manny said, sitting down on a bar stool.

"You're starting to sound as paranoid as I am. Ordinarily, I'd say he was probably taking a leak, but in Moore's case, every movement or delay has meaning.

"That's him now," Kyle said, pointing toward the stairs. "He sees us, get ready for anything."

Moore walked to within ten feet of where they were sitting and said, "Follow me." He didn't wait for a response. Manny and Kyle followed.

Moore practically ran to the parking lot, jumped into a van, and roared out towards I-35, waiving from the window for them to follow.

Manny drove and the Mustang barreled out of the parking lot.

"I smell a rat," Kyle said, watching Moore disappear ahead of them.

"Well, we came this far, I guess we may as well go the rest of the way," Manny said.

The two men saw the fire as soon as they crested a hill one mile from the Johnson County airport. It was the kind of fire you'd expect to see coming from a warehouse full of Christmas trees, flames and dark smoke shooting up to the heavens.

"Son of a bitch," Kyle said.

Manny pulled up behind Moore's van. They watched as Moore jumped out of the van and ran toward the burning hangar like a distraught father. It took four firemen to hold him back.

They didn't bother to get out of the Mustang.

"Look at that prick." Manny said.

"He's putting on a real show," Kyle agreed. "Those people standing next to their cars must be his committee members."

"I thought he might turn you over to the FBI," Manny said, gritting his teeth, "but it never occurred to me that he might use us as witnesses. It should have. Now I know why he wanted me here."

"Goodbye DVD, goodbye luggage and CVR tape, and goodbye every other frigging piece of significant evidence."

"He did a good job of it, I'll give him that much," Manny said.

"He wanted us for an alibi," Kyle agreed, shaking his head in amazement, "and we fell for it. Give credit where credit is due. The son of a bitch will probably sue the insurance company and we'll end up being witnesses there, too."

"You were right, Kyle, this guy's sickness runs deep. He must have had someone standing by to torch the hangar while we were on the way."

Kyle shook his head. "Well, we're back to square one. Let's just get out of here before he gets his jollies. I don't 'wanna give him the satisfaction of watching us suffer."

"Shouldn't we look in the hangar?" Manny asked. "It's possible the DVD or some of the luggage is still intact."

"I'm sure he destroyed all of that before he set the fire; he couldn't take a chance the fire wouldn't wipe them out completely. There won't be anything left for us to use, believe me. They'll be just enough left over from the crash to put together the final package. The only things he wouldn't burn would be the things he needs to prove his case. He probably has lots of old, unmarked luggage he bought at a second hand store, and enough aircraft parts without bomb damage to satisfy the FBI that there was no bomb. The FBI will be only too happy to oblige, I'm sure."

"The CVR tape," Manny said excitedly, that's probably still in the lab."

"We'll call the lab, but I doubt it. You have no idea how organized this guy is."

Manny keyed the ignition and they backed out of the parking lot.

Moore looked back at them, an innocent expression covering his face. He shrugged his shoulders as if to say: "What could I do?"

"Look on the bright side," Manny said, "at least you're still free."

Ten minutes later, as Manny's car zipped north on I-35, four FBI Crown Victorias blocked the highway, signaling for Manny to pull over.

In baseball terms, Moore's efforts could be called a home run: he stole the DVD, he conned his enemies into being his witnesses, he conned his committee members into being his witnesses, and he arranged to have the FBI arrest Kyle.

SIXTY FOUR

Kelly Edmunds had finally made it: her top ranked story about the DVD she had given Kyle had swamped the national news and rocketed her to the top. The fact that the DVD had been burned in a fire only made things more intriguing. She followed up on the story daily and hung on to it like a remora fish clinging to a ship's hull.

Edmunds stood in the street outside the Kansas City Air Route Traffic Control Center, about to address a national audience with a story she had always dreamed of.

An excited Wolf Blitzer made the introduction:

"You won't believe what CNN has learned about the man the government says used his radar as a weapon to deliberately kill several hundred people. Our reporter Kelly Edmunds has the exclusive story:

"Wolf, I've learned that it's not the first time air traffic controller Kyle Matthews has been involved in controversy. A source close to Matthews told me he's been the subject of close scrutiny for several years. My highly placed source, who refuses to be identified, said that the FAA has secretly, perhaps illegally, scrutinized Matthews and recorded his movements for over a year."

The word had spread throughout the center like Thunderbird wine in a room full of hobos. As Edmunds spoke, a startled group of controllers, watching from inside the center cafeteria, jumped from their chairs and ran to get a closer look at the TV. Staff members came running into the cafeteria as well, looking over shoulders.

Edmunds continued to speak while her TV audience saw a shot of Kyle being taken away in handcuffs.

"Was accused murderer Kyle Matthews destined to kill two hundred thirty seven people all along?" Kelly asked, holding a mike and pointing towards the center building. "And if so, did the government know it in advance? Should they have noticed the warning signs?

"My source tells me that the FAA has wanted to fire Matthews all along, convinced that he was the mastermind of a local strike that tied up air traffic for two days. According to this source, Matthews was the subject of a secret psychological study conducted by the FAA, although the FAA denies knowing anything about it. According to the same source, the study indicated that Matthews might have been suffering severe stress that could lead to errors in judgment. My source insists that if the study is accepted by justice department psychologists, it could lead to Matthews pleading guilty by reason of mental defect, which in turn might even lead to an acquittal. If that turns out to be true, the FAA would no doubt come under fire for failing to take action sooner.

"As I have said, the FAA in Washington denies the existence of any psychological report, and sticks to their original contention that Matthews was of sound mind and was solely responsible for causing the midair collision. The FAA also said that while it may be just a coincidence, the recent rash of bomb threats may be the unions' way of showing support for Matthews.

"This is Kelly Edmunds reporting from the air route traffic control center in Olathe, Kansas."

Rooster reached over and turned off the television set.

One of the controllers, Barbara Ferris, appeared ready to fight. "Holy shit," she said, "do people really believe this crap? How can these guys get away with that 'unnamed sources' bull shit?"

"We all know who the unnamed sources are anyway," another controller added. "It's some prick looking to make a few bucks or get his name in print. He'll remain 'unnamed' as long as they keep paying him."

"Is it possible that Kyle really was stressed out, Rooster?" Ferris asked.

The other controllers waited, expecting Rooster to go ballistic, but for once he remained outwardly calm. "He wasn't before all this, but who knows how he'll end up if they keep attacking him. A man can only take so much pressure, even Kyle."

One of the supervisors spoke up. "That woman may be full of crap, but you guys better get used to the idea that Kyle is going to jail for a long time."

Rooster gave the supervisor the stink eye. "Brown, how in hell could you possibly know that? It's been thirty years since you even looked at a radar scope. It's shit-heads like you that give this outfit a bad name. Why don't you go back to reading your management handbook? Start with the part that says: 'see supervisor run, see supervisor kiss Curtis Raymond's ass'."

"Careful Rooster, Brown said. "You may be the union rep, but you can't talk to me like that."

Morrisey cleared his throat and attempted to change the subject before Rooster got in any deeper, which seemed imminent. "Did you ever notice that all those media people do is ask questions? They ask things like, 'was he really crazy,' or 'what really did happen'? They never give any answers, just fucking questions, like we're supposed to do their job for them. Next thing those bozos will do is ask us to take a survey: 'Go to www dot Dumbfuck and tell us what you think'."

"Yeah," Ferris added. "NBC, CNN, all those assholes, they're all the same. After every crash, no matter how small or what caused it, they start the broadcast with a question: 'Are the skies really safe anymore'?"

Morrisey agreed. "Yeah, but they never tell you the answer; they just interview some grungy old science reporter who doesn't know jack shit and rambles on, stalling for time."

Dave Cannady wanted in on this:

"Chances are, it's the same old science reporter who was the 'health' reporter the week before."

Brown gritted his teeth and left the cafeteria.

"I wonder who the 'source' is this time." Dave Segal mumbled.

Rooster frowned. "I'll tell you who it is: someone looking out for his own ass; someone close to home, like Kyle's lawyer, that rat Tyler Harding."

SIXTY FIVE

Nancy had been lingering in a hotel room shower for some time, agonizing over Laura's accusations and Manny's questions. She didn't like being dominated by her father any more than they did, and yet what could she do? Where else would Kyle get the necessary funding for his defense? She remained convinced that she had no other choice; nevertheless, she wasn't proud of herself.

She turned off the shower when she heard a familiar voice coming from the TV in the next room. It took several seconds for her to realize the voice belonged to Tyler Harding. She listened carefully for another long moment while she hurriedly dried herself, and when she thought she heard her name mentioned, decided she couldn't wait any longer. She grabbed a towel and ran, dripping wet, into the next room.

She turned up the volume and was shocked to see Harding standing in front of a large group of reporters, smiling, gesturing, and telling the reporters his client was suffering "severe emotional distress." He talked at length about the FAA's psychological report.

"Why won't your client talk to us?" A reporter asked.

"He will at the proper time," Harding said. "In the meantime, I'm speaking for him."

"Is it true that he bragged about running two airplanes together?"

"We'll explain all that in due time. You have to understand that controllers work under very stressful conditions, and with poor equipment. The suicide rate is high. It's hard to tell what someone will do under stress; sometimes they don't even remember what they did themselves."

"Then why doesn't he just say that? The public has the right to hear it from him," another reporter said.

Tyler answered with his most reassuring smile. "He will tell the whole story when he testifies at trial."

"You're going to let him testify, then? What about the story on CNN? Is it true that the FAA has known all along that Matthews is suffering from stress? Were they really going to remove him medically? Were you the source of that story?"

"No, I was not the source of that story, but I personally believe it to be accurate. The FAA has been worried about Mr. Matthews all along, and knew he should not have been working a radar position. That is really the essence and strength of our case. Mr. Matthews will eventually tell the world of the terrible stress and unsafe conditions controllers work under, and the FAA's study will back him up. We will eventually read that psychological study in court. In the meantime, I suggest you might ask the FAA about the report. Ask them how long they have known about Mr. Matthews' condition and why they didn't do anything about it."

"What dangerous conditions? What's unsafe?" The questions started coming like a waterfall. Every reporter started talking at once.

"Who is Nancy Corey? Is she Matthews' girl friend?"

There were more questions about Nancy. The reporters were like a hundred sharks with one, tiny piece of meat.

"Everything will come out in due time," Harding said smugly. "That's all I have to say at the moment."

Nancy knew that Kyle would never have authorized Tyler Harding to hold a press conference and talk about stress, not even to save his own life. He had made that perfectly clear on more than one occasion. Harding had jumped ship; that was the only way to explain this breach of faith.

What would Kyle say when he heard about it? How would he react? Would he fire Harding? Where would that leave her? And what will her father say when he learns that Harding is bringing up the stress thing? Is Harding really so cowardly that he would wait until Kyle was in jail and unable to defend himself before pulling a stunt like this?

SIXTY SIX

Kyle and Manny sat in the local U.S Attorney's office, watching TV coverage of a mine accident in Utah and waiting for Kyle's attorneys. Two FBI agents hovered over them. The program was interrupted by Harding's press conference.

There, standing in front of a large gaggle of reporters, stood Tyler Harding, talking about "controller stress." "My god," Manny said when he finally recognized Harding.

Kyle jumped up from his seat at the same time and almost attacked the TV set. One of the agents grabbed him from behind and pushed him back down. "The son of a bitch is doing exactly what I told him not to do," Kyle shouted. "He's making me sound like a character from 'One flew over the cuckoo's nest'."

"He's a man enjoying a million dollars worth of free advertising instead of showing up on time for our meeting," Manny fumed.

"Can you believe the nerve of that little jerk?" Kyle went on. "Why isn't he telling them about the bomb, the CVR tape, or the other things we've been telling the FBI about, instead of selling me out for a little free publicity?"

"I'll kill him, myself," Manny agreed.

Kyle jumped up again when Harding started talking about impossible working conditions, but the agent pulled him back down again and turned off the TV set. "If I could get out of here I swear I'd chase that moron clear out of the state. I can't wait."

Harding strolled into the office twenty minutes later, looking pleased with himself. He actually grinned at Manny and Kyle.

Kyle was back on his feet in a second. He grabbed Harding by the collar and lifted him off of his feet, his index finger jabbing at Harding's face. The two agents quickly tackled him from behind and dragged him until all four ended up on the floor. Manny hovered over them, hoping to get in one good punch.

After a long moment, Kyle regained control and allowed himself to be dragged to his feet. One of the agents handcuffed him.

"You promised not to talk to the press, you liar. When this is over I'll shove those goofy glasses down your throat."

"Just sit there and be quiet, Matthews," one of the agents said.

"I . . . don't understand why you can't see this," Harding stammered, backing away to where he had protection from the two agents. "I'm your lawyer; I had to respond to the CNN story about the psychological evaluation. Besides, we just gained a million dollars worth of free publicity. We have no choice now but to go forward with the strategy I suggested."

"You mean respond to the story you gave them, don't you? You initiated that press conference to force me to change my mind, so don't give us that crap."

Harding didn't even bother to deny it.

"You could fuck up a two car funeral," Manny threw in.

After a long moment, Harding reloaded. "You heard how the media reacted when I mentioned the blackouts and how the FAA covered up. The press is just dying to attack the government. All they need now is to hear it from you, Kyle."

"But they're never going to," Kyle said. "You're making me look like some kind of nut case. Next thing you know I'll be on that commercial about California nuts. And where did you get that stuff about poor equipment? It didn't come from me."

"I was. . . speaking in general terms," Harding said.

"Were you speaking in general terms when you told them my friends said I was under severe pressure?"

"Why not? Didn't you see the reaction I got? The press is on your side!" Harding eyes pleaded with the two men.

Manny just shook his head. "You were interested in Tyler Harding, that's all. You wanted to get on national TV and resurrect your sorry ass career."

"Auditioning for your next case," Kyle agreed, "that's what you were doing. If you were really representing me instead of you own interests, why didn't you tell the press about the DVD, or the CVR tape? And why not ask them to investigate Butch Moore's background, something that might help?"

Harding started to respond, but Kyle held up hand. "Because that didn't fit with what you've been planning, that's why. Manny and Nancy are the only ones working on my behalf."

Harding saw that it was no use; he sat down and slumped in a chair.

Nancy came hurrying through the door a minute later, waiving her arms. "Did you see it?"

"If you mean Harding's fifteen minutes of fame, yeah, we saw it," Manny said.

Nancy stood over Harding while he cowered in his chair, wrestling with his tie.

"Why?" she asked, staring down at him.

Harding just shrugged his shoulders.

Nancy studied Kyle's expression, wondering why she didn't see a stronger reaction.

"Never mind, it's done now," Kyle finally said, sounding mysterious.

Nancy dropped into a chair and continued to stare at Tyler, her eyes blazing.

Tyler just shifted in his seat, each nervous movement reflecting his guilt.

SIXTY SEVEN

After a less than scintillating meting, during which Harding just sat there looking embarrassed, two federal marshals arrived and took Kyle back to the federal detention center.

Manny drove Nancy back to her hotel.

After riding in silence for several minutes: "I hate to admit it, but the little runt is right about one thing."

"Harding?" Nancy asked. "What's he ever been right about?"

"Kyle no longer has a choice; he needs to let the public hear his side of the story."

"Kyle doesn't agree; he insists he'll tell his story in court."

"Well, if our defense is that he didn't do it, then he needs to convince prospective jurors who *did* do it, and how. He can't wait for a trial to change people's impressions; he'll be dead before he even walks into the courtroom. He needs to get on some talk shows, tell people about the DVD, the bomb, and all that; get prospective jurors thinking about it. All they're thinking about now is the tape recording."

"He'll never do it. He'll consider it begging. He doesn't want people feeling sorry for him."

"This isn't begging; this is war. He's expecting the public to think for themselves because that's what he does; Harding's made that impossible: the public's been brainwashed."

He gave Nancy time to think it over. He guessed that she was worried about Kyle's sponsor, wondering if he would agree.

"Well?"

She began to slowly shake her head up and down: "You're right; we tried working within the system and it had no effect; I guess it's time to put to bed the things Harding said and lay out what we have. If we don't, it'll be too late. Kyle needs to explain the anomalies in the tapes and give prospective jurors some time to buy into it. He's the only one who can explain it."

"The up-side is that the government will have to prove him wrong," Manny agreed. "Their own expert, Andes, won't be able to do that. At least he couldn't when we last talked to him. It won't be easy; he'll face some tough cross examination. But the thing he has going for himself is that he's an expert in these things. He also has a ton of experience in front of TV cameras; jurors will be shocked when they see how normal he is, compared to the impression Tyler has created."

"Plus, he's innocent."

Manny was surprised to hear her say it: maybe she was about to become the lawyer he had always thought she could be, rather than someone's puppet. "We need to get Diane Sawyer or one of those other big wheels to interview Kyle, someone who can draw a large audience."

"I have an idea," Nancy said. "Kelly Edmunds gave Kyle the DVD; let's let her find someone. I'm sure she'd love to be a part of this."

SIXTY EIGHT

Kelly Edmunds couldn't believe what she was hearing; Nancy Corey was offering her the story of a lifetime, an exclusive. She slowly hung up the phone and stared into space. The "Sky Killer" exclusive was hers; Kyle Matthews was finally going to tell his side of the story.

It wasn't as if the phone conversation had been entirely pleasant: Corey had ripped her for making Kyle seem like a nut case. She even forced Edmunds to admit that Tyler Harding had been her "reliable source." Nevertheless, Kelly got the assignment.

Edmunds sat at her desk and stared at the phone, patting herself on the back for having left WDAF when she did. It had been a gamble and it had taken guts, but this was her reward. She decided that she would drop Bob Lewuellin a note, reminding him what an asshole he had been: something like, "Go to hell, Bob, hope you enjoy my exclusive, to be shown on any other network than yours." She sat and smiled for a long time, just thinking about it.

Now, who should she choose to do the interview? Which TV biggie would generate the largest audience? She was in the driver's seat, so even the biggest of the big would have to jump when she called. All that was left now was to find someone who could light up a switchboard.

SIXTY NINE

Barbara Walters didn't hesitate; she not only agreed to do the interview, she even agreed to allow Kelly Edmunds to produce the show for the network and do some local spots. The only disagreement was over the location: Walters wanted to do it in Kyle's prison cell, but Nancy said "no." Nancy thought that interviewing Kyle in jail would leave a "convict image" with potential jurors.

But if they couldn't do the interview in jail, how would they ever get permission from Mallek for Kyle to leave prison and be transported to the local ABC affiliate? Fortunately, Edmunds hadn't chosen Walters for her drawing power alone; Walters had the kind of clout that could move mountains. She soon created such a political furor that Mallek was forced to fold. The interview would be conducted at KCMO TV, in Kansas City, Missouri; Lewuellin and WDAF had been left out in the cold.

The week preceding the interview was filled with continuous promotional spots on the ABC network. The other networks, including Lewuellin's, clamored for a piece of the action, aggressively hounding ABC and their local affiliate for inside information. When they were turned down flat, they scrambled to find family members who might be naive enough to give them some crumbs.

Kyle's team was equally uncommunicative. No matter how hard reporters from the other networks tried, the lid was on.

Both sides kept their silence for the long week that preceded the show.

SEVENTY

A limousine with two FBI agents aboard delivered Kyle to the KCMO studio an hour and a half before the Monday night, 7 P.M., prime time broadcast.

Once inside, Kyle was introduced to a staff determined to make him comfortable and in a talkative mood. ABC was anticipating a ratings bonanza; they were not about to antagonize their infamous guest.

After the preliminary introductions, the show's producer led Kyle and his FBI escorts to a small room in the back of the studio, where coffee, cookies, and soft drinks were spread out on a table. The producer informed Kyle that Barbara Walters had arrived at the Kansas City International airport and was on her way. She smiled and told him to "holler" if he needed anything, but as far as Kyle could see, he'd been sequestered so far away from other human beings it would be impossible for them to hear him. The FBI apparently wanted to keep him away from potential escape routes. A swat team had cordoned off the entire block.

SEVENTY ONE

Kyle's legal team chose to evaluate his performance with an audience, thinking that an audience's reaction might portend a future jury's reaction. They chose the *PLAZA THREE* restaurant on the Country Club Plaza, midtown Kansas City. Small and always crowded, the restaurant and bar were perfect for their purposes.

The five minutes preceding the interview reminded Manny of waiting for the kickoff before a Notre Dame-Southern Cal football game: ninety five percent of the patrons were standing, staring at the TV screen. This would be the first time the public had had a chance to hear the story from the Sky-Killer himself. Nancy concluded that the bar's patrons weren't really interested in hearing Kyle at all; they just wanted an opportunity to confirm his guilt. There were boos whenever his name was mentioned.

It would be a tough sell.

Harding's press conference had made Nancy's father so angry that he had threatened to find another lawyer. It took every verbal skill she possessed just to convince him that there would be no change in strategy. When she reminded him of her objection to hiring Tyler Harding in the first place, he became even angrier; she could feel his cold stare go right through her. He finally agreed to watch the special before deciding whether or not to continue backing "the controller."

While waiting at the bar, Nancy couldn't help but think about Kyle's buddies and how loyal they had been: she smiled when she remembered Andy rummaging around in a dark office trying to find the letter; Kyle telling the story about Karen Davies running through a parking lot scared out of her wits; Rooster, a little guy who would fight anyone who disagreed with Kyle's explanation, and Morrisey, who, while he had only one leg, had the guts of a burglar. Those people were giving everything they had for Kyle. She had never seen such loyalty; it made her question her own. She wasn't exactly sure what had eventually convinced her of Kyle's innocence, but she thought that the loyalty of his friends might have had a lot to do with it: they were standing by him in spite of the fact that they knew nothing more than what they had heard on the tape recording.

*   *   *

Controllers and supervisors from the Kansas City Center packed a private room in the Bigger Jigger. They sat talking quietly with family and friends, waiting for the interview. They were excited; a close friend was about to be interviewed by the famous Barbra Walters. There was plenty of beer, yet the atmosphere was surprisingly subdued.

Ron and Mary were there, as were Paul Hilger and family.

The Bigger Jigger management, afraid of another commotion, scheduled extra security personnel. They even forked over freebies to keep their best customers happy.

The media would not be allowed in this time.

SEVENTY TWO

Barbara Walters came strolling in with her entourage. She had on a blue jacket, blue slacks, a white blouse with a large collar, and high heels. Even with the shoes, she was shorter than Kyle had remembered.

Big smile; polite handshake from both.

Walters didn't recognize Kyle at first, but he remembered her: he had been a guest on *"NOT FOR WOMEN ONLY,"* a local show Walter's had hosted in New York. The other guests on that occasion were an FAA representative and an airline pilot who identified himself as "Captain X." The captain wore a "Lone Ranger" mask and claimed to have seen dozens of near mid-air collisions. He said he wore the mask to prevent retaliation from his company, Mokawk Airlines, but everyone in the industry, including Mohawk Airlines executives, knew who he was.

Walters had been tough on the FAA representative during that show, angry because he had stalled whenever one of her questions pinned him down. She had berated the FAA rep, questioning his honesty and forthrightness. Kyle had no doubt she would try the same thing on him tonight.

"Have we met?" Walters asked after studying Kyle's face carefully.

Kyle decided this was not the time to reminisce.

"No, I don't think so."

"Shall we get started? My understanding is that I'm free to ask whatever I want."

"Take your best shot."

"Count on it." She smiled confidently.

The producer stepped forward, said, "Kelly Edmunds will be conduct-ing interviews from a remote site." She turned to Kyle: "She might have some questions for you, as well."

Walters hesitated. "I didn't agree to that, but I guess it's OK."

Kyle just shrugged his shoulders.

The director walked in with two of his assistants, all three wearing headsets and carrying clip boards. "We'll be doing the interview in an old, abandoned studio, there's more privacy there." He motioned for Walters, Kyle, and the two agents to follow. They passed through hallways clut-tered with lights, cameras, and assorted props, arriving at a small, make-shift stage. It was more like a platform in the middle of warehouse, with two chairs, a couch and a coffee table. It was comfortable looking, but certainly not ostentatious. Cables ran from the set in all directions and cameras on wheels rolled toward strategic locations, each one manned by a man or a woman dressed casually, some wearing flip flops.

Kyle got the message immediately: the location had been chosen be-cause it was a spot where he would have very little contact with station employees or the public. Mallek's imprint was all over it; the deputy at-torney general apparently didn't want Kyle influencing anyone.

Informal as the setting was, Kyle considered it more like a dentist's office under the circumstances: a place to extract something newsworthy from the "guest's" mouth. He looked around and saw the window of what he assumed was an old control room. It was covered with dust, but dozens of eyes looked out. On second thought, this was more like a gas chamber: everyone trying to get close, but not close enough to inhale the gas.

The FBI agents stepped aside and reluctantly allowed Kyle to climb the two steps to the platform. Walters pointed to the couch and he sat down, crossing one leg at the ankle. She sat in a chair opposite, and they both waited while two women brushed their faces with a soft, powdery substance. The one working on Kyle took the longest, frowning and look-ing him over like an executioner.

Walters took a few minutes to look over several sheets of paper. Fi-nally, she looked up and told Kyle there be might some lapses in the conversation while ABC showed file tape or broke for commercials. She told him to look directly at the camera, but not to be too concerned about it.

Kyle had heard it all before; he'd been interviewed many times. Nevertheless, this was different. This time his very life was on the line. He looked down and noticed that one of the camera operators had on dirty jeans with holes in both knees. It had the effect of bringing him back down to earth. Flip-flops, holes in the knees, these were just ordinary people after all. He experienced a kind of transformation at that moment. It occurred to him that he might have been thinking too much about defense and not enough about offensive. He was sick and tired of defense. It was then that he decided not to mince words when answering Walter's questions. He had come there concerned about making accusations without proof, but now he realized that accusations might be the only thing that would get the government's attention. The public wanted specific answers; they weren't going to be satisfied with anything else. He would have to give them specific answers, regardless of how angry it made the government. What more could they do to him?

He watched Walters studying her papers again. No doubt she thought this was going to be a one-way conversation: she would try to pin him in a corner, destroy his confidence. That was what everyone wanted, wasn't it? She was probably expecting him to act remorseful, too.

Kyle slowly inched his way forward on his seat. He decided that if this was intended to be an ass kicking contest, Kyle Matthews, air traffic controller, would be he number one seed.

SEVENTY THREE

Less than one minute until broadcast time.

The studio lowered its collective voice; soon there was total silence.

In the dark, the set looked like a living room in a parking lot, lit only by spotlights. The two participants were all that mattered now; everyone else had disappeared into the shadows. Prying eyes and ears listened as the two prospective combatants chatted quietly, voices subdued.

The seconds ticked away.

The cameras began inching in, guided by mechanical arms. Walters asked Kyle about Laura and the children. She remarked that they must be very worried about him. Kyle smelled the trap: she was loosening him up; playing the sympathy angle and checking to see how responsive he would be. The hard questions, the ones the public wanted, would come once the cameras started rolling. There would be questions about Nancy Corey too, the woman's angle, hoping he would reveal something personal, talk about the separation from his wife.

Kyle's mind flashed back to a live interview he once did on a Washington, D.C. TV station: it was a six o'clock news program the evening after the crash of TWA flight "Five Fourteen." Everyone aboard the aircraft died when it crashed into a spot called Mt. Weather while on an approach to the Dulles airport. Kyle was being interviewed because he had been assigned to the NTSB investigation team.

The key element in the investigation centered on the responsibility for separating the aircraft from the mountain. The regulations state that it's the pilot's responsibility to keep his aircraft at least one thousand feet above any terrain. He or she does this by following an approach chart, one that depicts the proper altitude for each particular geographic location. Nevertheless, when the pilot of TWA Five Fourteen found himself in heavy turbulence, hail, and ice, he immediately descended the aircraft and crashed into the mountain. The station's producer had been warned in advance that Kyle was not allowed to discuss the inadvertent descent until the NTSB released its findings. But just as the cameras began rolling, Kyle noticed that a large reproduction of the approach chart had suddenly appeared behind him, and realized that the anchorman was about to break their agreement.

When the anchorman's very first question was about the inadvertent descent, Kyle simply got up and walked off of the set without saying a word.

Expect some surprises from Barbara Walters too, he thought.

The director's hand became two fingers.

The bright lights came up.

Kyle heard the "tease" and saw motion on a monitor.

Show time!

SEVENTY FOUR

"Good evening.

"Tonight, in this exclusive interview, we will hear from the air traffic controller the FAA says is responsible for causing a mid-air collision in the skies over Kansas City, Missouri. Controller Kyle Matthews continues to insist that he is not responsible, but until tonight has refused to tell his side of the story.

"The mid-air collision on the night of September first represents one of the most tragic events in aviation history. . . "

The television monitor began showing background shots of the crash site; investigators were shown sifting through debris and staring down at a row of body bags.

Walters introduced Kelly Edmunds with a live shot and explained how Edmunds had been following the story from the beginning. Edmunds got enough of a buildup to insure her future success.

Then the cameras focused on Kyle.

"Mr. Matthews has assured me that he will answer whatever questions I ask," Walters explained. She then introduced him and described his background as an air traffic controller. She explained that he had been instrumental in suggesting improvements to the air traffic control system. The introduction was brief and professional, without embellishment. Walters was well aware that the public knew all about him, anyway.

"Mr. Matthews, why don't you tell us in your own words exactly what happened on the night of September first," Walters said conversationally.

Kyle explained that he had been attempting to pull a prank, and that it had failed. He ended his explanation by apologizing for the "stupid prank," but assured the TV audience that his ill-advised joke had nothing to do with a mid-air collision: "I regret that two aircraft exploded and that many people were tragically killed, but I can't accept blame for anything but my own act, which was inexcusable in itself."

"You said, 'exploded'," Walters corrected. "I assume you mean after the collision?"

"There was no collision, not unless the two aircraft got together after they started down."

"Started down? I don't understand."

"I don't actually understand it myself, I jut know that a bomb exploded on one of those two aircraft. What happened after that is still a mystery."

"A bomb? You're telling our audience that a bomb actually caused the collision after the fact?"

"Not exactly, because I don't know exactly what happened. I just know that at least one bomb exploded before those two aircraft went down and that there was no mid-air collision."

"Can you prove that?"

"I could if the evidence from the crash site hadn't been destroyed in a fire. Washington is doing its best to keep their investigation a secret; they don't want the public to know what really happened."

"Are you suggesting that this whole thing is some sort of plot directed by the government?"

"You're putting words in my mouth. All I'm saying is that there are people high up in the government who are happy to see me taking the blame for whatever happened. At least one NTSB official saw evidence of a bomb at the crash site, evidence that might have exonerated me, but the government conveniently assigned him to work with the Russians in Siberia, or wherever. Someone is using this opportunity for their own purposes."

Barbara Walters' eyes flashed excitement. This was good stuff. Anything anti-government was always good for ratings. "Is that just a gut feeling, or did you actually see the proof yourself?"

"No, I didn't see it myself, but I was standing right there when my private investigator and an NTSB investigator saw it. I doubt if the government would agree, though, even if the evidence hadn't been destroyed. They made up their minds as soon as they listened to the center tape recording."

"Why would they want to blame you?"

"Because of the views I have expressed about the computerization and modernization of the air traffic control system."

"But your own lawyer, Mr. Harding, told reporters you might have made an error you don't even remember. He insists you were under severe stress at the time."

"Mr. Harding's comments were never authorized by me. He was dead wrong in saying what he did. I have told Mr. Harding repeatedly that I was not under that kind of stress. I knew exactly what I was doing."

"You admit you knew exactly what you were doing?"

"Yes, absolutely, I was pulling a prank, but that's all. Like I've said dozens of time, I'll take the blame for that."

"But isn't it true that your profession is stressful and that you could have just made a mistake because of the pressure?"

"First of all, there have been studies which show that the air traffic control profession is no more stressful than any other profession. One such study was called the 'Rose Study.' It was done in Boston and took over five years. That study proved that concern over paying your mortgage, driving to work in heavy traffic, or any other such activity, can be just as stressful. As for me, I have stress like everyone else, but nothing that would cause me to do something sadistic. There have been occasions when I've handled thirty aircraft at a time and felt perfectly comfortable, and other times when all I had to do was walk into the building to feel stressed. The night those two aircraft went down I felt fine, good enough to make a fool of myself, I guess."

"At what level do you claim the government is covering up?"

"It has to be pretty high up, certainly higher up than any government agency, because no individual in one of those organizations would have the motive or the clout. Someone close to the White House wants to see me get the blame and has managed to either destroy evidence or at least allow it to be destroyed. Whoever that is, he or she has managed to keep the wraps on investigators working for the NTSB and the FBI."

"Give me some examples of what you call a cover-up."

"I had a DVD that clearly showed there was at least one explosion on one of the two aircraft, before either of them went down. There was also evidence at the crash site: bomb fragments imbedded in luggage and pieces of metal that had been scarred by a bomb blast. All of that was destroyed in the hangar fire, a fire that was no accident. The NTSB and the FBI insist that any bomb evidence resulted from an explosion caused by a mid-air collision, but my expert knows better."

The television cameras moved in tighter as Barbara Walters edged forward in her chair.

"The DVD you're talking about, is that the one our reporter, Kelly Edmunds, gave you?"

Kyle shook his head: "Yes, she made it from TV footage taken on the night of September first."

Walters turned and looked into the camera: "Our reporter, Kelly Edmunds, was the first person to break this story about the DVD. She's standing by now at the crash site:

"What about the DVD, Kelly? Did it actually show that there was a bomb on board one of those flights?"

Kelly Edmunds stood in front of several TV trucks with their satellite dishes. Walter's face appeared alongside hers on the split screen. "Barbara, I only managed to get a brief look at the DVD before I gave it to Mr. Matthews, but it did show several flashes of light, one of which could have come from an exploding bomb. Unfortunately, the DVD was destroyed in that hangar fire. That DVD was the only copy, and the video footage I used to make it from has since disappeared. I did talk with the secretary for Mr. Matthews' lawyer, Mr. Harding. She said a Mr. Moore from the NTSB commandeered the DVD before she had a chance to make copies."

Walters turned back to Kyle: "Exactly what was on the DVD?"

"There were two or three, separate flashes of light in the background. My private investigator thinks that at least one of them was from a bomb exploding."

"Or lighting, perhaps?"

"We checked with the weather bureau: there wasn't any lightning that night. My private investigator witnessed the accident himself and remembers hearing several loud noises that could have been explosions."

"Kelly, where did the video footage you used to make the DVD come from?" Walters asked.

"It was taken by a cameraman from a television station in Kansas City on the night of September first. He was a colleague of mine, shooting video footage of a wedding."

Walters looked into the camera:

"Perhaps someone out there in the public also took a video on the night of September first that could corroborate Mr. Matthews' story. If so, we hope you will contact us."

Walters turned back to Kyle.

"You say there was no lightning that night?"

"That's correct: no lighting and no thunder. But even if there had been it wouldn't explain the bomb damage at the crash site. My private investigator, Mr. Manny Vigil, an expert in such things, told me the markings were identical to what the FBI found after the Lockerbie crash. He participated in that investigation."

Walters kept stealing glances at her producer, hoping that by now, someone had called in with more video. She had less than twenty minutes for a miracle that would turn the interview into a bombshell. Station personnel were scurrying to answer phone calls from the public.

"Has the FBI determined who set the fire that destroyed the hangar containing the evidence?"

"The FBI doesn't communicate with me, so I doubt if I'll ever find out. A special prosecutor is going to be necessary if we're ever going to find out what happened."

"Do you believe it was arson?"

The camera changed to a close-up of Kyle.

"I know it was arson. Given a chance, I'll prove it."

"Will you be able to present evidence of your innocence in court?"

"Bring it on, I can't wait."

Walters changed the subject, stalling while her people answered phone calls and scrambled to find more video.

"Let's talk about this new air traffic system you support. Briefly, why do we need such a system?"

"Because human beings can't handle high volumes of traffic efficiently. We need to use the technology we already have to increase our ability to keep a safe, even flow of air traffic. I'm talking about using computers, because when air traffic volume is light, the job can be is easy, but when air traffic volume is heavy and complex, humans can't keep up. The result is that the FAA has to keep aircraft on the ground. That's why we have delays, and that's why airlines are going broke. Computers have no limitations: one home computer could conceivably formulate and deliver air traffic clearances for every aircraft in the sky and maintain an even flow at the same time. It will eventually happen anyway, it's just a question of time. Meanwhile, the FAA continues to attempt to improve the systems with things like radar platforms that cost the taxpayers millions and have proven to be a bust.. . . . "

". . . Explain 'radar platforms'."

"Similar to what controllers have now, just radar consoles with all kinds of unnecessary dew-dads that provide information controllers really don't need. Now they're going to spend a billion dollars so that pilots can have their own TV screens and enjoy watching controllers work. That kind of Razzle-dazzle doesn't do a thing to improve efficiency or safety; it's just a toy for pilots."

"How can you be so sure computers can handle that task?"

"Because it's already happening in the space program: look at how computers deliver the Discovery vehicle to the space station or the Rover to Mars. In the future, controllers will manage the system and act as a fail-safe, but they won't issue clearances. Unfortunately, the FAA has already spent millions of dollars on a system that was obsolete the day it was put into service; It's like putting fur linings in garbage cans."

Just when Kyle thought Walters would continue to focus on improvements in the air traffic system, she made a right turn and went on the attack:

"What about the rumors coming out of Washington; rumors that you and your friends are putting pressure on the FAA by calling in bomb threats?"

"That's nonsense: All I had time to do before they put me in jail was to run from the media and the FBI. I would never do anything like that, anyway, regardless of how provoked I might be."

"I've heard the FBI has received dozens of bomb threats lately, most of them coming since you were indicted. Did you have anything to do with that, maybe use it to pressure the Justice Department into reducing your charges?"

"No; most bomb threats are called in by business people late for a flight, anyway. The idea is to delay the flight until they can get to the airport. The rest of the bomb threats come from harmless whackos. The FBI knows that."

"You're telling our viewers that ordinary citizens are the ones making bomb threats?"

"Not every bomb threat, of course not. But many of the bomb threats you hear about are made by ordinary citizens, and for the reason I just stated. There are even occasions where an executive will have his or her secretary make the call. I remember one incident when a secretary called an airline and said: 'Mr. Smith says to tell you there's a bomb on board flight so and so.' There are very few bomb threats that are legitimate. Ask the FBI, they'll tell you the same thing."

SEVENTY FIVE

Butch Moore watched the show from his hangar. He wasn't seeing the ass kicking he had expected Walters to dish out. She was milking the story for all it was worth, waiting expectantly for some citizen to call in with another DVD. He wasn't too pleased about the hangar fire references, either.

Moore had been waiting for over twenty-five years to get even with Kyle Matthews and his father, Eric. Troy Moore, Butch's father, had been fired following the 1981 PATCO strike, and he blamed Eric Matthews, who was a director in PATCO at the time. The elder Moore had been convinced that because Eric Mathews was so highly regarded by the FAA, he could have brokered a settlement that would have saved the controller's jobs. But he didn't, and Troy Moore ended up broke and destitute, sleeping on the sidewalks of Washington, D.C. until he finally committed suicide. Meanwhile, Eric Matthews, who Moore insisted went on strike just to keep his union job, was eventually rehired because of a legal technicality.

Now, Moore was in position to get even: all he needed was for Walters to expose Matthews. Once that was done, the government would stop looking for an alternate suspect, Matthews would be out of the way, and Moore could finally relax in his new job, compliments of Mr. Brock.

But his desire for revenge didn't stop there: his sick mind included a detailed plan to make others suffer too, including any FAA manager responsible for the PATCO firings. He even considered running for NATCA president to show the FAA how to run a real strike.

He smiled when Kyle mentioned the DVD. He was proud of the way he had convinced Matthews and Vigil to come to the hangar, then made them witnesses to the hangar fire. It had been one of his better moments: two birds with one stone. He smiled, remembering the look on their faces during the second act, the one where he had to be restrained by firemen. Matthews and Vigil were too embarrassed to even leave their vehicle when they realized how badly they had been duped. He had always seen himself as smarter than everyone else, anyway, and now he had proven it.

The center tape recording was all that mattered now; it couldn't be contradicted no matter what Matthews and Vigil said to Barbara Walters. He had taken a ton of heat for allowing evidence to be destroyed, but nothing he couldn't handle. There was always Brock and Ramsey to cover for him. He was smart enough to know that someone in the NTSB, probably Fred Bell, would eventually spill the beans about the bomb fragments, but with Matthews in jail or dead, there was no way the government could turn back, even if they had to create another cover-up

Nothing had come easily, though; the last thing he'd even considered was that some hound dog bitch of a TV reporter would come up with something that might incriminate him. It was just dumb luck on Matthews' part. Now, the same bitch was scoring big with her exclusive.

He consoled himself by remembering that in the end it wouldn't really matter; Matthews and his stooges still didn't know how he brought down the two planes. They could never understand something that complicated.

Moore clicked his gold pen as he watched and waited. In a way, it was like he was being interviewed himself. After all, he was really the main player in all of this.

Just imagine, Butch Moore being interviewed by Barbara Walters: Could happen.

SEVENTY SIX

During the final commercial break, Walters received word that the interview was causing significant public excitement. She needed to finish strong. It was time to move in for the kill:

"You demanded a public hearing with Deputy U.S. Attorney Spencer Mallek. You charged that the air traffic control tape from the night of September first was either the wrong tape or had been doctored. You turned out to be dead wrong. If you were dead wrong then, why should the public believe you now?"

"I wasn't wrong then, and I'm not wrong now. The voice heard on the center tape recording was mine, I'll admit that, but I didn't put it there because I didn't issue that clearance. I don't know how it got on that tape or what tape it was, but that clearance to climb wasn't broadcast by me on the night of September first."

"So you do admit it *was* your voice?"

Kyle nodded. "Yes, it was."

"Then I don't understand."

"There were two separate transmissions; I learned that when my private investigator and I were allowed to listen to the cockpit voice recorder tape and the center tape played simultaneously. If I had the cockpit voice recorder tape now, I could prove it to you or anyone else."

"Two separate transmissions?"

"Yes, and I know that because the two were different: one, the cockpit voice recorder, had a read-back from the pilot, and the other, the center tape, didn't. There was also a two or three second delay between the two."

"How does the NTSB explain that?"

"The NTSB investigator who listened with me *couldn't* explain it. Now he's disappeared."

"Disappeared?"

"That's right. He can't verify what we heard because we can't find him or his ex boss, the man I mentioned before, Fred Bell. Seems the second man is out of the country, as well. As for the CVR tape, it was destroyed in that fire."

There was just enough time to wrap things up:

"Who is paying for your defense?" Walters asked suddenly. "It has to be more than a fired government employee could afford."

"I wish I could tell you, but I don't know. Far as I know, it's just a generous individual who insists on anonymity."

"In some people's eyes, it looks like it's a reward for committing murder. And doesn't the fact that you won't say who that person is make you appear even more guilty?"

"I can't worry about what people think. Besides, I just said I didn't know who it is myself."

Barbara Walters smiled and leaned forward in her chair. The final questions represented the long awaited woman's angle: "Who is Nancy Corey? Why is she involved? Some media reports say she is an old flame of yours from the time you spent in Washington, D.C."

"I never saw or heard of Nancy Corey before this. I'm sure that if I had, your network or some other network would have come up with some sensational rumor by now."

Walters wasn't fazed by the put down. "Is she the reason you're separated from your wife?"

"No," Kyle said emphatically.

The answer was so decisive that Walters seemed afraid to follow it up.

"If I can sum all of this up, you think someone is out to get you, whether it's the government or not. In short, that means you think someone actually conspired to kill three hundred twenty seven innocent people and blame you. That's difficult to believe."

"Or someone was out to kill Deeter Noonan and I was just a bonus. Whatever the case, the unfortunate victims of the crash just happened to be in the wrong place at the wrong time."

SEVENTY SEVEN

Butch Moore stalked the room and he was no longer smiling. He clicked his ubiquitous gold pen and mumbled to himself: *A one or two second difference? He knows there were two transmissions? How in the hell could he know that?*

"That fucking Matthews," he shouted out loud!

He straightened out his workbench for the hundredth time, picked up a stray wrench and meticulously placed it in its proper place. Then, suddenly, he picked it back up again and fired it across the room. It stuck in the wall.

He figured it out. He'll have them looking deeper into it now.

He gathered himself and walked around some more, thinking. *Where would they look next? I still have some tapes I had intended to destroy, but those are hidden. Could they possibly find them? They might go looking for those tapes. They found the video, who says they won't find the tapes?*

He thought about it and smiled. *Well, if they did he would leave them a little surprise. Matthews thought he was so damn clever. I'll show him how dangerous it can be to get involved in Butch Moore's business.*

He stalked the hangar for an hour before he finally came up with a detailed plan.

Then he ran from his hangar and jumped into his van.

SEVENTY EIGHT

For the first time, Warren Ramsey realized what a formidable foe Kyle Matthews could be, and it frightened him. He could see that Matthew's credibility could be a major obstacle. There would be more interviews now, and Matthews had the communications skills to sway viewers. According to ABC, they were already being flooded with phone calls from surprised viewers; the largest number of calls following one of their interviews in twenty years. According to their poll, not many of the callers believed that the government had anything to do with the mid-air collision, but they did believe they could be hiding something. Worse yet, national broadcasters and reporters were beginning to express their own doubts.

Ramsey knew from sad experience that when the media latches on to a juicy government conspiracy story, they won't let go until careers are destroyed.

Time to cut and run.

Ramsey didn't dare call from his office. He stepped outside the building and called on his cell phone.

"Did you watch the interview?" He asked.

"Yes," Peter Brock answered haltingly.

"She made him look like St. Jude. Meet me for breakfast tomorrow at 9 A.M. You know where."

SEVENTY NINE

Brock ordered room service under an assumed name and waited for Ramsey to arrive. His Hay Adams hotel room offered a magnificent view of the White House and Lafayette Park, but he wasn't in the mood for sight seeing today.

Ramsey barged in without knocking, threw his dark blue suit jacket on a bed, and plopped down in a plush chair. The two men had always enjoyed the peace and privacy they found in this small, private hotel, but rumors floating around between agency heads and talk show blabbermouths had eliminated any possibility of peace or privacy today.

"The newspapers and talk shows are killing us," Ramsey said, opening and closing the clasp of his Rolex watch. "I hate having to hide out like this all the time." Ramsey's watchband made an annoying "snap" each time, adding to Brock's nervousness.

Brock shook his head. "I know."

"I can't believe they're making a hero out of this guy," Ramsey went on. "*NIGHTLINE* is about to do a show on air traffic control deficiencies. This is exactly what the president didn't want. He's called me three times today."

"It's alarming, I agree," Brock said. "Unfortunately, the man handled himself well. He sounded believable."

"You sound like you're on his side, for Christ's sake."

Brock felt the rebuke. "I'm just saying what the public is saying; it doesn't change anything. Why are you putting this on me?"

Ramsey twisted in his seat and looked out the window, trying to control himself. When he looked back his face had hardened.

"Did you know that Moore was once fired for making false radio transmissions?"

"False transmissions, I don't understand."

"What? You put this man in charge of a mid-air collision investigation and you didn't know a damn thing about him? It took me one phone call to learn about the false transmissions."

Ramsey realized he was raising his voice. He looked around, forgetting for a moment that they were alone.

"I told you everything I knew about Moore right after I put him on that committee. I haven't had time to do a complete background check; it would have been too late, anyway. Everything happened so fast."

Ramsey sighed and shook his head. "I told you before we could be considered part of a cover-up; now I'm telling you we could even be considered co-conspirators. What if that fire was no accident? What if Moore deliberately destroyed the evidence? If he did, and if the FBI can prove it, they might connect *us* with Moore. Think of what Matthews' lawyer could make of that."

"But we haven't really done anything; we're in the clear."

"You've got to be the most naive person I've ever met," Ramsey said. He took several long seconds to cool down. "Well," he finally said, "I never thought I would even consider something like I'm going to suggest now, but I can't take any more chances. We're going to have to do something drastic."

Brock wasn't sure he wanted to hear it. "Well, we do need to have all our ducks lined up," he added stupidly.

"I'm not talking about ducks, I'm talking about drastic action, you moron."

"I just meant . . . "

"Never mind!"

Brock wondered if Ramsey might be on the verge of a nervous breakdown. He turned his head away, afraid to look Ramsey in the eye.

Ramsey, still fuming, "Our damned careers are at stake here. I'm not just talking about our jobs; I'm talking about our careers! We could even end up in jail for obstructing justice. I don't know about you, but I really don't care to see that happen."

"I think you're exaggerating," Brock blurted without thinking first.

"Oh?" Ramsey shouted contemptuously: "What about the 'two second thing' that Matthews mentioned, or the difference between the two recordings? Did you forget to tell me about that, too?"

Brock shook his head. "No. . . , of course not. It's the first time I've heard either of those things mentioned. Maybe we should talk about this later, after we've had time to assess the situation."

"We can't wait until 'later,' goddammit. We're already up to our assholes. Where are those two NTSB investigators Matthews talked about right now?"

"Bell is still in Russia helping with a crash investigation. The Russian government asked for him. Under the circumstances, I thought it would be a good idea to keep him there."

"And the other?"

"He resigned. He's on vacation somewhere. Can't be reached."

"Great, just great; nothing like sending the principle NTSB investigators off somewhere and giving the job to some fucking madman. That won't look at all suspicious, will it?"

"The NTSB checked the cockpit tapes thoroughly before they were destroyed," Brock said earnestly. "As far as I know, they didn't discover anything about a two second delay."

"Did it ever occur to you that this Butch Moore might have thought otherwise and deliberately destroyed the tapes?"

Brock's expression reminded Ramsey of a scolded child's.

"And what about Hufnel?" Ramsey added. "He was supposed to convince Matthews to plead guilty."

"Maybe I should talk to him again," Brock said.

"It's too damn late for that. We could be headed for jail if we don't do something immediately. We have to make a deal with Matthews' lawyer and get Moore out of the picture for good."

"But if Matthews gets off easy, he'll be back shooting his mouth off again. The president needs him in jail, permanently."

"The deal we make will include a promise to keep his mouth shut. Most people believe Matthews is guilty by now, anyway. We won't have any more problems if we can just get him out of the spotlight. I'll have Potorf call Judge Stone and tell her we're considering making Matthews an offer. If he agrees to plead guilty, we'll make up some mitigating circumstances that will explain the collision, some technical problem beyond his control. We'll think of some type of punishment consistent with pulling a prank and that will be that. His lawyer needs a win; we'll promise to make him look like a genius."

"Mallek will have a fit."

"Who gives a shit about Mallek? I'll have the Attorney General tell Mallek the president wants it this way. Mallek thinks the President is god almighty, anyway."

Brock suddenly realized what else Ramsey had said: "You mentioned something about 'getting Moore out of the picture.' Exactly what did you mean?"

"Moore is a runaway freight train. I'll have someone pay him a visit."

"What for?"

"You don't want to know."

EIGHTY

Spencer Mallek stormed out of a meeting with Attorney General Matt Potorf and stalked the halls of the Justice Department, ranting, raving, and ignoring anyone he happened to bump into. Potarf had insisted the president wanted him to "prepare" an offer to Kyle Matthews, just in case the government decided to go in that direction. How dare Potorf, or even the President of the United States, consider allowing a mass murderer to just walk away from such a heinous crime? Mallek visualized Matthews lobbing tennis balls in some federal country club and bragging about what he'd gotten away with. What kind of punishment was that? After all, didn't the government have the 'smoking gun,' the tape recording that Matthews' lawyers had been unable to refute?

The more he thought about it, the more he realized his instincts had been correct: some politician had been caught with his pants down, and the repercussions were a threat to the president.

Mallek had begun to feel uncomfortable right after Matthews' assault oh his office. The feeling skyrocketed after he had called the NTSB and listened to some pathetic story about how Fred Bell was so important to the Russians that the NTSB could allow him to interrupt a major airline investigation. Mallek knew better, this was what Washington insiders referred to as the White House squeeze: someone at the top had squeezed the president, and now the president was squeezing everyone below until the fire was out. As a result, the man at the bottom of the squeeze, Spencer Mallek, might have to surrender the biggest case of his life and take the blame when the feces hit the fan.

Well they weren't going to get away with it. He would go ahead and prepare the offer, but not before he arranged to channel the blame to wherever it belonged.

From the time his flight left Washington until it landed at the Kansas City International airport, Mallek took his anger out on everyone he came in contact with, including Jerry Rhinehart. The flight crew was only too happy to see him go.

As Mallek's limo made its way down Interstate I-635, headed for his Kansas City office, Rhinehart studied the fall colors outside his window. He was tired of Mallek's harassment; his insistence that he knew who was behind the proposed offer. He looked over to see if another attack was immanent, but for once Mallek seemed to be concentrating on something else, no doubt going over a list of his enemies.

Mallek was deep in thought, recalling the events of the past week and wondering what had changed. In spite of all of his contacts and the chits he'd called in, he had been unable to get at the truth; not a single soul in Washington would even discuss the case with him. Worst of all, the coroner in Kansas City had announced that Danny Houston had died from drowning, rather than the fire in Matthews' garage. If what Matthews had said in his office was true, if there really was evidence of a conspiracy, everyone in Washington probably knew about it except him. But why hide it from the chief prosecutor? Maybe he could have helped, guided them to a solution that wasn't a complete wash. He tried to rationalize things by reminding himself that it wasn't his fault; he had a duty to follow the president's orders. Still, he wasn't going to give in that easily. It was time for him to bring in the usual suspects and grill them until one or more spilled his or her guts. He would put them on the spot; ask the kind of questions where equivocation was impossible.

His limo had barely made it to the curb before he jumped out and stormed through the front door of the federal building. Rhinehart had to run to catch up.

"It's so wonderful to be working with professionals," he mumbled over his shoulder as they stormed down the hall.

They entered his temporary office and he pointed to a large conference table stacked with files.

"Am I supposed to go over those?" Rhinehart asked.

"No, just sit down," he barked, before sitting himself and shoving several files to the floor.

Rhinehart waited while he stewed.

"Well, then, is there something else you need for me to do?"

Finally, Mallek leaned over and glared at him. "I'm going to ask you once more: do you or do you not know why I'm being forced to prepare Matthews an offer?"

Mallek's paranoia was beginning to anger Rhinehart; he wanted to tell him to go to hell. He took a long time answering, his way of showing his own frustration. "No, I do not. I've already told you that, twice."

It irked Mallek to have to drag information form a subordinate. He wanted them to think he was always in the loop. Rhinehart picked up some files from the floor and ignored his glare.

"So what is all this talk about a DVD," he asked quietly. "What is it they think they have?" For the first time, his question didn't carry its usual sarcastic tone, a sign he badly needed the information and might even be willing to grovel a little.

"Supposedly, it was made from video footage taken by a TV station," Rhinehart answered. He knew the details, but intended to be deliberately vague. He wanted to make Mallek work for it; make him suffer the indignity he always felt.

"That's all you know?"

"It was taken on the night of September first. It showed flashes of light in the background."

"Flashes of light? Matthews' lawyers are banking on 'flashes of light' on a video? That's why Potorf asked me to prepare an offer?"

"Matthews' private investigator claims there was a bomb on one the aircraft. . . "

"Never mind, I know about the luggage and all that. Typical defense garbage; I'm not concerned about that stuff." Actually, he was very concerned.

"Barbara Walters asked the public for videos. Did anything come of that?"

"No. All the network got from the public was junk they couldn't use."

"What else?"

Rhinehart's pauses always equaled Mallek's, another way to counter his abusive behavior. "Matthews' private investigator claims to have seen the collision. He says he heard a bomb go off."

Mallek turned up his nose. "We'll tear him apart if he testifies to that; a jury will never believe a defendant's private investigator, anyway. Tell me about this two second discrepancy, or whatever it was Matthews brought up during the interview."

Rhinehart waited until he put it in the form of a question.

"Well?" he said.

"What about it?"

His eyes got tighter. "Tell me what he meant, and stop acting like *you're* the defendant."

"All I know is that the NTSB thinks it was probably radio interference."

Mallek frowned. "Radio interference? Well, if that's all they have, and since you seem to be in the know, maybe you can tell me why I've been ordered to prepare an offer for this man."

Rhinehart shook his head. "All I know is what I've learned second hand. If Potorf didn't tell *you*, he certainly wasn't going to tell *me*."

"There's nothing new on the air traffic control tape recording is there? I mean, they haven't changed their mind about that?"

"Not that I know of," Rhinehart said.

Mallek paused, studied Rhinehart's eyes for a long moment, said, "Are you sure you're telling me everything? Can you think of any reason Washington would want me to make a deal with this man?"

"No."

"Well, you better be telling the truth. I'm going to get to the bottom of this. God help you if you're lying."

Mallek sat for several, long seconds before he suddenly reached into his pocket and pulled out a piece of paper. He set it on the table in front of Rhinehart.

"What's this?" Rhinehart asked.

"A list of the people I need to talk to. Get them here tomorrow, and don't take no for an answer."

Rhinehart studied the list. "What is there left to talk about?"

"Just do it," he said.

Rhinehart was afraid the volcano was about to blow, and when the volcano is about to blow, you stand back. Nevertheless, and even if he was angry with him, he knew that underneath it all Mallek was still a dedicated man. He couldn't just stand by and see him jump off of a cliff. "These are very important people; they'll never agree to come once they know about the proposed offer. At the very least, they'll want to know why we didn't discuss this with them while we were in Washington."

"Because I'm the Deputy U.S. Attorney prosecuting a federal crime and I hadn't decided to question them at the time. I'm tired of being left in the dark, so just do as I say. And if they give you any trouble, just tell them I suspect a conspiracy; they can either come or I'll subpoena them."

He stomped out of the room.

Rhinehart sat staring at the list. Potorf's mandate had done something to Mallek. Had he underestimated him? Was Mallek really that interested in justice, enough that he was willing to ruin his career, or was he just angry because he hadn't been consulted? Rhinehart considered warning him again, questioning whether or not he really wanted to step on the president's toes. But after thinking it over and remembering the look on his face, he decided it wouldn't do any good, anyway.

There would be hot lava flowing from the volcano tomorrow, he could feel the burn already.

EIGHTY ONE

The following day, the FBI Director, the FAA Administrator, the head of transportation security, and the Chairman of the NTSB met with Mallek in a conference room, one at a time.

Rhinehart watched with amazement as the lords of government marched into what was essentially a battleground. Loud denials reverberated through the wall; shouting could be heard from both sides. Then, after only a short time, each one left with a red face, slamming the door behind them. If any of them knew anything that would necessitate making Matthews an offer, Mallek didn't seem to have discovered it.

Late in the day, the last victim, the Chairman of the National Transportation Safety Board, arrived for her turn. The FBI Director was just leaving as she entered the war zone. Mallek stood in the doorway and watched to see if the two exchanged signals. They didn't appear to.

The Chairman took her seat while Mallek did his best to act unconcerned. She was in her mid thirties, very pretty, and was dressed in a stylish pants suit, white shirt and a "Save the Children" tie. She had a reputation for being intelligent and perceptive. Mallek wondered how anyone so young could achieve such an important political position, even if she did have a Yale degree. He decided to be very circumspect, sensing she was very much in control. He didn't mention anything about the proposed offer, hoping she might be caught off guard and reveal something. They discussed the mid-air investigation, but only in general terms. At one point, he moved from the other side of the conference table and sat next to her, smiling. He studied her carefully, watching for signs she might be nervous.

Finally: "I'm sorry you had to come all this way," he said, "but I'm concerned about your investigation." He looked into her eyes, but her expression didn't indicate concern. "Do you know why I asked you to come?"

She shrugged and smiled.

He came right out with it: "The president has decided he might offer Kyle Matthews a deal. Have you heard about that?"

She nodded "no."

"I'm trying to figure out why he thinks such an offer is necessary. One of the things I've considered is that one of your top investigators, a Mister Fred Bell, may have compromised the investigation by allowing a friend, a private investigator, to look at some luggage at the crash site."

Her eyes slid away from him while she thought about it: "I've heard that some private investigator thinks there were bomb fragments in some of the luggage, but I talked to Mr. Moore, the man who took over the investigation for Mr. Bell, and he assures me that he and his experts inspected the luggage themselves, long before the hangar fire. He insists the damage to the luggage resulted from an explosion caused by the mid-air collision and was nothing more than what one would expect. The explosion sent small shards of metal and plastic everywhere, including, of course, the luggage."

Mallek studied her expression and smiled. "That's what I've heard, myself. But I'm wondering if Mr. Bell said anything different before he left the country?"

The Chairman smiled back. "I didn't talk to Mr. Bell myself; I've been relying on Mr. Moore. He told me he received a complete briefing from Mr. Bell before he took over."

Mallek stared her down for several seconds, looking for the lie, but couldn't find one. "Well then, do you think Matthews' private investigator might have scared Washington off? Maybe Mr. Bell agreed with the private eye and was sent packing to keep him quiet."

"That's not possible; Mr. Bell would have informed me if he thought there had been a bomb."

"That same private investigator claims to have witnessed the collision and heard a bomb explode. Have you heard anything of that nature?"

She shrugged. "No, just what Matthews said during the Barbara Walters' interview."

"Matthews' lawyers seem to think the DVD would have proven that there was a bomb." He smiled; "I believe they call that the 'Pygmalion Principle'."

"Yes, the 'self-fulfilling prophesy', that's exactly what it was," she agreed. "But that will never fly. They no longer have the DVD, and no jury is going to take their word for it." The chairman realized she was starting to sound like a schoolgirl sucking up to the teacher.

"Exactly the way I feel," Mallek said. He examined the chairman's expression once more; if she was lying, she was good at it.

"And the cockpit voice recorder, I know it was destroyed, but is there anything I should worry about there?"

"No. We will definitely have to take the heat for allowing evidence to be destroyed, but that can't be helped. The airport authority is suing the company that failed to remove the oil and gas drums in time; that should lessen the impact there."

"And the 'two second thing?'"

"Just a signal delay or something."

"You checked Mr. Moore's background? I hope you realize he could be an embarrassment to the president if the public thinks we didn't exercise due diligence."

"I had nothing to do with putting Mr. Moore in charge. Peter Brock was responsible for that. I can only assume he checked on the man's background thoroughly."

Mallek almost came out of his chair. He had to restrain himself. "Who told you that?"

"It was passed along in the usual way, through the chain of command."

"Did the chain of command also mention who sent Mr. Bell to Russia?"

"No, I took that call myself. Peter Brock said it was an official request from the Russian government. I've been asking around to see when he would return, but they keep referring me to the State Department, and the State Department doesn't seem to know. They said it might be a year or more."

The fog was beginning to lift.

"Did Mr. Brock say why *he* put Mr. Moore in charge of the investigation? I would think that would be your job."

She paused while she thought about it: "I think he mentioned that Mr. Ramsey had ordered it; he needed Mr. Moore because Moore is an electronics expert, something to do with black boxes."

Mallek took a few seconds to control himself: "Can I assume there's been nothing new regarding the center tape recording, we're still sure it hasn't been tampered with?"

"Yes, absolutely, Mr. Moore confirmed the FBI's findings."

"And both the FBI and the NTSB are convinced that in spite of the fire, the evidence that was destroyed, and all that, the center tape recording will suffice for a conviction?"

"Yes. No one has given me a reason to think differently."

Mallek was out of questions. He sat staring at the wall.

"Is there anything else?" the Chairman finally asked.

"Well," Mallek said, standing with a big smile, "I just wanted to insure that there will be no surprises and that Mr. Bell is out of the country on legitimate business. We need to insure that all of our musicians are playing from the same sheet of music.

"And. . . ," he said, "we need to make sure there is only one conductor." He made like a bandleader, grinning and waving his imaginary baton as if he'd just won the lottery.

The Chairman wondered about his sanity.

EIGHTY TWO

Judge Stone wouldn't take "no" for an answer; she ordered Tyler Harding to be in her office at 9 A.M. the following morning.

"And bring that woman with you."

Stone was still reeling from the attorney general's phone call. He had acted as if the call was routine at first, then threw her a bombshell, saying, "How have you enjoyed your brief career as a federal Judge, not counting tomorrow?"

The interpretation being that there might not be a "tomorrow."

"I'm not sure what you mean, sir."

"We might have to offer Matthews a deal if he refuses to plead guilty." Then he asked if she had talked to Matthews' attorney, and reminded her that a guilty plea would look good on her record. He also mentioned that if she could change his mind, the government might be willing to offer Matthews a deal and reward her, as well. "The only condition would be that he would have to promise never to lobby for changes to the air traffic control system again." He then went on to explain the overall terms Washington was considering.

Stone reluctantly told him that she hadn't heard anything about Matthews changing his plea, and that she hadn't really thought about approaching him or his lawyers.

Potorf went on to mention how pleased the president would be if Matthews changed his mind. He hinted, without actually saying it, that it was actually the president who was responsible for his call. He had sounded disappointed by her response and suggested it might be time for her to start thinking about talking to Mathews' lawyers.

She immediately started thinking about it.

*　　　　　*　　　　　*

Tyler did bring Nancy, though he had been tempted not to. Nancy had become a more newsworthy person than Harding himself lately, and he resented it. She was even featured on the prime time TV show, *EARLY EDITION*. Meanwhile, Harding's only publicity had come from local and national commentators who constantly ridiculed him after Kyle Matthews refuted what he had said in his press conference.

Stone sat behind a desk in her temporary office, not bothering to offer the two lawyers a seat. She looked Nancy over carefully, surprised by Nancy's rock-solid persona. Her bony face peered out at the two lawyers over her reading glasses.

"I just wanted to get a few things straight," she said. "I'm just a temporary appointment, as you both know, so I'm sure you can understand that I want to do the best I can while I'm here. Without in any way suggesting it, I'd like to know right now if the defendant intends to change his plea to guilty. This case has drawn a mountain of publicity; the press has agitated the situation until it's now a bigger deal that the O.J. Simpson case. We don't need that; no one will profit from another mind-boggling year or two of second guessing, period."

She studied each lawyer's expression; one long look at a time.

Both nodded affirmatively, not knowing what else to do, but beginning to understand what the punch like would be.

"Mr. Harding, does your client intend to change his plea to guilty or not?"

Tyler looked surprised. "No, your honor. He says he's not guilty."

"I see. And you believe him?"

"That's what he says, I have no choice."

"Do you really mean you have 'no choice', Mr. Harding, or are you anxious for a trial so you can pull one of your patented 'off the wall' defenses, some whacky scheme designed to get your name in the law journals. Because if that's what you're up to, you can forget it."

"All I know is that he doesn't intend to change his plea; he insists that he's not guilty."

"Would either one of you enlighten me on that, for god's sake? How can someone so obviously guilty be stupid enough to say otherwise? Sources have informed me that the government might even be willing to make your client a generous offer if he changes his mind. Considering that he's responsible for killing hundreds of people, I'd say that's something you should strongly consider."

"We heard the rumor," Harding answered meekly, "but we haven't been approached, and our client isn't interested, anyway. He says that he made no transmission to . . . "

"I know all that," Stone interrupted. "Don't waste my time with that crap. Just tell me why he's being so intransigent?"

For the first time, Nancy answered for Tyler: "Because it's his decision and we respect it. We're going to defend him with everything we have."

Stone threw Nancy a cold stare: "Can you tell me what the nature of that defense will be?"

"Not at this time. We're still preparing."

"I hope you don't think that crap your client gave Barbara Walters will save him. And considering Mr. Harding's reputation, I don't see how he has a chance of winning. You, Mr. Harding, could redeem your career by convincing your client to take the government's offer. No matter what that offer is, it's bound to be better than the alternative. You'll get credit for brokering a good deal and your client might escape the death penalty. You're a fool to waste this opportunity. It could well be your last."

She waited for a response, but Harding just stood with his mouth open.

"I remind you once again, I have no intention of becoming the laughing stock of the judicial system by allowing some absurd defense. If you're planning to bring up some highfalutin theory and expect me to allow it, you are barking up the wrong alley. I assure you that if you disregard my advice you will get no slack from me in the courtroom."

Stone had just verified that she would be the trial judge, something they were hearing officially for the first time. She paused to let it sink in. It gave Nancy cold chills.

Stone leaned back in her wooden chair, extending her bony arms and legs straight out to the edge of her desk. She balanced the chair on its two back legs.

"You know, I'm amused that you think you have a case here. I've tried to give you a message, but you don't seem to get it. You remind me of one of my husband's fishes, floating around in a little tank, thinking he or she sees the whole universe. Meanwhile, the observer looks down at nothing but an object that can be eliminated by urinating in the tank.

"Fish live in their own little world," she went on, "just like the two of you. You're just two little fishes swimming around, waiting for the flood."

She stopped smiling and let her chair fall forward, slamming the floor.

Harding winced.

"I may well be the one to do just that."

She waited for the thought to sink in.

Nancy's anger had reached the boiling point. She looked over at Harding and nudged him with her knee. How much crap was the little fish going to take? Apparently, a whole lot.

The judge adjusted her glasses. She saw Harding cast a nervous look at Nancy.

"And you, Ms. Corey, you look like an intelligent young woman. Do you agree with Mr. Harding on this?"

Nancy paused. "I considered several options, at first," she lied, "but now that we've discovered the truth, I've changed my mind; my recommendation is that we go all the way."

"Well then, Miss Corey, I'll give *you* the same advice I gave Mr. Harding: convince Kyle Matthews to plead guilty and take the government's deal. That's the last advice you'll get for nothing."

"That's up to our client," Nancy bristled.

"And it's your obligation to do what is best for your client. In this case I am making that easy for you. I can tell you what's best, because I can see into the tank better than either of you. The government is ready to deal, even though they have a solid case. It's in everyone's interest not to drag this out. I can be the intermediary; I'll tell the attorney general your client will consider a deal and make the transition as easy as possible for you. He might even throw in some goodies; who knows."

"We don't even have any idea what the offer is," Harding said eagerly. All we have are rumors."

"I'll let the deputy attorney general explain the details. All I'm asking is that you consider his offer. Your client will probably spend some time in one of those country club prisons where he'll play tennis and live on the government's dole." She caught herself. "Let's make something perfectly clear, I'm not ordering you to accept anything, I'm just suggesting that if there's cooperation here, it might be a solution for everyone; maybe even save the careers of some of Mr. Matthews' friends in the FAA."

Stone's eyes wandered back and forth between the two lawyers for a long moment.

Harding stood like a pane of glass, unable to move for fear he might crack, but Nancy made a face to show how revolted she was.

"Every possible consideration would be given to the fact that your client has served as an air traffic controller under stressful conditions," Stone added. "His guilty plea would be couched with mitigating circumstances that could be worked out between you and the prosecutor. No one wants to see the man die."

Nancy suspected that Stone had one more shoe to drop. "And. . . ?" she asked.

Stone hesitated, eyes dropping, "There would have to be complete agreement that Mr. Matthews would drop all attempts to cause disruption within the Department of Transportation," she said offhandedly.

Nancy frowned. "What does that mean, 'disruption'?"

"Your client could probably tell you more about that than I can. I only know that the government is quite concerned about some of his public views."

"So, in other words, shut your mouth and we'll let you live?" Nancy blurted.

Stone blanched and threw Nancy a savage look.

"We'll talk to our client. It's his decision," Harding interrupted, grabbing Nancy's arm.

"You do that," Stone said, "but don't take too long because this is the only chance you'll get. It could save your client's life."

Nancy jerked her arm away. "No, that's not going to happen," she said with a fierce look. "We're not taking any deal."

Stone hesitated, gave each of them another scorching look, then put her head down and waived them away.

The two lawyers started to leave.

Nancy couldn't resist. She stopped and looked back at Stone. "Thanks for giving us little fish the big picture."

EIGHTY THREE

Nancy leaned against the wall of Kyle's cell, fighting mad. "The nerve of that woman, predicting what will happen before the trial even begins. 'Country club prison,' my ass; she'd like to send Kyle to Alcatraz, even if it is closed. Whatever anyone gets from that bitch, they better get it in writing." Everyone but Harding was eating a hamburger and fries, smuggled in under Manny's coat. Harding just leaned against the walk, sulking.

Laura, standing next to Nancy, shook her head. "Maybe we should ask for a different judge."

"Finish eating before the guard gets in trouble," Kyle interrupted, sitting on his bunk next to Manny. "He's doing me a favor letting you guys bring in food. I'm not going to plead guilty no matter what anyone says, anyway, so who cares what Judge Stone wants. Let's just discuss where we go from here."

"*You* better care," Nancy said. "Stone is going to be the trial judge. And don't underestimate her; she wants to kick your ass so bad it makes me sick. She actually said that she was going to piss in your tank."

Manny said, "Your interview must have scared the government a lot more than we thought, Kyle." He smiled: "You were good, for a controller."

"And yet here I am," Kyle said, smiling weakly.

"Yeah, here we all are," Nancy agreed.

Manny: "Can't believe they could hide all that evidence. This is like shoveling shit against the tide. I thought the FBI had more integrity than to just ignore evidence."

"Agencies don't cover-up, people do." Kyle suggested.

"Like Mallek?" Nancy asked.

"No motive," Kyle said. "He wants a trial, a chance to show what a murderous scumbag I am and what a defender of truth and justice he is. He would never offer me a deal if he had his way. If there's an offer brewing, it isn't coming from Mallek, it's coming from whomever my interview frightened the most. Someone is apparently feeling very threatened."

Manny: "Ok, but who?"

Kyle: "Whoever put Moore in charge of the investigation would be my first guess."

Nancy: "Or the individual Moore threatened, who in turn went to someone higher up for help, who in turn asked someone even higher up for help. The threat has to have been a real good one, that's for sure; good enough to make someone think their ass is in a crack."

Manny: "Couldn't have been the NTSB Chairman, she hasn't been in office long enough to bump up that kind of threat."

"You're right; it has to be someone above her," Kyle agreed. "Maybe even the president, for all I know."

Nancy said, "I think we can all agree that whoever is willing to make us an offer knows by now that there was no mid-air collision, or at least suspects it. He wouldn't be working that hard to shut you up if he didn't. We just need to climb the bureaucratic ladder until we find the individual who has the clout to make an offer."

"It's not going to be an offer; it's going to be a threat, 'take it or leave it,'" Manny said. "We can't trust anyone."

"You better think this over, Kyle," Harding insisted. "If the person you're talking about is that threatened, he might be offering the deal of a lifetime."

"That your recommendation, too, Manny?"

Manny hesitated, sighed. "No, this isn't some parking ticket. The best you could get from the government would be life."

"We need to be realistic," Harding repeated.

"What about you, Nancy?" Kyle asked.

"Tell them we'll settle for community service and time served. If they won't agree to that, tell them to shove it."

"Well then, since Tyler suddenly seems to fear going to trial, are you ready to take his place?"

Nancy, hurriedly, "No, that's not part of the equation."

"Well then," Kyle said, after a long pause, "I'm going to accept Nancy's recommendation and tell them to shove it. Better still, I'm not going to tell them anything; let them sweat." He roused himself from his bunk and stretched. "I'll take the stand and take my shot; make the government explain why there were two transmissions and a two second delay. Let's just hope I can explain why, myself."

"You better do more than that," Nancy said, "You better give them another target. The jury will come into the courtroom looking for blood; if not your blood, then whoever's blood they can get. You can't expect them to just walk away without hanging somebody, not when the public is this riled. If you say there was a second transmission, you'll have to tell them who made it and how. Otherwise, they'll assume your explanation is just another excuse."

"Butch Moore, that's who we have to give them," Manny agreed. "Tyler's right about one thing, though, we don't have a lot of time. If Moore's still alive, we have to find him and get him in the courtroom where they can see his ugly face. Since we know he made those false transmissions, that's how we should introduce him to the jury. Once they see him, they'll have a better chance to picture him committing the crime. We'll let them know what kind of man he really is."

Kyle, thinking, said, "What about that psychiatrist in Kansas City who treated Moore during the strike? I think his name was 'Marone.' Maybe he'll give us some ammunition, Manny. We should check out Moore's cabin in St. Joe, too. See if anybody there knows anything about him."

Manny stood up. "I think I'll talk to Alice Houston first; show her a picture of Moore. If she agrees he's the man her husband took to the center, that could tie things together a little better."

Nancy motioned to Tyler, "Let's go, Tyler, we need to work on some motions." She called out to the guard.

"Who in the heck is this Moore guy, anyway?" Laura asked with a puzzled expression.

"He was fired for making false transmissions during the strike," Manny answered. "You remember; it was all over local television at the time."

Laura put her hand to her mouth. "If you need someone to testify that he was at the center the day of the accident, I can do that."

"You saw him there? When?"

"It was the morning of the accident, about nine O'clock. I brought Kyle his softball equipment."

"Softball equipment?" Manny asked.

"Kyle was supposed to play softball right after work, but he forgot his glove and shoes, so I brought them to him. Moore was coming out of one of those rooms downstairs. I remember because he seemed shocked to see me. I just never made the connection."

"What room Laura?" Manny asked. "Who was he with?"

"I don't know, one of those equipment rooms near the cafeteria. He was by himself."

"We need to know the exact room?"

She thought about it for a long moment: "The one just to the right of the cafeteria."

"For the record," Manny said, "that's the recorder room."

"That's the missing link," Nancy said, grabbing Laura and hugging her.

"Are you telling me he's the man responsible for killing all those people?" Laura asked. "That's insane; he looks more like Santa Claus."

"Do you remember Danny Houston's wife mentioning a fat man with a red face?" Kyle asked.

"The realization hit Laura. "My god, yes!"

"Let's don't get ahead of ourselves," Nancy cautioned. "Even if we could prove that Moore was in the recorder room that day, we might never be able to prove what he did there."

"Well then, I guess we're just going to have to ask Moore, himself," Manny said.

EIGHTY FOUR

Funerals frightened Manny Vigil. He kept his phobia a secret for fear it might hurt his macho image.

After almost turning back twice, he found himself standing in the rain beside Danny Houston's grave in Olathe, Kansas. The rain came down softly, as if not wanting to disturb the mourners; nevertheless, Manny's new suit was soaked through and through.

There was a large crowd, which surprised Manny: he had heard that Danny didn't have many friends. He decided that most of them must be friends of Alice Houston's.

Mrs. Houston was standing just a few feet away. She was dressed in a dark suit, with a veil hiding her face. Her head bowed as the priest said a final prayer. She seemed dignified, not overly emotional.

When the service was over, Manny approached her, stopping short for a few seconds because he could see was crying. He waited until she began walking toward her car before following again. When most of the crowd began fanning out toward their own cars, he stepped forward.

"Mrs. Houston? I'm Manny Vigil. Very sorry for your loss."

Alice Houston looked up slowly, surprise and disgust registering when she realized who Manny was. She looked as if she was going to say something hurtful, seemed to change her mind, and just shrugged.

"I know this is a bad time, but would you mind looking at this picture and see if you recognize this man?" Manny asked, handing her the picture. "Is this the man you saw with your husband?"

Alice Houston backed away, refusing to take the picture for a moment. Finally, she took the picture and studied it halfheartedly.

"It was dark," she said hesitantly, handing the picture back. "I only saw him for a second or two."

She started walking again, but Manny stepped in front of her. A funeral home representative had been holding a limousine door open for her. He moved to get in between them, but the Badger's stare caused him to think better of it.

"But you do think this was the man you saw, don't you; the man you told Kyle and Laura Matthews about?"

Alice Houston seemed too tired to resist any longer.

"Look," she said, "Danny didn't introduce him to me. He wasn't good at that type of thing."

"Yes, I know," Manny said sympathetically, "but all I'm asking is if this is the man you saw with Danny. It's very important."

"Yes," she said, sounding annoyed, "that's him."

Manny was getting a prickly feeling. Up to now he hadn't held out much hope that they could prove Moore's involvement, but together with what Laura had told them, Alice Houston's identification might bring things together.

"Didn't you tell Kyle and Laura that Danny took this man to visit the center the morning of the accident? It was the day he didn't come home."

"I might have. Danny said the man was very kind, offered to take him fishing. Danny was usually uncomfortable around people. I was surprised when he took up with the man. But Danny didn't have anything to do with your friend's so-called practical joke, I can tell you that. Danny was a professional. He would never do something like that."

"Did they actually go fishing?"

"Yes. Once."

Manny took out his notebook. "Where."

"Danny said he had a cabin near St. Joseph."

Manny made a note.

"Thank you, Mrs. Houston. Once again, I'm very sorry for your loss."

"You may as well know," Alice Houston said angrily, "I hope they send your friend to the gas chamber. I feel sorry for that nice wife of his, but I hope they kill Kyle Matthews for what he said about my husband."

Manny listened politely, shook his head, then ran to his car and took out his cell phone. It wasn't the first time he'd heard about the cabin in St. Joseph.

It didn't take long to verify that Butch Moore did indeed own the cabin.

But was there anything there worth looking at?

EIGHTY FIVE

Dr. Nicholas Marone sat behind his desk and studied Manny suspiciously. Marone was short, slender, and had a hook nose. He squinted behind wire-rimmed glasses, said, "You must know I can't reveal privileged information."

"I'm not asking you to reveal privileged information," Manny stated. "I'm just interested in whether or not a certain man is capable of murder. Another man's life is at stake."

Marone got up from his cluttered desk and closed the door. He studied Manny again for several seconds before walking to his file cabinet.

He returned to his desk, pushed his chair back, and studied a thick file, turning the pages with a pen. Finally, he looked up, said, "I can't reveal anything I discussed with a patient. The best I can do is speak in generalities. I probably shouldn't even be doing that; it borders on malpractice."

"I can respect that," Manny said, softening his approach. "I just need to know if I'm on the right track. I'm involved in a case where the suspect could not only be a cold-blooded murderer, he could also be a genius. But I'm still not sure if any man is capable of planning and carrying out what this man planned and carried out, that's why I came to you."

Marone took off his glasses. "I know who you are, and I know who you're talking about, so let's not beat around the bush. I'm assuming you don't think your client is guilty, either that or you're anxious to point the finger at another suspect. Either way, I don't care, but I am curious. Do you really believe your client is innocent, even with that tape recording of the incident?"

"Yes."

"Interesting." He studied his file some more.

Manny could see that he was wrestling with his conscience. "If you're worried about getting sued, you have my word I won't reveal my source."

Marone turned the pages of the file, stopped when he came to a particular page, studied it, turned his eyes to Manny and said, "I've been wondering how anyone but a crazy man could ram two airplanes together. I can only think of one person I've ever been associated with who could be that irrational, and since you're saying it isn't your client, I'm going to assume you and I are talking about the same man."

He closed the file, set it on the desk, got up and started strolling around his office. "Since this involves a man's life, I'm going to make an exception here. But I won't name names; I'll only discuss it in the abstract. I'll call the man I have in mind 'John,' but if you ask me to testify, you can forget it, because I can always tell the court I was discussing a hypothetical man."

Once again, Manny indicated his agreement.

Marone pulled up a chair and sat close to Manny, looking him in the eye. "You want to know if my 'John' is clever enough to carry out a detailed scheme like the kind you must have in mind?" He paused. "Let me just sum it up by saying that my hypothetical 'John' is more cunning, devious, and brilliant, than any individual I've ever met. If what you're talking about involves technological skill, detailed planning, and an almost pathological determination, the man we must both have in mind is more than capable of it."

He paused and studied Manny's reaction.

Manny was getting that prickly feeling again. "What would be his motive?"

Marone thought about that for a few seconds, said, "It would take more than a psychiatrist to understand John's motives. John is what we psychiatrists sometimes call a 'devoid'."

"'Devoid'?"

"We use that term to describe a person with no feelings; there are more scientific terms for it, but I prefer that particular one. Devoids don't feel what you and I feel; they're actors following a script; going through a list of imaginary enemies and constantly conjuring up ways to hurt them. On the surface, devoids can be outgoing and congenial, but it's all an act, a very polished act. They practice on their parents for years, and by the time they're fourteen or fifteen, they can lie with conviction. They have no real sense of humor or concern for others, either, and yet they can laugh or cry whenever they need to."

"Is that because they've been abused, or what?"

Marone looked out the window for a second or two before continuing. "It doesn't have to be, but in this case it was. John was abused by his parents and just about everyone else. The older he became, the more his need for revenge grated on him, elevating his need to retaliate. Little things would set him off. 'John' once slammed a little girl's kitten down on the sidewalk just because she wouldn't give him a piece of gum. He couldn't understand why she wouldn't stop crying. Having no feelings himself, he couldn't understand hers. His family was forced to move several times because of similar acts. Psychiatrists and psychologists didn't really understand devoids until just a few years ago; they're kind of in the middle of the pack; somewhere between raving maniacs and people who set cats on fire."

"Even if his target has never done anything to offend him? What if the target is just an innocent bystander?"

"Doesn't make any difference; if he can't get even with the person who offended him, he'll take it out on someone else. He has to have his revenge."

"And he wouldn't care if several hundred people got killed along the way?"

"Not at all. He's not even thinking of them, he's thinking of his target."

"Are all devoids that dangerous?"

"No, and even the dangerous ones don't usually go to that extreme. But believe me, the 'John' you're talking about sure as hell is."

"Sounds like a real charmer."

"He can be, that's what makes him so dangerous. A devoid puts on a good front, acts out a smile whenever he needs to, sucks you in. Just don't mistake his smile for friendliness. Your John is not friendly, not unless you consider Ted Bundy friendly."

"Everyone I talked to said John is very neat and orderly, so much so that he drives people crazy. How does that fit this. . . devoid thing?"

"It's another symptom: the classic neat freak. He keeps his equipment and tools clean and in perfect order to avoid drawing attention to himself. He gets furious with anyone who doesn't do the same. It doesn't take long before people start avoiding him; which makes him even moodier and more dangerous."

Manny sat quietly for several seconds, thinking.

Marone said suddenly, "I know all about Kyle Matthews. My John, speaking hypothetically again, has a powerful grudge against him and his family. He talked to me about it. He never mentioned Matthews by name, but between what you've told me and that Barbara Walters interview, I'm able to put things together now."

Manny decided he had all he needed. He stood: "Thank you Doctor, you've been a big help."

The two shook hands and Manny started for the door.

"Hey," Marone said, "be careful: John once lost a ten dollar bet with a co-worker and the man found his dog hanging from his back porch. Check before you open your doors or start your car. John has a habit of following people, too. He probably has you on his list of targets."

"And by the way," Marone went on, "I'm not worried about getting sued; I'm worried about getting killed."

Manny heard the lock on the door click as he left the office.

EIGHTY SIX

Jim Brandt looked up from his workbench, said, "The things you see when you don't have your shotgun."

"Long time, no see, Jim," Manny responded with a smile.

"What in the world are you doing here, Manny? How are you?" Brandt was almost too tall to be a pilot, six foot eight. He wiped his hands on a shop towel and the two men shook hands.

"I'm hanging in there. It's been a long time."

"I haven't seen you since we worked on that committee in Washington," Brandt said, leaning against his work bench.

"Yeah, the 'Drift Off' Runway'; I've been trying to remember what the hell that was."

"A double wide runway where a landing aircraft can roll off to one side," Brandt said. "It was a great idea until the fucking politicians got a hold of it. We just didn't have the bankroll, Manny."

"Yeah, now I remember: less time on the runway means more landings in an hour. It could have doubled an airports' capacity. It worked, too; I remember when you tested it yourself at some air force base with an extra wide runway."

"That was McDill air force base, Tampa, Florida," Brandt agreed. "Would have been great for crowded airports; too bad we couldn't sell it. Just another great idea the experts couldn't wait to reject."

"The FAA probably thought *we* were the ones drifting off," Manny said.

They shared a laugh.

Brandt frowned. "Maybe they rejected it because Kyle was on the committee. They never did care much for his ideas."

"That's right; he *was* on that committee; I'd forgotten that. I'll be damned. I guess I didn't actually know him that well at the time."

Brandt said, "I saw him on that Barbara Walters' special. I heard you were working with his defense team."

"That's the reason I'm here. I understand you know Butch Moore?"

"Sure, I know Butch. He works on my aircraft radios. Strange man."

"Do you happen to remember if he was up flying with you on September first?"

"You mean the night Kyle. . . I mean those two airplanes ran together?"

"That's right."

"Yeah, he was. Matter of fact we were near the spot where the collision occurred, only a couple of miles away. I was certifying the engines. We were at twenty five thousand feet, something like that. I saw the flash and looked up."

"You saw the collision?" Manny asked excitedly.

"Not really; I just saw the sky light up."

"Can you remember what Moore was doing at the time?"

"Sure, he was testing my radios. He made a few radio checks, testing the power output, that kinda stuff."

"Were you having radio problems?"

Brandt paused. "Problems, no I don't think so."

"Then why check the radios?"

"Good question. I didn't really give it much thought at the time. I just assumed it was routine. Guess you'll have to ask Butch, if you can drag it out of him."

"Were you able to hear exactly who he talked to?"

"Not every time, but I remember he did talk to approach control and one of the airlines a few times."

"Those were the only transmissions he made? How about the center? This is really important."

"I don't know if he called the center or not. If so, I didn't hear it. He keyed his mike a few times when he wasn't actually transmitting. He was using a meter to check the signal strength; nothing out of the ordinary, I don't think."

"Think hard; was he keying his mike when the collision occurred?"

Brandt put his hand to his chin, thinking. "I really can't remember, Manny. I was pretty busy myself."

Manny visualized Moore sitting in the cat bird seat, just a short distance from where the bomb exploded, the 'locus in quo,' as the lawyers refer to it. He probably couldn't wait to see the fireworks, knowing he was far enough away to have an alibi.

"That's OK. Was he carrying any special equipment?"

"Not that I noticed. We didn't talk much. It was rather quiet, except when he starting clicking that damn pen of his. He said his mother gave it to him. It must be his Oedipus complex or something; drove me crazy. Of course, Moore could drive anyone crazy: clicks that pen and talks about how everybody screwed him. The more he clicks, the crazier he gets. I don't like to do business with him, to tell you the truth. I will say one thing though; he's just about the best electronics man I've ever known. I keep going back to him because he can fix things when nobody else can. Plus, he's a neat freak; everything is always neat and clean when he finishes. When you're sitting in the confined spaces of a Learjet with him, though, it can be an uncomfortable feeling."

"Why?"

"I can't really explain it; it's just that he's so secretive. He won't answer questions unless he's in the mood. How would you like to spend an hour or so in the cockpit with someone who doesn't talk?"

"No thank you," Manny said. "Any idea where he is now?"

"Probably in his hangar next store," Brandt said, pointing. "We keep the Learjet in here, but most of the electronic equipment is kept there."

"Does he use any electronic devices you don't recognize?"

"Hell, there isn't anything he uses that I recognize. I tell you what, as far as my electronic knowledge goes, there's a little man in the wire that either says 'no' or sends you some juice."

"Do you know if he has any experience handling explosives?"

"Explosives? My God, I hope not. The FAA is tough enough without my having to worry about explosives. I probably wouldn't know what explosives looked like, though, even if I saw them. What are you looking for, anyway?"

Manny wasn't sure himself.

"Has he ever made any threatening remarks toward Kyle?"

"No, but he's very angry about what happened after the controller strike. He just says 'every thing will even out eventually.' Butch is mean, but he's not stupid; he would never say anything that would incriminate him. I wouldn't care to be his enemy, though, he's pretty scary. How is Kyle handling this? It's hard to believe he would deliberately run two aircraft together. I guess I don't know what to believe now, after listening to that interview. Is there really some kind of conspiracy going on?"

"It's possible. I didn't believe it myself at first."

"And the FBI is involved?"

"Either that or they're just being kept in the dark. I'm not really sure. You heard about the fire in the NTSB hangar? They sure didn't do much investigating there."

"Yeah, but didn't they already know what happened after listening to that center tape?"

"That's the problem; they were so sure they knew what happened that they stopped looking. They may have even been *ordered* to close their eyes, for all I know."

"You actually believe the FBI would just stop looking?"

Many shrugged. "They may be under so much pressure that they don't know how to reverse course."

"A cover up; that's hard to believe."

Manny shrugged: "I know."

"What can I do for you, Manny; I know you're not shopping for a hangar?"

"Does Moore keep everything in his hangar, I mean, is there another place where he keeps things?"

"He once told me he had a cabin in St Joe. I think he also has a storage shack up there."

"But you don't actually know what he keeps there?"

"No, and knowing him, he probably has three or four locks on the door."

"Sounds like a job for Andy," Manny mumbled.

"Who's Andy?" Brandt asked.

"Just a friend; he dabbles in locksmith work."

"I didn't hear that."

EIGHTY SEVEN

Butch Moore felt the ladder shake and looked down to see Manny Vigil glaring up at him. His eyes immediately searched for an escape route, settling on an open hangar door.

"Forget it," Manny said, noticing where Moore's eyes had gone. "And don't say you don't recognize me or I'll pull this ladder down and you with it."

Moore stammered something unintelligible, his eyes still scanning the hangar for a way out.

"Come on now," Manny teased, "you remember me; I'm one of the guys who watched you burn down that hangar. You better be nice, I might be called as a witness when the FBI arrests you. I have to admit, though, you did put on quite a show."

"I know who you are," Moore stammered, refusing to look Manny in the eye. "Whadda ya want?"

"I hear you were good friends with Danny Houston?"

Moore hesitated: "He gave me a tour once, that's all."

"You seen him since?"

Emphatically: "No."

"Ever been to his house?"

Moore's eyes went wandering again. "I don't remember."

"How about that tour; that was in the center, wasn't it? What were you doing there?"

Moore started to shake; he was breathing hard. Manny could actually feel the ladder tremble. He started down, keeping one eye on Manny.

Manny stepped aside when he got to the bottom, then followed him to his workbench. He hovered over Moore's shoulder while Moore wiped his hands with a red towel.

Manny studied the workbench, looking for anything unusual in the way of electronic equipment. Moore opened a drawer and began to put his tools away, giving Manny a chance to look him over carefully. So this was the man Dr. Marone called a devoid? Moore's shoulders were wide and his hands were huge; tools disappeared in his grasp when he picked them up. His bib overalls were neat, clean, and pressed.

"Well?" Manny said, sticking his jaw up against the back of Moore's head. Moore ducked his head away. "I can't remember anything about the tour. I go lots of places. I can't remember them all. I didn't know Houston that well."

"When was the last time you saw him?"

"When he gave me the tour."

"That was the only time?"

"That's what I said."

"So when you went back to his house, what did the two of you talk about?"

"I said I don't remember if I went to his house, you're trying to trick me." Moore opened his briefcase and began nervously straightening out the fountain pens that were clipped to one of the flaps. The pens were already in a perfectly straight line, but he rearranged them, anyway. Everything in the briefcase had been organized to perfection.

"So you can't remember if you went to his house, but you do remember going into the recording room."

Moore turned quickly, a little too quickly. "What recording room? I never said I went into any recording room."

"You do remember there was a recording room, don't you?"

Manny's rapid fire questions were having an effect: Moore eyes had narrowed to slits. He was about to burst.

"No. . . *you* said there was."

Manny: "No I didn't. I asked if you remembered going into the re-cording room."

Moore appeared stunned, confused.

"Where were you when Danny Houston died in that fire?"

"Right here, working."

"Seems funny you can remember that, and yet you can't remember anything else? How would you know when he died, anyway? What time was that?"

Moore took a gold fountain pen from the pocket of his overalls and began clicking it nervously. "I just meant. . . I was here, I don't know the exact time."

"If I don't get some straight answers soon I'm 'gonna start thinking you're hiding something. When Kyle goes to court and we present our de-fense, our attorney is going to ask you the same questions. Kyle Matthews' wife will be there too, she'll identify you as the man she saw come out of the recording room the morning of the crash, maybe even remember if she saw you anywhere near the Matthews' home right before the fire started."

Moore turned his head and snuck another look at the hangar en-trance. "Why would your attorney ask *me* to testify?" he asked sullenly. "I answered your questions. I never said I didn't go to Houston's house, I just said I didn't remember. And I don't remember the exact time Houston was murdered, either."

"Who said he was murdered? I didn't say he was murdered; I said he died in a fire."

"I'm not going to answer any more of your fucking questions. Talk to my lawyer."

"You still insist you can't remember if you went to Houston's house?"

Moore was so confused he couldn't think. He walked away from his work bench and went clear over to the other side of the hangar. Manny followed on his heels.

"If you can't remember the time Houston died, maybe you're wrong about being here at the time of his death."

"I'm not wrong," Moore fumed. "I said I was here."

"How do you know that? You seem awfully confused."

Moore was holding a large wrench. Noticing the look in his eyes, Manny remembered Dr. Marone's warning and took a step back. "Maybe you can answer this one. Where were you around Nine O'clock on September first?"

Moore's attitude changed quickly. He was suddenly eager to answer. He turned and looked at Manny, his eyes wide. "You mean the night of the mid-air collision?"

"Yes."

"I was up flying. You can check with the pilot." He pointed in the direction of Brandt's hangar. "I was checking radios in the bird."

"Where'd you go?"

Moore, cautious, "We. . . it was a local flight, about Flight Level Two Five Zero. We flew around and then landed."

"Who was with you?"

Moore didn't hesitate: "The pilot, Jim Brandt. Check with him. He's in the next hangar."

"I believe you," Manny said. "See how easy that was?"

Moore offered a satisfied smile; he seemed to relax a little. Manny remembered what Dr. Marone had said about how a devoid can change personalities in a flash. Now that he had Moore calmed down, Manny went on the offensive again. "You hate Matthews because of some bull shit about what his father did to your father, don't you?"

Moored hesitated: "That's crazy; why would you say that?"

"Because when we get to court, our lawyer is going to quote several nasty things you've said about his father; the hatred you carry around because his father refused to settle a strike. We'll be talking about those false transmissions you made, too."

Manny turned and started walking away.

"Check with Brandt," Moore said, following quickly. "He'll tell you where I was when Matthews smashed those two aircraft." He was practically pleading now.

Manny took several more steps, stopped and turned around. "One more thing: how in the world did someone like you ever get assigned to a crash investigation? We'll be talking to several high-level Washington people about that. You might want to warn them."

"I was appointed to the NTSB investigative team. The rest is none of your business."

Manny smiled and resumed walking.

Moore took a deep breath and watched him cross the ramp.

EIGHTY EIGHT

Kyle's home for the past three months had been a federal detention center in the middle of a weed infested field in Kansas City, Kansas. Manny usually met with him in the visitors' room, a nondescript hole in the wall with Formica tables and a few metal chairs. But Manny was carrying precious cargo today, something to boost Kyle's morale. A marshal escorted him to Kyle's cell, and he found Kyle sitting on his bunk with his head in his hands.

"What's wrong?"

Kyle shook his head, sighed. "I can't take it anymore, Manny."

Manny opened his briefcase: "I brought you something. How does a Chick Filet sandwich with pickle and waffle fries sound?"

He dug out the sandwich and fries and held them out.

Kyle waived them away. "I can't eat that, Manny."

Manny stood up and glared down at him. "What in the hell is the matter with you? Eat the damn sandwich."

Kyle shook his head. "I can't."

"You ate the hamburger and fries that I brought you the last time."

"I can't eat, now. I can't sleep; I can't do anything, anymore."

Manny sat back down. He could see that Kyle was deeply depressed. One little shove might push him over the cliff. "You were all right when I last saw you, what's happened since then?"

Kyle turned his head and stared at the wall. After a long thirty seconds, "Even seen that movie *The Chamber*, Manny?"

"Yeah, John Grisham."

"That's all I can think about. I keep seeing that scene where this prisoner says goodbye to his lawyer, who is also his nephew, or something. He's going to the gas chamber to die the next day. That's it, he has twenty-four hours left and it's all over. Someone he doesn't even know tells him 'were going to kill you tomorrow,' and that's the end of it. The prisoner has no comeback, no chance to argue. No more wife, no more children, just goodbye."

"It's not going to go that far this time, trust me. You have to stop thinking negative thoughts."

"How could I not think negative thoughts? What else is there?"

"You have to fight through this. I thought you were going to spend your time figuring out how Moore triggered the bomb. Did you give that some thought?"

"Of course I did. I've thought of just about every possible scenario. I've been sitting or lying on this bunk twenty-four seven thinking about that. I've wracked my brain ever since I've been in here. I'll still be wracking my brain the day I go to trial. It's just no damn use. A remote transmitter; that's how he did it, either that or he had an accomplice on the ground. But it doesn't do any good to know that if I don't know the rest. What did Jay Brandt say?"

Manny hesitated, not anxious to bring Kyle more bad news: Moore has a perfect alibi; he was testing radios at the time of the crash."

"You see, it's his two places at one time alibi; the same one he used when he made those false transmissions. And if I could figure that out, I'd still have to figure how he triggered the bomb with Brandt sitting right next to him. I'd have to know those two things before I could even make a case."

"So then, you're going to just give up?"

"What's the use? I don't have a chance if I can't prove those two basics. All I have is speculation."

"You still have time to figure it out; concentrate on nothing but that for the rest of the time you're in here. I hate to say this, but if all you're going to do is sit and pout you really are going to die. Keep working on it, don't give up."

"I think it's time to pull the plug, Manny. I think I'll just go ahead and plead guilty."

"Well, fuck it then," Manny said, getting up and giving Kyle's bunk a kick that shoved it sideways, "if it really is that hopeless, I may as well give up, too."

He called for the guard and hurried out, banging the cell door.

EIGHTY NINE

Andy came crawling through the bushes on his hands and knees, holding a small tool kit.

Manny saw his head poke through and jumped a foot.

"Jesus Andy, you scared the shit out of me."

Andy stood, brushed off his clothes. He gave Manny a puzzled look, as if he assumed everyone crawled around in the bushes. His Huckleberry Finn face stared up at Manny: "Did you check the cabin?"

Manny pointed to a small cabin up on a hill. "It's completely empty; if there's anything useful here it must be in this shack." He pointed to an ugly, six foot high structure with a large lock.

Andy studied the shack: "He sure didn't want anyone going in there, did he? That thing looks like it was carved out of a tree."

"Yeah, I'm wondering why anyone would build a fortress like that just to store junk."

Andy took a closer look. "Maybe his neighbors were the nosey type. Not to worry though, we won't have any trouble getting in." He took a rechargeable power saw out of the tool kit and held it up.

Manny shook his head. "That should do it, all right."

Andy cut through the lock in seconds.

Manny opened the door and went in first, bending down to keep from banging his head. Andy followed behind. The inside was like an oven, with cobwebs everywhere, brushing against their faces like ghosts guarding a fort.

Manny turned on his flashlight, swiped at the cobwebs, and looked around. "I bet this isn't the first time you ever broke into someone's shack, is it Andy," he said casually.

"'Broke into' is such a harsh phrase."

"I thought you told me you'd been to locksmith's school?"

"I did, but I found out that a power saw is a lot faster, so I quit the course."

Manny stopped when he got to a second door, also locked. He stepped aside and pointed to an even bigger lock than the first one. "You're going to need a bigger power saw."

Andy noticed the brand on the lock and smiled. "I did learn one important thing at locksmith's school before I quit, steal the instructor's keys." He pulled out a large set of keys, fumbled through them, found the right one and opened the lock. He let Manny go in first.

"Jesus, look at all this stuff," Manny exclaimed. "This place is like Radio Shack."

"Yeah," Andy whistled, "and I bet every bit of this stuff is stolen. Most of it still has the FAA serial numbers." He aimed his flashlight beam on a large playback machine. "A Magnosync," he said, "just like the ones we use at work. This one came from the center. It was one of our spares, I can tell by the serial number."

"What's this other crap?" Manny asked, pointing to a pile of boxes neatly stacked in a corner.

Andy opened one of the smaller boxes: "Microchips, resistors, all kinds of electronic stuff."

Manny kneeled down, opened a much larger box and whistled. "I know what this is, it's Semtex. There's enough here to blast a tunnel through a mountain."

"Wouldn't have a problem blowing an aircraft out of the sky with that," Andy agreed.

"Well, the FBI can't ignore this, Andy." Manny said wondrously. "This guy's a bigger thief than you."

"I bow my head," Andy agreed. "Now I know where to go when I need supplies."

"He must be awfully confident to leave this stuff lying around. I thought he was smarter than this."

"He probably never dreamed we'd find this place," Andy surmised. "He thought we'd concentrate on his hangar."

"Is there power in this place? Can we play these tapes on that playback machine?" Manny wondered.

Andy looked around: "There is an outlet here, but we'd be here all day going through sixteen channels on each tape."

Manny sat down on a wooden crate. "I just happen to have all day."

Andy threaded one of the tapes and switched on the machine. They played five tapes, every one an old recording containing Kyle's voice.

"It's hot in here," Manny said. "Let's grab the rest of these tapes and go. We need to find a place where we can listen until we find the exact tape Moore used to implicate Kyle."

"Shazam," Andy agreed.

"And don't touch anything else; leave everything right where it is. On second thought, we better leave everything here and let the FBI take over. If we move anything they might accuse us of tampering."

"Can we trust the FBI?" Andy asked. "They haven't exactly gone overboard on Kyle's behalf."

"I'll bring the press here if I have to. Let's see if Moore can explain how he got all this stuff."

Andy shook his head and followed Manny toward the door. He stopped when he stepped on something. "What's this?" He got down on one knee. Manny did the same.

Andy turned an object over in his hand.

"What is it?"

"I think it's a miniature transmitter, like the ones I use when I fly radio controlled airplanes. Except this one is a hell of a lot smaller. I didn't know they came this small."

"I used to fly radio controlled airplanes myself," Manny said. "I never saw one that small, either."

"Moore must have made it himself."

Manny examined the circuitry; he had some knowledge of electronics, himself. "This thing is unbelievable. You could put one of these things inside a nail."

Andy smiled.

"What is it?"

"I'm just feeling a lot better, that's all. I'm pretty sure now that Moore had the capability to rig that center recorder. I always trusted Kyle, but I have to admit that center tape recording had me wondering. I was sure he had accidentally triggered his mike. This is like climbing out of a dark hole; I can't wait to tell the other controllers."

"Let's just get the hell out of here," Manny said. "Leave that thing right where you found it."

Andy was still on one knee. "Wait a second; here's another one, it's connected to a wire." Andy traced the wire. "It's coming from that closet. Let's see what's in there."

"No, let it go, Andy, don't touch that door," Manny screamed as he grabbed Andy's arm. But it was too late; the blast knocked them both backwards. Fortunately, the door provided some protection for Andy, and Andy's body provided some protection for Manny. But both men went flying out through the front door, anyway.

NINETY

Kyle was in full recovery mode. Manny's visit had been exactly what he had needed, although he hadn't realized it at the time. It wasn't the lecture Manny delivered, it was the two hundred sixty pound kick that put a dent in his bunk and left his ears ringing for days.

Manny had never shown that kind of anger before, and it startled Kyle, made him sit up and think. It took almost a week for him to get over his funk, but when he did, he realized that he had been acting like a submarine captain stuck on the bottom of the ocean, unable to get to the surface to fight back. His cell had become the ocean floor, and he had simply assumed that there was no way up. He had needed someone to remind him that he still had a brain; that he could still think, even in a cloistered cell. Manny had provided that reminder, and when Kyle finally realized what a wimp he had become, everything changed: his cell became his office. From that point on, he put aside every other thought and focused on how to get into Moore's brain, figure out exactly what Moore had done to put him in this position.

Sitting in a quiet cell with no distractions turned out to be just what the doctor ordered: he could think clearly here. In whatever time he had left before the trial, he vowed that he would learn exactly how Moore's trickery had resulted in him sitting alone in a prison cell. He had to understand everything, and he had to be able to explain it to a jury. It was several days after Manny left that he asked the guard for a pencil and paper and began drawing up schematics to show how one man could perform two tasks, in two different places, and yet be in only one of those two places at the same time. After a week and two dozens examples, he thought he had finally scratched out two possible ways it could be done, and one of them might even explain the two second delay. He still didn't know how Moore triggered the bomb with Brandt sitting next to him, but having figured out the first part, he knew he would eventually figure the second part, as well.

And then Laura showed up and broke the news that Manny and Andy had almost been killed in a bomb blast. That news nearly sent him back to the bottom of the ocean. He found it difficult to listen when she explained that Manny and Andy had received serious burns and were recovering in Research Hospital. Andy's burns were the worst: he would be in the hospital for some time. Manny's weren't quite as bad, but doctors had warned him that he would have to stay home for several weeks to prevent infection. Laura explained that, while they were searching Moore's storage shack, Andy had picked up a wire that tripped a bomb. It was actually a miscalculation on Moore's part, she said. Moore had intended for the bomb to go off after they entered the closet. According to the police bomb squad, killing was secondary, anyway: the bomb's primary function was to blow up everything in the shack. Unfortunately, it had done that very well. Like the hangar fire, every remaining piece of evidence in the shack was now history, including the Magnosync playback machine.

Laura had to leave after just a few minutes to pick up the children, so Kyle was left alone again to fight the battle by himself. But even her bad news couldn't undermine his newfound determination; he simply refused to allow it. He had to put aside everything she had told him for the moment and go back to work on his schematics. The trial was right around the corner; he had to stop agonizing over the things Moore had done to his friends, stop blaming himself, or let anything else get in the way of his trial preparation. His explanation to the jury would be his only chance to clear himself, and he had to be able to explain the details in such a way that it could be clearly understood by lay people. If he couldn't overcome the bias created by the center tape recording, then he had no chance at all. He would have to be at his very best; have everything figured out precisely.

And there was another thing he had to do: switch lawyers.

NINETY ONE

Rooster had become convinced that without Moore's testimony, Kyle's lawyers had no chance to convince a jury. He had to find Moore, and he needed Manny's contacts to do so. He spent three weeks waiting for Manny to recuperate. Finally, he could wait no longer. He fought off his wife's insistence that he shouldn't risk Manny's health by dragging him around town, then called Manny to say that he was going after Butch Moore, with or without him. Manny picked him up in his Mustang two hours later.

"You feeling OK now?"

"No. Where are we going?"

"To find Moore."

"What makes you think he's 'gonna let us get near him? He's probably in another country by now."

"No," Rooster insisted, "he thinks he's immune because the bomb wiped out any remaining evidence. He'll tell the cops you and Andy broke into his shack and accidentally set off the Semtex; we can't prove otherwise."

"I still say we're wasting our time. Where do you think he is?"

"I have no idea. I just know we'll both feel better when we find him."

"You have no idea? On second thought, I'll pass. I don't feel like driving around all day; just take the Mustang."

"I thought you were a tough guy. Hang in there a little while longer. You're not doing anything but watching TV, anyway."

After thinking it over: "I'll give it two hours and no more. We may as well start with his hangar; see if anybody there knows where he is."

After checking Moore's hangar and talking to a dozen people: "We're not getting anywhere."

"We'll find him," Rooster insisted.

"I'm 'gonna pull over and get some coffee."

Rooster noticed Manny grimacing, his eyes squinting.

"You look like you're going to pass out. Maybe I should take you home, I didn't realize you were hurting this bad."

"I'll be all right after I get the coffee."

"*I'll* get the coffee."

Rooster went into a Starbucks and returned carrying two, large, paper cups. "I'll drive," he said, but Manny shook his head "no" and drove off, one hand on the wheel and the other holding the hot coffee.

The more they drove, the more frustrated Rooster became. He took it out on Manny: "You let Moore sucker you, you know that, don't you?" he said thoughtlessly. "If you'd been more careful we'd have nailed that bastard by now."

Manny turned and burned Rooster with his eyes.

"Sorry," Rooster said.

After a long moment: "You're right, I should have known better, now shut the fuck up. Let's just find this prick."

Rooster couldn't resist: "Didn't that shrink warn you about him?"

Another turn of the head, eyes burning Rooster again: "Yeah, you're right again, things worked out just like the doctor said. Moore made the shack so inviting I just couldn't resist. I stepped right in. I should have known it was too easy; that shack was like a magnet. Now, like I said, shut the fuck up."

Roster started to say something more, but Manny stopped him. "Don't say it, Rooster. One more of your stupid, thoughtless remarks and I might forget about Moore beat the crap out of you."

Rooster finally shut up. Threats didn't frighten him; he was used to losing, but he did need Manny's help.

After a few, long moments: "I heard you and Kyle have a theory about the mid-air."

"Kyle has the theory, I just happen to agree with it. It would take too long to explain it."

Rooster snickered. "I got time."

Manny hesitated for several seconds while he thought of a way to explain it: "Moore used the same basic technique to destroy those two aircraft that he did when he made those false transmissions. It was all about being in two places at one time. He probably used a couple of those mini- transmitters Andy and I saw, transmitted a clearance to Transcon Three Eleven, and sent a signal to put Kyle's voice on the center recording at the same time. Seconds later, just as the two aircraft were due to pass, he triggered a bomb on one of them. Don't know how he did all that, but if he can make homemade mini-transmitters, then I guess it's certainly possible. Whatever Moore did to the recorder, Kyle's voice wasn't intended to go out over the air; it was only put there so he'd get the blame."

"So how come there was a read-back on the CVR tape, but not on the center tape?"

"Because the clearance on the center tape recorder was pre-recorded; something Moore was able to rig up when he visited that morning. After he cleared Transcon Three Eleven to climb, he probably kept his mike keyed so that Kyle wouldn't hear the read-back."

"Because otherwise Kyle would have heard it and wondered why Transcon Three Eleven was reading back a clearance Kyle hadn't even given him."

"You're not as dense as I thought you were."

"But how did Moore know that Kyle was planning the prank in the first place?"

"Houston told him; probably bragged about how he was going to help Kyle beforehand. Houston didn't have that many friends. He probably felt honored when Kyle asked him to participate; wanted to brag a little. Kyle thinks that Moore had been planning something for a long time, and when Houston told him about the prank, it triggered everything."

"Moore had to have had someone tell him when the two aircraft were about to pass."

"I'm sure Houston was somewhere in the center, keeping Moore updated."

"And Kyle's voice was actually copied from one of those old tape recordings you found in Moore's shack?"

"Exactly. Moore told Jay Brandt he needed to check out the Learjet's' radios, waited until the two Transcons were in his vicinity, which he was able to determine because Houston or someone else kept him advised, then triggered something."

"Pretty good alibi, I'd say. Fucking Danny Houston, if he had said 'no,' Kyle would never have done such a stupid thing. Then the prick hides out and gets himself killed."

"He never did anything anyway. When Kyle saw three seven zero on that data tag, he was seeing the aircraft actually climb following Moore's clearance. Afterwards, Moore probably drove Houston to St. Joe, held Houston's head under water until he was dead, then drove back and eventually threw him in Kyle's garage."

"Houston was murdered because Moore thought he would rat on him?"

"We'll probably never know exactly what happened there."

"Pretty damn slick; brilliant is more like it. Sick bastard even made sure he had a bird's eye view so he could enjoy watching the explosion. Except that he made one big error; the delay between the two transmissions: he should have triggered the center tape recording and the clearance to Transcon at the same time."

"He probably did and the delay was due to the distance between the Learjet and the center. I doubt if he cared anyway; he never dreamed Fred Bell's assistant would allow us to hear the two tapes simultaneously."

"On second thought, he made another error," Rooster said, "the readback on the CVR tape."

"No way Moore could have anticipated that we would hear that; we just lucked out because Andes let us listen to the CVR tape."

"Kyle's pretty damn smart himself, figuring all that out. And you did OK too, breaking into that NTSB lab. You're a stubborn old dog, Manny."

"Yeah, well, it's Kyle whose 'gonna have to testify at the trial, not me. Only someone with his experience could make a jury understand all of that."

Rooster sat quietly, digesting Manny's explanation. "Did Moore actually think he was going to get those two aircraft to run into each other? It's a real big sky out there."

"Hell no: he just wanted them close enough to make it look like a collision so he could blame Kyle. It was a bomb that brought those two aircraft down; although we're not sure how it nailed both of them."

"You were right when you said we shouldn't blame the government for not figuring this out, It's so damn complicated I'm still not sure I understand it, myself. Even Fred Bell's assistant couldn't figure it out, and he's supposed to be an expert on black boxes."

"We were lucky all around."

"Shit yes."

The two sat in silence for several seconds.

"All that just to hang a man," Rooster finally said.

"Kyle thinks Deter Noonan was Moore's real target. Getting back at Kyle's family was just for kicks. Noonan and the FAA were the ones who wouldn't reinstate him."

"How do we prove all this?"

Manny noticed a van going in the opposite direction.

"By catching that son of a bitch," he said, swinging the Mustang around and following.

NINETY TWO

After slowing down several times to let the three cars behind him pass, Butch Moore realized that they were actually following him. He could tell because they refused to pass regardless of how much he slowed down. He recognized the third car in line, Manny Vigil's Mustang, and he guessed that either Ramsey or Brock had something to do with the Crown Victoria right behind him. As for the car in the middle, a black Mercedes, he had no idea who that might be. Not that it mattered much now; he was a marked man and he wasn't about to trust anyone.

"Nice turn," Rooster said sarcastically. "Be careful, my wife still loves me."

"The woman has no taste," Manny mumbled, looking past the two vehicles to keep an eye on the van.

"Doesn't look like he's trying very hard to get away," Rooster theorized. "He's doing the speed limit."

"He probably knows we're following him and doesn't want a problem with the cops. I'll wait him out; I just wish the Mercedes and the Crown Vic would either pass or get the hell out of the way: I don't 'wanna lose contact."

"There's something odd going on here," Rooster said. "Those two cars are keeping pace with the van."

"Kyle's always talking about a Mercedes that hangs with him wherever he goes. He thinks it belongs to a relative of Nancy's and wonders if it might be the person paying for his defense. I have no idea who belongs to the Crown Vic."

"Can I assume you'll explain all this to me?"

"I can't explain shit. I'm just concentrating on Moore. We may have to get to him before someone else does."

"You said he wouldn't talk, anyway."

"Seeing him pisses me of so much I'm ready to beat the shit out of him and *make* him talk."

"If he does talk, it'll just be lies. If bullshit were snow, Moore would be a fucking blizzard."

Suddenly, the Crown Vic increased speed, came up alongside Moore's van, and sideswiped it, causing the van to lurch to one side. After several more broadsides, Moore's van veered off and left the highway. Moore didn't even try to get back on the highway; he changed directions and took up a northwesterly heading through a field, running over anything in his way.

"The Crown Vic driver must have been waiting for the traffic to thin out before he made his move," Rooster said.

"Ditto the Mercedes."

They watched as the Mercedes roared off though the underbrush and followed the Crown Vic and the van. Manny turned and followed the Mercedes, almost rolling the Mustang over in the process.

"Are you trying to get us killed?" Rooster hollered.

"I'm "gonna make sure we get to him first," Manny hollered back. "It could be worse, *you* could be driving."

Moore's van had disappeared from view. Manny was forced to follow the trail of dust from the Mercedes.

"We can't let whoever is in that Crown Victoria or that Mercedes get to Moore before we do," Many said. "We have to save the asshole so he can testify."

NINETY THREE

Moore pulled the Mustang into a Holiday Inn parking lot and went looking for higher ground. He needed to be able to see exactly who was after him.

He quickly parked and went inside, through the lobby and up the stairs to a third floor window. From there he would have a good view of anyone approaching.

He looked out the window, waited almost ten minutes, but didn't see the other vehicles. When he was sure he had lost them, he waited another couple of minutes before walking back to the parking lot, passing through a dark hall. He walked quietly, looking around constantly. There was a prickly, suffocating feeling in the hall, as if there was only enough air for one person and others were sucking it up.

He felt something brush up against him, but before he had time to react, his head reeled from a blow that left lights flashing in his brain like an Elton John concert. His ears rang and he found himself flailing his arms in a futile attempt to defend himself. More blows followed. He went down and began to crawl crazily, his arms attempting to ward off whoever was aiming at his head. He took a blow to the stomach, a kick that left him breathless. He tried to scream, but nothing came out. What followed was a shower of something wet, like a bucket of water. But it wasn't water he smelled, it was gasoline fumes.

He looked up, knowing instinctively what would come next. He saw the glow from a cigarette lighter and the shadows of two men, one of them holding out the light as if to say–"take this."

Poof, he was on fire!

He scrambled to his feet and began to throw himself against the wall, anything to put out the flames. His anxiety brought on an extra allotment of adrenalin. He rolled his body on the floor and slapped at the flames with his powerful hands. When that didn't help, he scrambled to his feet and ran for the door, using only the light from his burning clothes to find his way through the dark hall.

Once in the parking lot, he threw himself to the ground, rolling over and over to put out the flames. He thought about the kitten he had thrown to the ground many years ago. Funny he should think of that now.

He saw two men running toward him.

"You've threatened someone way above your pay grade," one of the men said, pointing a gun. "Next time, you might want to think first." There was a "swoosh" and Moore felt a pain in his side. Another "swoosh" and he grabbed his shoulder.

The Mercedes roared into the parking lot just as the gunman was about to fire again. The gunman withdrew his arm, turned and ran with the second man toward the Crown Victoria.

Manny's Mustang had followed the Mercedes into the parking lot. He and Rooster saw Moore on the ground and the two men running for the Crown Vic. Manny brought the Mustang to a screeching halt behind the Mercedes.

Two men jumped from their Mercedes and grabbed Moore. They threw dirt on him, dragged him to the back door and threw him in. Manny saw blood flowing from Moore's left shoulder. He jumped out and ran to the passenger side of the Mercedes with Rooster close behind. One of the men held up his hand as if to say "stop," while the other, a powerful looking animal, drew his gun and pointed it.

Manny continued to move forward, thinking at the same time how ironic it would be if he had to take a bullet for the very man who had tried to blow him to pieces. Ordinarily, he would have enjoyed watching Moore get his due, but Kyle needed Moore desperately.

Seeing that Manny wasn't going to stop, the two men quickly jumped into the Mercedes. Manny was there in time to grab the door handle, but a huge arm swung from the passenger's side window and knocked him to the ground.

The Mercedes roared away, leaving Manny lying there.

He rolled over and watched helplessly as their only witness was probably dead or about to be.

NINETY FOUR

Courtrooms are always cold and dark places, especially in February. But this federal courtroom on State Street in Kansas City, Kansas, went beyond that: it would have taken a blast furnace to heat it and a bank of floodlights to brighten it. Some argued that the furnace must have been installed in the eighteen century. The décor made things even worse: years and years of polish had turned the cherry wood dark, enveloping every piece of wood from the judge's bench to the chairs, tables, even the rail around the jury box.

The judge's bench sat like a mountain, looking down on the defense table to the judge's right and the prosecutor's table to judge's left, with the spectators in the middle, separated by a heavy, wooden rail.

Kyle sat like a scolded schoolboy, hunched up at the defense table, shivering and waiting for the judge to arrive. Funny how the principal's office had seemed so foreboding when he was a schoolboy. Oh, for something as innocent as that now. He tugged at his shirt collar and looked around. High up on the wall behind the judge's bench was the great seal of the United States of America. He had always considered that to be *his* seal. After all, a controller was a federal agent, a man keeping the skies safe, a representative of his country.

Now his country wanted a pound of flesh.

He tightened his suit coat, his long legs continually shifting in an attempt to create more space at the table. It occurred to him that the chill racing through his body wasn't from the temperature in the room at all; it came from somewhere deep down in his body, taking whatever warmth that was there and leaving a damp core of cold that penetrated the nerves and made it difficult to move the limbs. Five months in a prison cell without room to exercise hadn't helped, either: it made his body even more susceptible to the elements, less flexible.

He rubbed his hands together and looked over at Spencer Mallek and his entourage of assistants. They were hunched over, whispering quietly. Mallek turned, making eye contact for just a second, then quickly turned back again. He adjusted his body to avoid Kyle's line of vision, as if Kyle didn't matter.

You haven't won yet, you bastard, Kyle said to himself, but he wasn't sure he really believed it. He took a quick glance toward the back, hoping to see Laura. He avoided eye contact with the crowd, and when he didn't see her, quickly turned his head back toward the front. He lowered his head and stared at the floor, trying to gin up positive thoughts. The events of the past six or seven months flashed through his mind like a blur. The mid-air incident seemed like a lifetime ago. He had been alone with his thoughts since his capture and indictment; no visitors except his family, his lawyers, a few friends; and no trips outside the prison except for the interview. He hadn't even had a chance to tell his version of the incident to a grand jury, no chance to cross-examine or explain. Nancy had warned him that grand juries were misguided anachronisms anyway; a prosecutor's way of using untrained and sometimes uneducated citizens to help produce an indictment. There was nothing grand about a grand jury, Nancy had insisted.

He had to admit that it had been peaceful in jail, though, all things considered. It had given him time to think, strategize; reduce the stress that came from running from the FBI and the public. The downside was that there was no opportunity to care for his family, serving only to punish his family more than himself. His house was gone now; his wife and children were living with Laura's mother, held captive in their home by an angry public. No job, no income, it was guilt by association for the whole family. He wondered if he would ever feel in charge again. To top it all off, he was to be defended by two lawyers who didn't trust each other and couldn't seem to decide on a strategy. The best they could do was live out a truce.

In spite of everything, he had managed to smooth out the wrinkles in his plan of action during his long hours in prison. It was a long shot, a million to one chance, and it would require perfect timing and lots of luck, but it was all he had. His strategy was simple, but it relied on finding Butch Moore and getting him on the witness stand. It was the one thing that was actually out of his control, but he thought he knew who could get it done for him. After that, it was a matter of connecting Moore to the two transmissions and explaining to the jury exactly how he did it. It would mean getting the jury to buy into a very complicated scenario, but it had to be done. When he tried to explain how difficult it would be to Laura, she cried. She thought the task so improbable that he might as well just plead guilty. She argued that pleading guilty might be the only way to save his life.

Laura was probably right, and he knew it. It was a plan that depended upon Nancy, Manny, and, in some ways, even Harding. Nevertheless, he had no intention of pleading guilty. Laura had finally said she understood.

NINETY FIVE

Kyle let his eyes and mind drift as he looked around. The courtroom was jammed; there were so many people wanting to get in that the bailiff had been forced to hold a lottery. Some of the lottery winners eventually sold their seats for big money. On his way in, he had seen television cameras, everywhere.

The pre-trial frenzy concerning government cover-ups and blunders had faded into nothingness; the media predicted a short trial and a quick conviction. After Butch Moore disappeared, the prosecution never again mentioned a deal. Kyle and his lawyers were convinced that it was no coincidence. Nevertheless, Kyle hoped the prosecution was wrong, that Moore would reappear and that the result might be enough to change a jury's preconceptions.

"Are you all right Kyle?" Nancy asked. She was sitting on his right, looking very "legal" in her pin striped, gray suit and white blouse. Her hair was pinned back, making her look less glamorous but more business like.

He studied Nancy for a long moment, still not sure what to think of her, but convinced he could trust her. In spite of everything, Nancy had become a good friend and ally in the past few months.

"Compared to what?" he asked in a raspy voice. His throat had been hoarse for months; the prison cell hadn't allowed much opportunity for conversation. "It's important to look confident," Nancy said. 'First impressions,' remember? The jury is looking at you right now. Don't let them see you looking guilty."

Kyle sat up straighter in his chair and offered a short smile. "You're not going to give me that old saw about how you 'don't get a second chance to make a first impression,' are you?"

Nancy smiled back, glad to see that Kyle had retained at least some of his sense of humor. She had worried about him during their pre-trial preparation: he'd been acting strange, as if his mind was somewhere else, apparently analyzing things he wouldn't talk about. At other times, some idle thought would apparently pop into his head and he would come alive, like a fighter before a bout.

Kyle looked to his left and studied Harding for a long moment. He tried to comfort himself by remembering the positive things Manny had said about him. According to Manny, who was back in the hospital because of the parking lot incident, Harding had a sharp mind and was quick on his feet. Kyle had noticed the same thing while coaching Harding on air traffic control procedures, demanding that he *think* like an air traffic controller. Harding had proven to be a quick study. Maybe Harding would surprise him and do the job on his own, but he doubted it. In the meantime, he would prod Nancy in case Harding did as Kyle expected him to do.

He had been counting on Manny for moral support, if nothing else. Knowing Manny was back in the hospital didn't help his confidence any. Manny had been loyal almost from the start. Kyle suddenly remembered that he had never really taken the time to thank Manny. For that matter, he had never really thanked Nancy, either. He realized he had been ungrateful. The three had become good friends after a rocky start.

He turned and attracted Nancy's attention. "Whatever happens Nancy, I appreciate your help, and Manny's," he said self-consciously.

Nancy seemed embarrassed. She shook her head and smiled. "I wish I could have done more. I hope you realize that I was constrained somewhat, even if I'm not authorized to tell you why."

Kyle leaned over, forced a smile and whispered. "You mean restrained by Tyler Harding or the other guy?" His satisfied smile let her know he had figured out some things.

She smiled and changed the subject, pretending she didn't know what he meant. "Tyler's been pretty cooperative lately. I just hope he doesn't start going backwards."

"I agree," Kyle whispered, "but I'm not worried." A quick smile appeared at the corner of his mouth. Nancy noticed it. "If Manny were here he'd tell you to 'get real'," she said. "The last thing he told *me* was that Tyler would behave 'as long as we were sitting right next to him'."

"Everything will be fine," Kyle said confidently.

Once again, Nancy noticed the confident smile and wondered if jail has weakened his mind.

Kyle looked to his left again; Harding seemed to be engrossed in something.

Harding had been formulating his own plan. On the surface, he looked the part of the confident attorney, studying documents carefully and waiting for the bell to ring. But inside, he was boiling; he had no real conviction that the evidence Manny and Kyle had discovered would be enough to convince a jury, even if the judge allowed it, which she most likely wouldn't. As for the two-second thing, the jury probably wasn't sophisticated enough to understand the significance of that, not with the CVR tape having been destroyed. He didn't expect to convince even one member of the jury in that regard, much less twelve. The center tape recording was what they were going to believe, and that was it. He was faced with an impossible task unless he did it his way.

Harding looked to Kyle's right, where Nancy sat reading something. He wished she would suddenly disappear so he could do as he wanted. But with or without her, he was determined to have his own way.

Winning would make everything right.

NINETY SIX

A buzz, like air escaping from a pressurized can, came over the courtroom. The bailiff called the court to order.

"All rise."

Judge Maureen Stone came bursting through a side door, her tall, slender frame enhanced by a black, flowing robe. She appeared to float in like an apparition, her robe billowing from a fan somewhere behind her. She stood for a long moment looking defiant, surveyed the courtroom, and peered out over her half glasses like an eagle perched on a tree limb. The courtroom spectators detected a no-nonsense attitude; they stared up at her. Finally, she lowered herself into her high, leather chair, looking around as if she were aware of each and every individual there and knew each of their names.

"Be seated."

"The matter before us today," Stone said, "is the United States of America versus Kyle Francis Matthews."

Her first instructions were to the spectators: "Ladies and gentlemen, this trial has probably received as much publicity as any in history. I know there are strong feelings among the spectators, especially those who have lost family members or friends as a result of this terrible tragedy." She turned her head and looked at Kyle when she said the word "tragedy." "Nevertheless, there will be no talking and no noise in my courtroom. I expect you all to remain silent and avoid moving around. The disgraceful scene I witnessed in front of the courthouse today will not be repeated nor tolerated in my courtroom.

"I also expect counsel to conduct themselves in a professional manner, and to control those at their table." Her last statement was made with eyes directed at Kyle and his lawyers. She never once looked at the prosecution table. It gave Nancy a cold chill. Judge Stone appeared ready to deliver on her promise.

"Now, let's get on with it."

The bailiff read the charges.

Stone turned to the jury and gave them their preliminary instructions. She told them that Title 18 of the U.S. Code meant that a guilty verdict could result in the death penalty. She explained exactly what she expected of them, both in and out of the courtroom, and informed them that they would be sequestered for the entire period. The jurors, expressions taut, didn't seem surprised, but didn't seem pleased either. She finished with a statement that shocked the defense team: she told the jury that the trial "shouldn't take too long." Once again, she looked at the defense table when she made the comment.

Tyler and Nancy exchanged glances. They didn't dare look at Kyle.

"Mr. Mallek, you may make your opening statement."

Spencer Mallek smiled at the judge and unraveled his protracted body from a chair. He slithered toward the jury box, reminding observers of a "Slinky," one of those coiled up toys that can "walk" down the stairs one step at time. Like the toy, Mallek walked as if the upper part of his body had dropped off with each step, only to catch up on the next one. Others thought he walked like a camel, with all the parts seeming to work against one another.

"Ladies and gentlemen of the jury," Mallek said, smiling and gripping the jury box rail. "You are privileged, as are all jurors, to participate in the American judicial process. Most people call it the finest in the world."

He smiled again.

"Some will tell you that this is the trial of the century, or at least that's what I hear.

"But let me explain why this case is actually very simple: it's because we have the smoking gun; a tape recording of the defendant committing the crime!"

He turned to look at Kyle, raising his hands like a preacher: "This is a sad day for America; one of its most trusted servants, an air traffic controller whose job it is to keep our skies safe, has failed us all and committed a heinous crime in the process."

Now he glared at Kyle.

"No doubt the defendant or his lawyers will tell us that someone else did it, or that he was incapacitated at the time. That's just bunk; don't listen to that kind of nonsense.

"Our witnesses will tell you that Kyle Matthews is one of the most stable men you will ever meet. He was once an important director of the air traffic controller's union, NATCA, until that union, like its predecessor, PATCO, flew in the face of the law, and several of his cronies were either fired or suspended. That's the kind of person we're dealing with."

He turned and faced the jury again.

"Well then, you ask, if he's so stable, why did he deliberately run two airplanes together, leaving pieces of aluminum falling from the skies and bodies falling all over the city?

"We intend to show that Kyle Matthews was peeved, ladies and gentlemen; yes, I said peeved. He can't get the Federal Aviation Administration to listen to his views on how to improve the air traffic control system; a system he himself has at times said is already the best in the world.

"You see, once upon a time, Kyle Matthews held center stage when it came to impressing congress; his opinions were taken seriously. One congressman even considered a bill to implement some of the defendant's ideas.

"Now he is, or was before he murdered several hundred people, just an air traffic controller whose views are ignored. And so, he decided to kill the man responsible for his plight, the former Administrator of the Federal Aviation Administration, Mr. Deeter Noonan, who at the time of his death was president of Transcontinental Airlines.

"We will show that Kyle Matthews wanted to get rid of Deeter Noonan, bragged about getting rid of Deeter Noonan, and then took the necessary action to get rid of Deeter Noonan; not to mention two hundred and thirty six other innocent human beings.

"We will also show that the man who the defendant claims assisted him in that act wasn't even in the building when the deed occurred. As a matter of fact, that man has since been discovered murdered. What a coincidence, the only witness the defendant could come up with just happens to have been murdered.

"This was indeed a spectacular and gruesome crime, of that there can be no doubt. It is repugnant to even think of what the ill-fated passengers of the two Transcontinental aircraft went through as they fell to their death from thirty seven thousand feet. According to police reports, one body actually fell through the roof of a house and landed in a child's bed. Fortunately, the child was not there at the time. You will hear of many, similar occurrences as the trial progresses."

Mallek paused and surveyed the jury, six men and six women. He looked each one in the eye. Several of them seemed on the verge of tears.

"What I would like you to keep in mind, however," Mallek said as he spread his eagle like wings to the jury and then to the crowd, "is that this is not a complicated case at all, in spite of its spectacular and gruesome nature. The evidence is contained in one, conclusive tape recording, and it is persuasive."

Mallek pointed at Kyle, but continued to look at the jury.

"Ladies and gentlemen of the jury, I feel confident that you will have no difficulty in concluding that this defendant, Kyle Matthews, is guilty as charged, and that he deserves the ultimate punishment - death. Thank you."

NINETY SEVEN

"Mr. Harding, are you ready?" Judge Stone asked, sounding as if she couldn't stand to utter his name.

The jury was still shaking their heads: Mallek's opening statement had them breathless.

"Yes your honor," Harding answered. He walked quickly to the jury box and gave each juror a kindly and fawning smile, making eye contact with each one before he began.

"Ladies and gentlemen of the jury, have you ever seen a magician make an elephant disappear?" Mallek had had to practically look down when he addressed the jury; Harding's stance was the opposite, he had to practically look up. Nevertheless, his voice was strong and clear; the elephant reference got their immediate attention.

He paused.

"Ever wonder how in the world the magician does that? We all know the elephant doesn't really disappear, yet even the most perceptive and experienced of us can't explain it.

"Well, ladies and gentlemen, this is a case where a man made two elephants disappear, two giant aircraft and several hundred unfortunate people. I mean no disrespect when I say that.

"The magician in this case used a tool to perform his trick, a small, ingenious, electronic device with which he transferred Mr. Matthews' voice onto the tape recording the prosecutor mentioned, thereby convincing a gullible government that my client had gone mad and committed the crime. Our ingenious magician, you see, is really just a man with an extensive knowledge in electronics and a pathological urge for revenge."

Harding crouched like an actor in a stage performance, his head cocked upwards as if looking to the heavens. "But if all this sounds just too difficult to believe, think about your iPod, or your cell phone, and remember that we live in new, fascinating world of technological wonders. Men and women can do amazing things with electronic gadgets. For some people, making magic with electronics is child's play: who would have believed twenty years ago that today, any one of you could stand in the middle of a river and talk to someone in space?

"But wait, there's even more magic involved here. The tape recording was just an electronic distraction to put the blame on an innocent man. Meanwhile, our magician pulled off another, even more sensational trick to destroy those two aircraft and their ill-fated passengers.

"You see, in spite of what Mr. Mallek has said, this is not a simple case at all. Moreover, Mr. Mallek, who by now has to know that my client is probably innocent, will never reveal the magician's tricks for you. And since magicians never reveal their secrets themselves, it will be up to the defense to reveal how the magician performed his trick, and just exactly who he is.

"The magician the government is hiding is both a genius in electronics and a man so hard-hearted that in order to extract revenge on one or two people for imaginary offenses, he deliberately murdered several hundred innocents.

"Ladies and gentlemen of the jury, my client is an intelligent and capable individual, but he is not gifted in electronics. And please remember that Mr. Mallek himself has told you that Kyle Matthews is 'one of the most stable people you will ever meet.' Oh, and by the way ladies and gentlemen, we have a confession to make and we may as well make it now:

"My client readily admits that he was pulling a prank on his friends on the night of September first. No man or woman in this courtroom is as sorry about that as my client is, especially in light of what happened. But the prank had nothing to do with the disaster, nothing whatsoever.

My client feels a strong sense of remorse over his inappropriate behavior, but let me make this one thing clear: he feels no guilt whatsoever about what happened to those passengers. He feels sorrow, he feels anger, he feels confusion; in short, he feels the same as you do, but he does not feel guilt!"

With that, Harding placed both hands on the jury box rail and rested them there for a second, looking each juror in the eye.

"Ladies and gentlemen, it will take all of your intellectual effort, attention to detail, and imagination to learn the magician's trick and help me eliminate my client as a suspect in this repugnant crime. We will show that Kyle Matthews had no part in this. We will introduce witnesses to demonstrate that there was in fact, no mid-air collision at all, unless it occurred after the two aircraft had been blown apart."

The jury gasped and started to whisper among themselves, drawing an angry stare from Stone.

"We will show," Harding went on, his voice getting a little louder but still under control, "that someone else deliberately committed this act for their own purposes, purposes similar to the ones Mr. Mallek accuses my client of pursuing."

Now everyone in the courtroom was whispering.

Harding turned and walked slowly toward the prosecution table. He stopped and pointed at Mallek, who was grinning uncomfortably. Then he looked back at the jury.

"Stick around ladies and gentlemen, we are about to show you and Mr. Mallek how someone can make an elephant disappear. And when we do, even Mr. Mallek may start believing in magic.

"But please remember this: my client is an air traffic controller; not a magician."

Harding returned to his seat and a murmur passed through the crowd. It had been a very good show. Kyle gave him a pat on the back as he passed behind the table. Harding smiled: the pat on the back was the first complementary gesture he had received from any of them. He was back on top, at least for the moment.

Nancy was flabbergasted; she looked from Kyle to Laura, who was smiling from the front row. They both realized it had been an outstanding performance. Maybe she had been worried for nothing.

Suddenly, a voice came from behind the defense table: "I told you the guy's good on his feet," Manny Vigil said.

Kyle and the others turned quickly. Manny, looking pale, squeezed into a chair next to Nancy.

"What are you doing here?" Nancy gasped. "You should be in the hospital."

"And leave you alone with this bozo?" Manny asked, pointing at Tyler. "Not on your life. I came here to save you from him. Don't get too excited about that opening statement. Harding will get his game back very soon."

NINETY EIGHT

"Mr. Mallek, call your first witness."

No more promises. Game on.

The twelve jurors shifted in their seats, sneaking glances at one another. They were surprised and excited now. They'd been expecting a slam dunk, but Harding's opening statement had presented another possibility, something infinitely more interesting.

Mallek rose and sidled forward: "I call Zack Morrisey, your honor."

Morrisey, sitting in the second row, looked around as if finding himself in la la land, then slowly got up and limped to the witness chair.

Kyle allowed himself a small smile: Morrisey never limped unless he wanted sympathy. And since sympathy was something he ordinarily loathed, the limp had to be for Kyle's benefit.

Mallek walked toward the witness stand, stopped. He took a few seconds for his body parts to settle, then stared down at Morrisey. Morrisey looked as if God was about to get even with him.

Mallek flashed a toothy smile, then asked some preliminary questions, background, experience, all that. The preliminaries over, he got to the point: "Mr. Morrisey, you were working with the defendant at approximately nine o'clock on the night of September first, were you not?"

"I wasn't working *with* him, but I was working *next* to him."

"Tell the court what you heard with respect to Transcontinental flight Three One One and Transcontinental flight Three Five Four."

"Which part?"

Mallek frowned.

"Isn't it true that you heard the defendant issue instructions for Transcontinental flight Three One One to climb from thirty five thousand feet up to thirty seven thousand feet?"

The jury shifted in their seats, anxious to finally hear the details. Harding didn't bother to object to the leading question; better to stay on the jury's good side as long as possible.

Morrisey hesitated for as long as he could:

"He didn't really climb the aircraft, he was just pulling a prank. He had his. . . "

Mallek raised his hand, gesturing for Morrisey to stop. He turned and smiled at the jury, demonstrating his patience with an inexperienced witness. Most of the jury smiled back. "Just tell us what you heard; the jury will decide what he did." He smiled at the jury again.

"I think I'm going to puke," Kyle whispered.

Zack stalled for as long as he could, looked over at Kyle. Trapped. "I heard Kyle issue what I thought was a clearance for Transcontinental Three Eleven to climb to Flight Level Three Seven Zero, but,. .. ."

"So you're saying he told the pilot of Transcontinental Three One One to climb his aircraft to thirty seven thousand feet, an altitude which was already occupied by another aircraft?"

"Objection," Harding said. "Mr. Morrisey wasn't part of the accident investigation team. He can't testify as to whether or not the altitude was occupied, other than what he heard on TV. Besides, Mr. Mallek is both leading the witness *and* testifying."

Judge Stone glared at Mallek, then looked down at Zack.

"Do you know the answer or not?"

Zack looked confused. "Well, I guess so."

"Mr. Mallek is leading the witness," Harding persisted.

"Overruled. The witness will answer the question."

"I was afraid of this," Nancy whispered: "Mallek's going to walk the witnesses down the garden path and Stone is going to be his guide dog. She's never going to forgive us."

"Mr. Morrisey," Mallek said, "I ask you again, did the two aircraft end up occupying the same altitude?"

"I guess so, they hit, didn't they?"

The spectators tittered.

Mallek ignored Morrisey's bad taste and shifted gears. "Mr. Morrisey, how long have you known the defendant?"

"About eight or nine years."

"And do you consider him to be a friend?"

Morrisey turned and gave Kyle an uncomfortable look. "Of course, at least I hope he still is."

"Do you consider Mr. Matthews to be of sound mind; is he usually in control of himself?"

"Yes, of course. He's been a little depressed lately, but other than that he's been fine."

Mallek frowned; the "depressed" comment needed countering. "By depressed you mean unhappy because he was separated from his wife, not depressed to the extent that he wasn't aware of what he was doing?"

"He's been worried about the controllers who were suspended and the one that was fired, too. That's the kind of person he is."

Mallek, in order to stay as far away as possible from any further mention of depression, switched gears again, asked, "But didn't he lead the strike that led to the suspensions and the firing?"

"Objection, your honor," Harding shouted. "Mr. Mallek is leading the witness again and assuming facts not in evidence."

Stone glared at Mallek, trying not to be too obvious.

"Sustained."

Mallek got the message. He smiled.

"Just one more question, your honor: "In your opinion, Mr. Morrisey, did you at any time think the defendant's mental condition was such that he might do something drastic?"

Morrisey, between a rock and a hard place, "No," he admitted.

"So he was perfectly normal?"

"Yes."

"Nothing further."

Harding stood up quickly.

"Mr. Morrisey, do you know for a fact that Mr. Matthews actually cleared the aircraft in question to climb?"

Morrisey liked that question better.

"No, I don't. Like I tried to say, Kyle told me his headset chord was unplugged."

Harding moved quickly toward the jury box, indicating that he wanted the jury to pay special attention.

"Please explain to the jury what it means when you say that his headset chord was 'unplugged.' Don't you mean that it was only plugged in halfway?"

"Sure, it's the most important part of the joke; the controller puts the headset plug halfway into the console so that it won't really transmit; then he fakes some outrageous transmission. Nothing goes out over the air. We all do it."

Mallek: "Objection. Your honor, please direct the witness not to editorialize."

Judge Stone: "Just answer the questions, don't give your opinion."

Morrisey didn't look up: he wasn't going to give her the satisfaction.

Harding: "So, just to clarify, when you said unplugged, you really meant 'plugged in half way'."

"Yes."

"Thank you for clarifying that. Now, Mr. Morrisey, you said Mr. Matthews was worried about the controllers who were suspended and the one who was fired. Was the defendant in any way responsible for the local strike?"

"No, he was against it. He tried to stop it, just like his father did during the PATCO strike. But there was a handful of crazies out there who let things get out of control. They essentially overrode his wishes."

"Mr. Morrisey, were you aware the FAA conducted a psychological study of Mr. Matthews without his knowledge," Harding asked suddenly.

"Objection, objection." Mallek was on his feet, heading toward the bench. Harding followed.

"Your honor, there is no foundation for such testimony. This is one of counsel's famous dream sequences."

"Objection sustained."

Harding floundered. "But your honor. . . "

"Move on counselor," Stone said.

Harding went back to the defense table and looked down at his notes for a long moment: "Getting back to the headset chord, Mr. Morrisey, isn't it true that the idea behind controller pranks is just to shock visitors?"

"Either that or to see who's the best actor. We usually do it late at night when things get boring. It's harmless; nobody pays any attention, usually."

"Did they pay attention this time?"

"Not really, as far as I know."

"Because, as you said, they assumed it was just a prank?"

"Yes."

Harding looked at his notes again and changed course.

"Don't you usually get a read-back from the pilot, as controllers call it, acknowledging that he or she heard the clearance and will comply?"

"Yes."

"Was there one in this instance, to your knowledge?"

"Not on the center tape."

"And so, what does a controller do if there is no read-back?"

"He issues the clearance again."

"And did Kyle Matthews issue another clearance?"

"No."

"Doesn't that indicate that he never intended for the clearance to go out?"

"Objection," Mallek bellowed, "speculation."

"I'm not asking him to speculate," Harding answered, "I'm asking what the procedure is. He's an air traffic controller, he should know."

Stone was cornered and she knew it. "I'll allow the question."

"Yes it does," Zack said. "Kyle is always very careful. He would have corrected the situation and reissued the clearance if he really intended to climb the aircraft."

"Just to clarify, you're saying the transmission didn't go out, aren't you?"

"Objection, asked and answered."

"That's what it means to me," Morrisey said, ignoring the interruption and smiling.

Stone: "Mr. Morrisey, do not answer a question until I rule on the objection."

Morrisey did look at Stone this time, throwing open his hands with an innocent expression.

"No further questions."

"Re-direct, Mr. Mallek?"

Mallek jumped to his feet: "Just a couple more, your honor. Mr. Morrisey, are you aware that the so called read-back was clearly heard on the cockpit voice recorder tape?"

"I heard something like that," Morrisey answered dryly, but I was told the man in charge of the NTSB investigation screwed up and burned the CVR tape, so I didn't get to hear it. I just know it wasn't on the center tape recording."

Judge Stone allowed herself a small smile.

Mallek's jaw tightened. He realized he had made a big mistake mentioning the CVR, especially since it no longer existed. But it was too late now. He quickly changed gears, hoping Harding hadn't noticed.

"But you do agree that the clearance itself was clearly heard on the center tape recording?"

"I've never heard it myself," Morrisey persisted, "except on television. And who can trust them?"

"And isn't it true, Mr. Morrisey, that the reason the read-back might not have been heard on the center tape is that it was blocked out by another aircraft's transmission? I believe you controllers call that a transmission that has been 'stepped on'?"

Now Morrisey was trapped, so he decided to throw some muck of his own into the game: "Are you asking me about the CVR tape now, or the center tape? I'm confused."

Mallek wanted to strangle him. "I'm asking about the read-back on the center tape."

"There was no read-back on the center tape."

"Your honor, please instruct the witness to pay attention."

"I am paying attention. All I know is that if Kyle had really issued a clearance and didn't hear a read-back, he would have issued it again."

Mallek forced a grin, teeth barred: "You mean, if he hadn't been occupied with his own objectives. No further questions."

Harding rose, "I have a few more questions, your honor."

Stone shook her head. "Get on with it, counselor."

"Since Mr. Mallek brought it up, are you aware that there were some discrepancies on the cockpit voice recorder, or black box, as everyone calls it?"

"Objection," Mallek shouted, jumping up again. "We just heard the witness testify he didn't know what was on the CVR tape."

"I think he said that he hadn't heard the CVR tape. I'm asking if he knew there were some discrepancies on that tape," Harding corrected. "This is not the same question. Since Mr. Mallek brought up the CVR, the witness should be allowed to answer questions about it, to the extent he knows."

Stone had been cornered again. She glared at Mallek, reminding him it was his own blunder.

"Overruled."

"Then it's hearsay."

"Overruled, sit down Mr. Mallek."

Mallek sat down with a thump.

Nancy inched forward in her chair. This was the opening the defense had been hoping for, a chance to talk about the two separate transmissions and the two second difference between the CVR and the center tape. And it was Mallek who had inadvertently opened the door.

"Yes. I heard that Kyle and his private investigator, Manny Vigil, noticed several discrepancies on the CVR tape. They were allowed to listen to the CVR tape and the center tape simultaneously in the NTSB lab."

Mallek wanted to object again, but he didn't. No use calling any more attention to the CVR tape. The jury was already leaning forward in their chairs, waiting anxiously to hear more.

He needn't have worried; Harding just turned and walked back to the defense table. "No further questions."

Nancy's mouth was now wide open. She jerked her head and stared at Kyle in amazement.

Kyle didn't seem that surprised: he just shrugged his shoulders.

She turned to Manny, but all he did was give her an "I told you so shrug."

NINETY NINE

"Prosecution calls Rich Carpelski."

Carpelski marched to the witness chair, was sworn, and sat look-ing very "federal" in his three piece blue suit and large, white, name tag: *"RICHARD E. CARPELSKI FAA."*

Mallek smiled at Carpelski.

"Mr. Carpelski, you were the FAA investigator who first played back the tapes of the mid-air collision, were you not?"

"Yes," Carpelski said proudly, looking forward to his fifteen minutes of fame.

"And is the tape that is marked here as 'Exhibit One' the exact tape that you played on the night of September first?" Mallek knew that it wasn't, but he needed to make a point for the jury, show them how care-fully the tape had been guarded so they would know it had never been tampered with.

"No," Carpelski said smugly. "That is a certified copy of the original. We keep the original in a safe. We only make one copy from the original, in order to protect it."

"So, a certified copy is an exact duplicate of the original?"

"Yes," Carpelski said.

"Tell the court what steps you took in examining the original tape."

"Well, as soon as I arrived on the night of September first, I played the tape for the radar sector operated by Kyle Matthews. I heard him issue the clearance for Transcontinental Three Eleven to climb to Flight Level Three Seven Zero. I then informed my superior, Mr. Ron Adair."

"And when you speak of Kyle Matthews, you're speaking of the defendant who is sitting at that table?" Mallek pointed to Kyle. "You're sure it was his voice?"

Carpelski looked pointedly at Kyle. It was the moment he had been waiting for. "Absolutely."

"And if someone were to claim that the defendant's voice was put on after the fact, or that you or someone else spliced the tape, what would be your reaction?"

"That's not possible. Like I said before, we don't take license with original accident tapes; they're kept under lock and key."

"And is there a time channel that would show the exact time of each transmission?"

"Yes, and it's very accurate. The original source is the official time clock in Boulder, Colorado. It's the standard throughout the country, automatically corrects itself. We refer to it as the 'WWV time'."

Mallek smiled and turned to the Judge.

"At this time your honor, I would like to play 'Exhibit One,' the tape recording Mr. Carpelski referred to, and have Mr. Carpelski identify it."

The Judge nodded.

The courtroom went into silent mode when the bailiff turned on the playback machine.

Once again, Kyle had to sit, embarrassed, listening to his own voice:

"Transcontinental Three Eleven climb and maintain Flight Level Three Seven Zero. . . "

"Is that what you heard, Mr. Carpelski?"

"Absolutely."

Mallek smiled brightly. "No further questions. Tender the witness."

Tyler Harding came out of his chair quickly.

"Isn't it true, Mr. Carpelski, that you and Kyle Matthews have been openly hostile to one another for the past few years?"

"I . . . wouldn't say that, exactly."

"You were the manager of the Kansas City Center when the recent strike occurred, were you not?"

"Yes."

"Didn't the strike cost you your job, and didn't you blame Kyle Matthews for the strike, even though a subsequent investigation proved he had advised against it?"

"Of course not. I just said that as an NATCA officer, he should have done something to stop it."

"Rather than support his members? You expected him to be disloyal?"

Harding didn't wait for an answer. "Mr. Carpelski, I noticed that when you talked about examining the tape recording that was referred to as 'Exhibit One,' you said you went to the radar position 'operated by Kyle Matthews,' rather than to the radar position that had jurisdiction over the two flights."

Carpelski thought for a long moment. "OK, so what?"

"Doesn't that demonstrate that you were more interested in seeing the defendant get the blame than you were in analyzing what had happened?"

"Objection."

"Overruled."

Carpelski had come to the courtroom to condemn Kyle; he hadn't expected to have to defend himself. Harding's question had caught him completely off guard. "I don't. . . don't understand what you're talking about," he stammered.

"When you were the manager of the Olathe, Kansas, Center and the NATCA local went on strike, isn't it true you were accused of poor leadership for refusing to negotiate?"

"Objection, relevancy," Mallek said.

"Mr. Harding, where is this going?" Judge Stone asked, peering over her glasses.

"Goes to motive, your honor. I'm simply attempting to determine if Mr. Carpelski had a motive for wanting my client to be blamed for the aircraft tragedy. Allowing Carpelski to audit the tape was like using a wolf to guard the sheep."

Harding's attempt at humor bought him a few chuckles from the jury, but only a severe look from Judge Stone. "Mr. Harding, even if your little attempt at humor had any relevance, your question doesn't. What Mr. Carpelski's superiors did or did not think of his performance is of no significance. Mr. Carpelski is not on trial here. We are concerned with evidence, like Exhibit One, the tape recording from the center. You've heard of 'evidence,' haven't you? The objection is sustained."

"But you honor . . . "

"The objection is sustained!"

"No further questions," Harding said, throwing up his hands.

"Mr. Mallek?"

"Yes your honor, a few more questions, thank you."

"Mr. Carpelski, were you alone when you listened to the tape?"

"Yes, I was, at first."

"At first?"

"Yes, then three others listened to it: The center manager Mr. Raymond, Mr. Brockman of the FBI, and my superior, Ron Adair."

"Everyone is your superior," Kyle mumbled out loud.

Stone looked up quickly, but didn't catch who had said it.

"What happened then?"

"They took charge of it; I didn't see it again."

"Did you carry any equipment into the room with you, anything that could be used to splice or record over a tape?"

"No, of course not."

Mallek grinned at Harding: "And, Mr. Carpelski, just for the record, you aren't a magician, are you?"

Big smile from Carpelski and Judge Stone.

"No, I'm not."

Big smile for Mallek from the jury.

Smiles from the judge to the jury.

Pained looks from the defense team.

"No further questions," Mallek said, practically bowing to the jury before taking his seat.

ONE HUNDRED

The rest of the afternoon was taken up by testimony from FBI and NTSB experts in their particular areas of expertise, or committee chairmen responsible for certifying reports from their various committees. NTSB experts also provided an overall view of how aircraft accident investigations were conducted; routine stuff. They insisted that there was no evidence pointing to anyone else's involvement. None of them admitted to having seen anything out of the ordinary before the significant evidence from the crash was "accidentally destroyed."

Mallek's technique was not to push for every small detail. He was letting the jury know that they had all the facts they needed, playing the "what you see is what you get" strategy to the hilt.

On cross, Tyler tried unsuccessfully to introduce testimony concerning the bomb-scarred luggage. Having no success there, he demanded that the government produce Paul Andes or Fred Bell. Mallek countered that Bell was too busy providing expert assistance to the Russians to attend the trial, and that Paul Andes no longer worked for the NTSB and couldn't be located. Harding then insisted that the government find Butch Moore and force him to testify. Mallek said that Moore couldn't be located, either. NTSB witnesses stonewalled Harding at every turn: they either didn't know anything or they weren't saying anything.

Mallek accused Harding of a witch-hunt.

Judge Stone admonished Mallek for his inability to produce witnesses, but told Harding to move on anyway.

The situation was going from bad to impossible. Worst of all, the jury didn't seem to be listening anymore; it was as if their receivers had been turned off.

The final two prosecution witnesses for the day were center manager Curtis Raymond and the cafeteria cook.

Raymond was sworn in and gave his background and current FAA duties.

"Mr. Raymond, have you seen any indication during the past several months that the defendant has been anything other than stable in performing his air traffic control duties?" Mallek asked.

Raymond shifted in his seat before answering. "No, he's just the same as he's always been. He stirs the other controllers up, though; always getting them excited about one thing or another. They think he's a god, or something; like he's going to save aviation."

"Yes, well, so you see no reason for us to believe that he was under any particular strain, and you had no reason to believe that he might do anything drastic?"

"You mean was he sane? I suppose so," Raymond said reluctantly. He'd obviously been warned to stay away from mentioning stress.

"Are you aware that the defendant bragged to his friends that he was going to run two aircraft together?"

Raymond was between a rock and a hard place now: if he said "yes," Harding would ask why he hadn't taken action; if he said "no," he might weaken the testimony of some of Mallek's best witnesses. He decided to protect his own interests:

"Not before the crash. If I'd known that, I would never have let him work."

Mallek, gritting his teeth before he spoke: "Based upon your long years of experience as an FAA manager and an expert air traffic controller, can you sum up for the jury exactly what happened on the night of September first of this year?"

"Well, there's not a whole lot to sum up: Matthews, the defendant, just climbed one aircraft until it ran into another one. End of story."

"And you have no doubt that that's what happened, no doubt about the tape recording itself?"

"No."

Mallek turned and broadcast his smile to the entire courtroom: "No further questions, thank you, Mr. Raymond."

Tyler Harding stood and picked up a manila folder from the table. He appeared to be studying it.

"Mr. Raymond, are you familiar with a psychological report commissioned by the FAA, the one that describes the defendant as being depressed and recommending his removal from the center?"

Mallek jumped to his feet, checking with his assistant prosecutors to make sure he hadn't missed anything. Curtis Raymond stalled, looking to Mallek for help.

"Objection, your honor," Mallek said. "If Mr. Harding has something in that folder we should know about, we should have been given a copy."

Judge Stone glared down at Harding. "Why don't you show us what you have there, counselor?"

Harding looked up, his eyes pure innocence. "I didn't say I had anything, your honor. I just asked Mr. Raymond if he knew about a psychological report."

Judge Stone fumed: "I know what you're attempting to do with that folder Mr. Harding. Everyone in the courtroom knows. We've all seen that tactic on *MATLOCK*. Don't try that again."

Harding didn't seem fazed. He'd been expecting the judge's reaction, but at least she hadn't cut him off yet. He asked, "Mr. Raymond, do you know if such a study exists, or did exist?"

"Objection."

"Sustained."

Harding sighed and returned to his seat.

"I have no further questions."

Kyle whispering to Nancy: "How bad did that charade hurt us?"

"Probably not that much. At least he gave the jury something to think about. What mystifies me is why he keeps backing down. He starts out well, but keeps changing directions. He's dodged every opening; he had a chance to mention the read-back on the CVR tape and he passed on it. He's playing right into Mallek's hands."

"Or maybe he's had something else in mind, all along," Manny interjected.

Mallek called his last witness for the day, the cafeteria cook. The cook verified that Kyle had bragged about running two aircraft together. He quoted Kyle as having said, "I'm getting tired of this job. I think I'll run two of those big sons-of-bitches together."

On cross, Harding tried to get the cook to agree that Kyle was only joking. The cook seemed embarrassed; he did everything he could to keep from accusing Kyle and still tell the truth. All he could do, he said, was repeat what he had heard.

The prosecution rested their case.

ONE HUNDRED ONE

The defense had been meeting for over an hour, hunkered down in an eight by ten room down the hall from the courtroom. Federal marshals kept watch outside. It was late; everyone appeared to be too tired to think.

"How far down are we?" Kyle asked.

"We're so far down, fucking Captain Nemo couldn't find us with his submarine," Manny answered.

Vigil was boiling over. He hovered over Harding, his face close enough to bite. "You shit, I know what you're up to; you could fuck up a two-car funeral. But I'm not going to let you get away with it this time. You promised to play this straight, but that act with the manila folder proves you're up to your usual, cheap shit, amateur theatrics. You don't pull that 'guess what I have here in my folder' crap unless you at least have something to keep the judge off of our backs. Then, there's the opportunity the judge gave you when she practically handed you a chance to attack the tape discrepancy. You walked right away from it."

Harding stiffened. "I planted doubt in the minds of the jury," he whined. "The jury has to wonder if there was something in the folder. I saw them looking at one another. There were questions in their eyes."

"Well the jury knows what was in the folder now; nothing but pure, unadulterated crap that left us looking like liars. How can they believe anything you say from now on, you fucking idiot?"

Kyle pretended to support Harding while throwing out some bait for Nancy at the same time. "Actually, I didn't think what he did was that bad."

"What?" Nancy said, jumping up from her chair. "How can you say that? He just put a nail in your coffin."

Kyle stifled a smile; Nancy's reaction was exactly what he had hoped for.

Manny: "Jesus, Kyle, can't you see what this little shit's up to? He's trying to pull that 'stress' crap, can't you feel it?"

Not only could Kyle feel it, he'd been hoping for it all along; Tyler was actually carrying out his plan, the last leg of a journey he had mapped out while sitting in jail all those months. And if he read Nancy correctly, she was about to cut the strings and be her own person. If not, all was lost. It all depended on Nancy now; it had actually depended on her from the very beginning.

Nancy sat down and shifted in her chair uncomfortably. Kyle and Manny weren't the only ones who had suspected Harding might revert to his old tactics. As she watched him perform, she was reminded of her first law school case in property law: it was about a pet fox that escaped from its owner and ran into the woods. The question the students had to answer was whether or not the fox was still someone's pet, or had reverted to its natural state and now belonged to whoever found it. She thought Harding was like the fox, just waiting for an opportunity to escape, to revert to his natural state. He couldn't help it; it was just the way he was. But as bad as Nancy wanted to take over, she wasn't quite ready to challenge her father, sitting in the first row and watching her carefully. He had already refused her latest attempt to change his mind.

She rationalized things by remembering that Harding had made some good points when questioning Morrisey and Carpelski. With the exception of several unexplained lapses, she thought he was doing pretty well. His opening statement had been brilliant, and she had been impressed with his understanding of a "read-back" and the other technical matters. The CVR questions were on point, too, he just hadn't gone far enough.

Or was she just rationalizing because she felt guilty?

"As far as I'm concerned, Nancy, it's your call," Kyle said casually.

Nancy's head shot up. "I . . . don't know what you mean."

"He means he wants you to take over," Manny said abruptly. "That's our only chance."

Nancy seemed shocked and embarrassed. "No," she said. "I can't, I've told you that. Let's just get on with it. What's our strategy? Do we have a case on appeal? Stone is obviously prejudiced; she hasn't given us a damn thing."

"She's given us just enough to *avoid* an appeal," Manny disagreed. "I'd say she's covered herself pretty well."

"Judges are always wary of an appeal," Harding added peevishly. "I doubt if you'll find anything in the transcript that would help. She even gave us a few wins, making sure each time that they weren't significant. Now, let's talk about how I'm supposed to proceed, since you people won't let me do my job and the judge won't let me get at what I need."

"After that bonehead act of yours, we need to let the jury know we're not liars," Nancy said. "We have to recapture Kyle's reputation; call managers and supervisors who will attest to his good character and such. Spend some time building him up to the jury. Mallek can't do much objecting there, he's been saying all along how stable Kyle is."

Kyle focused on Nancy's expression; he knew she was struggling with her conscience and hadn't quite reached apogee yet. He expected Harding to supply the final thrust tomorrow.

"After you get through with those preliminaries, it will be time to put Kyle on the stand," Nancy continued.

Harding shook his head. "I don't think that's a good idea."

"See what I mean," Manny said. "He doesn't want Kyle on the stand because he wants the jury to think Kyle is nuts. He's still hasn't given up on that insanity shit."

Kyle noticed Nancy subconsciously shaking her head up and down every time Manny ripped Harding. He thought it was a good sign. He only had one chance for acquittal, one shot at the target.

And Nancy had to be the trigger.

ONE HUNDRED TWO

It was the defense's turn.

The following morning, Tyler seemed to be following the script. A parade of character witnesses trotted back and forth to the witness stand. Tyler asked pertinent questions and supervisors from the center answered them in a straightforward manner, bragging about Kyle's work performance and character. They described him as one of the top two or three controllers of the more than three hundred in the center, a man who would volunteer to work extra hours when they were short staffed.

None of the supervisors, except Curtis Raymond, believed that Kyle was guilty, although they couldn't explain what had happened. They verified that practical jokes were a part of the business, including the type that Kyle had pulled. They expressed shock and even some anger over what he had done, but supported his explanation. They were in agreement that it must have been pilot error.

Manny Vigil took the stand. He talked about the loud "booms" he had heard the night of what he called, "the bombing," and compared it to the matching flashes of light on the DVD from WDAF. Harding tried to sneak in questions about the luggage, but the judge disallowed it. She disallowed almost everything else Harding asked.

On cross examination, Mallek ridiculed Manny's analysis of what he had seen and heard, suggesting it might have been "too many late hours at law school." Manny had to agree under cross that he wouldn't be able to prove what the DVD showed, even if it still existed. Mallek's questions served to remind the jury that Manny was Kyle's private investigator, and that his testimony was therefore one sided, wishful thinking.

Harding made another motion for the prosecution to deliver Fred Bell and Paul Andes. There was a heated sidebar: Mallek continued to argue that Bell was indisposed, and that Andes wouldn't know anything more than the expert witnesses who had already testified. Judge Stone rolled over on the defense on that one like an elephant stomping on a mouse.

The court recessed at five o'clock.

It was all but over.

ONE HUNDRED THREE

"The defense calls Kyle Matthews."

There was a rumble in the courtroom. Jury members came to life as if awakened from a deep sleep, edging forward for a closer look. After hours of conflicting opinions, they were anxious to meet the man the world was talking about.

Judge Stone rapped her gavel; the noise faded to silence.

Kyle walked quickly to the witness box, keeping an eye on Nancy the whole time. Nancy noticed Kyle eyeballing her and lowered her own eyes.

Their last meeting had been tense, with Tyler arguing against putting Kyle on the stand and Manny and Nancy arguing back. When it was finally agreed that Kyle would testify, Nancy attempted to prepare him. But he seemed disinterested, as if he knew what the outcome would be, so she had finally given up.

Harding began by asking routine questions about Kyle's career. Then, he attacked the strike issue head-on:

"Since Mr. Mallek brought this up earlier, let's get it out of the way right now. Did you encourage the controllers in the center to strike?"

"No," Kyle said, and went on to state NATCA's objectives. He said his own interest in the union was to achieve controller benefits through insurance programs and a secondary retirement plan, not by illegal strikes. He then explained that another officer in the local had pushed for a strike to pressure congress for a raise. He said the NATCA national policy was to avoid strikes, and that the local strike was just a few individuals throwing their weight around.

"Mr. Mallek told the jury you were 'peeved' because no one would listen to your ideas for improving the air traffic control system. Is that true?"

"No, they were only suggestions, not something I would endanger lives for."

"Isn't it true that back in 1981 your father also fought a strike that ended up with almost the entire work force fired?"

"Yes. He was a national director of PATCO. The FAA offered controllers a huge pay raise, but they voted it down. My father insisted they take the deal, but the controllers went on strike, anyway. I didn't want to see that happen again."

"Why did PATCO controllers turn it down, Mr. Matthews?"

"The hard-liners wanted more. They kept telling the controllers, 'they can't fire us all,' until it became their mantra."

"So what Mr. Mallek is saying is incorrect, you did not lead or encourage the local strike because you knew the same thing might happen. Then why do you think Mr. Mallek is working so hard to convict you? Is it something personal?"

Kyle looked over at Mallek. "I believe Mr. Mallek really did think I was guilty, at first. But now he's just being dragged along by someone who wants all this to end before the real truth surfaces."

Mallek looked a little uneasy, but didn't object.

Harding walked over to the jury box.

"Tell the jury what happened on the night of September first."

Kyle went on to repeat what he had already said a hundred times, including the part Danny Houston was to play. He kept it simple so the jury would understand."

"You were in the courtroom when Mr. Morrisey said that he heard you clear Transcon Three One One to climb, were you not?"

"Yes, but I didn't have my microphone plugged in all the way, so the pilot couldn't have heard it."

"Mr. Matthews, I'm going to anticipate the question that Mr. Mallek will soon ask you: how do you explain how your voice got on the center tape?"

"It was put there by someone who wanted to blame me; the same person who put a bomb on at least one of those two aircraft."

The spectators started murmuring among themselves again. Judge Stone rapped her gavel.

Mallek started to rise but Stone waived him off. "Ladies and gentlemen of the jury you are to disregard that last statement. There is no evidence to support the witness's claim that there was a bomb." To Kyle: "Mr. Matthews, you are to answer only the questions put to you and refrain from making unsubstantiated claims." To Harding: "Mr. Harding, you're going over some well trampled ground here; let's move this along."

Tyler shrugged his shoulders, smiled sheepishly, then turned back to Kyle.

"Now, Mr. Matthews, we're going to get into some details that might be a little confusing to everyone; it was difficult for me to understand some of them myself, even after you explained them several times." He was telling the jury to pay close attention. Without anything the jury could actually see, he was going to need their complete concentration.

"First," Tyler said, "a simple question so we can understand the terminology. What does the term 'Flight Level' mean?"

"Anything above seventeen thousand is called a 'Flight Level,' so as not to confuse it with numbers below seventeen, like seven thousand. Eight thousand is eight thousand, but eighteen thousand is Flight Level One Eight Zero, that sort of thing."

Tyler nodded his understanding.

"Now, I want you to explain to the jury why you say the clearance on the center tape couldn't have come from you, even if your headset chord had been plugged in all the way. But first, with the courts permission, it might be easier for us if we played the center tape again while you explain."

Judge Stone looked surprised, but nodded her consent.

Nancy was feeling a little better. She thought Tyler was doing well. It was smart to show the jury he wasn't afraid to play the tape.

The bailiff put the tape on the playback machine. The jury heard the tape recording once again.

"There was no read-back," Kyle said. "A pilot is expected to read back a clearance so the controller knows he or she received it."

"So when you don't hear a read-back, what do you do?"

"Give the clearance again. The fact that I didn't shows that I didn't issue a clearance in the first place."

Nancy paid close attention to the jury. It was hard to tell if they were following the testimony or just astonished that controllers played games to relieve boredom. In any event, they were listening carefully.

Tyler went on: "Are you sure you do that every time? Are you saying it's automatic?"

"Of course. Each clearance is critical; you don't just sit there and hope the pilot heard you."

"And that's how you know the clearance was never transmitted?"

"That's the main reason, but there are others."

"There were others" was a rehearsed prompt reminding Harding to ask about the "two second difference."

"You heard me question Mr. Morrisey about the discrepancies between the center tape and the CVR tape, did you not?"

Mallek was on his feet immediately. "We object to this line of questioning, your honor; this has been tried before. It's nothing more than hearsay about time differences and such."

Judge Stone had already sustained a similar objection from Mallek, so she knew she should sustain this one. But the press had been referring to her as 'one sided' in the papers. She thought she would let Harding get in a few shots and then cut him off at the knees. Besides, she was kind of enjoying this: she thought the government deserved what they got for allowing the cockpit tape to be destroyed. Harding wasn't getting anywhere, anyway. She could afford to be a little lenient.

"Overruled."

Nancy leaned forward in her chair. She couldn't believe Stone was giving them a second chance at the two-second thing.

Harding walked toward the defense table, looked at Nancy and Manny as if deciding what to do, started to say something, changed his mind, and turned back to Kyle.

"Mr. Matthews, are you aware that you were the subject of a psychological profile, and that the FAA recommended you be removed from duty because of stress?"

"Son of a bitch," Manny said out loud. His voice could be heard all over the courtroom.

"Objection." Mallek was out of his seat again and running toward the bench. "Sidebar, your honor?"

Kyle wasn't shocked by Harding's sudden change of direction; he'd actually been counting on it. He knew Harding wasn't going to follow the agreed upon plan without a fight. The only question had been 'when.'

Judge Stone waived Harding to the bench. She was actually enjoying this. She, too, suspected that Harding would eventually take the plunge. Nancy started toward the bench with Harding.

Stone motioned for her to stay away. Nancy could swear she saw the judge's lips form the words "little fish."

The argument at the bench was boisterous: Mallek argued that no such psychological report could be produced and that the objection had been sustained previously. Harding said he could produce witnesses who could quote parts of the evaluation. Judge Stone finally said she would allow Harding to proceed, cautioning him not to go too far.

Nancy leaned over and whispered to Manny, "I wonder why she's being so generous."

Manny wasn't listening; he was busy focusing on Harding.

Nancy thought for a second, then answered her own question: *Because she knows he's going to go off the deep end and she's enjoying it,* she said to herself.

Manny tried to get Harding's attention, but Harding kept his eyes away from the defense table.

"Isn't it true, Mr. Matthews, that you were under great stress on the night of September first, and that the FAA knew all about it from a psychological evaluation?"

"No. I've already told you it was a prank, does that sound like stress to you?"

Judge Stone smiled. Harding's own witness was arguing with him! The defense was about to go down in flames, just as she had predicted. It hadn't been so bad watching Mallek get ripped, either.

Harding seemed disappointed. "I'm talking about an evaluation done by FAA psychiatrists that concluded you were under stress and could be dangerous, that you might suffer blackouts. Do you recall that now?"

The jury was starting to look at Stone suspiciously, wondering why she was changing course and allowing Harding to go on. Stone noticed it and decided to change course again.

"That's enough, Mr. Harding."

"But your honor. . . "

Stone: "Can you produce a copy of the report, Mr. Harding?"

"No, but like I said before, I can produce a witness who has seen it and can quote parts of it."

"That's not good enough," Stone insisted.

Harding looked as if he was going to argue further, but stopped suddenly. He looked up at Stone and threw open his hands.

"No further questions." He didn't dare look at Manny or Nancy as he took his seat.

Spencer Mallek couldn't wait to get out of his chair. He quickly walked toward the witness box, stopping a safe distance away as if Kyle might infect him. He looked at the jury and shook his head angrily, suggesting that they should be angry as well.

"Mr. Matthews, do you really expect this jury to believe your 'somebody else did it' theory?"

"I just told the truth; I have no control over what the jury will or will not believe."

"Regarding your testimony concerning what you think you might have said over the air, I guess I'm just a dullard. Haven't you ever missed hearing a read-back because one aircraft blocked out the transmission of another?"

Mallek had made a good point. But Kyle was ready for him: "That would only occur if other aircraft were transmitting. I had no other aircraft except the southbound, and he had no reason to transmit."

"OK, Mr. Matthews, suppose the jury were to believe that your radio transmission didn't go out over the air. And let's suppose we believe that someone else put your voice on the traffic control tape after the fact. Do you have any evidence at all to support your allegations?"

"Only what I've already said. The cockpit tape was destroyed. If I had it, that tape, played simultaneously with the center tape, would have proven there were two different transmissions. Unfortunately, someone put a maniac in charge of the NTSB investigation and he destroyed all of the evidence, leaving me with nothing to work with."

Mallek had opened the door again, an invitation for Harding to walk right back in on cross-examination. He blanched, knowing he'd make another big mistake, but went right on: "That's what this is really all about, isn't it Mr. Matthews? It's about credibility. Do we believe our own ears when we hear an official tape recording, or do we believe these mythical claims of yours that have absolutely no backing?"

He didn't wait for an answer.

"There's something else that has me puzzled, Mr. Matthews: You and your attorney can't seem to agree on your mental state at the time of this crime. You say your mental state was good. Isn't that correct?"

Kyle had been left high and dry, not that he hadn't counted on it.

"My mental state at the time of the accident was excellent."

"Yes it was. And you just decided to murder all those people by causing those two airplanes to collide, didn't you," he shouted. "You deliberately murdered two hundred thirty seven people!"

"Nancy found herself jumping to her feet. Objection," she said, without really thinking about it. It was her first utterance in the courtroom.

Mallek went back to his seat with a wave of his hand.

Kyle looked over at Nancy and allowed himself a small smile.

The sleeping giant had awakened.

ONE HUNDRED FOUR

Kyle stood and walked toward the window, holding his chin and thinking. He stopped and looked out longingly, enjoying for a few seconds the blue skies and the look of freedom. He turned and faced Nancy, hands on hips: "Well," he said.

She hid her eyes. "What?"

"You know *what*. Are you going to just sit there and let Harding pull this crap? I thought you were supposed to be a lawyer."

No answer.

"If you're going to just sit and let me get convicted, I may as well go in and change my plea to guilty right now."

He waited. Nancy had her head down now, staring at the floor.

He hesitated for another long moment, then looked at the others and proclaimed, "Nancy is taking over." The others turned to Nancy, expecting an argument, but she remained silent.

"Tyler, you can sit second chair," Kyle said. "I don't want the jury to think there's any conflict between my lawyers. But I don't want you to say a word, either. Just sit there; understood?"

"I have an opportunity to talk about the two second thing now; Mallek brought it up."

"Too late, your ship has sailed."

Harding lowered his head and shook it up and down, slowly.

"Nancy, go see the judge. Ask for a postponement. Threaten her if you have to."

Nancy looked confused.

"How can *I* *t*hreaten *her*?"

"Use you considerable family influence; like your father did when I was unexpectedly released on bail. I'd appreciate it if you'd also ask your father to pull off another miracle and produce Butch Moore, as well."

"Moore? How's he supposed to do that? Besides, you said Moore was shot, maybe even killed."

"I changed my mind when I saw you talking to that elderly man and his two bodyguards. I assume the elderly man was your father, and the two bodyguards were the ones who carted Moore away from that parking lot. Just tell your father he won't get the truth he's looking for unless he brings Moore to the courtroom and convinces him to testify."

Nancy started to argue, but Kyle put up his hand. "We don't have time to argue about this. I have an idea that might work, but I can't carry it out without you and your father. It took me a long time, but I think I've figured out how to shock Moore into talking. He's convinced he's smarter than us; but if I can show him that I know exactly how he triggered a bomb, he might fall apart. I need him in that witness chair, right in front of the courtroom. Will you do it or not?"

Nancy kept her head down, but shook her head "yes." She finally raised her head, looking relieved. "I have to warn you, I'm not sure how my father will react. I've always done just as he's asked; even if I haven't always known exactly what he was after."

"That's OK; I'm pretty sure I know what he's after now."

Nancy grabbed her coat and ran out.

Harding followed in a huff.

Manny studied Kyle for a long moment. "You had this planned all along, didn't you? You let Harding put his foot in his mouth until Nancy couldn't stand it any longer. You even knew exactly when she had made up her mind: it was right after Harding pulled that brown file crap. That's why you've been acting so disinterested for the last two weeks: you wanted this case to turn to shit so that Nancy would finally have had enough." Manny shook his head. "You conned me into thinking I was the only one concerned and I fell for it. Couldn't you have at least warned me?"

"I couldn't take the chance. I needed you to help provide the pressure that caused her to fold."

"Yeah," Manny said. "You're the arsonist, but you let me supply the gasoline."

"Well then, let's just hope Nancy can supply the match."

ONE HUNDRED FIVE

Nancy jumped into her father's black Mercedes limo and told the driver, Dominick, to shut the privacy window.

As soon as the window was up: "I need Butch Moore in the courtroom tomorrow, in the front row," she said. "Don't tell me you can't arrange it, because I know you can."

Corlini, eyes down, "What makes you think that?"

"Let's just say the man I'm representing turned out to be much smarter than you and I suspected. I still don't know how he put everything together, but *he* says it was when he saw the two of us with Benny and Dominick."

Corlini sighed, "I was keeping Mr. Moore safe for you."

"Is he in good enough shape to testify?"

"Of course. I thought I might shorten the process a little, so I had Benny ask him a few questions. He's a very stubborn man, doesn't seem to feel pain. He denies everything, even though we've been very persuasive. Give me a little more time and I'll get the job done. I must warn you though; he will make a very reluctant witness."

"We don't have time: we need to get him in front of the jury now. Matthews thinks he can shock Moore into talking if we can get him on the stand. I'm just guessing now, but I think you might even be able to convince the judge to let him testify."

Corlini looked as if he wanted to deny it, but didn't. "I have some influence. He'll be there; he'll testify."

"I also need a postponement until tomorrow."

Corlini paused for a second. "Wait an hour, then go and ask the judge, she'll give it to you."

*   *   *

Laura left the courtroom just as Nancy climbed out of her father's limo.

"Who was that?"

Nancy hadn't wanted anyone else to see her with her father." Just a relative," she said.

"Did you get your postponement?"

"Yes."

"I thought we were going for coffee?"

"We are: Tuscany's OK?"

Laura shook her head and they started walking.

Nancy felt bad about deceiving Laura. Finally: "I lied; that was my father."

"Oh, is everything all right?"

"I hope so, we'll know tomorrow. Let's hurry and get that coffee; I need to get back. If I'm going to take over for Tyler tomorrow, I need to learn exactly what Kyle has in mind."

After coffee, the two women resumed walking, looking around for a cab. They passed the courthouse where media types were gathered in bunches, networking and drinking coffee before heading home.

"It's early," Laura said. "Maybe we should just walk and relax for a minute. There's a cab stand in the next block."

"Want some ice cream?"

"Sounds good," Laura said. There's a Baskin Robbins on this block."

They walked until they found the ice cream store. Nancy ordered a banana split, Laura a vanilla cone.

"You'd pass up a banana split for a measly vanilla cone?" Nancy asked.

"That's me, plain vanilla."

"Yeah sure," Nancy said.

The two were becoming good friends; they had spent a lot of time together while Kyle was in jail. Nancy was grateful for Laura's help, and Laura thought Nancy was brilliant, with values similar to hers.

They finished their ice cream and resumed walking: "How can you eat, knowing you're taking over tomorrow? I'd be a wreck."

"I eat when I'm a wreck."

They passed a ramshackle building that was badly in need of paint. A grungy looking woman stood in the doorway, wearing a long, cotton dress. A neon sign read: "Your fortune-Tarot card readings."

"Not even a crystal ball," Laura remarked.

"Do you know what your future holds?" the toothless woman asked as they passed by.

Laura didn't believe in fortunetellers, nevertheless, she needed a good laugh. A sudden impulse caused her to grab Nancy by the arm and drag her inside.

"I don't believe in this junk," Nancy insisted, but allowed herself to be carried along. "Besides, I don't think I could stand any more criticism right now."

"Come on," Laura said, continuing to pull Nancy's arm.

The inside was as disappointing as the outside: just a couple of wooden chairs and a table. No crystal ball inside either, nothing but a tall bottle filled with something blue, and windows that had been covered with dirty sheets. There were cats wandering around everywhere. The smell was deadly. The two women glanced at one another in disgust.

The fortuneteller had disappeared momentarily, but reappeared wearing a cheap crown and a tattered robe with splotches of bright silver and gold. She seemed bored. She motioned for them to sit.

"You go ahead, Nancy," Laura said, pushing her down.

Nancy reluctantly lowered herself into the rickety chair. The woman seemed shocked when she got a good look at Nancy's face. Her eyes began to glow as if they were on fire. Nancy noticed it and scooted back in her chair, wanting to get as far away from the woman as possible. The woman took her hand and Nancy felt a tingle go up her arm. If it was an act, Nancy thought, it was a damn good one. The woman was having a hard time studying Nancy's palm because she couldn't take her eyes off of Nancy's face. Eventually, she managed to finish her examination. "Someone in your family is in the banking business," she said earnestly.

"No," Nancy said, smiling. "Not my family, try again."

The woman didn't answer right away. Her eyes still had that strange look and she gripped Nancy's hand even tighter. Laura was impressed with her act, too.

"Something important in your future has to do with gold," the woman said. "I don't know exactly what it is, but the vision is strong, very strong. I see someone holding something up, and I see you staring at it. It's a gold coin, or perhaps a gold medal. Whatever it is, it's going to be very important to you."

Nancy didn't believe a word of it; nevertheless she couldn't help feeling nervous.

"Very important for what?"

"For you future; to help you accomplish something; maybe even save your life."

"Help me? How?. . . Save my life?"

The woman's hand started to shake; she seemed to be on the verge of collapsing. Her far-out look was beginning to frighten them both.

"Something in your future is gold," she repeated. "It's the only thing that can save you, or someone close to you. You must find the gold."

"I'm a little busy to go gold prospecting," Nancy said, giggling but still feeling nervous.

Laura giggled, too, but the panicky look on the woman's face was sobering to both of them.

The woman continued to stare at Nancy's disbelieving expression for a long time. Finally: "You must not take this lightly," she warned. "Pay attention to what I say."

Once again, Nancy saw genuine fright in the woman's eyes.

"Let's go Nancy," Laura said, grabbing her hand and pulling her up from the chair. She was sorry now that they had come.

Nancy offered to pay, but the woman brushed her hand aside as if afraid of her touch. She waved them off and ran into a back room.

"That was strange," Laura said as they left the building.

"Yeah, what kind of fortune teller refuses to be paid?"

"Maybe she's a trainee," Laura said. She felt safer now that they were out of the building.

"Well, at least she made me forget my problems for a few minutes," Nancy said. "I wish she could have told me more, though."

"I thought you didn't believe in that stuff," Laura said, surprised.

"I don't. But the look in that woman's eyes scared the crap out of me. I'm just glad I'm out of there."

The two women searched for a cab.

Had they looked back they would have seen the fortuneteller peeking out of the doorway, watching them until they were out of sight.

ONE HUNDRED SIX

Nancy rose: "The defense calls Butch Moore,"

"Objection," Mallek shouted.

Stone was surprised to see Nancy rise, until she noticed Tyler Harding with his head bowed and his eyes downcast.

Stone had had a long night. Just as she had been preparing for bed, she got a call from Attorney General Portorf, telling her that Butch Moore would be in court the next day and ordering her to allow him to testify. He told her that Mallek had been given the same orders. She wanted to argue, but she didn't dare.

She looked out toward the spectators and saw who she assumed was Moore, sitting in the front row. Moore looked like the victim of a train wreck. Next to Moore was a man whose picture she had seen in the paper recently, something to do with his testifying in a money laundering trial.

Moore was studying Spencer Mallek expectantly.

"Your honor, Mr. Moore is not on the witness list," Mallek argued halfheartedly. "We've had no time to prepare."

Nancy: "We just learned of Mr. Moore's whereabouts ourselves, your honor."

Stone sighed, said, "Overruled."

Moore rose furtively, like a trapped animal wanting to make a run for it. He looked over at Mallek hopefully and slowly stumbled forward, his face bruised and his arm in a sling. Reporters in back of the courtroom began to question each other, speculating as to who Moore was and what he might testify to.

Moore took a seat and was sworn. He sat like a bird in a cage, surrounded by imaginary bars. He held his injured arm and adjusted his body as if trying to create more breathing room.

Nancy hurried toward the witness stand, taking a quick glance back at her father. For the fist time, she put everything else out of her mind but the witness. The puppet master was no longer in control; this time she would be her own person. The defense team would be working for the defendant and only the defendant.

"Your honor, I request to treat Mr. Moore as a hostile witness."

"But this is *your* witness," Stone answered bitterly, remembering Nancy's nasty retort as she was leaving Stone's office.

"I understand that your honor, but we have reason to believe Mr. Moore will be a reluctant witness. We ask that we be given some leeway. I respectfully remind you that this is a capital case."

"Mr. Mallek?" Stone grumbled, carrying out Potorf's other order to make it look good.

Mallek rose slowly, searching his mind for something to say that wouldn't anger Potorf and still keep him from looking too bad. He looked to his assistants for help, but they just looked back with blank stares. He turned to Stone, shrugged as if to say, "What's the use," threw up his arms and sat back down.

Nancy didn't waste any time.

"Mr. Moore, isn't it true that you were in the center tape recorder room the morning the accident occurred?"

Moore looked over at Mallek: "Maybe."

"Your honor, would you please instruct the witness to answer the question?"

Kyle was watching Nancy work for the first time. His initial impression was that her style was forceful, and her voice confident.

"Answer the question," Stone barked.

Moore hesitated, trying to decide how much the defense team already knew. "I visited the center once, but I can't remember the exact date or what rooms I went into."

"I'm talking about the room where the air traffic control conversations are recorded."

"I wouldn't know one room from another," Moore replied smugly. Corey's question had actually been a relief; he'd been expecting something much more threatening. He wondered if that was all Corey had.

"Come now, Mr. Moore, isn't it true that you are an expert in electronics? Are you telling this jury you wouldn't recognize a room full of recorders when you saw them?"

Moore shrugged. "I know something about radios, but that doesn't make me an expert on tape recorders."

"Would it surprise you if I called a witness who will testify that you had a Magnosync tape recorder, like the ones in the center tape recorder room, right there in your storage shack?"

Moore began to squirm a little, wondering why Mallek wasn't objecting.

"And would it surprise you if I said there were numerous copies of FAA tape recordings in that shack, all with Kyle Matthews' voice, and all with air traffic control instructions?"

Jury members began to look at one another.

Moore brightened, remembering that the tapes didn't exist anymore. "I never had any such thing," he said confidently.

"They were in that storage shed you rigged to blow up!"

"You. . . you have no. . . no right," Moore stammered.

Mallek had heard enough, Potorf or no Potorf: "Objection. . . "

But Nancy kept right on going.

"Mr. Moore, isn't it true that you were once fired for making false transmissions over air traffic control frequencies, transmissions that could have caused a serious accident?"

"I wasn't fired for that; the case was dropped," he said confidently.

"Your honor," Mallek said.

"All right, but didn't the government accuse you of making false transmissions using another controller's voice?"

Moore tugged at his collar and continued to look to Mallek for help.

"Mr. Moore, you haven't answered my question: I didn't ask if you were convicted, I asked if you were once accused of making false transmissions."

Moore reached into his jacket pocket, pulled out a gold pen, and began clicking it nervously.

Kyle smiled and edged forward in his chair.

Nancy looked back, saw Kyle smiling, and wondered why. He had refused to tell her his plan, insisting that she might accidentally give it away.

"Mr. Moore, isn't it true that you harbored a grudge against Deeter Noonan, the former FAA Administrator killed in the aircraft crashes?"

"I. . . I didn't like him very much," Moore conceded.

"And isn't it true that you also had a grudge against Kyle Matthews? Didn't you swear to get even with him because his father refused to help settle the PATCO strike?"

Nancy didn't give Moore time to answer: she roared on like a flood. "Mr. Moore, isn't it true that it was you, and not Kyle Matthews, who was responsible for the disaster that killed Deeter Noonan and hundreds of other passengers?"

Moore stood and pointed his one good arm at Nancy.

"No. I was up in a Learjet performing checks on some equipment when that mid-air occurred," he said confidently. "You can check with the pilot, Jim Brandt."

Judge Stone said, "Sit down, Mr. Moore."

Nancy was in uncharted waters here, and she had no idea where the shore was. Her only instructions from Kyle were to keep plowing ahead until Moore "lost it." She had to trust that he knew what he was doing.

"Exactly what kind of 'checks' were you performing?"

"Radio checks," Moore answered belligerently, as if talking to an idiot. "I was checking to see if the radios were functioning."

"Didn't your geographical position and altitude put you very near to the accident?"

Every time Nancy asked a question Moore didn't like, he clicked his pen furiously. He had the gold pen at top speed now: "I guess so. . . . I didn't hear about it until I was back on the ground. So what?"

Judge Stone made a feeble attempt to act judicial, in spite of Potorf's orders: "Ms. Corey, where are you going with all this?"

"I'm getting there, your honor, just a few more questions."

Nancy turned and saw Kyle motion for her to come to the defense table. She walked over to the table and picked up a piece of paper.

Kyle whispered, "We need to stall until tomorrow. I just thought of something that might make Moore go ballistic, but I need time to prepare."

"How in hell do I do that?" Nancy whispered back.

Mallek unwittingly saved the day.

"Your honor, perhaps we could take a recess until tomorrow," Mallek pleaded, walking toward the bench. "The witness is obviously in some discomfort."

Nancy acted as if she was about to object, but threw up her arms instead. "If Mr. Moore isn't feeling well, the defense certainly doesn't want to take advantage of him. We'll agree to a recess."

"Court is adjourned until tomorrow at nine a.m.," Stone said, "but I want to caution both parties that I expect to hear only relevant testimony from this point on."

ONE HUNDRED SEVEN

"I was starting to drown out there," Nancy complained.

"I know, I hated to put you through that, but I needed you to keep going until Moore came unglued."

"Then why stop when he was almost there?"

"Because I'm sure I know how Moore triggered a bomb without Brandt noticing, and I've just thought of a way to drive him over the edge. It's crazy as hell, but it just might just work if I can get a few hours to prepare."

"He'll never admit anything," Nancy insisted. "He has an alibi. Don't leave me hanging like that again."

"Maybe not, but maybe I can do something that will jolt him to his socks. Did you notice what he does every time you hit a nerve?"

Nancy was frustrated. "Yeah, he clicks that damn pen, but what does that do for us?"

"Tomorrow, I want you to pressure Moore like he's never been pressured before. Keep pounding him with follow up questions just like you have been: ask a follow up question before he has time to answer the previous one. He's capable of going ballistic in seconds; you just need to create that one big moment where he's about ready to lose it; I'll do the rest."

Nancy looked like she wanted to argue, but Manny jumped in first: "What about me? I 'wanna be in on this."

"Don't worry, you will be, because you're going to steal that gold pen of Moore's and give it to Nancy."

"Oh, is that all?" Manny asked.

"No, you're also going to become an assistant aircraft manufacturer."

ONE HUNDRED EIGHT

The following morning, Manny brought two paper mâche models of Boeing Seven Seventy Seven aircraft to the front of the courtroom. He set them on a table in front of the witness box, adjusting them until they were nose to nose. But these were more that just paper airplanes; they were first class models, all painted and covered with Transcontinental Airlines emblems. It had taken several men and ten, long hours to make them.

Mallek walked in and immediately hovered over the models with his assistants, examining each one closely and poking at them with his index finger until he was satisfied they were harmless. Still, he looked over at the defense table suspiciously before he went to his seat. After he sat down, he went into animated conversation with his assistants, gesturing and pointing to the two model aircraft.

Judge Stone entered and quickly recalled Butch Moore to the stand.

Moore had obviously been well briefed in the interim: he looked calmer, more confident, wearing a suit that was obviously brand new, and a tie he hadn't picked out himself.

Nancy started right out: "Do you remember our conversation about your knowledge of electronics, Mr. Moore?"

Moore nodded his head.

Nancy kept one eye on Kyle and Manny while she asked her questions. She noticed that Manny had taken something out of his briefcase and handed it to Kyle. Kyle signaled for her to come closer.

Nancy drifted over, but continued talking. "And it is true, is it not, that you have an extensive knowledge of electronics."

"I guess so."

"May I have a moment, your honor?" Nancy asked.

"Make it quick; you've asked these same questions before."

Nancy turned to Kyle and he handed her Moore's gold pen.

"What the hell do I do with this?" she whispered.

He pointed to the models. "Ask a few questions about those models.

"Like what?"

"Anything. Use your imagination, but get him agitated, even if you have to insult him. When he starts to lose it, hand him that pen. But whatever you do, don't give it to him until you think he might be ready to blow."

"I don't like this. Why won't you tell me what this is all about?"

"It's a long shot, and it's more likely to work if you don't know in advance. Just improvise a little and pray that Moore blows it. Manny and I will do the rest. Remember, this is it. Don't worry about what Stone or Mallek say, just kick ass and keep on kicking."

"Can't you even give me a clue?"

"Sure: Roy Rogers horse!"

"Do you recognize these two models, Mr. Moore?"

Moore hesitated. "They look like models of Boeing triple seven aircraft."

"Yes, just like the ones you blew up on the night of September first."

Mallek started to object, but Stone did it for him: "Ms. Corey, I must warn you, you are very close to contempt."

Nancy was in too deep to stop now; she ignored Judge Stone and studied Moore for signs he might be about to crack. She could tell he was close, because he'd begun to search his pockets like a man looking for heart medicine."

"Looking for something, Mr. Moore?" Nancy asked, holding up the gold pen. "Is this yours?"

Moore checked his pockets again. "It looks like mine, but I'm not sure," he stammered.

"It has your name on it," Nancy said. "I found it after you left last night."

Moore knew it was a lie, and it made him very nervous: his eyes began to dart back and forth. How did she get it? How much did they know?

"Give it to me," He cried out. Everyone in the courtroom jumped a little, startled by the intensity of his outburst. All eyes locked on to the witness chair, including Judge Stone's and the jurors.

"Just a minute," Nancy said calmly. "Why don't you tell the jury why you're so attached to that pen?"

The jury sat in rapt attention. This was better than a movie.

"I. . . don't know. . . what. . . you're talking about."

Nancy wasn't sure herself.

Over at the defense table, Manny carefully leaned down and reached into his briefcase. He clasped a small black box with a toggle switch.

The timing had to be perfect.

Nancy was operating on complete faith. All she could think about was *Roy* Rogers' horse. . .

Roy *Rogers' horse? "Trigger," she thought to herself, his horse's name was "Trigger!"*

She looked back at Kyle, openmouthed. Kyle nodded his head and smiled.

Nancy looked at the gold pen and everything came into focus at once. She practically ran toward Moore now, almost as if she was going to attack him physically.

"Mr. Moore, isn't it true that the gold pen I hold in my hand is actually the trigger you used to bring down those two aircraft?"

Moore began to rise from his chair, but sat back down when he noticed Stone's threatening look.

"No. . . what the hell are you talking about?"

Nancy glanced quickly at Kyle, then back at Moore.

"Well. . . prove it to us then, Mr. Moore. Here's your pen." She handed it to him. "Hold up the pen and show it to the jury. When I tell you, click it."

"Ms. Corey, I hope you know that you're doing here," Stone said, scooting her chair back and looking anxious. Jurors also began to squirm.

Moore took the pen and stared at it.

"It's just a pen," he said a little too eagerly. "My Mother gave it to me. See. . . " He held the pen up to show the jury.

"Well then, click the button Mr. Moore. . . Go ahead and click the button. Show us how it works."

Moore stared at the pen. He looked at the Judge and then out into the courtroom. He held the pen up, looked at it more carefully, then clicked it.

Suddenly, there were two explosions on the table in front of the witness box. The two model aircraft leaped into the air like geysers and disintegrated in a cloud of smoke and floating debris! Everyone in the vicinity, including Nancy, jumped in surprise and covered their ears.

The judge disappeared behind her bench.

The spectators and the jury dove for cover.

Moore was on his feet, stunned. He ignored the sling on his arm and stood up, throwing both hands up to cover his face. He looked from the evaporating models to the pen, then from the pen back to the empty table.

Suddenly, he saw something floating right in front of his eyes. Tiny paper airplanes, stuffing from the models, came circling down. He watched them float to the floor. One fell on the rail in front of him and then skidded off, landing on his shoe.

"Isn't that the way you did it when you triggered a bomb while sitting in a Learjet the night of September first?" Nancy shouted as she recovered her composure. "Didn't you use that pen to trigger the explosion so that even the pilot of the Learjet wouldn't notice?" She was shouting so that her voice could be heard over the din of the recovering spectators.

Airplanes! The pen! Moore's mind tried to take it all in. He looked at Nancy, then at Kyle and Manny. They both had smiles of satisfaction.

THEY KNEW EVERYTHING

Moore got control of his reflexes, and with one leap vaulted over the rail, showing remarkable dexterity for an injured man. He bolted toward the door and managed to dodge the bailiff, but not the next two men.

Kyle and Manny stood like two defensive tackles.

Moore started to go around them, but Manny rammed a shoulder into his gut and he fell backward onto the floor. Manny's weakened condition caused him to fall backwards onto the floor himself.

Moore staggered to his feet as the courtroom went wild. Shocked reporters were running in every direction, trying to protect themselves and still see the action. The Judge and jury were nowhere to be seen.

Moore wheeled and began running forward; he jumped over the prosecutor's table and started for the door in back of the courtroom. But the other defensive tackle was ready. Kyle stood poised, fury in his eyes. He bellowed out all of his frustration as he lowered his shoulder and rammed Moore into a wall. "You son of a bitch, you killed all those people."

Moore bounced off of the wall, fell over a table, and flopped to the floor again.

Antonio Corlini was suddenly standing in front of Moore, a big, silver gun in his right hand. As Moore tried to get to his feet, Corlini stepped forward and raised the gun to eye level.

"You. . . you killed the woman I loved," Corlini screamed. The crowd held it's breath as he moved closer.

Nancy stared at her father in disbelief.

"The woman I loved?" she said out loud. "What is he talking about? She was already moving, even as she asked herself the question. She had to stop him.

In one last, mad dash, Nancy covered the distance between her Father and his intended victim.

Moore was getting up slowly on the other side of a fallen table. Nancy grabbed her father's wrist with both hands.

Corlini shouted, "No. . . let go of me! He killed Betty. Don't you understand? We loved each other."

"Don't," Nancy screamed, "don't!"

Her scream was drowned out by the sound of the gun, a sound that deafened the ears and numbed the brain.

The bullet that killed Butch Moore didn't just kill him, it literally blew him apart. He flailed against the wall, a huge, gaping hole in his chest.

It was hard to tell if it was Nancy or her father that had actually fired the fatal bullet. His hand held the gun, but both of her hands held his wrist as she wrestled him onto one knee in a gallant, but feeble, attempt to stop him.

In that one instant, it all became clear to Nancy: her father wasn't interested in defending Kyle at all, he only wanted revenge. He wanted to personally kill the man or woman responsible for killing his lover, and he wanted to do it in full view of the spectators. That's why there was to be no plea bargain; that's why there had to be a trial. He wanted a public execution.

Something else flashed through Nancy's mind: The fortuneteller had said "something gold" would save the life of someone close to her. It must have been the gold pen she was talking about, but how could she have known?

As Butch Moore's body lay shattered, two small paper airplanes, blown around in all the activity, drifted and finally landed. One fell on Moore's chest; the other landed on the floor next to his lifeless head.

Kyle couldn't help but notice the irony: they were at two, different altitudes, just like he had always said!

ONE HUNDRED NINE

Court was adjourned for the day. But any thought that Moore's death meant acquittal was quickly dispelled. Judge Stone ordered the courtroom cleared and then announced that the trial would continue the following morning at 9 A.M.

Butch Moore's life and death were analyzed by every media reporter in the world. Kelly Edmunds, who was now Kyle's most ardent supporter, made headlines by questioning why an ex-controller, fired for making false radio transmissions, would be allowed to chair an important NTSB investigation. She demanded that the FBI examine the relationship between Moore's false transmissions and the tape recording from the mid-air collision. Talk show hosts followed up with similar demands.

Nancy Corey filed a motion to dismiss. With the public now firmly on Kyle Matthews' side, Spencer Mallek intended to support the motion. He was angry, convinced that he had been deceived. He still thought Kyle might be guilty, but that was beside the point.

A call from Washington changed everything: Mallek was told to continue the prosecution. He had the impression that Washington was relieved that Butch Moore was dead.

By now, the public just assumed that Kyle would be cleared as soon as the trial resumed. Even Judge Stone was ready to dismiss the case. She was sick of Harding, Mallek, and the whole mess. She had received so much criticism from the media that she even looked forward to going home and watching Al's fishes swim around. She might even piss in his tank.

But before the trial could resume, the Attorney General called Stone again. He suggested that since there had been no actual confession, the jury had a right to decide the case.

The next day in court, Stone denied the defense's motion to dismiss and ordered Nancy Corey to resume presenting her case, admonishing the jury not to consider Moore's outburst as anything more than the act of an emotionally distressed witness.

The defense was taken by surprise and asked for a continuance. This time it was denied. Nancy had no choice but to rest her case.

After two days of closing arguments, the Judge gave final instructions to the jury, reminding them that they were to consider only the evidence they had heard during the course of the trial, and to disregard the bizarre tactics of the defense team. In short, she told them that nothing that they had seen or heard with regard to Butch Moore had any significance.

The Jury deliberated for ten days. Loud arguments could be heard coming from the jury room. Almost all of the jurors wanted to acquit. They sent messages to Judge Stone asking for clarification and demanding to consider Moore's testimony. The response was always the same: no element of Moore's testimony or actions could be considered.

Having no other choice, the jury returned to render their verdict.

In a courtroom overflowing with anxious citizens, the jury foreman shocked everyone when he announced the verdict:

GUILTY.

ONE HUNDRED TEN

Spencer Mallek was now a marquee figure. There weren't enough hours in the day to respond to all the requests for interviews or autographs. He was credited with successfully prosecuting the most notorious criminal since the Lindbergh kidnapping. His picture graced the cover of TIME magazine. It was something he had always dreamed of.

Still, he felt terrible. He brooded for days, trying to understand his own feelings.

Mallek's wife, Gloria, had never seen him so despondent. She tried everything to cheer him up. She told him to count his blessings and suggested he pray for guidance.

Mallek prayed, but it didn't help. He tried to tell himself that he should be celebrating, but the guilty thoughts came anyway, like water from a leaky pipe.

It wasn't just the thought that he might have convicted an innocent man that bothered him; it was just that he had spent most of his life defending the legal system, a system that hadn't worked. He was also convinced that the judge had sold out and that the government had conspired to convict Mathews whether he was guilty or not. Their lack of professionalism sickened him.

Mallek didn't attribute all of his feelings to a guilty conscience; he knew that his ego was also hurting: inferior intellects in the White House had gotten the better of him.

He sat around for several days, hoping the feelings would go away. He hid from congratulatory phone calls, in spite of his wife's objections.

Then came the one call he couldn't turn down, and it changed everything: "Spencer, I just wanted to congratulate you on a wonderful job. This was something we needed to get done. I'm proud of you."

"Thank you, Mr. President. I just did my best."

"Well, you handled things well. I only hope you haven't decided that this was your greatest accomplishment, because I think your greatest accomplishment is still to come. There's always a need for a man of your talents. Come and see me when you get a chance."

Mallek wondered if the President might actually be laughing at him.

It was the last straw: he walked out the front door of his Maryland home without even saying goodbye to his wife.

ONE HUNDRED ELEVEN

Mallek ignored the receptionist and walked right into FBI Director Perkins office. Perkins sat up quickly, his eyes wide.

"I have some questions and I want some straight answers," Mallek said. "Tell me what the FBI has learned about Butch Moore."

Perkins stiffened like a marine caught sleeping on duty. He pointed to a chair, but Mallek waived his hand away.

"We checked everything we could," Perkins said.

Mallek stalked the office, his head bobbing, his brown suit rumpled. Pictures of former FBI directors hung on the wall, including a picture of the ubiquitous J. Edgar Hoover. Mallek stared at the picture and thought about the old days, when everyone at least *thought* that justice was blind. He looked out the window and examined the Justice Department building with tired eyes. "Has anyone in the White House ever discussed with you the things Matthews talked about the day you were in my office. . . you know, about a bomb, the luggage and such?"

"No," Perkins said. "I looked into it myself, but ended up going along with what the NTSB had said; the damage was caused by the explosion from the mid-air collision."

Mallek shook his head, wheeled and looked as if were about to leap onto Perkins' desk. "I'm beginning to think Matthews was right; because of that tape recording, we were all so convinced he was guilty that we stopped looking."

Perkins started to argue, but Mallek cut him off.

"Weren't your agents suspicious of the fire in the NTSB hangar? Did they think that was just a coincidence? And how in the world did a man like Butch Moore ever get assigned to such an important committee?"

"Well. . . I guess if we knew then what we know now. . . but then, when the evidence was accidentally destroyed. . . you yourself said. . . "

"Never mind what I said; it was your job to learn the truth. You failed; we all failed."

Once again, Perkins wanted to argue, but saw that it was useless. "What can we do about it now?"

Mallek held his chin and thought for a long moment: "Where are Moore's effects, I want to see them."

Perkins stammered, "Right now? They're put away somewhere."

The FBI storage room was like the catacombs, except that it was filled with rows and rows of dusty boxes in poorly lit aisles; everything from Al Capone's tax returns to notes written by FBI traitors.

Almost every known possession of Butch Moore's was there, languishing in cardboard boxes. The family had been notified, but nothing had been claimed. One box contained several manila envelopes. Mallek sat in a chair for an hour rummaging through them, his skinny fingers tossing the obvious ones aside.

Perkins stood looking over his shoulder. "There isn't much here, I looked at all this stuff myself; just some old letters. We checked through all of them. I even took a look at Moore's gold pen, or what was left of it after he fell on it; nothing left but scrap. It's in one of the boxes."

"What about his tools, and his electronic equipment, where are they? There must be more than this."

"His tools are still in his hangar; we checked all of them; there's nothing significant there. If he owned anything else, it was destroyed when his shack blew up. Moore's ex-wife doesn't even know where he was living at the time of his death."

Mallek lifted his head and frowned at Perkins. "You haven't even found out where he lived?"

Perkins looked chagrined: "We assumed it was the cabin where his shack was, but we had no reason to check it out at the time."

"Please leave me alone for awhile," Mallek said quietly. "I want to study these documents. I'll let you know when I leave."

"As you wish," Perkins said. He walked out and closed the door.

Mallek continued to sift through the envelopes. The only thing that seemed to be of any importance was the title to the cabin in St. Joseph, Missouri.

Mallek leaned back in his chair, thinking. He rubbed his chin, his wire glasses hanging down over his nose.

Something that Matthews' lawyers had said during interrogatories popped into his head, something about "Danny Houston" and a "cabin" in St. Joseph, Missouri. It was one of those things the defense had insisted he check, but he had ignored them. He wasn't in a "checking mode" at the time. He jumped up and left for Reagan National Airport with Perkins and a team of agents.

The cabin was small, with no heat, furniture, or indoor plumbing. The place had been scrubbed as clean as a hospital room before it was listed for sale.

It took almost seven hours before Mallek and the FBI agents found the envelope that had been hidden in a wall. It was one of Moore's reluctant neighbors who finally remembered the hiding place Moore had showed him, right after they had been fishing. Moore had bragged that he hid money from his wife there.

The FBI didn't find any money, but they did find a "to whom it may concern" letter.

Mallek read the letter carefully and then handed it to Director Perkins.

"Do whatever you want with this," he said. "I have all the answers I need."

Mallek slowly picked up his jacket coat and started walking toward the door. "I'll be traveling with my wife for a while," he said, not bothering to look back. "I'm going to leave you an address and telephone number. I'd appreciate it if you would keep my whereabouts to yourself. Call me only if it's something urgent."

He scratched his number on a piece of paper, then walked out the door and disappeared.

The letter bragged about how Moore had plotted the death of Deeter Noonan, describing each and every detail. He insisted he was seeking revenge on behalf of every air traffic controller Reagan fired. He quoted a book written by a German professor that showed how the PATCO strike could have been handled without firing anyone. He said that Frank Zimmer and Peter Brock were aware of what he had done. He said Brock had promised to help him get a good job. He went on to explain that he planted plastic explosives in the baggage section of each aircraft. He verified that he intended to make the crash look like a mid-air collision, even before Kyle was included, and that Kyle was just a throw in. He bragged about using Transcon's own access codes to enter secure areas when he planted the bombs; access codes that were never changed, even after employees left the company. He said that he didn't think the FBI or the NTSB would ever figure things out, and that he wanted to enjoy watching them fail. Unfortunately, he didn't explain how or where he had hidden the bombs, which might have been useful in the fight against terrorism.

Director Perkins delivered the letter to Matthews' lawyers just as soon as it was authenticated by the FBI lab.

Then he resigned.

He wouldn't be the last.

Epilogue

One year later:

There was a big party in the Matthews' new home.

Laura, Kyle, and all the other players were there, including a host of controllers and their wives.

Tyler had been invited, but declined. He was now working for a law firm in Topeka, Kansas, handling divorces. The word was that he was doing well.

Kyle and Laura were back living together. They sat next to one another on a couch, Laura looking very comfortable in her Levis, running shoes, and favorite Kansas City Royals baseball cap.

Kyle sipped on a Pepsi like he didn't have a care in the world. His only post-release interview had been with Kelly Edmunds. He was back to work but still hiding from the rest of the world.

Nancy kept an eye on them all evening. She wasn't sure if she should be happy or sad. She liked Laura very much, but she knew that she was going to miss Kyle more than she wanted to.

Laura called everyone to attention and said she had an announcement to make:

"I want you all to know that when Kyle runs for president of NATCA, I'm going to be his campaign manager. If necessary, I'll even go back to Washington."

There were cheers all around. Rooster and Morrisey beamed.

"And I have an announcement of my own," Kyle said.

"I have decided that I have already spent too much time away from my family. My children need a good father, one who is there for them. Everyone knows my opinions and ideas. Now, it's time for someone else to offer theirs. I don't intend to run for office anymore. I'm resigning from the FAA and going to law school. From now on you can read about my opinions in the book I intend to write."

Laura was as shocked as everyone else. "Are you sure?"

"I'm sure," he smiled.

The two hugged. It was obvious that Kyle was determined.

"I guess Morrisey and I better go and remove all those damn campaign posters," Rooster grumbled.

As the party subsided and the crowd dwindled, members of the defense team, minus Tyler Harding, rehashed the entire event.

"OK Nancy," Manny said, tell us why you didn't use your real name."

"I didn't want you to know it was my father paying the bill," she said. "It was his plan and his money; I just did whatever he wanted. I had no idea that he had a lover, or that she was killed on one of those flights. Apparently, the two of them had been meeting in secret for years. He wanted to be sure who the guilty party was before he shot him or her. If he had found out there were others, he would have killed them, too. He said it's his 'code,' or something."

"I guess he didn't trust the courts to do their job," Kyle said.

"What about those two guys who followed Kyle around?" Manny asked.

"Those were my father's bodyguards. He gave orders to protect Kyle until after the trial. He was afraid some member of the public might shoot Kyle before he was able to learn the truth."

"Did he give the orders to beat me up, too?" Kyle asked.

"No, they did that on their own. I don't think he minded, though, as long as they didn't go too far. He was pretty sure you were the only guilty one, anyway."

"So that's why they got that crowd to beat me up outside the grocery store, and then stopped them before it could go too far?"

Nancy shrugged.

"What about the Crown Vic Manny and Rooster saw when Moore was taken by your father?" Laura asked.

"I think we have to assume that someone in the government wanted Moore out of the way until the trial was over."

"Then why did they let him testify?"

"Because the government needed my father badly; he was to be a key witness for the government in several, big money laundering cases. They didn't dare turn him down when he demanded to have Moore testify. They probably didn't think Moore's testimony would matter that much anyway."

"Think of the irony here," Manny said. "If Butch Moore had just ignored that little explosion while he was on the witness stand, Mallek would have never have searched his cabin."

"And I would have spent my life in jail, or worse," Kyle added.

"And I guess we can say my father accomplished something, too," Nancy said. "In the long run, he did discover the guilty party."

"Well then," Kyle said. "I guess we can say that Butch Moore gave his life for me, too."

Manny laughed. "That would make Moore turn over in his grave."

"What about your father, Nancy, what will happen to him?" Manny asked.

Nancy looked thoughtful for a minute. "He's in jail, of course, and I still don't know exactly what's going to happen. I can't believe he did what he did; even if I have been suspicious of him at times. He always told me he was just a businessman, but businessmen don't go around killing people. Things don't look too good for him; I may have to plead temporary insanity or something like that."

Nancy noticed that Kyle and Laura were smiling. She looked at Manny and found him smiling, too. She finally caught on.

"Oh no you don't, you guys; I know what you're thinking," she said.

Kyle could hardly keep from laughing. "I know a lawyer in Topeka who is really good at insanity defenses!"